Time's Revenge

the sequel to

Time Portals of Norwich

David Viner

Published by
Viva Djinn (Horde) Publishing
vivadjinn.com
Norwich, UK

ISBN: 978-1-913873-06-6

British Library Cataloguing in Publication Data available.

Design and layout: David Viner

Time's Revenge

When and Where?

A Rude Awakening

Cassie woke with a jolt and groaned in pain. She kept her eyes shut and lay as still as possible. The migraine, or whatever it was, insisted upon pummelling the inside of her skull with a lump hammer.

Whatever was afflicting her didn't restrict itself to her head. Her entire body felt wrong.

What on Earth did I do last night? she thought. *Was I out with Georgia and Mark, or even Jason?*

Recent memories refused to surface and those she could drag up felt ancient.

Just what the hell am I sleeping on? Lying on her left side, her right hand explored the bed. The sheets – *they don't even feel like sheets* – had the texture of used rags. Whatever was underneath them wasn't a mattress, either. Her left arm was limp across her face and the fingers of that hand were touching something that reminded her of cat fur. *Why am I covered by fur?* Whatever it was made from, she was buried within it, which at least kept her warm.

Well, warmish.

She raised the covering with her left hand to be rewarded with a shaft of light accompanied by an icy draft. Shivering, she dropped her arm and tried to inch her body deeper to get away from the cold.

That tiny movement made her discover something else as her body moved under the cover. And that was it – her entire body moved against whatever was covering her.

Her right hand moving up her leg to her hip confirmed her lack of clothing.

Oh my God, I'm naked. Naked and not in my own bed.

Struggling to suppress a tide of panic, she told herself there had to be a rational explanation for all this.

She heard noises not far away – in the same room – but the echoes were wrong, an impression of a larger space. Not a room – a hall? The noises resolved into the sound of women's voices but they were soft and Cassie couldn't make out what they were saying. Whatever it was, it didn't sound like English.

Where the hell am I? And why does my head hurt so much?

A persistent itch above her right ear diverted her attention. Attempting to scratch the spot, her fingers detected movement. A tiny creature squeezed from beneath her thumb to scuttle away across her scalp. Her fingers followed it and that brought a new discovery. Her hair was no longer straight. But it was more than just frizzy. It was matted and greasy to the touch, and far longer than normal.

Have I switched bodies or something?

Considering what life had previously dealt her, that wasn't an idea she could reject out of hand. There was one way to check. She caressed her right cheek with the tip of a finger, seeking out the scar that had been a part of her since she was six. Falling from her pushbike to the pavement, a sharp stone had sliced into the flesh of her cheek. She located the scar – the small ridge of harder skin felt no different to normal. Cassie didn't know whether she felt annoyed or relieved at that confirmation.

An intense cramp passed across her abdomen. She clenched her teeth.

Her hands, moving down towards the source of the pain, recoiled upon encountering breasts that were far larger than they had any right to be. Her fingers brushing past her nipple felt a sticky dampness. But the pain in her belly intensified and her hands continued their descent to discover an unexpected bulge and movement within.

She screamed long and hard. Seconds later the covers were stripped away. Grey light, originating from somewhere behind her, coupled with the pain in her head, was still bright enough to make her squint. But it wasn't enough to hide from her eyes the distended shape of her belly.

Struggling to pull herself upright, she stared down at her body in disbelief. Seeing the pregnant mound, she sucked in another breath and screamed again, unable to prevent it.

An Endless Dream

Both the pain and the scream passed. With her breath spent, Cassie's eyes rose to meet those of the person who had pulled the cover from her body.

She encountered dark brown irises surrounded by a wide, olive-skinned face. The cheeks were picked out with raised scars, four lighter lines with a dot between each, symmetrically arranged on either side of the nose. The face was itself framed by black hair, almost as matted as hers felt.

Cassie blinked, unable to comprehend what she was seeing, but blinking didn't cause the apparition to go away. So her eyes continued their explorations.

Bare to the waist, with breasts that hung limp, Cassie's eyes tracked down to a stomach that showed signs that it had borne at least one child in the past. The woman's skin was lined and leathery as if she had spent far too much time exposed to the elements. Her face, too, was wrinkled around the eyes and mouth. Though far past her youth, the woman's eyes still sparkled with life. She wore only some sort of animal skin as a skirt, yet didn't appear to feel the cold.

Cassie did, and pulled the cover back up around her body. She could see it, too, was made from animal skins, sewn together with a coarse thread. She gripped it close to her neck trying to exclude the cold air and hide her nakedness, as she tried to take in the rest of her surroundings.

The woman said something using sounds that had never known any connection with English. But, somehow, Cassie understood her. Little more than articulated grunts, within her head the noises became, "Okay. Light in eyes. Wake proper." Except that the woman really had said something that sounded like 'okay' before the grunts and noises that followed it.

The woman moved the cover to one side again and put a hand on Cassie's swollen belly, adding, "Baby soon."

A large flea hopped onto Cassie's left breast. The woman's long fingers pinched it away before Cassie had time to react to the horror of seeing it. Manipulating the insect between the nails of her thumbs, the woman applied a moment's pressure and, with an audible click, the flea was flattened. Its remains were wiped down the woman's excuse for a skirt.

Cassie pulled the cover back around herself and tried to make out her surroundings in the dim light. The walls were smooth rock and led up to a vaulted ceiling almost lost in shadow – a large cave of some sort. More than a dozen bundles of animal fur, similar to what she was sitting on, were distributed around the floor of the cave.

Nearer the source of the light, two more women were tending a fire that crackled as twigs and small branches were added. Each was dressed in a similar style to the woman beside her. None of them apparently embarrassed about the skimpiness of their clothing. One of them held a baby in one arm.

Cassie looked past them, her eyes following the smoke from the fire. She watched it curl up to the roof of the cave before drifting towards the entrance where, unhindered by any sort of door, it escaped into the freedom of the world beyond. Behind a line of trees, a dense wall of dark green, rose a snow-coated mountain range.

This can't be happening, Cassie told herself. *I have to be dreaming.*

She shut her eyes and tried to will herself into waking up. But the cave, the woman and her own nakedness persisted when she opened them again.

With trepidation she touched her stomach under the cover, feeling the tautness of the flesh. She handled the fullness of her breasts, they were heavy and painful. She gasped as her hand came away wet – but when she brought her fingers into view, the liquid on them was pale yellow and sticky.

Something else – images, memories – crept into her mind.

I remember this, she thought. *I remember a dream of being here. But, where is here, and when am I going to wake up?*

The woman looked at Cassie, her head tilted a fraction to one side, and spoke again. "Fire in sky. Wake okay. Okay wait. Ka'Chull come. Baby. Soon."

Cassie stared at the woman.

How can I understand her?

But then she frowned. That word – Ka'Chull – was familiar. Looking at the woman's face popped another word of similar construction into her head: Em'Kell. What did that mean?

"Em'Kell?" Cassie said.

The woman's face lit up with a broad smile. She sprang to her feet and rushed towards the cave entrance where she chattered to the other women. All three came back and sat beside Cassie's bed.

"Okay," said the youngest one, pronouncing it more like 'Oh'Kay' with a distinct pause and a click between the two syllables. The first woman had also said it like that – like they were saying 'Oh Kay' which made Cassie's mind conjure up an image of the older, white-haired Kay. Coincidence?

Cassie stared at the girl. She couldn't have been more than about thirteen but her face, too, had been deliberately scarred – two lines on each cheek with a row of dots above her eyebrows. Her belly showed signs of pregnancy, though nowhere near as full as Cassie's. The girl patted Cassie's shoulder with fingers that were slender and long, an attribute shared with the other two women.

"Baby," Cassie said, pointing to the girl's stomach.

The girl said something in the grunt language that, to Cassie's ear, also meant 'baby' – the same word used earlier by the older woman. Cassie repeated the 'baby' grunt, and all three smiled and laughed.

"Oh'Kay talk. Oh'Kay wake. Fire in sky wake Oh'Kay," said the woman Cassie thought of as Em'Kell.

"Em'Dor," the girl said, pointing at herself. Cassie repeated what she presumed was the girl's name, and then realised that the name, like Em'Kell's, was also familiar. The girl responded with a laugh and a wobble of her head that was neither a nod nor a shake.

"Em'Jex," the third woman said, her free hand pointing to her chest while her other arm cradled a naked, sleeping infant. Again, the name was no surprise to Cassie. The woman was somewhere between the ages of the other two, though Cassie couldn't put an exact number on it. However, what she could see was that the woman's breasts were as full as her own. Cassie stared at the baby held in the woman's arms – again, a name popped into her head.

"Em'Tull," she said and Em'Jex squealed in delight.

All of them, including the infant, possessed common facial features that made them consistent with each other but, to Cassie's eyes, misproportioned. Thickset around the jaw, wide across the cheeks and nose, they also possessed overlarge teeth, receding chins and foreheads that were sloped more than normal. There was just a hint of the oriental around the eyes, too.

"Cassie," Cassie said, pointing at herself.

All three erupted in laughter, shaking their heads with that strange wobble.

"No," Em'Kell said. She pointed at Cassie and said, "Oh'Kay."

"Huh?" Cassie said, which reduced the three to laughter again.

"Oh'Kay," Em'Dor said. "All Oh'Kay say since thirteen moons past is Oh'Kay. You Oh'Kay." Not that the girl said *thirteen* – it was more like hand-hand-fingers-three – but Cassie's mind translated its meaning automatically.

"But fire in sky make Oh'Kay wake," Em'Kell said. "Is Oh'Kay not Oh'Kay now?"

What the hell are they talking about?

"I'm Cassie."

"Ka'See?" Em'Dor said. "Man name. No, you Oh'Kay."

"Cassie," she repeated. "I'm Cassie. And I'm not okay." She was speaking in English and it was plain from the sudden look of shock on all three of their faces that none of them understood a word she was saying. But that didn't stop her. Her voice inched up in both scale and volume, and she felt as if she was losing a battle against a tide of conflicting emotions. "I'm Cassie," she shouted, "and I don't know where I am, or who you are, or where we are, or anything. My name is Cassie. Cassie! And how the fuck did I end up with a baby inside me?"

The dam burst as tears flooded down her cheeks. She clutched her arms around her knees which, given the size of her belly, wasn't achieved without some difficulty, and sobbed her heart out.

Baby

Cassie was still crying many minutes later. The three women tried to comfort her, making soothing sounds and patting her hands, shoulders, back and, in Em'Kell's case, rubbing the swelling of her belly through the cover.

Then they brought her some water in a shallow dish that, Cassie could see, had been carved from wood. The water it contained tasted fresh, though it did little to stop her head from pulsating. She drained it and handed the dish back.

"When will I wake up? Please let me wake up," she muttered in English.

"Baby soon," Em'Dor said. Then she patted her stomach and said, "Baby come three moons." Then she pointed at Cassie and said, "Oh'Kay baby here soon. Today?"

Moons? What does that mean? Three moons, thirteen moons. These people, whoever they were, measured time in moons. Was it how long it took the moon to go around the Earth? A value of twenty-eight days popped into Cassie's mind – about a month. Thirteen moons. Did that mean she'd been here more than a year? Why couldn't she remember?

Cassie tried to lay back down but another spasm hit her. She whimpered and held her breath until it passed.

Oh, my God, she thought, as she lay there gasping. *That had to be a contraction. I really am about to have a baby.*

Then another realisation hit her hard and her thoughts screamed, *I must have been raped. Who the hell is the father? Was it one of these people? Some bloody caveman? I don't even remember. Why can't I remember?*

Noises came from outside the cave.

"Ka'Thon, Pa'Tay, Ka'Char, Ka'Chull," Em'Jex said. "They laugh. Hunt good."

Cassie raised her head and heard the babbling get closer. She wiped the tears from her face with her hand, noticing the accumulation of filth upon her skin.

Filling the cave entrance were four taller men, surrounded by others whose ages ranged from children to adults even older looking than Em'Kell. Two of the men dropped the large body of a deer they'd been carrying onto the ground. It was picked up by three women and taken off out of Cassie's sight.

I know them all, Cassie thought. *How do I know them? Have I really been here for a year?*

Em'Kell rushed to meet them and accosted one of the hunters. She dragged him by the arm towards Cassie. She shrunk under the covers, trying to hide her nakedness from him.

"Oh'Kay," his voice boomed as he squatted beside her. Across his shoulder were slung the limp bodies of several cat-sized animals, tied together with something that wasn't quite string. Dried blood was spattered across their fur and even more dotted his bare arms.

She stared into his face, at the darkness of his features, at the delicate yet familiar pattern of scars on his forehead and cheeks – though the latter were half concealed by beard growth. Cassie forced herself to breathe again as the certainty grew that she was staring at her rapist. She swallowed. He was, like the others, tall, strong in the jaw and broad across the face. Neither handsome nor ugly.

Just wrong.

Without any doubt, she knew his name was Ka'Chull.

Am I guessing or remembering that? she asked herself.

Cassie closed her eyes again. *What in hell has happened to me?* She racked her thoughts trying to locate something – anything – that would unearth even the tiniest answer. But her thoughts were interrupted as the man placed a hand under her chin and raised her face. *How dare he?*

"Oh'Kay has eyes now," he said, his face only inches from hers. "Fire in eyes like fire in sky. Awake. Fear, too. Scared."

Releasing her face, he pulled the cover from her and placed his hand on her stomach as if he had every right to do so. She flinched at the touch of his spidery fingers upon her.

"Baby come soon," he said. "Ka'Tor if boy, Em'Char if girl."

"Don't I get a choice in its name?" she said, in English.

"Hah," Em'Kell said, "I tell true. Oh'Kay talk now."

"Mad talk," Ka'Chull said, patting Cassie's belly and smiling.

Another contraction caused her to pitch forward and then she felt something worse. It was as if she had wet herself.

"Baby," Em'Kell said, pulling the cover away. "Men go. Baby come now."

The next few hours were torture; several kinds of torture all mixed up together: pain, embarrassment, pain, cold and yet more pain.

Cassie was surrounded by women. They wouldn't leave her for a moment. They made her lay down, stand up, walk, sit, bend over and squat. They pushed and prodded at her abdomen and, even worse, inserted their bare fingers between her legs as they determined the state of her labour. Her ears were filled with their constant chatter along with her own screams, as waves of agony hit her at decreasing intervals.

As the minutes crawled by, she prayed for all this to end and wished total oblivion upon herself. She craved sleep and never to wake again. Anything to get away from the pain, not to mention the indignity. But there was no respite and her whole body shuddered to the spasms of the increasing contractions. She was sure she passed out at least twice – small blessed reliefs that were all too brief. But the women wouldn't let her remain that way. She wasn't allowed to slip away into the darkness she so eagerly sought.

In between all this, she became conscious of the cave filling as more people arrived – their faces stirring memories. Also, she detected the twin aromas of blood and cooking. The thought of either made her physically sick, though she only retched as her stomach felt empty of nourishment.

At times, Ka'Chull would come into view, a smile plastered across his broad features – not an expression of sympathy, more one of amusement. It held indifference, too, if not total unconcern, for what she was going through. She screamed blue murder at him but it was obvious he neither understood nor exhibited any concern about the words that flowed from her mouth. At times people would come to stare at her – men, women and children – many of them talked of the fire in the sky or of broken trees, but Cassie was in too much pain to take in what they said.

The night was drawing in when the baby made its way into the world. Dancing shadows that only a large fire can conjure decorated the entire cave, accentuating the uneven floor, walls and ceiling, and emphasising the darkness building up outside. However, the fires – for there were now several dotted around the interior of the cave – did little to prevent the evening cold from numbing her bare skin. The women forced her into a squatting position and she felt something shift inside her, the pain moving lower. Hands on her cold but sweating body prevented her from falling one way or the other. More hands guided the child's head as it entered the world and then, with a flop and a splash, it was out of her. The women encouraged her to lay back onto something softer than the hard floor. She gasped in relief as the agony began to subside.

Her eyes opened wide when Ka'Chull strode towards her with two rocks, one in each hand, that in his left somewhat larger than the other. She screamed as he approached, thinking he was about to attack her. Instead, he took the still connected umbilical cord in his hand, positioned it on the larger rock and brought the smaller one down with a swift chop, dividing it. There was a mixture of cheering and whooping sounds from everyone else. The noise almost drowned out the baby which, taking its first breaths, screeched its lungs out.

"Boy," Em'Kell announced, examining the child.

Ka'Chull lifted the still-bloodied infant into the air with one hand and repeated the declaration at the top of his voice, "Boy. Ka'Tor." There was more cheering.

He then passed the baby back to Em'Kell who, along with the other women, cleaned it utilising dried grasses to wipe off the blood and mucus. Another contraction expelled the afterbirth and then more grass was used to clean blood, and worse, from her body and legs.

The baby was placed against her breast and Em'Kell manoeuvred Cassie's nipple into its mouth and its cries were silenced.

To her relief, Ka'Chull left her side. The women surrounding her wrapped her shaking body in warmed animal skins that limited the bite of the cold. Once they had completed this, the child, too, was enclosed within the coverings. Only its – his – head remained on show.

Em'Kell patted the baby's head saying, "Ka'Tor. Good naming."

"Why Ka'Tor?" Cassie asked, trying to pronounce it as Em'Kell had done.

"Ka'Chull father name Ka'Tor. Mother name Em'Char," came the reply.

"Oh," she said. *A family name?* "Where they?"

"Dead – four, five summers past."

"Oh."

Cassie stared down at the infant suckling inches from her face, knowing without a doubt that it had come from her body but, at the same time, unable to believe that fact.

What do you have to do with me? she thought.

After all the pain she had gone through, she felt numb. Shouldn't she feel love for this child – this boy that was hers? Maybe, if she'd remembered experiencing the pregnancy from beginning to end, that love might have come naturally. But, of the nine months that preceded her awakening earlier in the day, her head held almost nothing. Her mind could dredge up mere snatches – vague glimpses that hinted at what might have taken place. But she had no concrete recollection of how she had come here, or even when and where 'here' might be.

Exhausted, her eyes closed and consciousness slipped away.

In a dream, a wolf ordered her to *stay dangerous*.

Eyes

Cassie was nudged awake. She opened her eyes – the world outside the cave entrance was devoid of light but dancing fires lit up the interior. The baby's mouth was still attached to her breast, though he no longer suckled.

Em'Dor, sitting beside her, nudged her again and offered her one of the two wooden bowls she was carrying. The smell of cooked food accosted Cassie's nostrils and, this time, despite the feeling that her entire body had been put through a mangle, Cassie realised she was hungry.

Once Cassie had managed to free a hand from inside the coverings, she sat up and accepted the bowl Em'Dor offered, Cramming the food into her mouth with her fingers, she found it consisted of a mixture of meats, root vegetables, mushrooms and cooked leaves. What the origins of those ingredients might have been, Cassie neither pondered nor cared.

Damn, Cassie thought, *when was the last time I ate anything?*

Inside her head, she was still numb. A part of her wanted to be running away as fast and as far as possible – but, instead, she just lay there stuffing food into her mouth.

Sitting beside Em'Dor were two younger girls, whose faces were free of scarring. The first girl, whose name of Em'Lo popped into Cassie's head, was eating from a bowl while staring at Cassie. Apart from the lack of scarring, she and Em'Dor could have been sisters.

Wait – they are sisters, aren't they? How do I know?

Cassie struggled to remember the other girl's name so she pointed at Em'Dor and then Em'Lo and said, "Em'Dor, Em'Lo."

Then she pointed at the other girl.

"Ge'Tal," Em'Dor said.

Oh yes, I did vaguely know it.

Cassie repeated the name in between eating and the girl smiled.

Isn't she the daughter of that man over there? What's his name? Oh yes, Ti'Pik, I think. No idea who the mother is.

"Oh'Kay now Ka'See," Em'Dor explained to Em'Lo and Ge'Tal, who both frowned.

"Man name?" Ge'Tal said.

Why do they think it's a man's name? Their names are all constructed simply – two syllables. What's wrong with Ka'See, as they pronounce it?

The meanings of the names were beyond her. Anyway, the food was going cold, so she forced it down, clearing every last morsel. She handed the empty bowl to Em'Lo. The girl had only eaten half of her meal.

"Full?" said Em'Dor to her sister, who nodded.

Em'Dor handed Em'Lo's unfinished meal to Cassie, who polished it off without hesitation. As she handed the bowl back, Cassie shivered as the hint of a memory passed across her mind.

Oh, déjà vu, she thought. Something about finishing off someone else's half-eaten dinner – but not in a cave – more like a restaurant or café. *When was that?*

She lay back, dislodging the baby, who started bawling out his discontent. Em'Lo watched as Em'Dor repositioned him back in place where he began to suckle, an expression of contentment on his face. Ge'Tal chuckled and stroked the boy's head. Then Em'Dor looked around and made a quick grunt sound to the other two. Without a further word all three left Cassie's side to collect empty bowls from those who had finished eating.

Cassie gazed down at her son as a multitude of thoughts flashed across her mind.

Where am I? When is this?

She tried to concentrate, a fleeting memory of having a built-in calendar passed across her mind. Was that her imagination or had it ever been real?

Past or future?

Was this back before the dawn of civilisation? Or could this be some sort of nightmare future where mankind had degenerated back to living in caves?

Future or past?

The faces of the people gave her no clue.

Who are they? What are they? Are they dangerous?

Something about being or staying dangerous flashed through Cassie's mind, but it was gone an instant later.

She had vague recollections of seeing reconstructions of Neanderthals and other prehistoric human-like species on TV but, to her knowledge, scant as it was, none resembled the occupants of this cave.

Still compatible enough to make babies, though, she thought, stroking the wispy dark hair that adorned the baby's head. At her breast, he continued to draw nourishment.

Who are you? Why am I your mother?

As if he might have heard her, the baby moved and, for the first time, opened his eyes wide for a few seconds. Cassie gasped, catching sight of the intense blue of the boy's irises. Even in the flickering firelight, the colour was unmistakable.

Oh, she thought. *Well, that proves you're definitely my son.*

Everyone else in the cave possessed brown eyes. She looked around and her mind brought the faces close. Some, like Em'Lo, had names that came into her head as she pictured them, evidence confirming that she had already spent a long time with these people. That boy of about ten helping his father, Pa'Tay, make spears was Ko'Lak. Her eyes scanned across the faces and alighted upon a child of about six dancing around his mother's legs as she tended one of the fires. Te'Set, like all of them, was olive-skinned, broad across the face and possessed brown eyes. Against her breast, it was obvious that the baby, too, was endowed with the same olive colouring given the contrast between his face and the paleness of her own skin. However, even in the low light, she was sure he was a shade or two lighter than everyone else. But, unlike Ka'Chull, Pa'Tay, Ko'Lak and even Te'Set, his face was free of the symmetrical scarring that adorned every other male. Her eyes fell on a girl seated next to Te'Set. After a moment, the name Ge'Tek came to mind. She appeared to be between the ages of Em'Dor and Em'Lo, and her face was already marked with decorative scars. The man known as Ka'Thon sat with them and Cassie had an inkling that he was the father of both Ge'Tek and Te'Set.

I know many of their names, but why can't I remember how I got here?

She shut her eyes.

Just what can I remember?

Memories flashed through her head – Grandad, of course. And Georgia, her best friend since early childhood, whose skin was far darker than any of those in this cave. Then Kay, the device and the time portals.

Well, I could hardly forget those, could I?

Jason – she remembered him all right, but it was a remembrance tinged with disappointment. No, not disappointment – something else. Despite her concentration, that *something else* escaped her, though her heartbeat increased as her mind pictured him.

And wasn't there something about Robert Kett as well? She tried to pin his face down in her mind – but, for some reason, he seemed to have several. How could that be?

Then she remembered something else.

She remembered holding it in her hand – a flat, metallic disc with writing around the edge. Plain on one side but on the other...

She recalled stabbing at the big red button in frustration whilst sitting on the parched grass on top of Castle Mall in her home city of Norwich. The button had refused to do anything.

Another memory leaked into her consciousness. And, in that memory, which felt like it had happened a long time later, she recalled the button depressing with a resounding click. But where and when that had happened was beyond her ability to recall. She glanced around, wondering if the disc was still in her possession.

I don't think so.

The night drew on and the remaining food was consumed as the fires grew dimmer, reducing the light within the cavern to a few glowing points. Only the larger fire at the entrance was kept burning. *Keeps wild animals like bears and wolves away,* Cassie remembered and then frowned. That felt more like a recent memory and not one from before she had come to this world. Something that had emerged from the fog of the past year.

The people – there were around three dozen of them – sat around talking for a while. Occasionally a few would go outside and return a short while later.

They always went out in twos or threes, never alone, even the men.

No inside plumbing, Cassie concluded, *not that I cared about that when I was giving birth to the damn baby*. But then a few vague memories stirred of using bushes outside the cave and further down the incline. *Small things are coming back. Not enough.*

Around her, the conversation still buzzed. Her limited understanding of their language meant she could pick up only a little of what was being said, though the frequent mention of the fire in the sky piqued her interest.

What's that got to do with me? How did it wake me up?

Every so often, others would come close and stare at her and the baby. One boy, who she thought looked like he might have been about four or five years of age, approached. Cassie was shocked to see the puncture wounds that patterned his face and forehead. They looked recent as the one on his left cheek was oozing pus. A flash of memory of the boy screaming while one of the men sliced into the boy's face made Cassie gasp. Then, the man that Cassie's erratic memory thought might be called Za'Lak, came across and collected the boy as if he didn't think he should be associating with her.

Before long the members of the tribe took to their animal skin beds, a few singly, many others in pairs or even larger groupings. Those with younger children appeared to bundle together, with entire families sharing the same bed. Not that all were complete family units as Cassie saw Em'Jex cradling a young baby to her chest as she bedded down alone. Cassie was relieved that Ka'Chull had a separate bed and didn't disturb her. She was pretty certain he hadn't gone to bed on his own but with another woman called El'Car.

Suits me fine, Cassie thought. The lower half of her body felt like it had been through a war, which, in a way, it had. Her head, though clearer, still pulsated as if she had a hangover. *What I'd do now for some paracetamol.*

Cassie wanted to sleep but, despite her exhaustion, sleep wouldn't return.

Am I afraid I might forget everything again if I sleep? Would that be so bad?

The last of the smaller fires died to glowing embers, hardly distinguishable from the background blackness. An animal howled far beyond the cave – the eerie noise causing her to shiver.

I've got to get out of here, she thought. *Can I still travel in time? But when is now? Past or future?*

Suppose I go the wrong way? That idea that she'd once had a built-in calendar emerged yet again.

Yes, after Kay died and I spent several days trying to figure out how to get all the portals created. I kept jumping all over Norwich's past – pretty certain I knew down to the minute when I was.

But what about this place? It definitely feels more like the past. So, maybe I need to go forward in time. Can I be sure of that?

The baby at her breast scrabbled to find a different position. *This is my son. If I leave, it would mean abandoning him.*

She frowned. *I really should feel something like love for him, shouldn't I?*

But the knowing of what she should have felt and what was going through her emotions at that moment, couldn't be reconciled. It was a baby, and there were plenty here who would take care of it – him – should she disappear.

Another memory came to her – images of a woman dying as she gave birth here in this cave. The new baby had been parcelled out to another woman, barely more than a child herself, who had recently given birth to a baby of her own. Cassie remembered spotting a girl nursing two babies of different ages while they ate their meals earlier on. Yes, the younger boy, who the father had named Zo'Mar, had been the motherless child.

So, if she left, she knew her son would be looked after.

Cassie closed her eyes and, as she had done many times in her past – which might still be in the future – began to initiate a move to a different time.

Nothing.

She tried again.

Still nothing.

Maybe I'm just too worn out after giving birth. Then she remembered another occasion when her ability to time travel and teleport had failed her.

I need to remember everything that I've either forgotten or, maybe, has somehow been taken away from me.

As sleep overcame her, her mind drifted back to one thing she had no problem remembering. It was what had occurred on the last day of June 2018 after the device had abandoned her.

What Cassie Did Next

A Close Brush With Death

Sitting on the parched grass that covered part of the Castle Mall shopping centre in Norwich, Cassie turned the disc over in her hands, marvelling at its weight and construction. Heavy enough to have been made out of lead, the body of the disc itself was the colour of brass.

She read the inscription that ran along the edge several times as if each re-reading would make it clearer. How could it be any clearer than what it already said? 'For use in emergencies only.'

That's pretty unambiguous.

Despite that, her thumb hovered over the button. Big and red, it cried out to be pressed. Should she do it? She had lost the ability to travel in time and space. Did that constitute an emergency?

Of course, it doesn't, she told herself. The hot summer sun pounded down upon her and she knew she was going to have to move pretty soon.

Then, without realising she was going to do it, she stabbed hard at the button. It didn't depress as much as half a millimetre. In frustration, she thumbed it several times more.

Nothing.

With a grunt, she tossed it back into the jacket pocket where she had first discovered it.

Her forehead was beaded with sweat and her tangled hair was sticking to her face. She stood and, wondering why, in this heat, she was still wearing the jacket, pulled it off and folded it over her arm.

She glanced at the City Hall clock – it was a quarter to twelve. Maybe Georgia, Mark and Jason were already in Castle Mall.

I can't meet them like this.

Her eyes, squinting through the brightness, fell upon the castle and followed the roofline looking for Robert Kett's chained body. There was a shimmer of something, but she couldn't tell if it was him or the sun playing tricks on her.

Not wanting to bump into her friends, she strolled towards the castle gate seeking somewhere shaded but, with the sun overhead, found precious little.

People meandered along the pathway towards the Castle Meadow side of the keep. Cassie went the other way, passing the point where, in 1970, she'd created the portal that had taken her to the library. She stopped in a small sliver of shade under some trees.

"Back again?" came a voice, causing her to jump.

Cassie snarled, turning to see the familiar translucent face of Robert Kett. "I thought I'd seen the last of you."

"Why would you think that?"

Cassie sighed. "The device has gone."

"So? You didn't have the device when you first saw me hanging in my chains all those years ago."

"No, but it was still around."

"Was it?"

"What do you mean?"

"It was 2011 when it came into your possession for your trips through the portals. Where was it between 2011 and now?"

"I don't want to even think about it. Anyway, how do you know all that?"

"I'm sure you once told me about it."

"I'm sure I didn't."

"Maybe you haven't yet and I'm remembering something you'll tell me in the future or maybe future you will tell me in the past. Time does get rather messed up around you."

"Yeah, and don't I know it."

"I like your hair."

"What?"

"It reminds me of a serving wench back when I was alive. Name wasn't Cassie, though." Kett stopped and frowned. "Something similar, possibly. Oh, and her hair was shorter."

"Shut up."

"Could do with a brush, though."

Cassie glared at him and also through him.

"I haven't got a damned brush. Wish I had."

"There's one there," Kett said, pointing a few feet further on. "Someone must have dropped it."

Cassie frowned. There was indeed a hair brush – bright green in colour – no, not *that* shade of green. It was just lying on the ground.

Surely that hadn't been there a moment ago, had it?

She picked it up. It looked clean, almost new in fact.

"Bit convenient, isn't it?" she muttered.

Kett shrugged. A Kay shrug, Cassie thought. *Is he really the ghost of Robert Kett or just something left over from all that portals stuff?*

"I'd brush your hair for you if I could," Kett said.

"Go on, then," Cassie said holding the brush out for him to take. The ghost's hands attempted to clasp it but failed. "You're not even trying," she snapped.

There was a ping from her phone and she dropped the brush. Kett's hands grasped to catch it but it fell through his fingers to the ground. As she pulled the phone out of her pocket, Kett tried to pick the brush up. She turned away from him, using one hand to shield the phone's screen from the glare of the sun. The message from Georgia said: *hey foxy were here u close? j wasnt come is now x*

Cassie snorted, suppressing a chuckle. Georgia had been her best friend since childhood and had grown into one of the most beautiful girls she'd ever known. But punctuation in general and apostrophes in particular had never figured prominently in her use of English, written or typed. She had a good excuse, though, having been diagnosed with dyslexia when she was eight. But Georgia had refused to let it limit her. Georgia tended not to let anything or anyone limit her. Those who tried to taunt her for her dyslexia, or even the colour of her skin, soon found out that she'd put her sporting skills and martial arts lessons to good use. She wasn't afraid of anyone.

Should I meet them? Cassie sighed. She had so been looking forward to it, especially now with Jason being there. But she knew she wasn't in a fit state – mentally or physically – to do any socialising. She considered sending a reply saying she was stuck at home… or some other excuse.

Her thoughts were interrupted as something tugged at the knots in her hair. Out of the corner of her eye, she saw a transparent hand wielding the brush that was already aiming for a second swipe.

"I tried harder," Kett said, a grin spreading across his lips.

Cassie was too stunned to stop him and let him continue attacking her hair.

"Your friends are waiting for you," Kett said from behind her while brushing even more vigorously.

"Yeah," was all she could reply.

"I think you should go and meet them."

"Why?"

"You try to do your best for others. You don't like letting people down."

Cassie frowned. No, she didn't – but how could the ghost of Robert Kett know that?

"But I'm far too sweaty."

"Yes," Kett said. He swiped twice more with the brush and then stopped.

"You finished?"

"No," he said, "but maybe this will help."

There was a sudden cool breeze as Kett stepped into and through her. She squeaked as the heat returned.

"Is that better?" he asked.

Cassie touched her brow – it was dry.

"How on Earth did you do, uh... do whatever it was you just did?"

"It's said that ghosts are supposed to make places colder," he said, returning to the task of brushing her hair. "I thought I'd put it to the test for myself."

"But you walked right through me."

"Yes," he said.

"How dare you? It felt obscene."

"But it worked, didn't it?"

"Yes," Cassie whispered.

Kett smiled. "So, will you meet them?" he asked as he continued brushing.

"Maybe," she mumbled.

Two minutes later the brushing stopped and she used the phone's selfie mode to examine the results. She raised her eyebrows in surprise. Somehow, Kett had managed to impose some sort of order upon her hair. While it was still curled and frizzy, it was far less untamed than it had been. Also, and of more importance, she was no longer drenched in sweat.

In fact, she looked almost presentable.

She glanced away from the screen. "How did you…?"

But she was alone again.

Despite the heat, she shivered as if he had just walked through her a second time. *Spooked by a spook,* she told herself, trying to make light of it.

She looked back at the phone's screen but, for some reason, the camera app was no longer running and she had to restart it. She checked her image again to make sure that, with Kett's disappearance, her hair hadn't returned to its previous state. It hadn't, and what he'd done made her feel just that little bit more human. She closed the phone cover having noticed that the time was several minutes gone twelve.

What should she do?

She took a step but her foot kicked something. It was the brush. After picking it up and pocketing it, she came to a decision.

Map App Flashback

"Hey, Cass. Over here." Cassie heard Georgia's voice call from somewhere to the right as she entered the restaurant level of Castle Mall. Her eyes located the table where the owner of the voice sat.

Beside Georgia, with his right hand holding her left, sat her boyfriend Mark. His blond hair and pale skin, characteristics he'd inherited from Nordic ancestors, were a complete contrast to Georgia. She'd often joked that if ever they had kids they'd come out looking like zebras. Mark had once countered saying, "She understands as much about genetics as she does English." Laughing, she'd punched him on the arm for that – he'd had a bruise for days.

Over the years, Cassie had seen Georgia inflict far more damage than that on those who thought they could pick on her. She remembered that time when, both aged fifteen, two men had attempted to mug them one night in the city centre. Cassie had screamed but Georgia had sprung into action, lashing out with incredible fury. It wasn't Georgia who'd ended up losing several teeth or having a finger broken. Cassie had gasped as her friend kicked one of them in the crotch as a parting gift and then laughed as he'd crawled off in agony. After the story became common knowledge, no one dared taunt Georgia. Because of Cassie's close association with her, some of that protection surrounded her as well.

Jason, sprawled out on a chair on the opposite side of the table, nodded to her. He was, as usual, attempting to look cool – his fashionably-torn skinny jeans were tight around his legs, and the t-shirt stretched across his chest.

Is that merely one or two sizes too small? Cassie wondered as she neared the table.

She was pretty certain he did it deliberately. He always claimed that he was still growing, which was also true as he towered over almost everyone else at school, including many of the teachers.

Between Georgia and Jason, an empty chair beckoned.

"What the hell have you done with your hair?" Georgia shrieked, her face lit up in amazement. "It's even frizzier than mine."

Well, that was no lie. Robert Kett's valiant taming attempt had been quite spectacular considering what he'd had to work with, but Cassie knew it needed to be straightened again – if she could afford it. Given the state of her finances, that was far from likely. She wished she'd picked up some of that spare money lying around in Kay's old house. *Could I go back in time and grab some? Can I even still time travel without the device?*

As she joined the others, she was aware of a couple of girls at another table who eyed her with worried looks on their faces. Had they been here half an hour or so ago when she'd stormed out after the device had disappeared? She did her best to ignore them and sat down.

"Well?" Georgia demanded, her free hand fondling Cassie's tearaway locks.

Cassie shook her head. "Don't ask. Really."

"I *am* asking," Georgia said, grinning.

"It looked even worse ten minutes ago."

"Why?" Georgia persisted.

"Long story. Too boring to tell," Cassie muttered. "Maybe one day…"

"Hah – Foxy Fox being mysterious as usual," Jason snorted, using his habit of referring to her by her surname only. "Probably stuck her fingers in a plug socket or something stupid like that."

Shut up, you jerk, Cassie thought but forced a smile instead. *Why do I think I fancy him when he says things like that? Okay, being tall and so bloody gorgeous might have a lot to do with it. But does he have to be a jerk all the time? And does he really have to wear sunglasses indoors?*

The conversation moved on to food. Georgia and Mark decided to order chicken and chorizo burritos with chips, while Jason settled on a beef enchilada. Cassie counted the change in her pocket by feel alone and tried to order just a cheaper starter stating she wasn't that hungry.

"Yeah, right," Georgia said, seeing through the white lie. "Have what you want. It's on me."

"No, you keep pay–"

"Shut up, Cass," Georgia interjected with a laugh. "No argument. I insist."

"Thanks," Cassie mumbled, embarrassed. Georgia was fully aware of the struggles Cassie had with finances and, far too many times, had lent her money that Cassie was never able to repay.

When the food arrived Cassie devoured her burrito and finished first. Then, as perpetually-thin Mark claimed to be full after consuming less than half, Cassie finished his off as well.

Jason, popping the last of his meal into his mouth, said, while still chewing, "Want to lick my plate as well?"

"Thanks, I'll pass," Cassie said, forcing another smile whilst thinking, *Jerk,* but knowing she didn't mean it.

What is it about him?

She knew he'd had a string of girlfriends, and had often broken up with them, leaving them in tears. *Am I just asking for yet more punishment? Why can't I be more like Georgia and find someone like Mark? I must be mental...*

But the few boys Cassie had gone out with had never resulted in a proper relationship.

Maybe I'm just too weird for them, she thought, remembering the time a boy called Joshua had seemed keen on her but the three times they'd gone on dates he'd either tripped over his feet or spilt drink down himself. He'd claimed he'd felt someone push him or the glass. What Cassie couldn't tell him was that she'd seen the bus man doing those things. *Great-grandad Charlie trying to look after me, whether or not I needed it.*

After they'd eaten, Georgia, Mark and Jason sat fiddling with their phones, their discussion flipping from one random subject to another. They talked about school, clothes, Georgia's progress in her martial arts sessions, the state of the world, climate change and how powerless they felt about the way various aspects of their lives were going. They all nodded in agreement when Mark said he always felt sidelined and ignored when the world appeared to be going to pot. He also started muttering about how his casual job of filling supermarket shelves was already driving him crazy. He'd only started the previous weekend after taking the last of his A-Level exams. He was a year older than the rest of them and was hoping for a university place once his exam results came through.

Jason added to this by complaining about his mum – how she was an embarrassment to him, and that he was still angry that she'd voted for Brexit two years ago despite his arguments as to why it could be nothing short of a complete disaster. Mark and Georgia nodded in agreement.

Cassie wanted to scream, *You should try living my life.*

She ached to tell them that she'd met her dead mother, fought off her previously unknown father bent on taking her life and body for himself, seen that same father killed by a cloned future version of herself, and travelled in time as far back as fifteen-something-or-other to see Norwich's city wall when it was still intact. Not only that, but she'd seen dumb copies of herself being cut down and dragged through the ground to their deaths, and had barely escaped that fate herself on more than one occasion.

"That's the older generation for you. They never even think we've got our own opinions," Mark said with a sigh, even though Cassie knew he got on well with his parents, as did Georgia.

Instead of joining in, though, Cassie contributed little to the conversation, hardly more than a nod of agreement here or a shrug there.

"It's like they just don't see any urgency in things," Georgia mumbled. "Like, it will be our world one day."

"If there's anything left," Mark added.

As a diversion from what she was feeling, Cassie had also opened up her phone – it felt wrong not to. Though, after what she'd just been through, the attraction had dulled more than a little. This was the same phone she'd taken off the prototype Kay just over an hour ago. It seemed reluctant to open some apps.

Maybe, Cassie considered, *it's only twenty per cent real.*

She remembered the device splitting four clones from her, each with their own set of clothes and phone. *Hold on, if that's right, then did that mean I'm only twenty per cent real myself? No, surely that can't be right. I've got to be the original one – and still one hundred per cent real.*

She decided that maybe the first four cloned duplicates were twenty-five per cent real instead of just twenty. And, if that applied to the phone as well, it was more amazing that it still managed to function. She sighed, knowing she'd never figure out how it all worked. She still wasn't certain whether she had been controlling the device or it had been controlling her – sometimes it had felt more like a battle of wills.

She tapped the map app and, to her surprise, it loaded without hesitation, using its GPS to deduce her correct location, centring on Castle Mall. She swiped at the map with a finger until the market came into view. Despite feeling full on the burritos, thoughts of fish and chips entered her head. She activated the satellite view and then homed in on the memorial gardens between the market and City Hall. Her finger touched the exact spot where she had become reacquainted with the forty-year-old version of Kay. A marker pin appeared on the screen where her finger prodded it. She remembered Kay telling her that her old abandoned phone had sprung into life with a map displaying the market. When had that happened? She pictured Kay munching on chips and saying the year had been 1982.

Maybe she saw this exact map, Cassie thought. Then another idea struck her. *What if this really is the actual map Kay saw? Could that be possible? How could a phone from now pick up a map in 1982 long before the mobile networks were in place?*

She expanded the map thinking, *Kay, this map is for you – I'm waiting for you there in 1982. Come and find me.*

A sudden bout of vertigo hit her, followed by a flash of double vision as if she was seeing the phone from two different angles. Then she was back in her own head just as the phone's display flashed before going dark.

"Whoah," Cassie squealed.

"What's wrong?" Mark said. Georgia's eyes were full of concern.

"Phone crashed, by the look of things," Jason said, plucking it out of Cassie's shaking hands without asking. "Not surprised – this old thing's ancient. Didn't you, like, get it for your fifteenth birthday or something? About time you got a new one. Ah, but you're completely skint, aren't you?"

Cassie glanced away from him, embarrassed. *That's it, let the whole world know.* Anyway, she knew his own family were far from rolling in money. Like her, he had been brought up by his mother alone. She didn't know what had happened to his father – he never spoke about him.

Jason examined the phone. "Okay, it's restarting on its own."

He handed it back to her and Cassie watched as the phone powered itself back up. She unlocked it with her fingerprint and it seemed to be working again. The battery said it still had 45% charge, so a lack of power hadn't been the problem.

No, she thought, *the battery was definitely not the cause.* She was sure what she'd experienced hadn't been vertigo, either. It had been more like the feeling when she'd travelled through time – not in the time portal manner – the direct way.

What had she done?

She'd imagined herself talking to Kay using something like telepathy. Maybe it had worked, but in a way that was more than the phone could handle.

She swallowed. Without the device guiding her, she felt scared. Were things like this going to keep happening to her?

The Urge To Confess

"You wouldn't believe me if I told you," Cassie muttered. They were on the top deck of a bus taking them homewards. Mark and Jason had wanted to stay in the city but Cassie had said she was knackered – which was true – and wanted to get back. So Georgia, sensing something was far from right, insisted on coming along as well.

I know she means well, Cassie thought, feeling guilty. Georgia was more than just a close friend – she was more like a sister. They had first connected at nursery school and had been best friends ever since.

"You weren't like this yesterday," Georgia said as the bus lurched around the corner of Prince of Wales Road and onto Riverside.

"Yesterday?"

"Mmm, at school."

Cassie was silent for several seconds. Then she muttered, "Yesterday. Yeah, I suppose it was yesterday for you."

"What d'you mean?"

Cassie sighed. The urge to tell someone was eating away at her. Cassie had confided to Georgia about some of the strange things she had previously experienced. But was this going too far? Would it freak her out too much? She looked out of the window and down at the boats on the river. She didn't know what to say. Then, she felt Georgia's fingers on her arm.

"Thank you," she whispered, leaning her head on Georgia's shoulder.

"So. Are you going to tell me about it?"

"Seems more like a fortnight," Cassie muttered, so only Georgia could hear. Wondering where her mouth was taking her, she couldn't help adding, "No, not even *seems* – it *was* a fortnight, give or take a day or two."

Georgia frowned. The bus was already half the way along Riverside Road. Soon they would pass the Lollards Pit pub on the right with Cow Tower coming up behind the shops and houses on the left.

"A fortnight? Is this still something to do with the problems you had after we went on that ghost walk last year?" Georgia said.

"Worse."

"Yeah, going by your hair, it must've been."

Cassie, sensing the approaching turmoil, closed her eyes. She still experienced the fear the location produced in her. But, when they'd gone on that walk, she felt the experience had awoken something in her that had always been buried there. As a child, she'd suffered from occasional nightmares about being engulfed in flames or being crushed in with what, in the dreams, had seemed like hundreds of other people. She'd always felt uneasy around this area but it had become more tangible last year as if the nightmares had become an experienced memory of a real event. She kept her eyes closed and teeth clamped together and said nothing until she felt the bus halting at the Kett's Hill roundabout. Once the feelings of dread and fear subsided, she let out a sigh.

"Better now?" Georgia asked as Cassie reopened her eyes.

She nodded and then pointed to the small building on the northern side of the roundabout as the bus passed it. "Used to be a police station," she said. She could picture the clone police streaming out of its door when she had been with Kay sometime back in the 1970s or whenever it had been – she was beginning to lose track.

"Oh," Georgia said. "What's that got to do with it?"

"I was there back when it was."

"Huh?"

"Told you, you wouldn't believe me."

"No offence, Cass. But sometimes – with you – I really don't know what to believe anymore."

"Yeah," Cassie said. "Me too."

The bus rumbled up the hill failing to get anywhere near the twenty-mile-an-hour limit.

"Er, you want to come to mine for a while or have you got to get back to your grandad?" Georgia said.

"Oh, Grandad," Cassie said, with alarm in her voice. *How could I have forgotten?* She hadn't seen him for well over a week. When she'd left him he'd been recovering from her removal of the repression Laurence had inflicted. She remembered the device saying he had been weak – was he still okay? She had to know. "I've got to get back to him."

"You *are* getting back to him," Georgia said, "by bus."

"No, I mean right now."

"What?"

Cassie felt something happening around her – she was involuntarily trying to teleport and this time it felt like it was going to work. She saw the horrified expression on Georgia's face and forced the process to stop.

"W-What the absolute fuck just happened?" Georgia whispered. "I swear I could see right through you for a second."

Georgia's hand gripped Cassie's arm as if trying to keep her grounded.

Cassie closed her eyes again, trying to force the panic away. *Keep calm*, she ordered herself. *It may have been several days for me but, for Grandad, it can't have been much more than a few hours.*

"Sorry. Too much has happened," Cassie said, her voice breaking. "I-I saw my mum."

"Saw her? How?"

"Saw her, spoke with her. Even hugged her."

She opened her eyes and knew they were filling with tears.

"I need to tell someone," Cassie whispered. "All of it. Before I forget. Not right now, not here, though. I've got to get back to Grandad."

Georgia's worried eyes scanned Cassie's face. "You're serious?"

Cassie nodded, unable to speak.

"Tomorrow? Can you come to mine tomorrow or shall I come to yours?" Georgia asked.

"Mine," Cassie said, adding, "if I manage to wake up."

"Right, no excuses. I want to hear all of it. No matter how mad it sounds. Promise?"

Cassie inserted the front door key into the lock and turned it. As she pushed the door open, she dreaded what she might find inside.

"Grandad?" she called.

There was no reply.

She crept into the lounge and saw him in his chair, head back and mouth open. Her breath caught in her throat. Was he dead? She couldn't see whether or not he was breathing.

"Grandad," she shouted, rushing across.

"Er, what?" he spluttered, waking up.

"Oh, thank goodness. You're all right."

She grabbed him around the shoulders and hugged him.

"Why shouldn't I be all right?" he said. "Just taking a nap. Anyway, you fixed that thing that Laurence—"

He stopped and scrutinised her face, before glancing at the clock on the mantelpiece. It said the time was just gone half two.

"Okay," he said. "I last saw you, what, just over three hours ago? Yes, I think that's about right."

His eyes bored into hers for several seconds and he reached out with one hand and caressed her hair. It was not quite as frizzy as it had been the last time she had been here. Then he said, "How long has it been for you?"

Cassie sighed and flopped onto the sofa. "More than a week," she whispered.

He nodded and sat up. Then, with an expression that was part smile, part grimace, he said. "You keep this up and you'll be eligible for a bus pass by the end of next month."

Then his smile turned into a full grin and she couldn't help chuckling. That was like something he would have said five years ago. Elated, she was daring to believe that her proper grandad was back.

"Are you going to tell me all about it?" he said.

She shut her eyes. Would Grandad understand any more than Georgia? She now regretted her promise to her best friend. Grandad was family – he knew about the device, about what it had done to Mum – he deserved to be told. But Georgia and her parents had stood by her after they'd lost Mum as well as later on when Grandad had appeared to turn senile. Georgia deserved it as much as he did.

"Later," Cassie said. "I need a damn good bath and then I need to sleep for a whole day, maybe even a week."

Fire In The Sky

Bath Time

The first thing Cassie noticed when she woke up was the smell. Then she remembered where she was and groaned. At least her head felt almost normal and the piledriver headache from the day before was absent. However, her entire body ached and she was still sore down below, which wasn't too surprising.

It was light again and a glance around the cave showed that it was almost empty. Em'Dor was tending the entrance fire along with Em'Lo and Ge'Tal. While the elder girl was building up the fire, the younger two were collecting the old ash together for some reason. Cassie could also hear voices outside.

She turned her attention back to the smell.

"Oh, bloody hell," she shouted, lifting the animal skin cover. The baby had soiled himself or, more precisely, he had soiled her. He started screaming as she lifted him off her. She gagged staring at the dark, sticky mess that was spread from just under her left breast down to her hips.

Em'Dor, seeing Cassie's state, laughed before grabbing the child by his unsoiled arms to whisk him outside, leaving Cassie naked and filthy, and wondering what to do with herself. Em'Lo and Ge'Tal continued their ash-collecting and, although Em'Lo smiled at Cassie, she made no move to help.

A minute later Em'Dor returned with Em'Jex in tow. They helped Cassie to her feet, her legs unsteady after her ordeal of the day before.

They led her outside – she had to take small steps to prevent aggravating the soreness she felt in the lower half of her body. To her surprise, the rough, stony ground didn't hurt her feet as much as she expected. Em'Jex also carried out the soiled covers from Cassie's bed. These were dumped on a pile along with several others in the open area in front of the cave entrance. They guided Cassie towards the trees as they followed a path that descended towards the stream that flowed down the hillside.

I vaguely remember this, Cassie thought. *I'm sure I also remember them washing me as well. Couldn't I do anything for myself?*

The chill of the water on her bare skin made Cassie gasp. At least no one else other than Em'Dor and Em'Jex was around to see her. But her memories of being washed here also included glimpses of several people swimming and washing together at the same time – and many of them were male.

Em'Jex rubbed something into Cassie's skin – a gunky, oily substance that seemed to work like soap.

After the dipping and cleansing in the icy water, the air felt warm by comparison. Then she was warmed further as they dried her off using something that may have been woven from animal hair.

"Clothes," Cassie said as they walked back to the cave. She used the term in their language that referred to the wraparound skins that most adults, if few children, wore around their waists.

Back inside, Em'Lo was instructed to take Cassie to a place further back in the cave. Em'Lo pointed at several small piles of skins that appeared to have been stitched together into shapes that could, with a bit of manipulation, be secured in place. The first Cassie picked was too large but the second managed to stay up. She continued searching through the skins, looking for something that resembled the cloaks that she'd seen a few others wear but drew a blank.

She tried to ask about a bra but there was no word for that and, even after she'd tried to indicate what she meant, Em'Lo looked at her without understanding.

Topless it is, then, she thought with a shudder, pondering if she had the skills to concoct a stone-age version of a bra for herself. She then wondered whether or not she'd spent the last year completely naked.

No wonder I got pregnant, she thought, accompanied by a shudder.

Taking her hand, Em'Lo led her across to a second pile of skins and she was relieved to find one that could be used as a cloak. Although it was large and the arm holes weren't in the right place, she wrapped it around herself, tying it at the neck and waist with the attached strips of fur. After adjusting the fit several times until she'd got it about right, she felt the closest to being dressed, not to mention warm, since she'd first woken up.

Em'Lo then helped her select more skins from a third pile to replace the soiled bed covers. She was about to slide back under their protection when

Em'Jex returned and scolded her. Dragging Cassie back outside by the arm, they stopped beside the pile of filthy skins. Em'Jex picked up some of them and indicated that Cassie should do the same with the remainder. She shook her head, almost unbelieving.

"Surely I shouldn't be doing this so soon after having a baby," she said in English.

"Oh'Kay mad talk," Em'Jex stated, butting at her with her shoulder towards the skins. "Oh'Kay wake now. Work."

Cassie sighed and, with a wince, stooped to pick up as many of the skins as she could, leaving a handful behind. Em'Jex grunted her disapproval, but they remained on the ground while Em'Jex started back towards the stream. Cassie followed on legs that may as well have been made of jelly.

What was the point of washing if we've now got to handle all these? Cassie thought a few minutes later as Em'Jex dumped her load on the bank indicating that Cassie should do the same. Em'Jex then picked one of the skins from the pile and squatted down beside the water where rounded boulders, some several feet across, lined the edge of the stream. Then she dunked the skin in the water and applied some of the same soap-like stuff on it, massaging it in and manipulating the material to persuade the dirt, and worse, to come out. Then she thrashed it against the stone letting the water carry away the dislodged dirt and remaining soap.

"Wash," Em'Jex grunted and Cassie attempted to do the same but almost slid into the water as the boulders were smooth and slippery.

Just how many centuries have these boulders been used for washing clothes? she thought as she worked, marvelling that the rock was worn so smooth. The first skin she washed was thrown back at her and various spots where she'd missed something were pointed out. But, after a few attempts, she managed to perform the task to Em'Jex's satisfaction.

As she knelt she also glanced at the soles of her feet, shocked to see the layer of hardened skin on them. *No shoes*, she thought. *No one here wears shoes at all.* But she also spotted something else on her left foot – a discoloured patch of skin that looked like a burn mark. About three to four inches long, it ran up from her outside ankle towards her shin. She picked at it but there was no discomfort.

It looked old. When had that happened?

As the pile of unwashed skins shrunk Em'Jex would, once in a while, pick at something and flick it away. Cassie examined the skin she was washing and spotted a movement – another flea – she pointed it out to Em'Jex who clicked it dead between her thumbnails. Cassie was also shown another creature living on the skin, which made her shudder as she recalled the outbreaks of lice at school when she was six or seven.

They were almost through the pile of washing when Em'Kell and another woman, whose name Cassie couldn't recall, walked up the incline towards them. The other woman, who was no more than a girl, resembled an older copy of Ge'Tal. She carried two young, nappy-clad babies as she walked, one at each breast. There was something vaguely familiar about one of them. They stopped next to where Cassie and Em'Jex thrashed the last of the skins on the boulders and swirled them in the water for a final rinse.

"Ah, Gu'Tun," Em'Kell said. "Oh'Kay Ka'See work now. About time."

The 'about time' phrase consisted of a long whine, click and whistle, but Cassie's mind translated it, including the implication that it was also something of an insult.

Em'Kell then tapped Cassie on the arm indicating that she should stand. Then she wrestled one of the babies out of Gu'Tun's arms. The child screamed and momentarily opened its eyes.

Oh, Cassie realised, seeing the distinct blue irises, *no wonder I thought it was familiar.*

She took her baby – what had Ka'Chull called him? Ka'Tor? – opened her cloak and held him to her breast. He clamped himself back on and continued feeding as if unconcerned that his source of nourishment had been substituted.

She sighed. *At least, he's no longer covered in shit.*

Awakening

Over the next few days Cassie somewhat reluctantly found herself getting into a daily routine. Most of it was drudge work: cleaning, washing, preparing food, caring for and feeding not only her own baby but, on occasion, expected to have to feed Em'Tull and Em'Ban while their mothers, Em'Jex and Gu'Tun, were tasked with other duties. Sometimes the babies were just dumped on her and she'd have to feed one whilst cleaning another at the same time as making sure a third wasn't crawling off and getting into trouble.

While it wasn't strictly enforced, there seemed to be a definite gender demarcation when it came to the work. Women did the drudge work while the men spent most days hunting though, occasionally, some of the women joined them. The thought of hunting made her shudder – she didn't have the stomach for killing animals.

I've only got the stomach for eating them. Good job I never stuck with being a vegetarian, she thought, remembering the experiment that had lasted for less than a fortnight when she was fourteen.

It was becoming obvious that the other women treated Cassie as if she was barely a child herself. She couldn't blame them. The few fleeting snatches of memory that occasionally entered her head suggested she had been next to useless before *waking up.* Her stone-age skill set was comparable only with the younger children in the tribe.

They grew up with it – I've got to learn it from scratch. Maybe I'm like some wild animal they're trying to domesticate. No, more like the other way round – it's like I'm too domesticated, I suppose, for their wild way of life.

The days seemed to be growing longer and, as she became more adept at expressing herself in their simple language, she started trying to find out what had happened to her over the past year. Em'Dor, whose stomach grew as Cassie's shrunk back to something resembling its previous dimensions, was the one who provided the most answers.

"Men find Oh'Kay in woods," Em'Dor explained one day. She was showing Cassie how to mix fine ash from the fires with animal fat to make the soap they used for washing both themselves and their clothes. "Fourteen moons past. Naked. Tribe not known. Say nothing. Dumb. Except, sometimes, Oh'Kay. So name Oh'Kay."

"Why, how baby?" Cassie tried.

"Not know how baby made?"

"Yes. Why Ka'Chull?"

"Men say Oh'Kay ugly."

Thanks, Cassie thought, biting down a response that would have been wasted on the girl.

"Men say Oh'Kay white like spirit. Za'Lak say bad spirit.

Oh yes, he's the miserable one with the angry face.

"Men say Oh'Kay eyes are sky ice, not brown like warm bear and warm earth. Em'Jex say men scared."

"Not Ka'Chull?"

"Yes, Ka'Chull same. Then Ka'Chull see Oh'Kay cold. Ka'Char also but Ka'Chull bed Oh'Kay first. Warm. Oh'Kay like warm. Many times."

Shit – it sounds like I jumped into the first warm bed that offered itself.

Em'Dor continued, "Oh'Kay have new bed. Baby grow in Oh'Kay. Then El'Car want Ka'Chull again."

"Again?"

"Yes, El'Car and Ka'Chull make baby before Oh'Kay come."

"Which one?"

"Dead."

"Oh. Why?"

Em'Dor shrugged. "Born dead. Happens. Me – brother dead. Same."

"You had brother?"

Em'Dor nodded, touching her stomach. "Happens."

Cassie glanced at Em'Dor's pregnant mound and timidly asked, "Alive?"

Em'Dor grinned. "Yes, kicks."

"Good," Cassie replied, not knowing what else to say but wondering what the mortality rates, both infant and adult, were like in the tribe.

"Why I wake?" Cassie asked, deliberately changing the subject.

"Fire in sky."

"Yes, hear many times. What fire in sky?"

"In sky. Fire goes whoosh," Em'Dor said, accompanying the sound with a swift arc of a pointing finger. She gave Cassie the impression of something that had shot across the sky from west to east.

"At night?"

"Nearly night. Fire turn night day. Boom."

"Boom?"

"There, past hill," Em'Dor said, pointing eastwards towards the incline that was, like most of this world, covered in trees. There were mostly pines at this altitude though, on the lower slopes, Cassie could see other species mixed in with them. Where the land rose to the mountain peaks they were replaced by bare rock and, on the higher ones, snow. The peaks were mainly visible on the other side of the valley to the south but, on clear days, Cassie had spotted more mountains to the north behind the hill into which the cave had been dug, along with at least one more to the west whose peak was mostly hidden by the closer trees in that direction.

"Far fire, burn," Em'Dor said.

Probably a meteor or is it meteorite? Cassie thought, trying to remember the difference before recalling that a meteo*rite* was the one that came *right* down to the ground. Wasn't that something her grandad had told her years ago? Or maybe, as she still had no idea of *when* she was, her grandad would tell her that at some point thousands of years in the future.

"Men go see," Em'Dor continued.

"That night?"

"Morning. Za'Lak, Ka'Gar take Pi'Tut, Ja'Mutt." As she mentioned Pi'Tut, a boy who was a little older than Em'Dor herself, she smiled and her hand caressed her swollen belly. Cassie wasn't certain but she assumed Pi'Tut might be the father of Em'Dor's baby. The two certainly spent time together although they rarely shared a bed.

"What men find?" Cassie asked.

"Far. Many far. Men come back. No thing."

"No thing?"

"Find no spirit of fire. Just where spirit touch. Trees fall, broke. Land burnt. Nothing but burnt."

"Oh," Cassie said. *Does she mean a meteorite that was destroyed as it landed?* She remembered one that had caused a few problems in Russia when she had been around thirteen or fourteen – there had been lots of dash cam videos of it on the Internet. *Oh God, I really miss the Internet*, she thought, but Em'Dor was still talking.

"Fire boom wake Oh'Kay. Shout, mad talk, hold head. Lots."

"Then?" Cassie asked, having no recollection of what Em'Dor told her. *I only remember waking up the next morning.*

"Cry. Sleep. Wake morning. More mad talk. Baby come."

"Why fire make me wake?"

Em'Dor made a face. "Know not."

Well, at least I woke up, Cassie thought. Then something niggled at the back of her mind. She frowned trying to capture it before it completely escaped.

But then it crystallised into a certainty.

I was never meant to wake up at all.

She gasped. *Where had THAT come from?*

"You mad face," Em'Dor said, a puzzled look crossing her features.

"I've just remembered something important," Cassie whispered, in English.

"Mad talk."

"Me, head, come back," Cassie translated, pointing to her skull, wondering if she'd got the meaning across.

"Good. Now make soap," Em'Dor said, returning to the task at hand.

But, in Cassie's head, that thought kept returning, *I wasn't supposed to wake up at all.*

She was certain something had become unlocked.

Maybe it's like Pandora's box or that dead or alive cat that some scientist put in a box – oh yes, Schrödinger. Damn, I can remember his name. Why can't I remember really important things?

Whatever it may have been, Cassie's head found it elusive.

"Make soap," Em'Dor repeated.

"Okay," Cassie muttered.

"See, Ka'See says Oh'Kay," Em'Dor laughed. "Now make soap."

Cassie sighed and applied herself to the task.

While her hands stirred the mixture of fat and ash with a wooden stick, her mind thought about things escaping from boxes. And then the memory of one specific box, a large wardrobe-sized one built into a wall, popped into her head.

A Letter or Two

Write It Down

Cassie's promise to herself to sleep for a week hadn't worked out as planned. Georgia turned up before eleven the next morning – a Sunday – as she couldn't wait to hear all about what had happened. First, though, Georgia had to come to terms with how much better Cassie's grandad, Bill, was looking and acting.

"What happened to him?" she whispered to Cassie while he was in the kitchen putting the kettle on. "When I last saw him a couple of weeks ago he could hardly even remember my name."

"It's all part of what happened," Cassie said.

"Well, you'd better get on with it, then."

Reluctantly at first and spurred on with cups of tea brewed for them all by her Grandad, Cassie began to recount as much as she could still remember.

At least, this way, I won't have to tell it twice, she thought.

However, she found she had to backtrack as she kept missing things out.

Georgia said, "You seem to be forgetting bits of it already."

It was true. There were some events where Cassie couldn't remember the precise order in which they had taken place. Not the portals she had gone through – it was the other stuff – like when certain conversations with Kay had taken place and, nearer the end, where time had looped around and around.

"Write it down," Bill said, with a laugh. He was getting his own back on her for the number of times she'd said the same thing to him over the past few years.

"Yeah, good idea. You can't remember whether you were coming, going or had already been," Georgia said, with a giggle.

"Yeah, all right," Cassie said, getting grumpy. "Look, you try going round in circles meeting older or dumb versions of yourself and seeing them die under your nose or whatever."

"Sorry, Cass," Georgia said, her hand resting on Cassie's shoulder. "It must have been hard. I still find it hard as well – hard to believe, that is."

"Oh, it definitely happened, all right," Bill said. "I saw older Cassie at her mum's funeral seven years ago."

"So did I," Cassie said. "I saw me and older me."

"Now I'm really getting confused," Georgia said, shaking her head.

"I was nine when Mum died. Then me and Kay went back to the funeral."

"Why did you go back?"

"Because, when I was back in this house in 2010, I saw the reflection of myself and Kay in the wardrobe mirror upstairs. We looked just like the people I remembered seeing at the funeral when I was nine. So I knew we'd go back and, when I told Mum about it, that was how she realised she could get Grandad to pass the device on to me."

"Yetch," Georgia squeaked. "That didn't help at all. I need a map."

Cassie tried drawing a diagram – a timeline to get it straight in her head but it got so complicated, she gave up. Bill also jotted down notes but he looked at what he'd written and shook his head.

"Maybe you should take notes as well," he said to Georgia.

Cassie laughed. "Waste of time," she said. "She has enough trouble reading her own writing afterwards. And her typing's almost completely indecipherable."

Georgia, after sticking her tongue out at them, said, "I know. Let's record it." She turned her phone on and opened the voice recording app.

With a short break for lunch and several cups of tea later, it was mid-afternoon by the time Cassie thought most of it had been documented in some form. She used her phone to record it as well, hoping it wouldn't go wrong again. She also made Georgia promise she wouldn't let anyone else hear her copy of the recording – ever.

Well, at least it's no longer just inside my own head, Cassie thought.

All three of them fell silent, staring at the disc that sat on the table, its red button uppermost. Both Bill and Georgia refused to touch it.

Bill broke the silence. "I don't like what it says," he said.

"What do you mean?" Cassie asked.

"Giving it to you implies that the device thinks you will have need of it. Now that we've heard the whole story, I just don't want to imagine what might constitute an emergency."

"Nor do I," Cassie murmured.

"Promise me you won't do anything stupid," Georgia said, which initially annoyed Cassie until she saw the worried look in her eyes.

"I'll try," Cassie said.

"No, I want a promise – there is no try."

"I promise," Cassie whispered.

"Good. You'd better keep it," Georgia said and stood to envelop Cassie in a hug, wrapping her arms around her best friend as if she was afraid to let go. "Oh, and one more thing."

"What?"

"Let me try to do something with your hair, otherwise you'll be the big topic of conversation at school tomorrow."

"Oh God, school. I don't know if I can face up to that," Cassie said, feeling close to tears.

"Yes you can," Georgia said, "I'll look after you. I won't let anyone get to you. I'm good at that."

Cassie smiled and returned the hug.

Letters

There was a letter waiting for Cassie after she returned from school the next day.

She opened it up to find three sheets of folded A4 paper. Two of the sheets were completely blank but the one sandwiched between them contained inconsistent and somewhat wobbly hand-printed text. It read:

> fire today twice
>
> Second time LUcky
>
> Common first four Are the key
>
> if Nothing is ignored

Cassie frowned and showed it to her grandad. "Make any sense to you?"

He read it aloud. "Fire today twice, second time lucky. Common first four are the key if nothing is ignored." Then he shook his head.

He picked up the envelope and examined it. It was slightly yellow, as if quite old, but it had been stamped using a franking machine and the posting date was 28 June – last week. Cassie's name and address were handwritten in the same style used on the letter's contents, but neither of them recognised the writing.

"Parts of it – like the N in Norwich – are how I do it," Cassie said.

"It looks more like a child scrawled it," her grandad replied, and she was forced to agree. "The paper looks old as well," he added. "And there are depression lines on one of the blank sheets, probably from where something was written on the sheet above and pressed through."

"Weird. What do you make of it?"

"Hmm. A bit worrying. I don't think it sounds threatening but whoever sent it obviously knows where we live."

"Should I throw it away?"

"Maybe," he said. "No, on second thoughts, not yet. If any more turn up and they start becoming threatening, then we might need to inform the police."

"Another week over, thank goodness," Cassie said four days later, closing the front door. Her mind hadn't been fully on school work and Georgia had needed to chivvy Cassie along to encourage her to keep up with the rest of the class.

"There's another letter for you, Cass," her grandad said. "It's on the table in the lounge. Looked important."

"Another one? Let's hope it's not as stupid as the first one," she said. "Did you get the shopping done?"

"Yes, but I forgot to get the chocolate so we'll have to do without."

Cassie looked at him, her head tilted to one side. "What chocolate?"

"The big bar we can't afford and I shouldn't have anyway."

"Ah, that one," she said, grinning. "I bet you forgot the twenty bags of sugar as well."

He nodded and smiled. She hugged him. It was fantastic having her old grandad back. His memory had returned to normal, as had his sense of humour. He was already putting some much-needed weight back on, too. Only one thing niggled at the back of Cassie's mind. Where had Kay's version of him come from? Cassie recalled that the device had extracted Kay's essence from her body just before she'd died and then reinserted the memories into the clone Cassie had chosen. But what had been the source of that alternative Grandad? Cassie hoped there wasn't some strange timeline where that version of him actually existed.

"I saw the doctor this morning," he said.

"Oh, what did he say?" Cassie said, remembering that he'd phoned for an appointment a few days before.

"Young lady doctor this time," he said, a twinkle in his eye. "She had trouble believing I was the same person."

"Not surprised – you aren't the same person you were a week ago. Could she explain it?"

"No, and when she asked if I had any idea what had happened, I told her you'd knocked some sense back into me," he laughed. "Well, I couldn't tell her the real reason, could I?"

"Definitely not," Cassie said, picking up the letter and frowning at it.

"You're meant to open it – they're easier to read when you do that, I find."

"Shut up," she laughed, opening it up. "Oh, it's from one of those storage places. But I've never used them before."

"What's it say?"

"Apparently, they're storing something in my name."

"Sounds dubious. Do you have to pay anything?"

"Doesn't say – there's a phone number to call."

"Better ring them, then. We can't afford any extras."

"No, nothing to pay," Cassie said a few minutes later as she shut her phone off. She was still frowning. "It's all paid for up until the end of July but they'd recently been given instructions to send the letter out exactly when they did, even though they say the storage was set up several years ago."

"Years? That must have cost something. Who is it from?"

Cassie looked at what she'd scribbled on the envelope. "S. T. R. Boardal."

"Never heard of him."

"It's a woman, apparently."

"Never heard of her, either."

"Funny, but it rings a bell with me. Can't think why, though."

"Did they say what was stored and how much of it there was?"

"Ten square feet – they don't know how full it is or what's in it. Probably nothing valuable as she says they won't store money or valuables."

"And it's definitely addressed to you?"

"Yeah, by name – it even had a note of my date of birth."

"Probably too late to go today," he said, glancing at the clock.

"Well, I've not got anything planned for tomorrow – can't afford it. Anyway, the last time I went down the city – well, we all know what happened then."

"Indeed. Tomorrow it is, then. I'd better come with you and we should probably take some ID with us to prove who we are."

The Box

At the storage depot, they showed the letter to the lady on reception. She asked for ID and Cassie showed her birth certificate and student ID card. Her grandad also produced a council tax bill, his passport and forms showing he had been Cassie's legal guardian since the death of her mother.

The combination appeared to satisfy the receptionist who returned the letter to Cassie. She then led them through several security doors until they reached a wide corridor lined on both sides with locked metal doors. She stopped and gestured towards one door in particular whose designation label matched the reference on Cassie's letter.

"How do we open it?" Cassie asked, looking at the numeric keypad attached to the door.

"Haven't you got the PIN?" the woman asked.

"Huh?"

"The PIN code – the number that unlocks it."

"No," Cassie said. "We didn't know anything about this being here until your letter turned up yesterday. We didn't set it up."

The woman frowned. "Well, you can't get into it without the PIN."

"How long is it?"

"Four digits on those units," she said. "Didn't the original owner tell you what it was?"

Cassie's eyes met her grandad's.

"Ah," they said in unison, with Cassie adding, "We weren't given an actual number – more like a clue or riddle. At least, I suppose that's what it was."

"Right," the woman said.

"What happens if we get it wrong?"

"Oh, it just sets off some alarms. I'm used to it – people often enter them wrong even when they know what they should be."

"Will we get more than one go?"

"I'll keep an eye on you from reception and give you up to three goes," the woman said, pointing at a CCTV camera near the ceiling that Cassie hadn't noticed. Then the woman turned on her heel and left them to it.

"Can you remember what it said?" Cassie asked, softly.

He shut his eyes and said, "Fire today twice, second time lucky. Common first four are the key if nothing is ignored."

"You sure?"

He nodded.

"How on Earth did you remember all that?"

"Maybe you cleared out more than a few cobwebs when you freed me from the repression," he said. "I did the shopping yesterday without a list, you know."

"Impressive. And it does mention four being the key."

"But what does the rest mean?"

"Say it again," Cassie asked.

"Fire today twice, second time lucky. Common–"

"Stop."

"You got something?"

"Yeah, possibly. Remember I said the fires, the library one and that shop, whatever it was called, were on the same date, but different years?"

"Garlands?" he said. "Your gran loved that place before it burnt down."

"Yes, that was the name. Anyway, both dates were August the first."

"That explains the 'fire today twice' bit then. What about the second part?"

"Um, it took two goes to get to the library. 1994 was the year the library burnt down but I arrived in 1970 first."

"Okay, so maybe that deals with the 'second time lucky' part," he said. "Possibly, it's just there to confirm the first part. But, which four numbers are the key?"

"Well, it might be one and eight as that's August the first. But, as we need four numbers, maybe it could be 0108."

"Possibly – and they are common to both dates," he agreed.

"Oh, wait – could it be 0801?"

"Don't complicate things. Anyway, what about the 'if nothing is ignored' part? What could that mean? Does that tell us which way round it might be?"

"Doesn't make any sense to me at the moment," Cassie said. "What is there to ignore that we shouldn't be ignoring?"

Bill stood there thinking, tapping his bottom lip with a finger. Finally, the finger stopped tapping and was raised in the air. "Hmm – a zero is nothing. Maybe it's not saying *not* to ignore something but, instead, it's telling us to ignore the zeroes."

"But that only leaves us with two numbers – the one and the eight – or eight and one if they're the other way around."

"Yes, it does. Is there anything else common about those two dates?"

"Well, both the years start with nineteen," Cassie said. "Could that be it?"

"So, 1819 then."

Cassie shrugged, "You reckon?"

"No idea. Maybe the year comes first, followed by the month and day. In that case, it would be 1981. Who knows?"

"Not me, that's for certain."

"Yes, but we know what will happen if we get it wrong," he said.

"Yeah. Alarms, as she said. Hmm..."

"What?"

"It went 'common first four' – so the 70 and the 94 parts of the years would be at the end if the years came after the day and month. If the year came first, the 70 or 94 would be part of the first four, which doesn't match up. So the year must definitely be at the end."

"That makes sense. You sure?"

"Only one way to find out," she said, her finger poised over the keypad. "I think 1819 feels the most likely – it's the way I'd do it, anyway."

"Try it then."

Cassie slowly keyed in a one, an eight followed by another one. Her finger hovered over the nine.

"I think I want to put my fingers in my ears just in case," she whispered.

"Me, too," Bill said.

Cassie took a breath and, with a wince, pressed the final nine. There was a click and the unit unlocked itself. They both grinned at each other.

"I was really expecting those alarms to go off," he said, chuckling.

"Yeah, absolutely."

"Rather lucky getting it right first try. Or is something else going on?"

Cassie shrugged and said, "Possibly. Anyway, let's see what we've got."

She opened the door slowly and peered inside. The unit was about three-quarters full with two stacks of large cardboard boxes side by side, six boxes high. Perched on top of them was a single smaller box. Cassie started pulling down the top box and nearly dropped it as it was heavier than expected. It took both of them to lower it down onto the floor. She opened the lid, surprised to see that, despite the weight, it was only around half full. On top were several items of clothing, all black. As these couldn't have accounted for the weight, Cassie lifted them up and saw something familiar.

"Oh," she said, retrieving it.

"What is it?"

"Kay," Cassie said, with tears forming in her eyes as she showed him the broken mobile phone.

Pennies From Heaven

The phone's screen was cracked, and the rest of the casing was scratched and battered. Removing it from its case, she turned it over. Then she pulled her working phone from her pocket and did the same. She showed them to Bill.

"Scary," he said, seeing not only the same model number but serial numbers that were completely identical. "The exact same phone."

"This is the one I lost in the chalk caves. The original one that Kay used to find me on the market in 1982. It looks the same as when she showed it to me."

"You didn't keep it, then?"

"I really don't remember. It didn't work by then so probably not. At least I don't remember having it after that. The next time I had a phone was when I nicked Kay's one – this one – after the clones were made."

Cassie returned it to the box, placing it on top of the items of clothing. Then she turned her attention to what else the box held. It was filled with small plastic bags, each labelled with a number. She pulled out one at random and then pushed it back under the clothes just as quickly.

"Come closer," she whispered.

"Why? What is it?"

"Block the cameras from seeing this," she added.

She pulled the bag back out and showed Bill the label with 1998 written on it. The bag contained a fistful of coins and a few ten-pound notes. He lifted the clothes and pulled out another bag, keeping it close to his chest to hide it from prying eyes. That one had 2015 written on it. He opened it to find the coins it contained were more modern, though the smaller denomination notes were paper and not plastic.

A quick examination of one of the other boxes showed it was packed full with yet more money bags under a layer of innocuous black clothing. Given the weight of the other boxes it was possible they were all the same. If that was so, then they might have been looking at several thousand pounds.

"Wow," Cassie whispered. "Nothing valuable, they said. Looks like Kay broke a few rules."

"Indeed," he replied. "Are these the ones she carried around with her?"

Cassie nodded. "Yes, and the ones upstairs in her house."

He slowly shook his head, as if he couldn't believe what they were seeing.

"One question," he said, pulling out another bag and opening it.

"What?"

"This one's marked 1987 but has lots of coins from earlier than that." He showed her a handful. "Look, this two-pee coin is from 1975. Doesn't make sense."

"Ah, wait. I think the dates on the bags mean that the coins and notes are all legal tender for that year, not just the year they were made."

"Oh, I see. And I suppose that was how she could move money back into the past and bank it when it was worth more."

"Yeah, I still have problems getting my head around all that."

"Well, you obviously did figure it out by the time you became her."

"But I didn't become her, and never will do."

Bill sighed. "Yes," he said. "It's all extremely confusing." Then his voice dropped even quieter, "And if that lady is listening in on us, it should hopefully be too confusing to understand."

"No kidding. But how do we get all this back home?" Cassie asked. "There's too much to take back on a bus. And we can't afford a taxi."

"Can't we?" he said, with a nod to the boxes.

"What? Oh yes. I suppose maybe we can, now. This is going to take some getting used to. What if they find out Kay was storing money here?"

"Well, they can probably try to sue her or something," he chuckled.

He put the bag back and pulled out another labelled 1995. "Ah, Emily. Not a good year," he sighed, returning it to the box.

"I wish I'd met Gran," Cassie whispered.

"Yes, so do I," he said. "You really would have loved her."

Then he looked directly into Cassie's eyes. "Of course, that doesn't mean you need to go back and meet her in person."

"No, I promised," Cassie said.

He pulled out a bag labelled 2014 and whispered, "Well, we can't pay with the pound coins or paper notes in that one. Can you find any recent ones?"

They rummaged and found several labelled 2017 and 2018. The 2017 ones still contained a few paper ten-pound notes and a number of the old round pound coins. They left the paper notes and old coins in the bag, sharing out the rest between them. It reminded Cassie of when she did something similar herself just before she'd gone shopping in the Anglia Square of 1994.

"It feels like we're stealing it," she muttered, nodding her head towards the CCTV camera nearby.

"Yes, it does a bit," he agreed. "But, it's all in your name. And who else could Kay give it to?"

Cassie knew that was true. *Kay was a version of me I will never grow up to become — this money was hers so, logically, as Kay no longer exists, it must now be mine,* she told herself.

It still didn't feel right, though.

"What are we going to do with the really old ones?" Cassie asked, pointing out a bag with 1946 written on it. Inside, there were a couple of ten shilling notes, a pound note, loads of dull copper coins, some silver and the occasional brass of a 'thrupenny' bit.

"Well, maybe coin collecting might just have to become my new hobby," Bill said, with a smile. "You know, I did have a small collection when I was a boy. Lost interest when I got a bit older, though."

They heaved the small box back on top of the others in the storage unit and, after locking it, returned to reception.

"No alarms — you got it unlocked, then?" the receptionist asked with a grin.

"Yes, thanks," Cassie said. "Um, how do we get it all home? We haven't got a car and it's too much to take on a bus."

"We can arrange delivery, though one of you will need to come in and open it on the agreed date. Here's a price list for our delivery service."

Cassie and Bill exchanged a glance.

"When can you deliver it?" Cassie asked.

"You're quiet," Bill said as they sat on the bus back home. It was waiting at the traffic lights at the junction opposite the railway station, ready to turn left onto Riverside Road.

"Yeah," she said. "There are still things that don't add up?"

"What in particular?"

"Well, for a start — how did Kay get the letter with the clue sent?"

"What do you mean?"

"It was only posted last week. But she hadn't been to the house in weeks when I was there right at the end."

"No idea. Although…"

"What?"

"I think you can instruct solicitors to send things on specific dates."

"Yeah, could be."

"That might also account for the paper looking old and yellowed."

"But how did she figure out the riddle?"

"Did you tell her about the fires?"

Cassie thought for a moment. "Yes, I vaguely remember Kay saying it wasn't going to be a date I'd forget. Oh, wait…"

"What?"

"I remember her saying 'You'd better not' when I agreed with her."

"Well, that answers that."

"Um, no, it doesn't."

"How come?"

"Because the only possible time I could have told her was just before she went and…" Cassie paused, looking around at how far away the other bus passengers were. Then, keeping her voice low she continued, "…cut Laurence's head off. And she died almost straight after that."

He nodded slowly.

"So when did she have time to set it all up?" Cassie said.

He shrugged and shook his head. "No idea. Future you gets more amazing the more I find out about her."

"Yeah, I've got a lot to live up to. Not that I'm ever going to live that particular life."

The bus lurched into life and trundled around the corner.

"But that's still not all," Cassie said. "Where did that name come from?"

"What name?"

"The box people said the person who set it up years ago was called – oh, I can't remember now. Board-something or other."

"Boardal?"

"Yes, that was it – and there were three initials, S, T and R."

"You remembered that bit, then?"

"Yeah – when I first wrote it down it made me think of string or maybe star."

"Star?"

"Yep."

He thought for a moment, his eyes watching the boats on the river as the bus travelled along beside it. Then he snapped his fingers. "Star Boardal – ah."

"What?"

"Starboard is one side of a boat – the other is port."

"Huh?"

"Starboard followed by 'al'. And, of course, port followed by 'al' is…"

"Portal – hah."

"Clever."

"Me or Kay?"

"Both of you, of course," he said. "Oh, and me for working it out."

They both grinned.

"And maybe that's why we cracked the riddle so easily," he added.

"What do you mean?"

"Kay's thought processes must have been very similar to yours. So she knew she had to make up a clue that only you would understand."

"Well, you cracked a lot of it – I wouldn't have done it without you – especially the 'ignoring' bit."

"I expect you would have done it on your own, given a bit more time."

"Maybe – glad I didn't have to, though." Then she frowned. "But why go to the effort of doing the rhyme – why not just write the PIN down as plain numbers in the first place?"

"I suppose someone else might have read the numbers and raided the box before you could get to it."

"Yeah, I think she had a few trust issues," Cassie said, adding. "And I think old Kay was far cleverer than both younger versions of her. Definitely cleverer than me."

"Age brings wisdom and she obviously had the time to accumulate both that and the money," he said.

Cassie nodded as an image of old Kay passed before her mind's eye.

"So, what are you going to do with the money?" he asked.

"I haven't really thought about it – it still doesn't seem real."

"It will feel real enough once all those boxes are home. Not sure where we're going to put them all."

"Yeah, no kidding. Well, I'll give some to Georgia – I must owe her hundreds from what she's given me over the years."

Bill nodded in agreement. "Yes, Georgia – and her parents, of course – have always looked out for you."

"A new phone might be a good idea – I'm not sure I trust the old one as it's a clone. And there's one thing I definitely need to get done."

"What's that?"

"My hair. Oh..."

"What?"

"We're getting closer to Lollards Pit and the Cow Tower."

"They still affect you?"

She nodded and closed her eyes. Then, as the sensations started swamping her, she managed to whisper, "Another thing I must do is learn to drive and get a car."

"Why?"

"So I don't have to go past this sodding place on the bus anymore."

The boxes were delivered as promised the following Thursday morning. Bill had gone down to open the storage unit and, as the delivery van could accommodate three in the cab, they agreed to let him ride back with them.

By the time Cassie had arrived home from school, he had almost finished sorting them out. The usable cash had been separated from the older coins and notes that were no longer legal tender.

"How much?" she asked, looking at the two piles. The non-legal tender pile was, by far, the largest. "The stuff we can actually spend, that is?"

"There are quite a few fifties, more than a couple of hundred twenties, and even more plastic fives and tens."

"How much then?"

Bill shrugged. "Oh, a little over fifteen thousand."

Cassie gasped. Compared to the amount of money they'd had prior to this, it was an absolute fortune.

"And that's just the notes," he added. "Probably at least another five hundred in usable coins once we sort them out."

"Wow. We're rich."

"Hah, not really," he said. "Spending that amount wouldn't take much effort, I'd say. Oh, and look what I found in one of the boxes."

He handed Cassie a sheet of A4 paper – it had a crude map drawn on it.

"Ah," she said. "It's the map Kay drew for me to get to the chip shop."

"Looks like the same type of paper and handwriting as the letter," he said.

"Oh yes, it does. Her hands were so burnt from when Laurence set fire to her she could hardly hold the pen."

"Well, that explains that. But how come the map got put into a box when she gave it to you to find the chip shop?"

"That's because I didn't take it with me. Just glanced at it and figured out where I needed to go. Wasn't difficult – the chippy was just around the corner."

"If it was that simple, why was a map necessary?"

Cassie shrugged. "Dunno. Maybe she was so used to having dumbo versions of me around, she thought I might get lost or something."

Bill stood up and went to the mantelpiece. He retrieved the hand-written letter from behind the clock where it had sat since it had arrived. He examined the blank sheet that he had seen impressions on.

"Look," he said. "The map was drawn on the sheet above this one."

Cassie saw he was right. The indentations matched the hand-drawn map.

"So, she wrote the riddle in 1995 while I was out getting the fish and chips."

"But didn't you say she died straight after that?"

"Yes, but maybe she left another note for an earlier Kay to arrange to have it posted. Which, of course, she would have known about as she'd already lived through being the earlier Kay. So maybe she didn't need to have an extra note. Or maybe she would have done as the earlier Kay wouldn't have known what to do with it. Oh, I don't know."

"Another paradox," he said.

"Yeah, far too many of them," Cassie said. "Damned dangerous things."

"Indeed."

"Well, one thing's for certain," she said.

"What's that?"

"I'm going to keep my feet firmly on the ground from now on. No more portals or time travel whatsoever."

Her grandad smiled and drew her towards him for a hug.

Family History

Two days later they were still sorting through the coins.

"Hmm, wonder if all this makes you liable for inheritance tax," Bill said.

"What's inheritance tax?"

"I'll have to look it up."

"Yeah, but what is it?"

"Just a way for the government to get their dirty hands on your money. That's if they get to know about it, anyway."

"Oh. Do we have to tell them?"

"It might be hard hiding all this. And that's just the stuff we can spend. As I said, I'll see what I can find out."

"I reckon they owe us big time as I never managed to get any financial help for you when you were… you know…"

"Repressed," he said.

"Yeah – that. The forms were impossible and no one seemed to know exactly what we were entitled to. The system sucks."

"I sometimes think it's made as difficult as possible to get what you are legally entitled to, just to put people off from trying. Didn't you get Georgia's parents to help you with that?"

"No, I didn't want to burden them with more of my troubles. They helped so much, anyway."

"Such good people. I must get around to thanking them properly for all they've done over the past few years."

They were both lost in thought for a few moments and then he picked up a small pile of copper coins – pennies, ha'pennies and farthings. All were over one hundred years old. "To think my own grandad might have handled these very coins when he was a boy," he said.

"That would be amazing. Didn't you say he worked on the market?"

"Yes, fruit and veg stall. From what I can remember, the family ran it for about thirty or forty years until Grandad went to fight in the trenches in World War One. After he came back he got a job in a bank."

"That's quite a career change," Cassie said.

"It was all due to Nanna Lottie's dad."

"Oh, I remember hearing you talk about Nanna Lottie years ago. But I don't think I ever knew that much about her or anyone else in the family from back then. You've never mentioned that sort of stuff since Mum died."

"Forgot most of it donkey's years ago," he said with a sigh. Then he smiled, adding, "Well, I think I can blame you for stirring it all up again." He pointed to his temple. "But now it feels like there's a whole bunch of things running around up here that I'd thought had been lost forever."

"Well, you know what to do, don't you?"

"What?"

"Write it down, write it all down," Cassie laughed.

"Watch it, young lady," he said, his grin wide with amusement.

"So, who exactly was Lottie's dad, then?"

"Ah, I really ought to draw up the family tree sometime," he said.

"Ooh, yes. You must. I'd really love to see that."

"I think I can probably remember most of the names and some of the dates."

"In that case, you'd better do it soon just in case you forget again."

"Okay, okay. I could probably do a quick sketch for you now if you want."

"Oh, yes. Please do. I've never really known too much about our ancestors."

"Well, I can't remember any further back than my grandparents but I suppose I could start with what I do know."

"Go on then," she said, grabbing a sheet of paper from the notepad on which he had been writing down lists of coins. He picked up a pen and she watched intently as he began to map out something she had only ever vaguely known, though many of the names he wrote upon it were familiar to her.

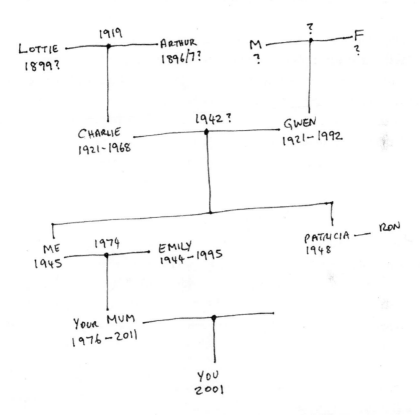

"Wow, we need to get onto one of those online things that do family trees and set it up properly," Cassie said, her fingers tracing the lines.

"One thing at a time. We haven't finished sorting the money out yet."

"I see you left Laurence off there."

"Yes, probably for the best."

"Absolutely. Okay, so tell me more about the rest of them."

"Well… my grandad – Arthur that is – met Lottie, or Charlotte, to give her her proper name, and they got married a year after the war ended.

"What was her last name?"

"Oh, um, Randall or Rendell, or something like that. Anyway, Nanna Lottie's dad worked at a bank – can't remember what that was called, either. I think there were lots of smaller, independent ones back then. Anyway, not long after they got married her dad got Arthur a job there. I don't think her dad liked the idea of Lottie living on the pittance that Arthur was earning on the market. So, an ulterior motive that helped Grandad in the long run."

"Why haven't you added Gwen's parents' names? Did you know them?"

"Not anywhere as well as Arthur and Lottie. Gwen's parents came from London and they were just Grandpa and Grandma to me on the rare occasions we saw them – her name might have been Millie, though his completely escapes me. I think they were a lot older than Arthur and Lottie as Gwen was the youngest of at least six. She was born down in London as well."

Cassie looked across to a couple of photo frames on a shelf. One was of her mum when she was around twenty and the other was of Gwen at about the same age.

"Apart from your eyes – hers were green, you know – you and Gwen could have been mistaken for sisters if you stood next to each other."

"Yes, Mum always reckoned I'd inherited her looks."

"Her dad had worked at Admiralty House for Winston Churchill and I remember her saying that he'd got her some temp work there. She'd sometimes done typing and note-taking for Churchill before he became prime minister."

"Really? Wow," Cassie said. "So how come she married Great-grandad?"

"She moved up to Norwich as she'd got a job at City Hall. It was not too long after it first opened, I think. That's how dad met her – of course, he was only a bus conductor back then, not a driver – he would have been about your age at that point. Arthur had wanted him to follow him into banking but he hated being cooped up inside and loved riding on the buses, and driving them, too. I remember both of them saying she was often on the last bus back out to where she was staying in Spixworth, which was a regular run for him."

"Yeah, when he was driving that bus, just before I knew who he really was, I could tell he loved doing that. How come we only had the one photo of him? I'm sure we've a few more of your mum, haven't we?"

"Yes. We did have more. I never did find out where they went. I would love to see them again. Ah, I really missed him after he, um, well, you know..." He stopped speaking and rubbed his nose.

"Sorry, Grandad. I shouldn't have brought it up."

"No, it's okay. Mum, Gwen that is, was never the same, though. She'd idolised him. And my sister, Pat, had only just moved out to Australia with her husband, Ron – Ten Pound Poms, they were – and they couldn't afford to come all the way back for his funeral."

Cassie put her hand on his arm. Then, picking up the sheet of paper, she said, "How come you didn't put any surnames on it?"

"Well, Emily's was Campbell and Gwen's was Page. And, of course, the rest of us are Foxes. As you said, we will have to sign up to one of those family tree websites and see if I can hunt them all down."

"I don't remember Mum saying what Laurence's surname was."

"No, I don't think I ever knew, either."

"Well, I suppose it wasn't his in the first place as he stole Laurence's body from the original owner."

"Of course. I tend to forget that aspect. Thank goodness you didn't become his next victim."

Cassie sighed, nodding in agreement, shivering as she remembered how she'd fought Laurence when he was trying to take over her mind. If it hadn't been for the device she would never have survived.

"Your mum was pretty determined not to give you anything of Laurence's anyway, least of all his name. She was under pressure to get his name on your birth certificate. But I suspect she used the device to get her own way."

"Yeah," Cassie sighed, "and suffered because of it."

"Yes," he said, "but let's not dwell on that. Nothing we can do now about it. Anyway, back to all this money. Hmm, talking of Arthur's career and all that, I think banks will take some of the more recent paper tens and fives."

"Oh right. And the rest?"

"Some of these rarer ones might be worth something, you know."

"Really?"

"Yes," he said, picking up a small pile of copper coins. Many had faded to a dark brown, though there was one that was still quite bright. "See these 1902 pennies?"

"What about them?"

"Low tide – see where the tide comes up against Britannia's legs. Now compare them with this one from 1926."

Cassie squinted at them. "Oh, I think I see."

"I did manage to look up a few things about them on the Internet."

"Blimey, you really are feeling better. Five years ago you said all that Internet stuff was beyond you."

"Hah, I did indeed," he laughed. "But it's simple when you put your mind to it, especially when that mind has been swept free of cobwebs. Anyway, it looks like there's plenty of guidance for identifying rare coins. And these ones might be worth a few bob."

He held up the one shiny 1902 coin. "This one is probably worth more as it's hardly got any wear on it."

"Really?"

"Yes. I'd say Kay must have picked it up when it was still new."

"How much? Hundreds?"

"Hah, no. Possibly as much as a fiver."

Cassie gave him a weird look.

Inventions

Calendar

Cassie awoke from a dream about boxes, coins and bags of money. She rolled over and sighed seeing the familiar rock that surrounded her. Several of the tribe were already up, despite the sun not having fully risen as yet. But it was already warm. The early light stealing into the cave mouth from a cloudless sky held the promise of a glorious day ahead.

On the otherwise unadorned wall near where Cassie lay was a set of patterns. She had cut them into the softer rock using a hard, sharpened stone that sat in a small recess just below the marks. Each pattern, apart from the last, was a series of five vertical lines crossed by two diagonals. The final one was missing the second diagonal.

Slipping out of the bed carefully to leave Ka'Tor sleeping, she retrieved the stone from its slot and, gripping it in both hands, stood before the marks. She didn't need to count the patterns – she knew there were fifteen sets.

Fifteen weeks, she thought. *Will I ever get away from here?*

She had attempted time travel several times over the weeks, without success.

She made a few deft strokes to cut the final diagonal on the last pattern and then placed the cutting stone back into its niche in the wall.

"Well, I guess that officially makes it Sunday," she muttered to herself. She turned to see one of the older children watching her – his name was Ka'Jat, an inquisitive boy of around eight years old.

When she'd first started making the marks she had tried to explain what she was doing to some of the other adults but they hadn't understood. They didn't seem at all concerned about needing to know the time of year. Knowing the season was enough – and that could be determined by the weather. It was, she was informed, always cold in winter, warmer in spring and autumn, and hot in summer.

"Wait until global warming," Cassie had told them, to blank stares.

Ka'Jat was the only one who seemed interested in what the marks meant, his wide brow furrowing as he tried to take in what she attempted to explain to him. The lack of suitable vocabulary was a real hindrance, but he seemed to understand what each grouping of symbols represented, though he did suggest that seven was a very silly value to use.

Holding his fingers up he said, "Five, ten. Better."

Cassie was beginning to understand the complex relationships within the tribe. Ka'Jat was the son of Em'Jex and the elder step-brother to Em'Tull. Cassie had recently learned that his father, Ta'Roo, had been killed in a hunting accident several years earlier. Em'Jex had fallen pregnant with Em'Tull via her on-off relationship with Ka'Chull's elder brother, Pa'Tay, though they no longer bedded down together. Pa'Tay also had a son, Ko'Lak, whose mother, El'Tak had died giving birth to Ko'Lak's younger brother who had been stillborn.

Cassie was beginning to wonder if she should attempt to draw out a family tree to get all the relationships straight in her head. She remembered her grandad doing one for their family but she knew that attempting to create a full tree for the entire tribe would be far more complex, especially as paper hadn't been invented. [1]

I think I'll stick to the calendar for now, she thought.

She had started the calendar around three weeks after her memory had come back, and then back-dated it to the day of her awakening – though she wasn't sure if she had accurately remembered how many days that had been, not that it mattered. Scratching a new line into it every morning as soon as she got out of bed had become a ritual. *Something to keep me sane, maybe – or possibly something that might drive me completely bonkers if I can't find a way of getting home.*

It wasn't all she had done.

Hearing Ka'Tor whimper, she returned and picked him up. The nappy he wore was doing its best at holding in the worst of the mess his digestive system seemed to produce in abundance. She'd been shown how to sew nappies from old torn skins and line them with dried grass to absorb the worst of the waste. Learning to sew using the crude bone needles the tribe had fashioned was a far

---

1 The full tribal family tree can be downloaded from https://www.vivadjinn.com by clicking on the book title and then selecting the support and resources link.

cry from twenty-first century seamstressing. Not that she'd done much of that in her younger years. Teaching the subject in schools had become almost obsolescent by the end of the twentieth century and even rarer by the time she'd attended lessons.

I wish I knew which century this was.

The top-cum-bra was still a work in progress but was still better than nothing. Her attempts at producing a papoose carrier, to make it easier to carry Ka'Tor around, had also resulted in something that was far from perfect. But it was a definite improvement on carrying babies by arm. Some of the other women had copied her design and even made a few changes that enhanced its usefulness. Also, their skill with the needles far exceeded her own. Some of the designs had been put together by others once they'd understood what she had been aiming for.

"Your tribe make these?" Em'Dor had asked seeing Cassie's first attempt at a carrier.

"Better," Cassie assured her. *Far better than I'll ever be able to make,* she added silently to herself, sucking on fingers that were sore and blistered from trying to manipulate the crude needles.

Over the past few weeks, she'd felt their opinion of her slowly shift. They no longer treated her as little more than a child. Instead, they'd begun to hold her in awe as she came up with each 'new' idea.

She carried Ka'Tor outside, her eyes automatically scanning the treeline to make sure no dangerous animals were lurking nearby. A couple of weeks ago a bear had been seen in the vicinity. The men and some of the older women had banded together to chase it off. Faced with more than a dozen shouting cave people armed with pointed wooden spears, some tipped with stone held in place with tree resin, the bear had thought better of staying around. Cassie hoped it wouldn't come back.

The sun was still rising above the tree-covered slopes to the east.

If this had been Norfolk, it would have risen an hour ago.

She had long ago concluded that this couldn't be England. The inclination of the sun was higher than it had ever been at home. She'd figured that she was still in the northern hemisphere, given the sun's changing position over the weeks. At night, however, she'd not recognised any of the constellations she remembered her grandad pointing out to her when she was young. Some groupings looked as if they may have been similar, but she was far from certain.

She hadn't tried to explain any of this to anyone – for all she knew these people probably thought the Earth was flat or, more likely, had never considered the question in the first place.

Along with Em'Jex and other mothers with young children, she headed for the stream, walking past the point where the water was drawn off for drinking. She waved to others swimming where the land's descent levelled out causing the water to slow and pool before it continued on its rush to the sea. Further down she reached the area the tribe designated for less pleasant needs such as washing clothes and mucky children. It had surprised her at first that these people understood some basic concepts regarding hygiene. However, she did feel sorry for any tribes that might be using the water further downstream.

I hope there are no tribes further up the mountain dumping their shit on us, she thought. But she had the feeling that they were probably the highest tribe around as, from what she could see from the clearing near the cave, not too much further up the incline the treeline started petering out.

She stopped and set about changing the nappy. Ka'Tor, as normal, cried throughout the process – it didn't seem to matter whether or not she was gentle.

Grumpy little sod, she thought, rinsing his behind in the cool water. Then she placed him on the bank where Gu'Tun agreed to watch over him.

She walked upstream and, after stripping off her papoose and skirt, joined a few of the other women for a swim. As she slipped into the water she startled several fish which darted off into the deeper areas, their silvery sides flashing as they swam for safety. Em'Lo, who was swimming nearby, noticed the fish and set off in pursuit, diving under the water until Cassie couldn't see her. Just when Cassie thought Em'Lo might be drowning, the girl resurfaced with a large fish twitching in her hands. The others cheered. Em'Lo swam to one of the boulders beside the stream and slammed the fish's head against it killing it instantly before tossing it onto the bank. Then, with Ge'Tal and El'Pak accompanying her, she dived back into the deeper water.

After a few minutes, nearly a dozen fish of varying sizes lay dead or twitching on the bank.

Well, I know what we'll be having for dinner tonight, Cassie thought.

After getting out of the water and drying herself, Cassie donned her skirt and went to retrieve Ka'Tor from Gu'Tun. She arranged the papoose on her front so he could suckle while she carried him.

As she made the return journey to the cave, she winced feeling a sharp pain from where he had clamped onto her. She had learnt first hand that breastfeeding a baby could often be a far from pleasurable experience. Although Ka'Tor was barely four months old, he had already started teething, which seemed to be common with the children of the tribe.

"Ka'Tor suck me raw," she said to Em'Dor as they passed. The girl had given birth to a daughter about ten days before. She was a slight pretty thing that the father, Pi'Tut, who was Gu'Tun's older brother, had named El'Tesh. Em'Dor laughed at Cassie's comment but, having wet-nursed Ka'Tor herself a couple of times, she had made it obvious she was reluctant to repeat the experience. Cassie, conversely, found El'Tesh a pleasure to nurse and idly wished she could do a permanent swap.

The sooner Ka'Tor is weaned, the better, she thought, and then felt guilty. *I feel more motherly towards El'Tesh than I do my own son.*

A tear formed in her eye. *Why don't I feel as I should towards him?*

Then, as she was looking down at him, his eyes opened. He looked back up at her and he smiled properly for the first time.

Well, that certainly helps, she thought, cuddling him closer but unable to stop a tear, along with several others, from falling.

Tribes and Shopping

"Where they go?" Cassie asked Em'Dor as five of the tribe, three men and two women, prepared for a journey early one glorious morning. Cassie had been trying to pinpoint the longest day to mark on her calendar and guessed it must be close.

Two days previously, she had marked an extra dot on her calendar to denote that her period, the first since giving birth, had commenced. She had occasionally seen some of the other women discreetly wearing a small, folded pad of old animal skin held up by twine, and had guessed the reason. Cassie had constructed her own version, which had been adequate, though nowhere near as efficient as the ones she had used in the twenty-first century. Normally, adults of either sex wore nothing underneath their wrap-around skirts.

The two women in the departing group were El'Po, the mother of Te'Set, and El'Po's elder daughter, Ge'Tek. Each of them, even Ge'Tek, who Cassie understood to be around twelve years of age, wore backpacks made of folded animal skins. All were armed with stone-tipped spears whose points were chipped sharp to do as much damage as possible. El'Po's partner, Ka'Thon, was one of the men accompanying them. The other two were Ka'Chull and his younger brother, Ka'Char.

"Ka'Thon valley tribe," Em'Dor replied, pointing downhill.

"Valley tribe?"

"Yes, Ka'Thon home. One day far, two back."

"Why they go?" Cassie asked.

"El'Po trade medicines. Herbs from valley – not grow here."

Cassie had noticed that anyone with any medical problems tended to go to either El'Po or her mother, El'Kek. Their family had knowledge of herbs and medical techniques. Cassie had often seen El'Kek passing on that knowledge to her granddaughter.

"Why Ge'Tek go?"

"Mate-meet."

"What?"

"Ge'Tek is of age and a summer. Valley tribe have boys, Ko'For, Zu'Mak, Ja'Pol, of age and two, three summers. Mate-meet."

"Mate-meet?"

"If she choose, they mate if like."

Damn it, Cassie thought, *she's not even a teenager yet.* But she was beginning to learn that she couldn't apply twenty-first century standards to these people. Without question, children here matured years earlier than those in her time. Ge'Tek's face was also marked with symmetrical scarring – three vertical lines above each eyebrow and two horizontal lines on each of her cheeks. Cassie couldn't remember seeing the girl without scars, so they must have been done before her awakening.

"If she doesn't like?" Cassie asked.

Em'Dor shrugged. "Ge'Tek come back. Find other boy. Mountain tribes. River tribes. Many."

"Ge'Tek not like men here?"

"Some, but good to mix far. Make better babies."

Wow, they understand all that stuff about not marrying within the family.

"Why Ka'Char go?"

"Knows path. Ka'Char travel lots." Em'Dor went on to explain how, when he was fourteen, Ka'Char had left to seek a permanent partner with another tribe. This he had achieved but both his partner and the baby had died in childbirth. After a period of mourning and then failing to find anyone else, he had travelled to other tribes but returned home a couple of years before Cassie's arrival.

"Ge'Tek not like Ka'Char?"

"A little. Not enough."

"What about Te'Set?"

"Not of age. Not mate yet."

"No. Who look after Te'Set?"

"All do. You, me. El'Po back soon. Six, seven, eight day."

"What they trade?"

"Many. Spear, skin, stone, food, twine."

"Many tribes here?" Cassie said. She had heard the occasional mention of names of people who were not part of the tribe and had come to learn that some members, like Ka'Gar, Ka'Thon and El'Pak, had originated elsewhere. So, she'd concluded that other tribes existed in the vicinity but didn't know much about them, how far away they were or how many they might be.

"Many. You met."

"When?"

"Oh, before fire in sky wake Oh'Kay. Before Oh'Kay is Ka'See."

"Ah."

"Not like you. Pale Ka'See tribe not here."

"No, I don't suppose they are," Cassie muttered in English. "I suspect 'my tribe' might not be around for several thousand years yet."

"Mad talk," Em'Dor laughed, nodding to one of the oldest women of the tribe, El'Kek, who was approaching them with Em'Kell not far behind.

Both of the approaching women had empty pouches slung over their shoulders and various wooden implements dangling from their belts. They were also each carrying spears. Cassie had observed regular parties similarly equipped heading out into the forest every day or two. They would return, several hours later, looking quite tired. But, by then, their pouches would be full of mushrooms, tubers and vegetables, along with anything else that might come in useful such as flints and sturdy lengths of wood.

As the eldest, it fell to Pe'Kat to intone something that wasn't quite a song to the trading party before they departed.

"What he say?" Cassie asked, realising she had no idea if they had a word that represented 'sing'.

"Make journey good," Em'Dor replied, adding. "Safe from bear, wolf and bad things."

"Oh, danger?"

"Many," Em'Dor confirmed as they watched the group take one of the downhill paths into the forest. Pe'Kat kept up the tonal song until they were out of sight.

"Come, need roots," El'Kek said as Pe'Kat's song finished. "Ka'See learn forage. About time."

"Oh," Cassie said.

"Ka'Tor with me," Em'Dor said. "Ka'See learn."

Em'Kell handed Cassie a pouch and a well-worn piece of flat wood.

Looks like I'll finally find out where they actually get this stuff from – I suspect it's not from the local supermarket.

El'Kek called out to her son, Ja'Mutt. He selected a couple of spears from the collection he maintained before joining them. Cassie understood that he would be their guard, keeping them safe from being attacked by any of the natural predators that lurked in the forest. The fact that he was needed in that capacity made Cassie nervous.

Over the next few hours, Cassie was shown how to spot places where edible roots and tubers could be located, and how to extract them from the ground using the wooden implements. They also hunted down various fungi. Em'Kell taught Cassie to recognise the differences between those that were edible and those that were not, especially those that were poisonous.

A while later, having picked a few on her own, El'Kek slapped them out of Cassie's hand. Given the volume of El'Kek's shrieking, these were some of the poisonous types.

Damn it, too many of them look the same to me.

By the end of the foraging session, Cassie could recognise some of the more obvious ones to avoid. But she still had trouble differentiating between the non-edible, non-poisonous ones and the fully edible ones.

"Not teach in your tribe?" Em'Kell asked.

Cassie shook her head, feeling useless. She couldn't explain to them that, in her century, mushrooms were grown by the ton indoors at specialised farms.

On the way back, they halted while El'Kek examined a bunch of close-growing plants with small blue flowers and long straight stems. Some of the plants were nearly waist height. El'Kek selected a handful of the tallest ones and yanked them from the ground.

"What they?" Cassie asked Em'Kell.

"Make twine," Em'Kell explained. Cassie had seen similar stems tied together and soaking in the pool near the cave. She had yet to see how it got converted into the twine that was used for various purposes.

By the time they returned it was late afternoon and Cassie was exhausted. Much to her relief, they hadn't encountered any wildlife more dangerous than a few timid rodents and trees full of birds.

Maybe this place isn't quite as dangerous as they sometimes make out.

Reality Bites Hard

A few days later, shouting awoke Cassie with a jolt, causing Ka'Tor to start crying. It was still before dawn and what light crept into the cave did little to illuminate what might be going on. Most of the tribe were still in bed apart from Em'Kell and a couple of the men, Ti'Pik and Ka'Gar, who were tending the entrance fire.

Gu'Tun rushed into the cave shouting, "Bear has Ko'Lak."

Suddenly every adult apart from Cassie was out of bed and on their feet, reaching for a weapon. Cassie got to her feet and, leaving Ka'Tor crying, she caught up with Em'Dor who, with the others, brandished a sharpened length of wood.

Em'Dor pushed her back.

"No, Ka'See," Em'Dor ordered. "No fight."

"But you are?"

"Yes, know how. Ka'See look after babies. El'Tesh, Em'Ban, Em'Tull."

Cassie retreated inside the cave, feeling helpless. Em'Dor and several of the other women, all armed with spears, arranged themselves across the cave entrance as the first false light of dawn tainted the sky with streaks of red. Out beyond Cassie's sight, there was more shouting and then screaming. One of the screams sounded like a child.

Ko'Lak. Oh, please let him be okay. Hell, he can't be more than about ten.

The noises retreated after a few minutes and the women at the entrance moved out into the cleared area in front of the cave. Within the cave, Cassie realised she was the only adult remaining. Ge'Tal, Ka'Jat and Em'Lo pressed themselves to the cave wall several yards back from the entrance. Most of the younger children were crying. Only Te'Set was silent but his dark eyes were focused towards the growing light. His breathing was fast and he was rooted to the spot. Cassie could see he was trembling and rubbing at a scar on his left arm. She'd noticed it before but had never asked what had caused it.

She approached him and he jumped when she placed a hand on his shoulder. Seeing her look at his scar, he said, with a quaking voice, "Bear."

No wonder he's scared, she thought. *He's not the only one.*

She gathered the younger children together near the back of the cave and wrapped her arms around them. Their cries reduced to whimpers, while the shouting outside grew in volume.

A round of cheering made Cassie jump. The children nearer the entrance rushed outside only to be ushered back inside by Em'Kell who scolded them and made them join Cassie.

Em'Kell said, "We kill bear. Is young. Good eating. Many skins."

"Ko'Lak?" Cassie asked.

"Ah," Em'Kell sighed and approached them. She held up Te'Set's scarred arm. "Bear bite Ko'Lak arm. It come off."

A few minutes later Pa'Tay carried his son's limp body into the cave. Ge'Tal screamed and Cassie almost gagged seeing how the boy's right arm had been reduced to a bloody stump. Ko'Lak appeared dead until she heard him groan as Pa'Tay lowered him onto a bed. Ge'Tal, tears streaming down her face, ran across to Cassie who put her arm around the girl.

Under the guidance of El'Kek, a group of women, including Em'Dor's mother El'Ra, Em'Jex and Em'Kell, gathered around the boy. They tied off the bleeding with strips of animal pelt and applied some pasty concoction that El'Kek had hastily prepared. Pe'Kat, who had been doing something with the main fire, wrapped a thick skin around his hands. He reached into the flames and extracted a large stone. He brought it across to El'Kek and El'Ra, who had wrapped their hands similarly. Horrified, Cassie watched as all three pressed the stone against Ko'Lak's wound. The boy screamed and his body arched twice and then fell limp. The heat from the stone seared and sealed the ragged flesh so that the flow of blood was reduced, though it didn't completely stop. Cassie had to turn her face away and swallow hard to stop herself from puking as the stink of burning flesh reached her nostrils.

Te'Set clung to her arm, whimpering, while Cassie tried to comfort Ge'Tal and the younger children. She wished someone would do the same for her.

By mid-morning, the bear carcass had been skinned, dismembered and dragged into the cave, piece by piece. Some of it had already been sliced into strips and was being boiled up with vegetables for a stew.

But, despite the abundance of meat, the mood during the main meal that evening was subdued. People kept sidling over to where Ko'Lak lay groaning and crying while Pa'Tay sat beside him, refusing to eat. Cassie avoided the boy, primarily because Te'Set was still dogging her every step. With El'Po away, he seemed to have latched on to Cassie as a surrogate mother. Meanwhile, Ge'Tal had retreated to the back of the cave and continued to weep.

As the light fell, Cassie hugged Ka'Tor and Te'Set to her in her bed but, with Ko'Lak's groans and occasional screams of agony, she knew none of them were going to get much sleep.

Several hours after darkness had fallen, Ko'Lak stopped making any sound. A few moments later it was Pa'Tay who emitted a deep cry that was taken up by others. The keening lament that went on for nearly an hour chilled Cassie to her core with its eeriness. Then, flaming torches were lit from the fire at the cave entrance, and a procession of the elder tribe members, with Pa'Tay at the head carrying Ko'Lak's body, ventured deep into one of the narrow tunnels at the back of the cave. With tears streaming down her face, Cassie heard them scraping and digging a hole in the ground. Around her, the lament was repeated.

It was nearly dawn before the ceremony was completed and everyone, except Ko'Lak, returned to the main part of the cave.

The next morning, after awakening from very little but nightmare-filled sleep, Cassie took a burnt piece of charcoal from the fire and added a black mark under the scratch that represented the previous day. Ka'Jat saw it and, with solemn eyes, nodded that he understood. He turned to Ge'Tal who was also watching what Cassie had added to the calendar and tried to explain it to her but, still crying, she walked off.

"Two, three summers more Ge'Tal, Ko'Lak mate," he said.

Oh no, Cassie thought. *Poor girl.*

Later, accompanying Em'Dor down to the stream, she said, "Teach me fight."

Em'Dor looked at Cassie's face and nodded.

The Sun Worshipper

Ka'Tor was crawling by the time Cassie added the twentieth week to her calendar.

"Learn quick," Em'Kell said one morning not long after, as she watched the boy negotiate his way from Cassie's bed towards the cave mouth. Cassie, still in bed, but sewing a few more skins to add to the communal stack of nappies, watched as Em'Kell steered her son away from the ever-smouldering fire.

"Ka'Tor like fire," Cassie said.

Em'Kell performed that strange nod they had that Cassie had yet to master.

Ka'Tor tried to crawl past Em'Kell but she picked him up and returned him to Cassie, whereupon he immediately started back towards the cave entrance.

Mind of his own, that one.

Over the past few weeks, her feelings towards her son had changed for the better. He was, at last, beginning to change from being an unwanted burden inflicted upon her, to something more. *I'm still not sure I can truthfully say that I love him as I should,* she thought, *but there is something there, I have to admit.*

She looked at the way Em'Dor and El'Tesh interacted with each other and ached to have the same rapport with Ka'Tor. Then her glance fell upon Pa'Tay who was sitting at the cave entrance chipping flint that would be used to tip the spears that sat in a small pile beside him. His countenance had remained clouded with sorrow and he had spoken little since the loss of Ko'Lak.

Would I feel the same if I lost Ka'Tor?

"Where Ka'Tor?" Cassie shouted a few days later as the cave dwellers got ready for another repetitive day. The others in the cave perked up and looked around.

"Outside," someone replied from nearer the cave mouth.

Cassie gasped, grabbed her wooden spear and rushed outside, glancing around in case of any danger. She saw her son just beyond the entrance, staring at the hills. Relieved, she scooped him up, wiping off the dust he'd picked up from crawling on his bare stomach and legs. His mouth was open and his gaze seemed locked on the rising sun.

"Where you look, Ka'Tor?"

He raised a pudgy arm and waved it eastwards. He accompanied the gesture with a gurgling noise and a smile.

"Yes, sun. Pretty, isn't it? Back to cave."

He gurgled some more.

Two weeks later, Cassie knew something more permanent needed to be done.

Unless checked, Ka'Tor would crawl for the cave entrance at every opportunity.

Her first thought was to try to create some reins to restrict his range. However, proper rope had yet to be invented and her amateur attempts proved flimsy. Even when tied up, Ka'Tor didn't take long to learn to thrash the leash, causing it to fray and eventually split.

A few days later a better idea hit her.

After trying to explain it to the others without any understanding getting across to them, she decided to be practical and do it herself. Recently, she had accompanied others when they sought out tree saplings to be whittled into their rudimentary spears. Some of the straighter ones were reserved for the addition of a stone tip, though most were nothing more than pointed sticks. All members of the tribe, Cassie included, carried one if they were going more than a few yards from the cave.

So, she organised the cutting of several larger saplings and many thin bendable branches, the latter being left to soak in a pool near the stream. Having seen what Cassie had done with the papoose, several women and younger men let her order them about – possibly they were just intrigued with what might come of this. The main thing was that they copied what she started and followed her lead.

Returning to the cave, Cassie marked out the best place. The cave was shaped like a bottle with a wider mouth where the fire burned, a short neck for several yards, after which it opened up for the main living area. Nothing of importance was kept in the narrow section, though the floor was relatively flat, worn down by generations of feet.

I wonder how many centuries this tribe has lived here?

Cassie dug a hole in the dry soil of the floor in the narrowest, most obstacle-free section. People crowded around her but she made them stand back mainly so that they didn't block her light. Using a sharp stick to loosen the soil, she initially shovelled the soil out with one of the wooden spades used for digging up roots. Once the hole was deeper, she utilised a flat stone she'd found outside the cave. While she was digging she hoped she wouldn't accidentally burrow into a grave. But, knowing that Ko'Lak had been buried in the tunnels to the rear, far beyond the living and sleeping areas, she was thankful that she encountered nothing more than compacted earth and stones.

She deemed the hole complete once its depth measured the length from her fingertips to her elbow. Then she positioned one of the thicker saplings in the hole so that its top was level with her chest. She piled stones into the hole around the base of the new post and, after stomping them down, backfilled it with loose soil. After five of these had been set up, which blocked off nearly half the width, she started weaving the thinner branches, now more pliable after having been soaked for several hours, around the posts in a wicker fashion. The others could see what she was trying to achieve and, under her instructions, started doing the same on the other side once she'd marked the places on the ground where the holes should be dug.

By the end of the day the fence, along with a working gateway had been put into place. The gate had been made by tying smaller saplings together into a frame, strengthened by cross pieces and weaving branches into the gaps. The gate was then attached to one of the end posts using leather straps. A loop of the same material served to lock the gate to the other end post, which was high enough to be out of Ka'Tor's reach.

Cassie stood back and tested the strength of her work. Then, after shutting the gate and making sure it was secure, called to Ka'Tor from outside the fence. Em'Jex, who had been looking after him further inside the cave, released him. After a few seconds, he was shuffling towards them. He tried several ways of getting through the new barrier but, to Cassie's satisfaction, failed to make any headway.

The others laughed and clapped their hands, understanding at last what she had made. Exhausted, she opened the gate, scooped Ka'Tor up into her arms and returned to sit on her bed.

A short while later some of the men returned from hunting and had to be shown how to operate the gate. Several of them, especially Za'Lak, had wanted to tear the whole fence down but the women, after much gabbling and gesticulating, finally managed to get them to comprehend the reason for its existence. Then the men stared at Cassie, frowned a bit, and finally nodded their acquiescence. After that, they treated the fence as if it had always been there.

Cassie, feeding Ka'Tor, chuckled to herself for a moment and then something pinged into her head.

If this is the past, she thought, *then I've probably just built the world's first enclosure.*

Then she frowned. Why had she thought of the word *enclosure* instead of something like *gate* or *fence*? But *enclosure* rang some sort of mental bell – was it important somehow?

The boy grew fast and, as summer changed to autumn, Cassie's wall calendar began to take up far too much room.

After thirty weeks – denoted by the five rows, each containing six groups of week marks – she decided on a new method. In addition to her growing skills with the spear and wrestling, which is how she thought of the way she had been taught to fight close up with others, she had been learning to knap flint. Apart from the inevitable cuts to her fingers and hands, which were thankfully few and minor, she was making good progress and could already make passable knives and axe heads. For her own use, and after several failures, she had made a drill of sorts that was sharp enough to make small holes in the softer rock of the wall.

Instead of making a new set of marks for each week, she drilled seven holes to one side of the main calendar area and pushed a wooden stick into one every morning. Once all seven were filled she emptied them and drilled a new hole next to the first week marker and stuck a stick in that. After filling the seven day holes once again, she drilled a new hole next to the second week marker and moved the 'week' stick to that. Of course, having already made thirty sets of week markers she knew she needed to reset the whole thing after twenty-two weeks and a day.

She ran a hand through her hair, the rough skin on her fingers catching in the strands. She stared at her hands, the fingernails chipped, the skin decorated with dozens of small scabs and cuts from her lack of knapping expertise, and sighed.

Oh, for some moisturiser and nail varnish.

She picked up another sharp stone and sliced off a few unruly strands of hair that were beginning to annoy her. It felt greasy and tangled – frequent washings in the stream were no substitute for shampoo. She rummaged around near her bed to locate the thing that she laughingly called a comb.

Maybe I should figure out when the winter solstice is and reset the calendar from that, she thought as she scraped the wooden, five-pronged device through her hair in an effort to tame it. *That is, if I don't manage to get away from here before then – or go completely mad instead.*

She picked a knot out of her locks and inspected it, ready to crunch any tiny unwelcome visitor between her fingernails. For a change, she appeared to be free of parasites.

If I don't get away soon I really am going to have to try and come up with something better than this damned thing.

She looked around the cave, at the primitive people, many of whom she was now beginning to count as friends and family.

They're not a bad bunch – apart from old Za'Lak, maybe.

She contemplated the possibility that she could be stuck here for a very long time.

I might be here until I die, she thought. It caused a shudder to pass through her whole body.

No Paradoxes Allowed

How Old?

"I preferred your hair as it was," Robert Kett said.

"Sod off," Cassie replied.

It was a Saturday, autumn half term, and she was leaning on the metal railing fence that stopped people falling down the side of the castle mound. Cassie's eyes gazed along Davey Place towards the market. Beyond that, the City Hall and its clock dominated the view.

"It felt nice to brush it the other day," Kett added.

"That was months ago," she said, glad that there was no one around to see her talking to thin air.

What if he really is just a figment of my imagination?

Kett frowned. "Surely not. It has been less than a week."

"Nope, it was back in June. We're now in October."

"October? Really? Time messes up around you."

"No," she said. "I don't do that anymore."

"You could, though."

"Haven't even tried."

"It's too short."

"What?"

"Your hair, it's too short."

"It's my hair. I'll wear it how I like," she said, one hand caressing its lack of curls. When she'd had it straightened back in July it had been cut to just below her jawline at the sides and hardly any longer at the back. It had already grown noticeably.

"Why are you here?" Kett asked.

Cassie wondered that herself. This had been the first time she'd come up here since the last day of June. Plenty had happened since then. The money, getting a new phone, starting driving lessons, and that volunteer first aid course that

Georgia had wanted to try out but hadn't wanted to attend on her own. Georgia had persuaded Cassie into accompanying her by reminding her that Bill wasn't getting any younger, and the things they'd learn might even end up making a big difference should he have an accident. Initially reluctant, Cassie found she'd enjoyed learning the various techniques required to save people's lives, though she hoped she'd never need to put any of them into practice.

The best part had been in August with their trip to London. Cassie had treated her best friend to three days and a couple of nights on the town. They'd even gone exploring and ended up finding Admiralty House where Cassie told Georgia all about her great-grandmother working for Winston Churchill.

If that was the highlight then, at the opposite end, there had been Jason.

Bloody Jason.

Bloody annoying Jason.

He'd finally asked her out properly on the last day before half term started. An actual date. They'd gone to see a film – just him and her. The film had been about Neil Armstrong and the moon landings. She'd enjoyed the film and, to an extent, Jason's company, though he could have communicated a bit more.

But, afterwards, they just happened to bump into some of Jason's friends from his previous school when he had been around ten, and he reverted to joking about things, sometimes at her expense. One of the boys had asked, right in front of her as if she wasn't there, if she was his new girlfriend and Jason had replied that she was just a friend. She'd bitten her lip, not being quick enough to think up apt retorts on the spur of the moment. She'd thought of plenty afterwards. It had been humiliating and she'd cried in bed after she'd got home.

"You've gone quiet," Kett said.

"Yeah. Oh, I don't know," she said. "Sometimes I think about all that stuff that happened and wonder why."

"Why what?"

"Lots of things. I wonder why I can see and talk to you when no one else can. What's the point?"

And, she thought to herself, *what's the point of Jason?* Why did she still feel attracted to him? He hadn't called to apologise or anything, and she wondered how she was going to face him when they returned to school.

"The point," Kett said, interrupting her thoughts, "is something you stick into your enemies before they stick theirs into you."

"Lovely," she said.

"No," he said. "We used to hurt each other – you still do the same. Just in different ways."

You're not wrong there. She turned to look at him, studying his face – partially transparent as it was – she couldn't quite make out his age.

"How old are you?" she said.

"Well, as this is 2018 – it is still 2018, isn't it?" Cassie nodded and he continued, "In that case, I suppose I must be well over five hundred."

"No, I meant how old you look. I'd say late thirties or early forties."

"I was fifty-eight when they executed me, when they tied chains around me and hauled me up to the top of this castle for slow strangulation."

Cassie swallowed. She'd seen him hanging there in the chains, waving to her with the one hand that was free only from the elbow down. Why had his ghost persisted this long? Was it something to do with her?

"Why don't you look it, then?" she said, finally.

"Why should I? I looked better when I was younger. I got fat for a while. But running a rebellion is revoltingly good for the waistline – pity I didn't get to enjoy it for long."

"What did you do, exactly?"

"Do?"

"To make them execute you?"

"You mean you don't know?"

"Well, you just said something about a revolution or rebellion or something. Is that why they killed you? Seems a bit extreme."

He sighed. "Your age and mine, Cassie Fox, are so very different. Some people... No, lots of people thought I was a hero."

"A hero? Really?"

"Yes, is that so hard to believe?"

Cassie shrugged. "Well, they killed you for a start. You must have annoyed someone. Did you do something bad to them?"

He gazed out over the city. "Maybe I didn't do enough," he said after a pause.

"I know they named a road on a hill after you. I don't think they'd name a road after some bad guy."

"That was near where the rebellion was – it was from the hill that we first attacked Norwich. It was my hill long before there was a proper road there. At least something lasted down the years."

"I can't remember them mentioning you at school in the history lessons."

"So much is lost," Kett said, looking older. "Maybe your world could do with more like me."

Cassie's eyebrows rose. "Why?"

"All your technology and yet your freedom means so little to you. They manipulate and control you. Do you realise that?"

"What are you talking about?"

"I should have been stronger," he said. "I shouldn't have misinterpreted that damned rhyme. I should have remained on the heights and defended them. Ah, Sheffield, I shouldn't have let that fool butcher kill him."

"Sheffield? You went all the way there to fight a battle?"

"No, not the place. I refer to Lord Edmund Sheffield. He was an honourable man, hardly more than a boy really, and could have been useful. Maybe if he'd lived, and had been made to see what injustices were being perpetrated, the outcome might have been different. And if I had won then maybe your world would have turned out differently – better."

"It's not that bad, is it?" Cassie said, staring out over the city, her mind dwelling on all the times her friends had complained about how bad things were. *Who am I kidding – it could be a lot better.*

"If you say so," he sighed. "If you say–"

Cassie looked around, but Robert Kett had disappeared.

"Hey, where did you go?"

There was no answer. She shrugged and waited for a few minutes more. Then, with Kett remaining absent, she left the castle grounds and went shopping.

The Play's The Thing

"I found out about you on the Internet," Cassie said, nearly two months later. Her hair was already starting to curl and frizz. She had already booked the appointment to have it straightened yet again.

This time the view across Davey Place and the rest of the city was augmented by Christmas lights. She still had some presents to buy but wasn't really in the mood for it. Her on-off relationship with Jason was currently a non-event so she certainly wasn't going to buy him anything.

Instead, she'd come up to the castle to see if Robert Kett would put in an appearance. He didn't always.

"The inter-what?"

"Oh, um, sort of like books you can see on a TV screen."

Kett frowned for a moment. "Ah yes, your technology. It sometimes slips my mind. Holding on to such things isn't easy."

"Why?"

"I forget," Kett said. "And what did you learn?"

Cassie, wrapped up in her winter coat, pushed her hands deeper into the pockets to keep them warm. It wasn't that cold, though.

"You tried to help the common people who were being pushed off their lands or something. They were building enclosures and chucking people out of them. Then you lost a battle. There was a bit about a tree as well."

Kett sighed. "Come around to the east of the castle," he said, walking in that direction. Cassie followed.

"See that water tower?" he said, pointing towards the white construction on the low hill in the far distance.

"Yes."

"The tree – my Oak of Reformation, they called it – was somewhere around where that now stands. They cut it down."

"Why? Was it dangerous or something?"

"In a way. The tree itself wasn't – it was just a large tree, though we'd built it up into a shelter and meeting place. No, it was the idea that it represented – what I'd used it for – that was where they thought the danger lay."

Cassie looked at Kett. His appearance had changed as he'd spoken – he looked older and she was certain he had become larger around the waist.

"They did a play about me and the rebellion."

"When was that?"

"Earlier in the year."

"I didn't hear about it. I was probably being attacked by nasties at the time."

"Actually, it might have been last year – anyway, it was before you went time travelling through the portals. They did the play several times. Twice they did it down in the moat."

"The moat?"

"On the other side of the castle, near the entrance bridge down in the gardens," he said.

"Oh, the Whiffler Theatre. I've seen things put on there before."

"One performance was near where we'd held the prisoners."

"Prisoners? What prisoners?"

"See, you know nothing of what went on. Over there," he said, pointing once again, this time quite a way to the left of the water tower. "You should go and watch the play – you might learn more that way."

"When's it on again?"

"No, go back and see it when it was first there."

"I don't do that anymore."

Kett looked at her. "You can, though, if you try hard enough."

"Maybe, but I won't."

"So you may say. But, in my experience, what people say they *will* do and what they *actually* do rarely coincide. You are no different."

She glared at him and snapped, "No."

"Do you deny your abilities?"

Cassie glared at him. "No," she said, "but that doesn't mean I will use them."

"So you may say. But I wager that you will."

She refused to respond and stalked off, annoyed.

Given the paucity of the clues, it took until just before Christmas for Cassie to pin down anything about the play and when it had been performed. But she'd eventually found references to it and the company that had performed it. It had been back in the July of 2016 – around two and a half years previously. Kett's grip on the passing years was somewhat slippery. It reminded her of Kay not having much of a clue to her own age – and Kett's ghost had been around for hundreds of years.

She'd also found some depictions of Kett conducting meetings at his Oak of Reformation. *Artists impressions*, she thought as in each depiction he looked completely different, as did the tree.

Maybe I should go back and take a photo of what it was really like, Cassie thought and, remembering Kay telling her off when she'd got her phone out in the 1960s, was then cross at herself. *No, I don't do that anymore. Too dangerous.*

But the idea, nagging at the back of her brain, was tempting.

Damn him – I promised.

It was several more weeks, what with Christmas, New Year, more driving lessons and school before she had time to investigate any further.

With school closed for half term, a cloudy but relatively warm February Thursday, the twenty-first, found her standing about halfway up Kett's Hill. She was far enough away from the base of the hill so that the effects of the Cow Tower were negligible – though she could still feel a sense of unease when she looked in that direction.

What the hell is it down in that area that spooks me so much?

On the concrete wall beside double metal gates, a sign announced Kett's Heights – something she'd not previously noticed, despite the number of times she'd been past it on the bus. The gates were unlocked and she ascended the stepped pathway under the trees until she reached a lawned area. She found a quiet secluded oasis hidden away from the world and, more significantly, the effects of Cow Tower and Lollards Pit.

This must be where it was.

She decided that the play might have been performed in the lower corner so that people seated on the grass had the best view. She tried to imagine the place filled with crowds watching the play and had to resist the urge to go back in time to see it for herself.

"Nope, not going there."

It had been nearly eight months since she'd lost the device and she wasn't even sure she could still do it, despite Kett's insistence that she could. Apart from that episode when she'd started to fade away on the bus in front of Georgia, her feet had remained firmly rooted in the present.

Anyway, now was not the time. A week ago Jason had asked her to go with him to his cousin, Erin's, birthday party this coming Saturday. She'd thought about it for a few moments and then said 'yes' while contemplating the chances that she was making a huge mistake. But, since then, she'd not only booked appointments to have her nails done and her hair styled but, two days previously and with Georgia's help, had already bought several new skirts, dresses and shoes. She'd even spoiled herself with some bangles and a couple of necklaces. Georgia had even convinced her to get some proper dark stockings along with a black suspender belt – a complete change from her usual tights.

"You'll slay 'em," Georgia had laughed, "especially if you wear that low-cut blue dress that really shows off your, uh, assets."

"Yeah, I only just fit into that one."

"If you've got it, flaunt it, that's what I say." Georgia looked down at her own slimmer, more muscular body. "Wish I had more up there."

So, Cassie thought to herself, *even if the situation with Jason goes pear-shaped yet again, at least I'll look good. I might even meet someone new. Someone who'll be good for me like Mark is for Georgia.*

Then she sighed out loud.

"Yeah, oink-flap more like. Stop daydreaming, you idiot."

Party Time

"I approve," Jason said, looking Cassie over. "Weird necklace," he added. "Is that supposed to be sharks' teeth or something?"

It was one of the necklaces she'd bought a few days before to match the dress. The shapes hanging from it did resemble sharks' teeth, though real teeth had never been that shade of translucent blue nor made out of plastic.

Jason was not hiding the fact that his gaze lingered on her cleavage for rather too long. Dressed up like this it was as if he was seeing her in a new light – but she was in two minds about the effect it was having upon him.

I'm not a piece of meat, she thought, now regretting her choice of dress. She pulled her coat closed to prevent further unwanted examination. But she said nothing and, instead, smiled sweetly as she waved to her grandad and closed the front door.

Jason, as usual, was attired in clothes that were too small. At least, they were intact and devoid of fashionable rips for a change.

Pity you didn't bother to shave, Cassie thought.

Jason had been one of the first boys in her year to develop the need to shave, not long past his thirteenth birthday. Some of the other boys in her class still had no need. Georgia's Mark, although a year older, had yet to start.

Poor Mark – his hair is so fair that no one would notice if he did grow a beard.

She got into Jason's car – it was secondhand and had seen far better days, if not years. But it was all he could afford and, she'd heard, the insurance had cost more than the car. He'd bought it only a few weeks previously, having passed his driving test on the first attempt. Her own test was still too far in the future – she was dreading the written part.

The party, celebrating Erin's twenty-first, was somewhere on the Dussindale estate – hardly more than a five-minute drive away. The house, one of the larger ones in the area, was quite crowded by the time they arrived. Jason didn't bother to ring the doorbell but just pushed the front door open and walked in, leading her through the crowded hallway. The guests were all ages though, being several months younger than Jason, Cassie felt certain she was the youngest person there.

"Hi, Erin. Happy birthday," Jason said, upon locating his cousin in the kitchen pouring drinks. Jason handed Erin a card and an unwrapped bottle of wine.

"Thanks. Ah, I see you've been raiding your mum's drinks cupboard again," Erin laughed. Cassie could see a slight family resemblance. Like Jason, Erin was quite tall and in possession of a strong jawline. Her hair, worn quite short, made her look like a tall elf. Her eyes were almost the same shade of brown as his – not that Jason's eyes were often seen without sunglasses covering them.

At least he isn't wearing them tonight.

"Nah, bought that one myself. They stopped ID'ing me since I went designer stubble," he said, scratching his chin.

"Oh," Erin chuckled, "I assumed you'd just run out of razor blades again having used them all up slashing your clothes."

Jason laughed back and they gave each other a brief hug, though Cassie felt Jason's laugh had been a bit forced.

"So, are you going to introduce us?" Erin said, tipping her head towards Cassie.

"What? Oh yeah. This is Foxy, er, Cassie Fox."

"Pleased to et cetera. Ooh, I absolutely love that necklace and dress," Erin said with a grin as she filled a couple of glasses containing something bubbly, offering them one each.

"Is that alcoholic?" Cassie asked.

"Yes," Erin said. "That a problem? You driving or something?"

"Well, no, but Jason is."

"Hah, it's only a couple of miles," he laughed. "And I've been drinking since I was thirteen. It's not illegal to drink at home, you know. You worry too much, Foxy."

"With your reputation, she'd be wise to," Erin goaded, at which Cassie frowned. Erin turned to her, "So, how do you two know each other?"

"School – sixth form," Jason said before Cassie could answer.

"Same class?"

"Some of them," he answered.

The doorbell rang.

"Right, I'd better see who that is. I'll catch up properly with you later, Jason. Show Cassie around and introduce her to the family," Erin said, adding, "Oh, and Jason…"

"Huh?"

"Apart from the loo, upstairs is out of bounds," she said, adding with emphasis, "if you know what I mean."

"Yeah, no problem," Jason replied, as Erin left the kitchen.

"What did she mean by that?" Cassie said.

"Um, just a family, er, joke," he replied, avoiding eye contact. "C'mon."

He led her out into the hallway where they were immediately waylaid by Erin's parents.

"Been going out long? You and Jason?" Erin said, catching Cassie on her own a little while later in the hallway. Jason was in the kitchen refilling his glass.

"No, not really. Only been out a few times – on and off." *Mostly off.*

"Yeah," Erin nodded. "About par."

"What do you mean?"

"Sorry, big mouth, that's me," Erin said and then sighed. "Look, I don't want to gossip but you seem a little sort of awe-struck with him. I wasn't kidding when I said he has a reputation. Are you really not aware of that?"

Cassie shook her head.

"Well, he may be family but sometimes he pushes the boundaries a bit too far," Erin said, adding, once again, "if you know what I mean."

Cassie frowned. She was aware that Jason had had a number of girlfriends over the past few years – not surprising, given his looks. But she'd not heard anything really bad – okay, there was the odd rumour but she'd not put too much credence in the gossip. But Cassie hated the gossip crowd – she was aware that she'd sometimes been the target of the conversation; about how she lived only with her grandfather, her previous lack of finances and especially regarding her hair just after all the portals stuff.

"How do you mean?" she said.

"Uh, tell you later. Here he comes," Erin whispered.

The doorbell rang yet again. "Ah, looks like another load of my university mob," Erin said, adding, "Look. Just be careful. Okay?"

Cassie nodded as Erin went to greet her friends.

"You really shouldn't," Cassie said a couple of hours later as Jason opened another can of lager. "I don't want to have to walk home."

"Oh, don't nag – I can handle it," he said, with a definite slur to his words.

Cassie was sure he was already far too drunk to drive. She felt slightly tipsy herself though she had only indulged in a few glasses of wine – she wasn't used to drinking. Jason had laughed at her a few minutes earlier when she'd decided to switch to water for a while.

Before Kay's money had turned up they could never afford the luxury of alcohol. Apart from some wine at Christmas, neither Cassie nor her grandad had thought to indulge even once they could afford it. *I just can't handle it.*

Even more of Erin's friends had arrived and the party was, by this time, in full swing. The whole house pulsed with loud music and voices doing their best to make themselves heard over it.

With the main rooms of the ground floor packed with people, Jason had led her to a utility room whose purpose, apart from housing a washing machine and dishwasher, seemed to be to separate the back door from the main hallway. While the hallway itself thronged with a mass of people moving between the kitchen and the other main rooms, no one else shared the room with them.

"Come here and stop being a bore," he chuckled, grabbing Cassie around the waist, pulling her towards him. With their faces barely two inches apart, he put on that damn gorgeous smile that Cassie found so hard to resist.

The gap closed and their lips met.

Cassie had fantasised about their first kiss for ages and, here it was at last, actually happening. But, after a few seconds, she realised the reality was falling far short of what she'd imagined. For a start, all she could smell was the lager on his breath and the roughness of his stubble against her face.

"Ow," she whispered, pulling away, her fingers touching his face. "It's like sandpaper."

"Get used to it," he grinned, closing the gap for another kiss.

"No, not here," she snapped, looking around to see if anyone else had noticed.

"Where then? Not upstairs, obviously," he said.

"What?" she said. Out of the corner of her eye, she caught a brief glimpse of someone in the hallway wearing a dress whose colour was identical to her own.

"Oh, I know. This way."

Dumping the empty can of lager on top of the washing machine, he encircled her waist with one arm and guided her towards the back door.

"It's a bit cold outside," she said, wishing she'd still got her coat on.

"Hah, I'll soon warm you up, Foxy."

Oh – I'm not sure I like the sound of that.

She let him lead her out into the garden. They passed a stack of logs that were destined for the wood burner in the lounge. Jason led her towards the shed and then past it.

"Where are you taking me?" she whispered.

"Somewhere private," he chuckled, as he pulled her behind the shed and out of sight of the house. Cassie shivered.

Pushing her up against the back wall of the shed, his lips were on hers again, his tongue opening them and darting inside her mouth.

She told herself to relax. This was what she'd wanted, wasn't it? To be out on a proper date with Jason, with him treating her as if she was a grown woman. She felt one of his hands sliding up from her waist, moving towards her chest. His hand reached its target.

"Oh," she gasped, breaking the kiss. It felt both right and wrong at the same time and she wasn't certain which she wanted.

"Now you're warming up," he said before his mouth slid from her face to her neck. But his breath stank and his chin against her skin felt like she was being stroked by a wire brush. At the same time, she felt his other hand move from her waist down her leg and then cross in front of her to lift the dress. His touch on her inner thigh above the top of her stockings caused her to freeze.

"No," she said. This was way too quick. Kissing was fine – well, sort of. But not this. She was beginning to understand what Erin had meant.

"Come on," he said, his hand moving between her legs, pulling up her dress. "You know you want it. You've been aching for it for months, haven't you?"

No, not like this, she thought. "No, Jason," she repeated. "Please stop. Please."

She tried to clamp her thighs together but he forced his hand further – too far.

"Stop," she gasped again, hoping time itself would stop as it had done for her on several occasions the year before. But time neither stopped nor slowed in the slightest, and his face was right in front of hers again. She turned her head away.

"You fucking little tease," he said. His hand grabbed her chin and pulled, wrenching her head back to face his.

How dare he?

"Anyone would think you're a virgin," he chuckled.

Oh God, he doesn't realise…

He jammed his lips back against hers, thrusting her head back so that her skull clunked against the wood of the shed. She tried to push him away but he leaned his upper torso against her, using his height and size to trap her. Her hands, flailing against him were like trying to attack a solid wall. She felt one of his fingers inside her underwear and, moments later, invading her body. She tried squeezing her legs together even tighter and fought to pry his hand away but his weight against her was too much. His other hand, no longer exploring her breast, reached down towards his crotch. She heard a zip being undone.

She tried to scream but his mouth was hard against hers. Panicking and desperate, her thoughts raced. *Can't move. Got to get out of here.*

She shut her eyes and tried to remember how to do it – how to teleport.

Home, she begged silently, as her hands were still trying to fend him off. *HOME PLEASE!*

Her fingers encountered hot flesh and it wasn't Jason's hand, either. Her eyes sprang open and he pulled back from the kiss.

"Take it, you little bitch," he grinned. "It's what you want. It's why you've been after me for so long, isn't it?"

She stared down at his groin, at what was just about visible in the near darkness. She was gasping and visibly trembling but Jason, pausing in his attack, gave her a moment of respite and that was just about enough to initialise the process. For the first time since that bus trip home after all the portals stuff, she felt it beginning to kick in again. She shut her eyes, willing herself to disappear. But Jason moved and, yet again, his weight pinned her to the wall of the shed, one hand trying again to force her legs apart.

Home, she thought, *It's taking too long. Home, Home, HOME!*

She desperately wanted to be back in the safety of her own house, her own bedroom. Why wasn't it working? Her eyes, open again, stared right into Jason's.

There was a loud clunk and Jason's head shifted sideways abruptly as if something had struck it. He crumpled to the ground, face down. Cassie gasped, seeing someone in a dark hoodie standing behind him.

What the hell…?

The light from the house wasn't enough to show the other person's face, though it did afford her a brief glimpse of the hoodie's torn pocket that flapped uselessly.

"Go," the other person whispered. "You can do it."

With Jason's weight no longer against her, Cassie finally felt herself fading away. As the transfer took hold she saw the other person chuck away the log they'd been holding. Then they stood behind Jason's prone form and kicked him right between the legs with their boot.

With a jolt, she was no longer in the garden but back in the darkness of her bedroom. From the position of the old LED clock glowing 10:15 on the bedside cabinet, she located the bed and, after slipping off her shoes, collapsed onto it. Tears cascaded down her cheeks and her body, unable to hold still, quaked and trembled as the shock set in.

How dare he? The bastard. How DARE he?

Loose Ends

Cassie dabbed at her eyes with a tissue. Ten minutes had passed but her heart was still racing, her hands and legs continued to tremble, and she had trouble controlling her breathing. All she could do was lay there, the events endlessly cycling through her mind.

A while later, a distant click and a slight increase of brightness in the room made her jump. She suppressed a squeak realising it was the upstairs landing light being turned on from the downstairs switch. Light seeped under the door.

She heard her grandad climbing the stairs. He was probably going to bed. Not knowing what time she'd be home, she'd told him not to wait up for her. She tried to be as quiet as possible, not wanting him to hear anything and come in. As he passed her door she was sure he would hear the thumping of her heart that pounded so loudly in her ears.

At the sound of the bathroom door clicking shut, she glanced at the clock – 10:39. Twenty-four minutes since she'd teleported home. What time had it been at the party? Her thoughts were still racing but she was reasonably sure she hadn't travelled in time.

I did it. I can still do it, she told herself, uncertain if that was a good thing or not. She hadn't wanted to. *I promised... but that bastard didn't give me any choice, did he?*

There was something else that was very important and, for a while, she didn't want to admit it. Instead, she lay there listening to the sounds of Bill moving around in the bathroom. She held her breath as he passed her door on the way to his bedroom, only daring to breathe again after he'd turned the landing light off. She sighed with relief as his door closed.

But that other thing nagged at her and she knew she couldn't avoid thinking about it.

The hoodie.

Not just the general style – no, that exact one – with the pocket torn in that particular way.

She waited another half an hour until the faint sound of snoring came from her grandad's bedroom. As she lay on her back, eyes open staring up into darkness, the time wasn't wasted. She figured out what she was going to do, what she knew she had to do.

I have no choice. I've got to finish it. I mustn't cause another paradox.

With the clock reading 11:45 and, as quietly as she could, she stood up.

I need a bath or a shower, she thought, feeling the trembling in her hands. She didn't want to wake her grandad but the need to scrub herself where Jason had touched her, invaded her, violated her, nagged incessantly.

Anyone would think you're a virgin, he'd mocked. She gritted her teeth, fuming.

After slipping the dress and stockings off in the dark, and dropping her necklace onto the bedside cabinet, she fumbled through her wardrobe for some jeans and a thicker top. Her hands sought and located the pair of tough walking boots kept near the wardrobe. She laced them up by touch alone. Then she grabbed the hoodie from the hook on the back of the door and put it on. With hands that still shook, she felt for the torn pocket on the left-hand side. She'd caught it on a tree branch a year previously when out walking through the woods on Mousehold Heath.

Pulling the hood over her head, she zipped the front up tight under her chin. She glanced at the clock: 11:54. *I need to do this now before I chicken out, while I still dare, while I still remember everything.* She closed her eyes and concentrated. *Ten o'clock*, she thought and, for the second time that night, felt it starting up again. It was a lot easier this time. Earlier, it had been as if she had almost been fighting herself in the effort to teleport home.

Ten o'clock, she repeated to herself. She needed to go back in time as well.

The garden was dark and her breathing was still deep and heavy. But, no one from inside the house would hear her over the music that was probably disturbing several of the nearer neighbours. She checked behind the shed to make sure no one was there already. Then she went across to the wood pile and selected a sizeable log. Solid, it felt good in her hands. Gripping it tightly to suppress the tremors in her hands, she swung it a few times and decided it could probably do a lot of damage.

"I bloody hope so," she muttered. *How dare he?*

Retreating to the rear of the garden, she hid behind some bushes. From there she could see anyone coming out of the back door but also monitor movement around the rear of the shed.

The frosted glass of the half-glazed back door prevented her from seeing directly in, but she detected fuzzy movement on the other side that looked like it was her earlier self and Jason. After a couple of minutes, the door opened and Cassie held her breath.

Yes, it was them.

Me, she corrected herself, *and that bastard.*

Her hands tightened on the log and she tried to force her muscles to relax. She had the urge to rush forward and crack him around the head with the log there and then. But she fought it, knowing she had to wait until the time was exactly how she remembered it.

No paradoxes.

"Where are you taking us?" she heard her voice say.

"Somewhere private," Jason replied as he led her behind the shed.

Not private enough, Cassie thought.

She heard Jason mutter, "Now you're warming up," followed, a few seconds later, by her gasp of, "No."

Cassie closed her eyes knowing what was taking place only a few yards away. She hardly dared breathe. *Not yet*, she thought, desperate to take her revenge.

"You've been aching for it for months, haven't you?"

"No, Jason. Please stop. Please."

Nearly, Cassie thought and then tried to calculate how long it would take to run across and position herself just behind him. *Surely he'll hear me, won't he? What if it doesn't work this time and he turns around and sees me? Can that happen?*

"You fucking little tease."

Wait, Cassie thought, *I don't need to run across at all.* Instead, she adopted an attack stance, gripping the log ready to swing it into action, waiting for *that* accusation. Concentrating on Jason's voice, she clamped her teeth shut when those words passed his lips.

Another few seconds, she thought.

She took a deep breath as he said, "Take it, you little bitch. It's what you want. It's why you've been after me for so long, isn't it?"

Now.

She concentrated and teleported, hopping the short distance. Materialising right behind him, she swung the log at his head, feeling the shock of the impact travel up her arms as it connected solidly with the back of his skull.

What if I've killed him?

He fell face down, letting out a groan as he hit the ground.

She looked at her earlier self, seeing her start to fade but remembering how slow the process had been.

"Go," she whispered. "You can do it."

Jason attempted to raise himself onto his hands and knees. Dropping the log and standing directly behind him, almost between his feet, she took aim and booted him right between the legs. He let out a squeal and collapsed face down once again. She looked around – she was alone with Jason.

"Not so fucking big now, are you?" she hissed at him as he curled up into a foetal position clutching his groin, groaning. Before he had a chance to roll over and see her, she concentrated and teleported back home making sure she arrived several minutes after her earlier self had left. The clock said 12:04.

She stripped off the hoodie, boots, jeans and top, and sunk back onto the bed, shaking and seething.

As she tried to calm herself down, something still nagged.

Damn, she thought. *It's not over. I still need to be at the party. If I disappear completely it might be even worse. I can't leave any loose ends. No paradoxes.*

But it needed working out properly. And, just like when she'd figured out the best way of sorting out the portals, her clones and Kay, she went over everything minutely. This time, though, she had to figure it all out for herself. There was no device and its resident *nearly-people* to help her double-check everything.

I wonder. She quietly opened the drawer in the bedside cabinet and felt around inside. Yes, there it was, next to that brush Kett had used on her hair.

In the dark, she had to feel for the side of the disc that held the button. She cupped it in her hand, her index finger poised over it.

Dare I? Does this count as an emergency?

Her finger hovered there.

Damn it, he was about to rape me.

She pressed hard on the button.

It didn't move a millimetre.

She stabbed it a couple more times before dropping it back into the drawer, wincing at the solid clunk it made. But the snores emanating from her grandad's room continued and she breathed again.

Not an emergency, then. But what would constitute an emergency? The tears were starting to form once more and she knew she had to go back in time yet again. If Jason had been hurt – and a large part of her hoped he had – then she also needed an alibi.

Alibi

She lay there for over an hour, trying to pluck up courage whilst constantly working the details over in her mind.

Climbing off the bed, she located her stockings, shoes and dress. Putting them on in the dark, she hoped her makeup hadn't been smudged too much.

With a sigh and noting the time on the clock – 01:07 – she closed her eyes and teleported. It was getting easier and, before arriving, she tried something new. Earlier, when trying to escape from Jason, the process had happened slowly, taking what seemed like ages for her to fade. Having seen that teleport from a second viewpoint she knew that her earlier self had been almost invisible at the point when she'd kicked Jason between the legs. But she remembered several seconds more from her earlier self's viewpoint.

So, in the upstairs hallway of Erin's house at ten o'clock, she tried materialising extremely slowly so that she stayed invisible. It took a bit of effort but it was a wise choice as there were a couple of people waiting outside the locked door to the bathroom.

Good job I didn't materialise inside the bathroom.

There was a shout from downstairs, "Someone's attacked Jason." The voice sounded like Erin's mother. There was more shouting followed, a couple of seconds later, with the music halting mid-song.

I need to go back a few more minutes.

Fifteen minutes earlier she found the hallway empty and the bathroom door stood open. Cassie materialised fully, slipped in and locked the door. But then she was horrified at her reflection in the mirror.

Her mascara had run and she had several large streaks down her cheeks from crying. Rummaging through the bathroom cabinets, she found some cleansing lotion and mascara, and started to repair the damage. After five minutes the bathroom door handle rattled.

"Won't be a minute," she called out hoping her voice wasn't shaking too much. She inspected the results in the mirror – far from perfect but, hopefully, it would do. Then she noticed she hadn't put her necklace back on – she'd left it back on her bedside cabinet.

I could pop back – but does it even matter?

She washed her hands, flushed the unused toilet and opened the door. One of Erin's university friends stood outside.

"Hi," he said, smiling.

She briefly returned the smile. The guy was quite good-looking – not in Jason's league but, under different circumstances, she might have stayed to chat. Instead, she forced herself to brush past him and down the stairs. Erin was talking to a couple of friends at the bottom, whilst drinking from a glass containing what looked like water.

"Hi, Cass," Erin, noticing her, shouted over the music that was blaring from the dining room. "Escaped his clutches for a while?"

"Yeah, definitely," she replied.

Erin frowned, looking at her more closely. "You okay?"

Cassie nodded.

"You sure? You look a bit, well…"

Cassie's lip trembled and she couldn't hold Erin's gaze.

"Sorry guys, chat later," Erin said. Then, with her hand on Cassie's arm, added. "C'mon, the lounge is a fraction quieter. This way."

As she accompanied Erin along the crowded hallway she glanced into the utility room, catching a glimpse of her earlier self with Jason. Entering the lounge Erin waved at a couple of girls seated on a sofa and went to join them.

"This is Cassie," Erin said, adding, "Holly and Megan." They parted, leaving a gap for Cassie and Erin to squeeze in between them. "She's with Jason."

"Not anymore," Cassie muttered, though not soft enough for them to miss hearing her, despite the noise of the music.

"Ah, thought so," Erin said.

Cassie almost burst into tears again. Instead, she swallowed and fought the urge. "Plenty more fish in the sea," she said, faking a smile, but fully aware of the quaver in her voice. Erin and the other girls nodded.

"That's the spirit," Erin said, resting her hand on Cassie's arm. "Where's your glass? You look like you could do with something stronger."

"No, um, water please, thanks," Cassie replied.

"Oh right, join the club," Erin said, raising a half-empty glass. "Sad to admit this, but more than a couple of drinks and I get ill."

"She's doing her best to give us proper drinking students a bad name," Holly laughed. Erin pulled a face at her.

"So, who was Jason drooling over near the back door, then?" Megan asked.

"I'm sure that was him with someone when I went past a few minutes ago. Similar dress to what you're wearing, I think. Same colour, anyway."

"Well, not me, obviously," Cassie said, hoping it didn't sound too much like a lie. "I just came down from upstairs. Fixing a couple of, er, smudges," she added, pointing to her face though she felt herself blushing under Erin's closer inspection.

"Yeah, he gets you like that," Erin said, nodding sympathetically. "What happened to your necklace?"

Damn, she noticed.

"I, er – it, er, broke. Had to take it off."

Cassie was fighting to suppress the tears, but Erin saw through her and wrapped an arm around her shoulder, pulling her close.

"It's okay, Cass. We'll look after you."

"Thanks," Cassie whispered, her voice breaking.

"It won't be the first time he's arrived at a party here with one person and, um, left with someone else," Erin said. "He may be family but, believe me, you'd be better off finding someone else – one who cares for more than just their own reflection in the mirror."

Cassie closed her eyes, knowing that her earliest self was probably coming to the same conclusion right about now.

"Right, let's get you that glass of–"

There was a scream from outside the lounge. "Someone's attacked Jason."

"Oh, here we go again," Erin said, as she bounced up to rush off after her mother. There were more raised voices, though Cassie couldn't catch what was being said due to the music. She gasped when it was suddenly shut off.

"Maybe he deserved it if what Erin says about him is true," Holly said, as several other guests followed Erin out of the lounge. Without the pounding music, the place felt completely different. Cassie became aware of someone approaching.

"Hi Callum, you met Cassie yet?" Holly said.

Cassie looked up to see the same face who'd said 'Hi' to her outside the bathroom earlier.

"Something's happening outside, apparently," he said. "I'm keeping out of it.

Erin's mum's going a bit crazy."

As more people left the lounge to see what was going on, Cassie wondered if she'd done the right thing in returning.

A few moments later Jason came storming in, pushing people out of the way. Seeing Cassie he staggered towards her. Megan and Holly immediately put themselves in the line of fire, protecting her. After a momentary glance, Callum joined them, holding a hand up to indicate Jason shouldn't approach any closer. But Callum was at least five inches shorter than Jason.

"You bitch," Jason screamed. There was mud on his face and his hair was, for once, a complete mess. He was rubbing the back of his skull where the log had connected. His fingers came away bloody.

Erin, who had followed him in, shouted back. "Leave her alone. It wasn't her. She's been in here with us for the past few minutes."

"What?" Jason shouted. "But we were... I... She was..."

"Was what?" Erin countered.

"She was kissing me. Yes, we were kissing. Behind your shed."

"Oh yeah?" Erin said, glancing down just below Jason's waist. "Is that why your flies are open?"

Jason snarled and zipped his trousers back up.

"So, then what?" Erin continued.

"She hit me on the back of the head."

"Oh really?" Erin said quietly. Then she screamed, "Liar."

"Huh?" Jason responded.

Erin, standing inches from Jason, poked him in the chest with a finger, and shouted, "Six foot six *you* was hit on the *back* of the head by five and a half foot Cassie who, because you were *kissing* her, was apparently both in front of you and behind you at exactly the same time."

"Er..."

"And all while she was in here talking to us."

"But..."

"You're drunk. I bet you've got absolutely no idea who or even *what* you might have been trying to molest. I'm calling you a taxi – it can either take you home or, if that knock on the head is as serious as it looks, it can take you to

A&E instead. Your choice. You can come and collect your car once you've sobered up."

Jason stared at Cassie for a moment.

"Bitch," he snapped, before turning on his heel and pushing his way back out of the lounge. The front door slammed and, seconds later, Cassie heard a car start and roar off into the night.

"Good riddance," Megan said.

Cassie closed her eyes and the tears flowed properly this time as Megan and Holly enveloped her in their arms. Callum brought them all some more drinks from the kitchen and, this time, Cassie was grateful it wasn't water.

Erin insisted on driving Cassie home afterwards.

"Thanks ever so much," Cassie said as Erin started the car. "Though you really didn't have to. I could probably walk back – it-it's not that far."

Cassie was aware that she was slurring her words. She was also sure she'd ended up drinking far more alcohol over the past hour or so than she'd ever had before in her life.

"Absolutely not," Erin insisted. "It's the least I can do. And no, it may not be far but I'd be worrying about you getting back safely. Anyway, despite it being my party, I was probably the only sober one there by the end, curse my inability to handle alcohol."

"Not sure I can, either," Cassie mumbled.

"Mitigating circumstances. You needed it."

"Yeah," Cassie said, flashing a quick smile as she pulled her coat more tightly around herself. The clock on the dash read 11:48 as the car left the Dussindale estate and turned left onto Plumstead Road East.

"Do you know who the other girl was? The one he claimed he was kissing?" Erin asked. "I don't remember anyone else wearing a blue dress that shade."

Cassie shook her head.

"Sorry," Erin said. "I should shut up. I don't expect you even want to think about it."

Not knowing how to reply, Cassie shrugged.

Erin was quiet for a while. Then, after they tackled the dual mini-roundabout at the junction with Thunder Lane and Woodside Road, she continued, "Even as a kid he was always a bit of a handful, from what I remember. Auntie Elise, his mum that is, never got over his dad, you know, and let Jason go a bit wild."

"I heard he'd lost his dad, somehow. He never really talked about it."

"Yes, that's right."

"What happened, exactly?"

"Well, his dad walked out on his mum when Jason was only a few weeks old. Just upped and left, apparently. I was too young to know anything about it at the time. My mum told me about it years later."

"Oh?"

"Mum said they were the happiest couple she knew, made for each other and really in love. They'd been married for several years before she finally fell pregnant with Jason. Then something happened and he took off. They never heard from him again – even the police never found him. Devastated his mum, of course, which is why Jason spent a lot of time with us while she tried to get back on her feet."

"Oh, I didn't know that."

"Is it right here at the roundabout?"

"Yes, thanks. So, why didn't she come tonight?"

Erin shook her head. "She's hardly done anything social for years. We did invite her. In fact, Mum phoned her several times to try to persuade her to come."

"That's so sad," Cassie said.

"You live with your parents?"

"Er, no. Just Grandad. I lost Mum when I was nine – c-cancer."

"Oh, Cass, I'm really sorry to hear that. And your dad?"

"No, he, er, died before I was born."

"Oh no, you poor thing. And I thought Jason had it tough."

"It's okay," Cassie whispered, unable to suppress the quiver in her voice.

"Sorry, shouldn't pry."

"No, it's, er, um… Oh, turn left at the junction coming up. That's it."

"Where's your place?"

"Bit further along."

Erin drove on.

"You can drop me anywhere around here. It's just over there," Cassie said a few seconds later, pointing out her house. Erin stopped the car and leaned over to give Cassie a hug.

"Look, if Jason causes any more problems for you, give me a ring. What's your number, I'll text you now so you get mine. Is that okay?"

"Yes, thank you," Cassie said and gave Erin her number. Erin added Cassie to her contacts. A few seconds later Cassie's phone buzzed as the text arrived.

"Promise me you'll look after yourself," Erin said as Cassie got out.

Cassie nodded and attempted to smile, but knowing that tears were on their way yet again, she turned and walked towards her house.

Erin didn't leave until Cassie had reached her front door. Then Cassie waved her off, making sure Erin's car was out of sight. Remembering the time on the clock when she last left the house, she moved forwards in time to 1:15 before letting herself in the front door.

Flopping down onto the bed for the third time that night, she silently sobbed herself to sleep.

Anyone would think you're a virgin.

The bastard.

How dare he?

Bonding

A Disappointment No Longer

"Bastard," Cassie screamed, punching the air. She gasped as Ka'Tor, disturbed by her sudden awakening from her dream, let out a wail.

Realising where she was, Cassie groaned and picked up her son, cradling him against her chest, trying to soothe his crying. But, she was on edge and shaking all over, which Ka'Tor must have sensed as he continued to bawl, which woke up several members of the tribe.

Cassie mumbled an apology and those disturbed began to settle down. As Ka'Tor's crying reduced to a grizzle, Cassie watched the glowing embers from the dying fires.

Damn, that felt so real, she thought – but that was the nature of dreams. Multiple copies of herself had been fighting Jason behind a shed but, resembling a bear and dressed in an animal skin, he had been defeating them all.

The dream had opened up a new raft of memories and her original assessment about him being a 'disappointment' had been far from adequate. Now that she fully recalled the events of that night, she couldn't stop shaking.

How long ago was that? More than a year? she thought, stroking Ka'Tor's hair – but how much longer? And what had happened between then and when she'd first arrived here?

I lost my virginity, obviously.

But, of that year she remembered nothing with any certainty and, of other events, she only retained bare snippets. She tried to dredge her memories but little surfaced: glimpses of Robert Kett; a knight in armour; a distinct recollection of pressing the button; and then a flash of a face, but one whose features were far more wrong than any of those here in the cave. She gasped as it momentarily coalesced into something solid, before slipping away as if her mind refused to tolerate it. And another thought dominated once again.

I was never meant to wake up at all.

This time, though, she was sure there was a clue as to why she was here.

Did I do something really bad? I know I broke my promise not to time travel. Am I being punished for it?

The idea made her quake once more and the animal skins that served as blankets were not enough to stop it. Cassie grabbed a cloak made from soft pelt and wrapped it around herself.

With the onset of wintery weather a few weeks ago, she had spent most of the time layered up in skins of various types. This one she had made for herself, managing to construct something resembling the long coat she remembered wearing to Erin's party. The sleeves had been difficult to get right and several of the pelts had been wasted before she'd succeeded. Some of the skins had come from foxes. Cassie had used their brown and red fur for the collar and to trim the ends of the sleeves. The others in the tribe had been intrigued by the effect as they normally just patched pelts together with total disregard for colour or style. They had also been bemused by the sleeves as these weren't something they made for their own cloaks.

After the attention her design had attracted, she'd thought, *So, I've invented fashion. Maybe the next thing I should introduce is the catwalk.*

However, the others had been just as interested in Cassie's addition of inside pockets into which she could stash useful tools whilst wearing it.

As Ka'Tor settled back to sleep, she tried to recall what had happened at the party at Erin's. Some of the *before* parts were now clear, especially the bits about getting the hang of teleporting again, but what happened afterwards was still hazy. She shut her eyes and, remembering she had regained the ability to teleport, set about trying to replicate it.

Ten minutes later she grunted in disgust. It still didn't work, despite being certain she was doing everything correctly.

Someone or something has taken the ability away from me.

She lay there seething, wondering if she was ever going to escape this life.

But, she thought, forcing herself to calm down, *it's not been all bad.*

She cuddled Ka'Tor closer. At least she was finally beginning to bond with her son. In the near darkness, she couldn't distinguish him from the general lumpiness of the bed. Maybe, one day, enough of her memories would return to help her understand how and why she had given birth to a son.

I'd never really thought about the whole having children thing. It was always years away – something that would happen when I was nearer thirty, possibly. Well, it looks like I escaped Jason's clutches but still ended up getting knocked up. And I don't even remember it.

In the near darkness, her eyes sought out the mound of fur skins that was the bed that Ka'Chull shared with El'Car.

She shuddered. *I don't want to, either.*

Unhappy Unbirthday

The days grew shorter and, in what Cassie estimated was mid-December, the first snows arrived overnight. Early the next morning, Cassie revelled in Ka'Tor's delight as he experienced it for the first time. Having recently learned to walk, though it was more of a stagger and tumble, he took faltering steps out into the freshly laid layer that was only a few inches thick. He picked handfuls of it up, throwing it around, falling back into it, laughing and oblivious to the cold on his bare skin. El'Tesh, who was still crawling, wasn't so sure about this new phenomenon until the older children joined Ka'Tor in playing and throwing it around. Then she advanced on hands and knees to the edge of the snow just inside the cave entrance, where she stared at it in wonder.

"Ka'Tor walk fast," Em'Dor commented. "El'Tesh slow."

"She pretty," Cassie said, wrapped up in her coat. She still felt the cold more than the others.

"Oh, he go," Em'Dor said, pointing at Ka'Tor who had started to toddle away from the cave entrance heading eastwards.

"Here we go again," Cassie muttered, running out into the snow after her son herself. But Ka'Chull, already outside and chopping wood, intercepted him, picking him up in one hand. He bounced the chuckling boy up into the air a couple of times before handing him back to Cassie with a laugh.

"Ka-kass," Ka'Tor said, using the name he'd started calling her weeks earlier.

By late morning the snow stopped falling. The day turned spectacular as the clouds parted and brilliant sunshine turned the view picture-postcard-perfect. Cassie wondered how close to Christmas it was and then chuckled to herself – if this was the past then the concept of Christmas would be an unknown number of centuries away.

She watched the sun carefully as it arced over the mountain peaks to the south. When it had almost reached its zenith, a position just to the right of one of the peaks, she moved back into the cave. She noted how far the shadow of the peak reached back onto a pattern of parallel lines carved into a large flat rock buried in the floor. It was barely any further than it had reached two days previously. Yesterday's cloud cover had prevented a reading but she suspected the date was either on or very close to the winter solstice. A few more days and she would know for certain. Then, the edge of the shadow would start moving back towards the cave mouth.

"What for?" Ka'Jat said, coming up behind her.

How can I explain this?

"Shadow now," she said, pointing at it. "Shadow two day past. Shadow four, seven, eight day past. Where one day soon, two day soon? Here, here, here?" She made motions showing the point moving slightly further inward and then more moving back out towards the entrance. Ka'Jat frowned. She made a hand motion which, in the tribe, was the equivalent of *wait and see*. He nodded.

"One day soon, two, three, four day soon," Ka'Jat said several days later, pointing further away from the back of the cave for each number.

"Yes," Cassie said, glad that he now understood what it all meant. And she had been proved right. Three days ago the midday shadow had changed direction and she had reset her wall calendar from the beginning once again. On that day she'd also said, *Happy New Year*, to everyone in English as there was no equivalent in the tribe's language. They had responded with 'Mad talk.'

Well, she thought, *at least we can now celebrate a new year on the correct day.*

A few days after resetting the calendar on the shortest day, Cassie daubed charcoal circles against a couple of her original week markings. The first one was at the end of the ten-week marker, the second was underneath the sixteenth.

If she had calculated things correctly, then Ka'Tor had been born around the first of March. Her birthday was April 15 and was represented by the second blob of colour. She tried to recall when El'Tesh had made her entrance into the world but, other than it being a week or two before she'd experienced Ka'Tor's first proper smile, she couldn't put an exact date on it.

"One year," she said on the date she estimated was Ka'Tor's birthday.

"How know?" Em'Jex asked. Cassie pointed to the charcoal circles on her calendar and tried to explain. Neither Em'Jex nor Em'Dor understood.

"You explain," Cassie said to Ka'Jat who had been listening in on the interchange. But he just grinned and nodded towards Em'Dor and his mother, Em'Jex, while making a hand gesture that, to Cassie's understanding, represented a lack of intelligence. Em'Jex rewarded him for his cheek by cuffing him around the ear. He laughed and ran off.

Oh, and it's also one year since I properly woke up, Cassie realised. *And probably around two years since I first got here.*

She looked across to her calendar, at the marking she'd placed for her own birthday. She walked across and placed a hand next to the blob of black.

How old am I?

But she could recall neither the date she'd left the twenty-first century nor how much time had passed between then and her arrival here. Also, having squeezed about two weeks into one day when she'd travelled around the portals with Kay, added further complications to the calculations.

Will I ever know? I don't even remember my eighteenth birthday. I could be well over twenty – maybe even more. Just how much have I lost?

She sighed, thinking about Georgia and Grandad. Would she ever see either of them again?

"Grandad," she whispered, feeling the tears well up. Seconds later she was sobbing loudly – she couldn't help it.

She felt Em'Dor's arm on her shoulder.

"Ka'See miss old tribe?" Em'Dor said in her ear.

Cassie placed her hand on Em'Dor's.

"Yes," she whispered, "Ka'See want see family. Ka'See want go home."

Temptation

Play For Today

"You're quiet this morning."

Cassie didn't reply. She sat poking at her cereal. Her head thumped a bit but the aspirins she'd taken earlier on were starting to take effect.

She'd got up early and run a bath, scrubbing herself all over several times. Afterwards, she'd applied foundation and a hint of mascara but the eyes that gazed back from the mirror were dark, almost thunderous. She felt soiled and violated, and no amount of makeup would obscure that.

"How'd it go last night?" Bill said and, when Cassie remained silent, persisted with, "I think I heard you come home in the early hours."

"I don't want to talk about it," she muttered.

"Ah, right. Not good, then."

"Good? No, it bloody-well wasn't good," she shouted, hearing her voice break as tears threatened to escape her eyes.

"Okay, okay. Sorry, I won't ask again," he said quietly, hands raised.

"Sorry, Grandad," she sniffed. "But he-he… oh, I hate him. How could he?"

Bill looked at her, questioningly. She shook her head.

I can't tell him. Unable to meet his gaze, she held her head in her hands.

"Hangover?"

"Yeah," Cassie said. Then she shot to her feet, saying, "I'm going out. I need to clear my head. Walk it off or something."

She stalked out of the kitchen and ran upstairs to her room. She threw on the jacket – the same one that Kay had paid for back in the early 1990s – and the pair of boots she'd used to kick Jason between the legs. She opened the drawer of her bedside cabinet and retrieved the disc. She stared at it for a few moments and was about to throw it back in the drawer but, instead, placed it in one of the jacket's inside pockets next to her phone and house keys. Then she took the phone out and put it on the cabinet.

I don't want anyone contacting me, she thought, *least of all Jason.*

After checking that her wallet was in the pocket of her jeans, she ran back down the stairs.

"Dinner will be around two," he called from the kitchen. "Roast chicken."

"Not hungry," Cassie said, opening the front door.

"You will be," he said, poking his head around the door frame. "Look, Cassie. I don't know what happened last night but… please be careful. Don't do anything… well, you know."

"Sorry. But I just need to walk it all off, somewhere quiet and peaceful. Bye."

As she went out the front door she heard her grandad shout, "Jesus Christ, Cassie, what's ha–"

The door slamming cut off anything else he said. Cassie stood on the doorstep for a moment, her eyes closed.

No, I can't talk to him about what Jason did. He'd go mad. Might even have a heart attack or something.

Gritting her teeth, she stomped out the front gate. It was still before nine o'clock but, being a Sunday in late February, there were few people about. Despite that, it looked like the day might turn out quite warm for the time of year.

She knew where she wanted to go.

I could walk there. It's not that far.

She glanced up and down the street – there was no one around.

Should I? Dare I?

She approached the row of shops set back from the pavement. With the sun low in the sky behind them, their fronts were in shadow. Peering in the first one, at the bows and other archery equipment that filled the shop, she wondered what it would be like taking up the sport. But in her current state, she knew what she might be tempted to do with a bow and arrow – and it would be far from legal.

Smacking him over the head with a log was 'far from legal' as well, but the bastard fucking-well deserved it.

She moved on to the next shop, which had changed hands at least a couple of times in the past few years. Currently, it was a tattoo parlour – the idea of needles puncturing her skin to inject ink made her shudder. Several of her school friends were considering getting a tattoo as soon as they were eighteen.

Not me. It's bad enough having that little scar on my cheek.

The third establishment was set further forward than the first two, so Cassie pressed herself into the corner where shops two and three met, hoping she was concealed. With her back to the shop window, she scanned the houses across the road for any sign of movement. Many of the curtains were still drawn but she could detect no faces behind the ones that were open.

To hell with walking.

She shut her eyes, concentrating on where she planned to go. But, as the process kicked in, she thought she heard her name being called.

I'll deal with whoever that was when I get back.

When she opened her eyes she was on the grass at Kett's Heights. She had only moved in space, not time – the same blue sky hung above her.

Her hands were shaking as she stood while a light breeze rattled the bare tree branches. Only the occasional chirp of a bird disturbed the near silence. There was no one else around.

Good job, she thought, *as I didn't check before materialising.*

She spent a few minutes reducing the rate of her breathing, the rapid rise and fall of her chest betraying the anxiety coursing through her.

I promised I wouldn't.

"I broke that promise last night," she told herself. "I didn't really have a choice."

Did I?

"Come on. Don't get cold feet. It worked last night."

Yeah, last night. I need to take my mind off what that bastard tried to do. If it hadn't been me, then it would have happened to someone else. Someone who couldn't retaliate the way I could. Anyway, it's only a few years – July 2016 – and just a play as well. I might even learn something new.

She closed her eyes and thought, *Back. July 2016. The ninth of July.*

The sensation of moving back through time enclosed her and she opened her eyes to see the flash of days accelerating. Sensing she was near the correct date she slowed down, remembering this time to keep herself invisible. Suddenly, there was movement all around her as a crowd appeared. It was early afternoon.

She continued backwards a few more hours and popped back into view when the grounds were deserted.

"I need somewhere hidden, where it will be safe to appear later on," she told herself. "Maybe up there," she added, spotting what looked like some ruins near the top of the hill.

Reaching them, she wondered what they had once been. Concealing herself behind the remains of a wall she moved forwards in time, only stopping when the ruins were deserted. Overdressed in her jacket and jumper in the warmth of a July day, she took both off. Then, with the local time at just gone two, she peered down onto the grassed area. It was full of people sitting on blankets or fold-up chairs, eating their picnics as they waited for the play to start. Strolling back along the paths as if she'd just been casually exploring the rest of the heights, she found a position off to one side, away from where the crowd was thickest. There, she folded up the jacket and sat down on the jumper.

Over the next couple of hours, Cassie began to learn what had taken place in 1549 in the months of July and August.

I was there, she thought, remembering when Kay and herself had been thrown back to that year by the device when it had been in Laurence's possession. Its later incarnation had helped return them to 2000 so Kay could cut off Laurence's head. But why the same year?

Coincidence or something else? she pondered as the actors broke into song.

This is more like a pantomime. How much of it is actually true?

Seated quite a distance from the crowd Cassie struggled to hear some of the finer points and she felt she might be losing the full benefit of the performance.

After the play finished, she explored the various pathways on the heights, seeking a secluded spot safe from prying eyes from where she could return to 2019. It took a while as others were also exploring the grounds, including the ruins she'd previously used. According to a discarded flyer, there was to be a repeat performance in the early evening but she had neither the patience nor the inclination to experience it for a second time.

I've probably got the gist of it, she thought.

A Request

"Why did you march all the way to Dussindale for the battle?" Cassie asked.

She had returned to February 2019 and hopped over to the castle mound walking around the walls looking for Kett, who took his time in materialising.

"What are you talking about?"

"I went back and watched that play all about your rebellion."

"See, I knew you wouldn't be able to resist. Oh, but something else isn't right, is it? You're angry, aren't you? Absolutely seething inside. Who or what has done this to you?"

"Leave it. None of your business. Not even going there."

"But it caused you to go there, didn't it?"

"Doesn't matter why I did."

"Doesn't it, really?"

"Shut up. I'm the one asking the questions."

Kett shrugged, smiled and said, "Go ahead. Ask."

Cassie looked around to make sure that no one else was up here with them. It was still early – the hands of the City Hall clock indicating a few minutes before half-nine.

With the city below them all but deserted, they strolled around the castle until they reached the eastern view. She stared across the Anglia TV rooftops and could just make out the dome of the railway station in the distance.

"So, why all the way out to Dussindale?" she asked again, pointing towards the eastern view. "It's miles away – even further out than my place."

"Do you mean out past the village of Thorpe?"

"Where else?" Cassie snapped. "You didn't even have buses then, did you?"

"Buses? You mean those big red things that carry people around."

"They haven't been red for years."

"No, but I'm sure they were red for far more years than they weren't. We had horses, wagons and carts – the occasional carriage – but no buses."

"No wonder you lost the battle if you spent time walking miles to get there."

"The battle wasn't out past Thorpe."

"But that's what they said you did in the play. You went to Dussindale."

"Ah, that rhyme again. Your generation has misinterpreted it, though not in the same manner we did."

"What are you talking about?"

Kett's eyes took on a faraway look, his features seemed to alter and grow older. If she hadn't already been talking to a ghost, it would have been spooky.

Along with his face, Kett's voice also changed and the words he uttered were accented in a different manner as if the vowels were all mixed up.

"The country knuffs. Hob, Dick, and Hick, With clubs and clouted shoon, Shall fill up Dussendale, With slaughtered bodies soon."

Some of it was familiar to Cassie. *Was that in the play?*

There was silence for a moment before he added, in a more normal voice, "We thought it meant Warwick's troops would be slaughtered by us. Not our own men by his. I shouldn't have let it sway me. Not that I was the only one. Even William believed it."

"Who?"

"My dear brother, may God rest his soul."

"Well, I didn't understand a lot of what you said, but you definitely mentioned 'Dussindale'."

"*Dussendale* is what the rhyme spoke of – not out past Thorpe, though I vaguely recall that there might have been some land out there of a similar name. Dussing's Dale, I think it may have been. But no, our last battle was not far from the city gates. I will show you," he said, starting to walk in the direction of Castle Meadow.

With the City Hall back in view, he raised an arm and pointed almost directly north. "It was in that direction, over there."

Cassie tried to figure out where he meant.

"What? Anglia Square?"

Kett looked at her askance. "I know of no square with that name."

"Near the flyover. Magdalen Street."

He frowned for a moment and then said, "Ah, the concrete atrocity that, not so long ago, sliced the heart out of the area."

"Not long ago? It's been there since long before I was born. Grandad's complained for years about it being an eyesore."

"Indeed, and back then the buses were definitely red. Sometimes I forget how different we are in age. Anyway, no, not the street. It was beyond that and Botolph Street. Magdalen Hill it was. Out beyond the gates."

"Gates?"

"When the city was mostly encircled within a wall, there were gates a-plenty in that wall."

"Oh yes, of course. I saw one of them. How many were there?"

"Cosn'y, Saint Augustine's, Magdalen," he said, "and those were just the ones defending the north. All gone now, of course."

"Saint Augustine's? You mean near that swimming pool I fell into?"

Kett sighed, repeating, "Shall fill up Dussendale, With slaughtered bodies soon," and then adding with a whisper, "It was carnage."

"What? The slaughtered bodies?"

"Yes, what else?" he snapped, suddenly looking even older. "More death than ever I had witnessed before. Too many good men cut down, some hardly more than boys."

"I suppose anything involving slaughtered bodies would look like carnage," Cassie muttered softly.

Kett was silent for a while. "It is told that three thousand and more died that day. Can you imagine what three thousand dead and dying look like? The cries of those still barely alive... the stink of the blood?"

"I – I don't think I want to."

"No," Kett said, his voice darkening, lowering in pitch. "I can still see them. I always see them. I will never forget. But you – oh, you people now. You are so soft. You don't have the stomach for such things, do you? Today you kill from afar, hurling death across continents, completely disconnected from those you would slaughter. In my day you would look into the eyes of those you killed even as you ended their life, as your arrows punctured them, as your sword slid between their ribs, as their blood spilled from their bodies."

Again there was silence. Cassie had never seen Kett act like this before. Was it more like how he had been when he was alive? She struggled to find a reply.

"Um, I'm sure cannons were mentioned in the play," she murmured, finally, in an attempt to break the tension. "Didn't you have guns and things like that?"

"Yes, we did. We broke through the walls in several places with the sakers, the cannons, as you call them. We stole them from Warwick's troops."

"Oh yes, I remember that bit. It was a lot to take in."

"For a few days we could hardly do any wrong," Kett sighed. "Ah, I really shouldn't have believed the rhyme. It was my undoing. If I could go back and do it again I would have disregarded it and ordered my army to hold the heights. And then make Warwick battle for every inch. What would the world be like now if I had succeeded? It can't have been worse than this, that's a surety."

"Too late now for regrets," Cassie said, though her thoughts were on much more recent events than Kett's battle.

"Indeed, yes," Kett said. He turned to face her, adding, "Or is it?"

"What?"

"You."

"What about me?"

"What good is your talent if you don't use it?"

"Huh?"

"Go back in time and warn me. Tell me to remain on the heights, to keep the camp intact instead of breaking it. Convince me the rhyme is a lie."

"No," Cassie hissed. "Absolutely not."

"You could."

"Maybe. But you can't change history," Cassie said, remembering the device saying something about events that couldn't be changed – oh yes, one of them had been the library fire, which she had tried to prevent without success.

"Are you certain?" Kett said.

Had the device been telling the truth?

No, I'm not. I wouldn't deny that I'd like to take another look at how the city used to be – a proper look this time – no dashing between portals – no nasties chasing me. But I dare not risk it.

"It's too dangerous," she said instead. "And I should know."

"But, you've already been back in time today, haven't you? To see the play."

"That was different. I didn't speak to anyone or do anything that could have changed history in any way."

"Really?" Kett said, his eyes taking on a faraway look. Then he continued, his speech quite slow as if he was having to think carefully about each word. "So, maybe during your trip today you might have stepped on a bug and killed it. If you hadn't gone back in time that bug might have bitten a child and caused it to die of infection. Now, because of you, that child will grow up and maybe murder someone else who would have lived had you not gone back in time."

"What? Are you nuts? That's just ridiculous. People don't die of insect bites in this part of the world. Australia, maybe. Not here."

"Oh. So, your trip back was completely safe, then?"

"Yeah."

Kett, staring out over the rooftops, smiled. "Well, then. How about a trip back to see the battle? Don't get involved. Just watch what happens from a safe distance away from the fighting."

"Why should I do that?" she snapped. *Shut up, don't tempt me.*

Kett spun around to face her directly, his face dark and thunderous. "So you can see how people really die."

Cassie flinched and swallowed. "N-no. I won't. I-I don't, er, see the point."

"So, you admit that you're scared to see how people die?"

"Well, yes. No. I mean…" *I've seen versions of myself dying. I saw Kay die. Christ, I watched my Mum fade away when I was nine years old.*

"Yes, you are scared to see proper death. To see the death of people who should have lived. People who were wronged and were fighting to right those wrongs. Back then we were willing to fight for our freedom. Maybe if I had won, you would have more freedom now. Instead, trapped here, I see that money still rules the land and the rich still build their enclosures and poison your minds against each other without you realising it. This world is naught but a shadow of what it could have become. Yet you, who has it within herself the ability to evoke such change, is too much of a coward to take that chance."

"No, please…"

"And have you ever thought upon why I am here and why only you have the ability to sense me? Why should I have remained if not for the purpose of speaking with you? What other reason could there be? And what other reason should you, with the ability to alter the past, be able to speak to me and listen to my own words? What if we two are the key to repairing this world? What if this is how it is meant to happen?"

Could he be...? No, stop it. I mustn't listen.

"Think on this, girl. What if the world that resulted from me losing that battle is the wrong one? How much injustice would there be upon your shoulders should you refuse to act? Do you dare turn your back on the possibility of a better world? Hmm, dare you?"

Can he really be right? Is this what I'm here for? Cassie's mind raced back to the conversations she'd had with her school friends over the past few years, especially with Georgia and Mark and, yes, even Jason. They'd all felt like they had no control over their lives or the state of the planet that seemed to be going from bad to worse. What would have been the difference if Kett had won?

Dare I do as he asks? Dare I risk it? No, no, no — the device said you can't change time. I can't change time. Can I? What if the device was wrong? Or had deliberately lied? Could it lie?

"Well?" Kett said, peering into Cassie's face as if he could see the turmoil raging through her mind.

No, I can't, I daren't.

"No, it's impossible," she blurted out. "I'm *not* going back. No matter what you say." *Don't tempt me... please?*

"No, of course not," he said, turning his face away from hers to gaze past City Hall. "You don't have the stomach for it. No one in this time does. This world no longer has any proper warriors."

"What? That's not true. We still got soldiers."

"Ah yes, those soldiers who fight from inside their protected shelters, whose weapons throw lead at enemies so far away that they do not know whether it is really their enemies they fight or a few unarmed villagers, or maybe even a herd of cows. Those are not soldiers, not like the men in our day, prepared to battle for hours or days while their own life may be taken at any time."

"Oh yeah? From what I heard, your own battle wasn't exactly much. It only lasted a short while and then you ran away."

"What?" Kett shouted, his face creasing and turning crimson with anger. "What abject lies they tell. I was there. It started hours before noon and we were evenly matched for much of it."

"Really?"

"Of course. I know what I saw, girl. Only by the late afternoon did the tide turn against us."

"That's not what they said, I think."

"More fabrications, damn them."

There was silence between them for several seconds. Then Cassie whispered, "I'm beginning to wonder just how much that play got wrong."

"They lie, willingly or unknowingly. The passage of time distorts truth. Ah, truth. But, of course, you will never know if I tell the truth or not, for you do not have the stomach to see for yourself, do you?"

Stop it.

Kett locked eyes with Cassie yet again. She glared back at him, ignoring the fact that she could see right through his translucent form.

"So, what is the point of you if you do not make use of your abilities?"

Stop tempting me, she thought, but still said nothing. *I saw the city when the wall still enclosed it. But only for a couple of minutes. Would it really hurt to see it again, properly this time? No, I mustn't.*

"Oh yes, you make use of your abilities when it suits you, don't you? Like that other burning you have inside yourself right now. Is that what it takes to make you travel?"

Cassie grimaced, clamping her lips shut.

"Your lack of denial is as good as an admittance," he said, turning away from her so that she couldn't see his face.

"Yes, okay," she shouted. "I had to get away from him."

"Him? So, a boy then. A lovers' tiff, was it?"

"Shut up," she hissed.

"A boy who refused your favours, perchance?"

"No." *Stop, just stop.*

"Ah, so you refused his advances instead, then?"

"He – he t-touched me…"

"Touched? Seems a minor thing."

"No. He fucking-well tried to rape me," she screamed, unable to prevent her outburst, feeling the tears well up yet again.

"Tried? He didn't succeed then? In that case, why did you need to travel in time if he didn't succeed?"

Cassie hissed back, "If I hadn't time travelled he would have done. It was the only way I could get away from him."

"And was history changed by him not taking his pleasure with you?"

That retort made her pause.

"Huh? Of course not." *Surely not... I hope.*

"You are certain? You have no doubts, whatsoever? Well, then. What's stopping you?"

Cassie ground her teeth together and, wiping her tears on the arm of her jacket, tried to stop herself shaking. But the beat of her heart that pulsated in her chest, throat and ears, was racing as fast as it had been last night as she'd endured Jason's hands upon and, she swallowed at the thought, inside her body.

"Tuesday, August the twenty-seventh, fifteen hundred and forty-nine, late afternoon. Take a look. Maybe your tears will be worth it then."

Kett diverted his gaze back over the city.

"I-I'm not listening." *August the twenty-seventh...*

"You don't have to talk to anyone or even be seen. Just go and take a look, a quick peek."

"No," she whispered, her breathing fast and erratic. *Fifteen forty-nine. I don't need reminding of the year. Oh hell, don't.*

"No, of course you won't. You haven't got the stomach. Even the women back then had more courage than your men of today. Maybe the anger that burns inside you is more due to the regret that your lover didn't try harder to win your affections," Kett said, facing Cassie again. "Is that it?"

"Fucking shut up," Cassie spat before closing her eyes, squeezing more tears away. *No, No, NO. I mustn't. I can't. Don't even think about it. August the twenty-seventh...*

Her eyes reopened to find the face of Kett's ghost only inches from her own. "Go back and look upon how real men fight."

His eyes, more solid than ever, bored into hers. Her imagination overlaid his face with that of her father's. It was almost as if Kett was trying to invade her body just as Laurence had done on her great-grandfather's bus.

No, Laurence is dead, gone.

"Stop it," she shouted, twisting away to break the spell.

But Kett wasn't finished. "See for yourself what your generation has lost. And, if it moves you to see such men dying, then go back a little further, just a few days and convince me the rhyme was a lie, a falsehood."

As if she was back on that bus, Cassie had an overpowering urge to escape by any means possible. But her legs felt rooted to the ground and Kett's voice pummelled her ears and the inside of her head.

"Go and make the world what it should have been, girl. Go and unlock a new future. Maybe only then will I finally be able to rest. Lord knows I have lived this life of vapour for so much longer than I ever did walking on corporeal legs."

Then she felt hands on her shoulders. As he had done when combing her hair, Kett had managed to make himself solid enough to physically interact with her. Cassie gasped as he spun her around to face him.

"Go and do your duty."

I've got to escape. Got to get away.

Inside her, the urge to abandon this place, this century, this world was overwhelming.

It's happening. I can't stop it. I can't fight it. Fifteen forty-nine.

"Do what you were born to do, Cassie Fox. Bring about a new world, a better world. And, after all these centuries, let me finally achieve peace."

A bout of dizziness made her sense of connection with the ground falter.

"I-I can't stop it," she whispered. *Do I want to stop it?*

"Go then, girl. Let you and your fate become one with mine."

"No," she whispered, as she let the sensation encompass her whole body.

"And off you go," Kett said with a smirk, flicking his hand as if that would help her on her way. Then he disappeared.

"Fuck you," she spat as she, too, faded away…

…and travelled.

Fifteen Forty Nine

"No, no, no," Cassie mumbled as the days flashing past her were reduced to a blur. I shouldn't be doing this. Another voice in her head added, *What's the harm? You've already been to that year once before.*

Hell. I knew even while I was arguing with him that I wanted to see it for myself. Must be careful. No paradoxes, no interaction whatsoever – just go, look and come back. Not a second too long. Nothing more. Mustn't do anything in the past to change the future.

But is it the right thing to do? I promised. Oh, God, I've got to regain control.

Cassie concentrated. The flashing slowed and then stopped.

She was, once again, looking out across the roofs of the city. But the City Hall and its clock were nowhere to be seen. Older grimier buildings crowded the area where it should have been.

It's 1912, summer, a Friday, about twenty to twelve. Wait? How exactly do I know? It's like I've got a built-in clock and calendar.

She hadn't thought about it when she'd flitted around Norwich the previous year after Kay had died. Nor the previous night at Erin's party or when she'd gone back to 2016 to see the play. But she hadn't travelled as far back as this. It was like that map that had appeared in her head when she most needed it – the one that none of her clones had possessed.

I told the device to put the map in my earlier self's head. But where did the clock and calendar come from? Can I do anything else that I haven't discovered yet? Do I really want to find out? Dare I?

But she couldn't resist examining the view. She was amazed at how different Castle Meadow appeared – it was almost unrecognisable. Gone was the wide sweep that encircled the castle mound. In its place ran a narrow curve of a road, its surface inlaid with two pairs of rails, their polished surfaces glinting in the sunlight. With her breath still coming fast and her heart thundering in her chest, her eyes followed a tram. It clanked along those rails amongst pedestrians who appeared to be in no hurry to get out of its way.

Most of the men wore black or brown suits, and the women wore dresses that reached nearly to the ground. Boys in flat caps and grubby attire were pulling and pushing their wares around on wooden-wheeled barrows.

I could have filmed all this on my phone if I'd bought it with me. In colour, too. I wonder what people would say if I put it up on YouTube. Probably think it was fake, like a film set or something.

She noticed a boy staring up in her direction as he pushed his barrow along. She wondered if he could see anything out of the ordinary. Maybe she was as invisible as she and Kay had been when they had been out of their own time. Or was that just an effect of the portals?

Can he really see me?

The boy stopped pushing his barrow and stared up at her, one hand shading his eyes. Then his other hand raised to wave at her.

Almost involuntarily, she raised a hand in response.

No, she thought, forcing her arm down, *no interaction. Come on, leave these people to their lives.*

But, down below, the boy still stared at her.

Do I return back to the present or carry on?

But, the urge to push further back dominated. She closed her eyes thinking, *Magdalen Gates, 1549,* and she continued her journey into the past.

Did that boy see me disappear? Too late now. Oh well, if he did then it will give him something to tell his children.

Time blurred as she moved in space as well as shooting back centuries, keeping her eyes shut to avoid the flickering.

"August the twenty-seventh, late afternoon," she muttered, homing in on that date. It seemed to take nearly half a minute to reach her target and each second drained her of energy.

Damn it, it's really hard to travel this number of years. Last year it seemed effortless. Did having the device around make it easier?

Finally, the centuries fell away and she arrived. Opening her eyes, she saw the city wall only feet behind her, with a gateway a short distance to her left, but she saw no evidence that any battle had been fought in the area. She frowned.

This is definitely the twenty-seventh. Isn't it?

Something felt wrong. But what? It was like having double vision – her calendar seemed to possess two sets of overlapping dates – one ten days out from the other. On the second, the current date appeared as the seventeenth and not the twenty-seventh.

Something nagged at the back of her mind.

Oh yes, last time I was here I asked the device the date and it said, 'Julian or Gregorian convention?' I remember something from school about the calendar changing for some reason. So I might be too early. How about ten days forward.

She hopped the difference and gasped.

No, no!

The city wall was again behind her but it was the scene in front of her that devoured her attention. The land that inclined gently away from where she stood was strewn with hundreds of bodies. Dead and dying bodies – some torn open with their innards spilling out of their shredded flesh, others spiked through with swords and spears. The blood hit her senses like a wall – the sight and the smell seeping into her so that she could imagine its stickiness clinging to her skin. Blood was everywhere: blood that had congealed, blood that oozed where it had yet to congeal, blood that covered the corpses as well as the barely living. Those still this side of death groaned or whimpered. But most of those she could see were far beyond the ability to groan.

Cassie gagged and promptly threw up.

"Witchcraft?" came a voice from close by.

Cassie squealed. While bile still forced itself from her throat, she swivelled to face the owner of the voice.

"Yo appair as from nawhah."

An armour-suited man on horseback approached from her right. His horse, its eyes wide and wary, appeared as scared of her as she was of it. Froth dripped from its mouth. The rider paused the horse's advance and his sword, brown with congealed blood, stabbed downwards – the whimpering was reduced by a minuscule amount.

"Are yo man or woman?" the horseman said, his accent like that of Kett's when he had recited that rhyme. "Your garb is nothing such as I have clapped sight on before prior to this dair. Your eyes trowly pierce."

Cassie took a step backwards. *No interaction – too late.*

"Hold. Dunna run," the man shouted.

Cassie wiped her mouth on her sleeve. *Got to get away.*

She closed her eyes as the process kicked in, though not quick enough to prevent her hear the man's shout. "What? Yo fahde as a ghaust. Witch, hold–"

She was gone, moving north by several hundred feet and back by a few weeks. According to her calendar, it was now Monday the fifteenth of July, though it told her it might also be the twenty-fifth. With a bit of effort, she found she could dismiss the calendar that was wrong. *How am I doing that?*

Opening her eyes, she was relieved to find herself alone. Located on the upper parts of the slope, she looked down upon the walled city of Norwich.

Is this Magdalen Hill? she thought, remembering the name Kett had mentioned. *I mustn't stay. Oh, my God, all that blood. Those poor people.*

She sat, wiping her lips on the sleeve of her jacket, glad that her breakfast that morning had been barely more than three spoonfuls of cereal. Her home felt a long way away.

It's like I can physically feel the years between me and 2019.

Her breath came in short gasps as if she had been running hard. But her mind couldn't expel the scene that had accosted her. She felt tainted as if she might never be clean again. The images that crawled through her head were even worse than the thought of Jason's hands on her body.

What am I doing here? Why did I come? Oh God, all those people.

She heard Kett's words in her head: "You don't have the stomach for it. No one in this time does."

He was right. I don't. I admit it.

The sun was low in the east. Morning.

But, I've seen it now. I won't ever be able to forget it. But what can I do? How can I help them? No interaction. No paradoxes. But I can't just ignore it, can I?

But she couldn't dispel the words that Kett had spoken: "Go back in time and warn me. Convince me the rhyme is a lie."

Dare I? What would happen?

The rising sun inched higher and began to bathe the shallow valley in light.

Could I really make the world a better place? No, stop, stop, stop. I mustn't.

She forced herself to sit, attempting to calm herself down. But she couldn't suppress the torrent of contradictory thoughts that crashed through her consciousness. *What if Kett is right and the world I know is the wrong one? What if I'm meant to come back here and fix things so that the future is a better place? No, no interaction. I promised. But, but...*

"Damn it," she spat, her voice quavering, tears forming in her eyes. "I don't know what to do. I don't know who to ask. I wish the device was here. Or maybe Kay – she always had answers."

But I'm a younger version of Kay. Oh, what can I do? Wait, maybe...

She reached into an inside pocket and pulled out the disc, holding it in the palm of one hand, staring at it. As her index finger hung over it, the rays of the rising sun caught the brass of the disc and the red of the button itself.

Is this an emergency?

She pressed it.

"Fuck it," she shouted as, like before, the button refused to depress. She tossed it back inside the pocket.

Gazing down towards the city she knew that, in a few weeks, the slope before her would be covered with death. *Can I prevent that? Do I have the right?*

She shut her eyes, muttering, "Those poor people."

Do I have the right not to try?

For several minutes, she sat there trying to think through what she should do. *Maybe I should just go straight back home.*

"Or maybe I need to take a proper look around first," she said, trying to suppress the tremor in her voice. "But how? I'll stand out like a sore thumb wearing this stuff. I need to find something more suitable."

Outside the city wall there were a few shacks dotted around but nothing that looked like a place that might contain spare clothes. Most of them resembled hovels that might, at best, have housed a pig or a goat.

I can't go inside the wall looking like this. But where else can I find something that won't look out of place?

She sat, barely moving, while the sun crawled up into the sky. Her mind pictured the houses she'd seen not far from Saint Stephen's Gate the first time she'd come to this year.

A noise broke into her thoughts and she saw movement as one of the city gates creaked open. Two figures exited before the gate was closed. Because of the distance, Cassie couldn't tell if the two were male or female. It didn't seem that they had seen her.

I need to get away before someone does spot me.

She willed herself away to where those other houses had been. Finding herself on the track that led to Saint Stephen's Gate, she spotted the buildings she remembered seeing before. Although ramshackle in style and distribution, they were still of a more solid construction than those north of the city wall. In case someone chanced to look in her direction, she ran for the cover of a bush.

I shouldn't be doing this. But, those poor people. Maybe this is what I'm supposed to do.

The nearer buildings appeared to be outhouses but, beyond them, was a larger dwelling, a cottage that was mostly roof. The thatch, which begun just above the lintel of the front door and was arched steeply upwards to a peak, was pocked by two small windows indicating the presence of an upper floor. The sound of animals – a horse and maybe a goat or two – emanated from the nearer outbuildings. Seeing movement, Cassie ducked down. A woman of indeterminate age, carrying a wooden bucket exited one of the smaller buildings. Chickens rushed from all directions to surround her. She plucked and threw handfuls of grain from the bucket, the chickens gobbling it up as soon as it hit the grass. For Cassie, watching the scene was like therapy, it was something normal occurring in the midst of all the chaos surrounding her.

Right now, I'd trade such a simple life for my own, she thought, seeing the satisfaction in the woman's face as the chickens around her feet fed themselves on what she provided.

A roaring noise back at the track made her jump. As the chickens scattered in alarm at the commotion, the woman screamed, dropping the bucket in her haste to run for the safety of the cottage.

Cassie peered out of the bushes back towards the track and gasped seeing a motorbike. The rider, dressed in black, shut off the engine a few seconds later.

"So, you didn't do this, then?" the rider said.

Cassie's mouth hung open as recognition dawned. She managed to suppress a shriek, and instead whispered to herself, "Oh, Kay, I wished for you and you're here. But how?"

But then she frowned. *Wait, this is familiar.*

Peering around some foliage to enable her to see a few yards further up the track towards Norwich, she thought, *Oh, I see.*

Her 2018 incarnation stood fifteen feet from the motorbike. The scene played out just as she remembered, though viewing it from this angle felt completely weird.

But surely it's no different to seeing my later self wallop Jason over the head or being that later version doing the walloping. Is it?

But those two events had happened close together. What she was now seeing had, in her own timeline, occurred nearly eight months previously. Unable to tear her eyes away and hardly daring to breathe, she bit her lip.

"What date is this?" she heard her own voice ask, followed by, "I don't know. Just give me the damned year."

I can't hear the device's side of the conversation – but it seems I didn't have the ability to tell the date back then. Or maybe I did – but hadn't figured out how to use it. When did that start?

After a few more seconds she heard the final words being said: "Okay. We need to hold hands."

"Sounds familiar," came Kay's response. "Getting your own back?"

That made Cassie smile briefly. "Oh, Kay," she whispered again, unable to prevent tears forming. "I really do miss you."

She wondered if the device in her earlier self's pocket had any idea that a later version of Cassie was observing them from a nearby bush.

She watched as they clasped hands and then, as if they had never existed, they were gone. There was another scream and Cassie's attention returned to the cottage. The woman again, but this time she was accompanied by a girl and two men who were similar enough in appearance to be father and son. The girl was probably no older than herself. They were peering through a gap in a hedgerow and it was obvious they had seen the disappearance.

"Say, ee said reet, hosbond," the woman shouted, her strangely accented voice laced with terror. "Deveels."

The man scratched his chin and shook his head.

"Mah we prah they have gun back to the hell that spawned they," he said.

"The black'un, that were Lucifer, I'll wager."

Cassie had no idea what he was talking about.

"Ee thot it wuss a croon," said the younger girl almost as incomprehensibly. But her quivering voice demonstrated how terrified she was.

She looks about the same height and build as me, Cassie thought, her eyes poring over what the girl wore. The simple dress, brown-red in colour and laced about her middle, descended almost to the ground. Partly concealed by the dress, she wore a top that might once have been white but was now grey through use. A bonnet of a similar colour enclosed her hair. Tied about her front was an apron with a single large pocket.

I wonder if she's got any spares.

Cassie examined the house.

If they're all outside, then I'll need to be quick. She teleported to the rear of the building and, finding the back door ajar, peered in.

Determining the room was empty, she stepped into the kitchen. It sported a stone sink, two rough wooden tables and five mismatched chairs. Pots, both iron and copper, hung from hooks driven into the exposed timber framework of the wall. A few more hung from ceiling beams that supported the upper floor. Another door led inside to an area dominated by a staircase. Hearing no one else, Cassie tiptoed upstairs to find the space divided into three bedrooms, one large, the others small. From a wooden rail in one of the smaller rooms hung a few more dresses similar to the one worn by the girl, along with an assortment of tops and undergarments. She stepped past the rail to peer out of the tiny window but the family were no longer in front of the house. Voices and the fall of footsteps filtered up the staircase from below.

Damn.

She selected a top and dress at random and was eyeing up the undergarments when there was a noise on the landing. Cassie's eyes met those of the girl.

"I only need to borrow them for a while," Cassie said, grabbing a spare bonnet to add to the top and dress. "I'll bring them back. I promise."

The girl screamed.

More feet rushed up the stairs.

"Deveels," the mother shouted.

"Yep, that's me," Cassie muttered as she disappeared, thinking, *So much for 'no interaction.'*

Safe House

Cassie hopped several hundred yards towards the south, materialising in a small wood. Detecting nothing more dangerous than a few birds singing in the trees, she hung the stolen clothes over a low horizontal branch and stripped off her jacket, top, boots and finally her jeans, adding them to the branch to keep them off the ground.

Before getting dressed in the girl's clothes, she thought, *It's a pity that normal teleportation doesn't do that thing the portals did.* She squatted down and relieved herself and, afterwards, utilised some tissues from the pocket in her jacket next to the disc. *Better than dead leaves, I suppose. But I've only got a couple of tissues left. What did they do for bog-roll in these times?*

She pulled the stolen top and dress over her head. Both were somewhat tight and she needed several attempts to figure out how to tie up the lacing. The bonnet took a while to get into place and, without a mirror, Cassie had no idea if she had it on correctly or not. After donning her boots, she picked the disc out of the jacket pocket intending to place it somewhere about herself. But the stolen clothes lacked pockets of any kind.

"Bugger. Should have picked up an apron as well," she muttered, putting the disc back into the jacket pocket and wrapping the jacket up so that the disc wouldn't fall out. She looked around for a suitable spot to conceal her modern clothing. However, the trees surrounding her were quite young and there was nowhere obvious to hide anything.

Carrying her clothes, she teleported to the edge of the tree line and, after several more exploratory hops, spotted another house with outbuildings not far away. She materialised closer and, noting the shabby state of the place, decided it was abandoned and worth closer investigation. The front door was open and only attached by one hinge, explaining the debris that layered the interior.

No one's been here for years, she thought, her nose wrinkling at the mustiness pervading the air.

She found a staircase whose first step creaked and moved alarmingly under her weight, so she hopped directly to the upper floor landing. An open door revealed the extent of nature's intrusion into what had once been a bedroom, where leaves had accumulated on the floor adjacent to a window whose frame was devoid of glass. There was little furniture apart from a spindly wooden chair tarnished with animal droppings, and a large double bed, its blanket equally as filthy and starting to shred. There were clearer scrapes in the debris on the floor as if something, maybe a large animal, had kicked some of it out of the way.

Opposite the open door was another, closed. Cassie twisted the handle and pushed. With a groan from long unused hinges, it inched open. Despite there being bright daylight outside, the illumination entering via the single tiny window, set mere inches above the floor level, barely crawled into the room. Part of the issue was that the room was crammed with furniture. In the centre a wooden bed frame was surrounded by a collection of tall free-standing cupboards, low chests as well as a couple of wardrobes standing next to each other, the larger one nearer the back wall.

The bed's slats, while mostly intact, had begun to warp. But the room felt dry enough at that moment. The glass of the window remained intact, preventing the fate that afflicted the rest of the house. There was also no sign of a chimney, another potential route for nature's ingress.

On top of the largest wardrobe was a mattress of some sort. It had been rolled up and tied with thick string.

"I don't ever fancy sleeping on that," Cassie said.

Opening the nearest wooden chest she found folded blankets. They, too, had escaped the ravages of nature, but smelt a little musty. She guessed that someone had tried to save the contents of the house by storing them in this room. Maybe whoever had done this would be back to collect them at some point. Or possibly the owner had died.

She eyed up the smaller of the wardrobes and squeezed between the bed frame and the wooden chest to get to it. She had to wrench the door open as, like the bed slats, time and winter dampness had warped the wood. The inside was empty and appeared devoid of anything that might eat through clothing.

Dropping her jeans, top and jacket inside, she noted the muffled clunk as the disc within the jacket hit the wardrobe floor. To force the door closed, she had to shove it hard, which caused the whole thing to shake alarmingly.

Should be safe enough for a few minutes, she thought, knowing that she could return to the same day and hour to retrieve her clothes once she'd finished here.

She looked around to see if the room held a mirror but couldn't find one. After another attempt at rearranging the bonnet to make it fit properly, she gave up and removed it, placing it on one of the bed posts.

"Now where?" she asked herself, and then gasped upon hearing a sound from across the room.

"Who's there?" she whispered, feeling as if she was being watched. She took a step and, below her boot, a floorboard moved, causing the wood to emit a creak further across the room.

"Damn it, now I'm spooking myself," she sighed. "Right. So where do I go? And what do I do?"

Accompanied by a vision of the dead and dying, Kett's voice repeated in her head, "Convince me the rhyme is a lie."

In her mind, she pictured something she had found fascinating since she had seen drawings of it. She had also heard it mentioned in the play and Kett himself had talked about it.

"The Oak of Reformation," she said and closed her eyes.

Blood

Morning Sickness Mistaken

Cassie stared at her reflection in the pool. The water, its surface glassy and still in the summer sun, was the nearest thing to a mirror this world possessed.

It was an extremely poor substitute. While she could make out the shape of her face in the reflection, it remained darkly indistinct. Picking out any finer detail than eyes, nostrils and mouth was impossible.

I think I've lost weight, she thought as she tried to reconcile the hazy shape in the reflection with what she remembered. *Not surprising the way he gives me the run-around.*

Her eyes rose from the water. Through the trees, she could hear her son's voice, along with those of Em'Dor and El'Tesh.

Easing herself to her feet, she winced as her back protested from carrying wood from the forest, from carrying Ka'Tor when the lazy sod refused to walk, and from all the other back, arm and hand-numbing chores she had been forced to learn. She was constantly tasked with nursing babies, knapping flint, mashing ash into soap, hunting for root vegetables and mushrooms, as well as collecting and chopping wood for the fires. The one she loathed was skinning and gutting animals. At least they were already dead.

She had recently started practising with the crude spears the tribe produced from the straighter lengths of wood. Although her aim was getting better, she refrained from any actual hunting. *I've got to draw the line somewhere.*

After he had pestered her for it, she had fashioned a short spear for Ka'Tor as well. He delighted in aiming it at anything that moved, including beetles, rats, rabbits, shadows and, occasionally until reprimanded, El'Tesh. It was a good job it didn't have anything resembling a sharp tip. Em'Dor was not averse to cuffing Ka'Tor around the head whenever he became too boisterous. Cassie couldn't blame her, the boy was prone to hyperactivity, far more than any of the other children in the tribe. Conversely, he would often drop into a dream-like state, his eyes gazing at nothing, thoughts away with whatever this age used as a substitute for fairies.

Cassie felt her arms and legs. *Definitely more muscle and far less fat. Am I turning into Kay? Will I be completely skinny in ten years? I really hope I can get home before ten years is up.*

She leaned against a tree and frowned. Last night she'd, once again, awoken from a vivid dream that had revealed another piece of her hidden past – only snippets remained but she now remembered returning to 1549. *I broke my promise,* she thought. *Did Kett trick me into travelling back to the past or did I secretly want to go myself?*

The full motivation still escaped her. *I do remember stealing clothes, so maybe I intended to do more than just observe.* Then an older memory resurfaced as she recalled claiming, 'I've never stolen anything in my life.' When had that occurred? It took her a while to remember it had been when she'd picked out that denim jacket in Debenhams, not long after she'd first met Kay.

"Not so innocent now, are you?" she muttered to herself, adding, "In more ways than one."

She left the pool – a tiny stretch of water that had probably been isolated from the stream at some point in the past – and strolled back towards its noisy parent. The torrent of water descending the hill was slower in summer but was still frenzied in its rush towards its unknown destination.

Having pinpointed the summer solstice quite accurately just over two weeks previously, it was early July. With all the tasks she was expected to perform in addition to being a mother, the time since the winter solstice had rushed past.

I must've been here in total for around two and a half years now. Hell, how much longer?

Under Em'Dor's watchful eyes, Ka'Tor was splashing at the side of the stream with El'Tesh. As usual, both children were naked, and so was Em'Dor as she was bathing. The tribe considered it a waste of time clothing anyone below the age of seven in summer. Even Ka'Jat, who was around nine, often went about bare during the warmest months.

Embarrassment about such things was almost totally absent from the tribe. Only Cassie still felt more than a twinge of awkwardness whenever she had to wash or went swimming in the stream when any of the men were around. Not that they sought to bother her in any way. She was, as some had told her to her face on more than one occasion, quite ugly compared to the rest of the women of the tribe.

Thanks a lot, she'd thought. *Well, at least it saves me from being a constant bedroom target like some of the others.*

They had told her that her narrow, pale face, unadorned as it was with any of the decorative scarring that all men and most of the women wore, was not at all appealing. The colour of her eyes was a further point in her disfavour. While such comments had mostly been made without any obvious malice, they still stung. Only Za'Lak seemed to bear a distinct animosity towards her.

It didn't affect just herself. Since Ka'Tor had been born she had often heard the odd comment that he had inherited the 'curse of sky eyes' from her. Some of the other children, especially Zi'Lar, the son of El'Pak and Ja'Mutt, delighted in teasing him not only about his eyes but for his slightly paler skin as well.

Nothing changes. People have always been complete bastards to each other.

She had seen the resentment growing in Ka'Tor's blue eyes. Despite trying to reassure him, she was often secretly pleased when he defended himself, lashing out at children older than himself when he'd had enough. It reminded her of seeing Georgia using her martial arts skills to defend herself when insults had gone beyond mere joking.

At only sixteen months Ka'Tor was far more advanced than children of her own time, especially in his ability to run, something he'd got the hang of only weeks earlier, but that was true of every child in the tribe. Em'Dor was still only fifteen, yet, to Cassie, she not only acted as if she was twice that age but, like many in the tribe, she exhibited far more wisdom than most adults could muster in the twenty-first century.

But wrong decisions here might mean the difference between life and death. We lived a cushioned existence – if people from my time were dropped here on their own then most would end up dead within a few weeks. Even now I wouldn't rate my own chances of survival as high if I was suddenly left on my own – and I know so much more now than I did a year ago.

Reaching the stream, Cassie sat down at the edge, her feet dangling in the water.

Ka'Tor, seeing her, squealed in delight and showed off his swimming skills. He had no fear of water and was as agile as a fish.

Doesn't take after me in that respect, she thought. *I was always a lousy swimmer.*

El'Tesh doggy paddled across to where Ka'Tor was diving but then let out a cry as he pushed her under the water and tried to prevent her from resurfacing. Em'Dor shouted at him as she launched herself at them both, cuffing Ka'Tor around the ear and reprimanding him as soon as she caught up.

"Deserved it," Cassie said to him when he started grizzling. He began swimming back to her but then changed his mind and headed for the far bank, pulling himself out.

Oh, here we go, Cassie thought. *The little sod's going to run off yet again.*

She slipped into the water and swam across, pulling herself out at the same place, but Ka'Tor already had a head start on her.

His attempts at escaping had been a constant battle ever since he'd figured out how to open the gate she'd constructed a year earlier. Several times she'd had to scamper after him after he'd sneaked off just before sunrise. Others who had been tasked with looking after him told of the same experience. Even at only sixteen months old he was more than capable of giving people the slip, even though he usually gave himself away by laughing as he ran.

This time, after having received a smack around the ear from Em'Dor, he wasn't laughing. Cassie tracked him via the trail of water dripping from his body along with the places where he'd bent a plant over here or where his feet had left an imprint in the soil there. Within a few minutes, she'd caught up to him, scooping him up in her arms and tickling him to make him start laughing.

By the time they had returned to the water, his sullen mood had dissipated and he returned to splashing around in the stream, attempting to chase the occasional fish that dared to come within range.

"He run fast," Em'Dor said.

Cassie nodded, "Too fast. Getting faster."

"One day he run to mountain."

"Always that way," Cassie said pointing towards the east.

With Ka'Tor settled for a few moments, Cassie and Em'Dor swam and washed each other's backs. After climbing out to dry off, Cassie chatted with

Em'Dor who remained in the water to keep a close watch on the children. Their conversation was interrupted by the sound of men's voices along a pathway a short distance away. Cassie peered through the trees to see Ka'Chull and two other men walk up the hill towards the cave.

"Good hunt," Em'Dor said.

She was correct. The latest kills hung from the backs of the men. Em'Dor looked pleased with this result but Cassie was of a different opinion.

Ugh, more skinning, she thought. Her nose wrinkled at the thought of her hands being covered in blood, the smell of it entering her nostrils. But her mind wouldn't let go of it and she felt light-headed and dizzy. She closed her eyes unable to shake the vision. It intensified and, for a second, she saw blood gushing from her hands, covering her body to flow across some open fields.

In her mind, the blood-soaked fields became populated. She gasped trying to suppress an image of acres of land strewn with dead and dying bodies. Her stomach convulsed and she couldn't prevent herself from throwing up.

"Ka'See," Em'Dor shouted. Cassie opened her eyes to see the girl climbing from the water to rush to her side.

"Oh, my God," Cassie gasped, as another set of memories flooded back. "Those poor people."

Em'Dor's arms were around her shoulders. "Sick in morning?" the girl asked.

Cassie groaned, unable to suppress the visions of blood.

"Hah," Em'Dor continued. "Ka'Tor get brother, sister. Yes?"

"No," Cassie whispered, her whole body shaking. "Not baby."

"Oh, not mated?"

"No, no. Not mated."

"Ah, no men want sky eyes. Poor Ka'See. You pretty to me. You wait. Men will see one day."

Oh my God, Cassie thought, staring wide-eyed at the trees and the flowing water, still struggling to dismiss images of death and devastation. *She thinks I want to 'mate'? One hyperactive kid is more than enough.*

"You pale spirit. Men still scared. Ka'Chull mated you. Other men will learn. I ask them?"

"No," Cassie sputtered.

"Oh," Em'Dor frowned. "But Ka'Tor need brothers, sisters. Look," she said with a grin, pointing to her own stomach and Cassie noticed the bulge that was beginning to show. "Pi'Tut plant brother, sister for El'Tesh. You want men to plant in you?"

"No, please no," Cassie whispered adding, with another shiver. "Not want mate, never mate."

Em'Dor's face was incredulous. Cassie sighed. How could she explain it to Em'Dor? In her mind's eye, the image of a blood-soaked, body-strewn field was replaced with Jason's barely-lit face, leering at her from behind that shed.

"Never again," she whispered, shivering.

Girl Scars

"What happen?" Cassie asked of Em'Jex one autumn morning. Almost everyone had risen earlier than normal, yet the dawn was still half an hour away.

"Em'Lo blood day," Em'Jex replied.

"Huh?"

"Em'Lo blooded herself a five day past. Em'Dor will tell."

Cassie looked across the cave seeing Em'Dor gathering up El'Tesh. The girl beckoned to her to follow them outside. Cassie pulled Ka'Tor from his bed whereupon he let out a howl of indignation. Then he clambered up her to allow himself to be carried along as he refused to walk.

Better than him trying to run off.

Catching up to Em'Dor, Cassie asked, "What is blood day?"

"Em'Lo become woman five day past."

"Become woman?" *Oh, her first period? She's about the right age.*

Em'Dor pointed out a bright star in the sky just above the horizon, saying, "Morning star high so blood day."

Isn't the morning star supposed to be a planet or something like that? Which one?

"Venus," Cassie said, remembering.

"Venus? Is what your tribe call morning star?"

"Er, yes." *Though I'm definitely not going to attempt to explain all about the solar system – the little I remember will probably still be too complex for them to understand.* "What happen to Em'Lo?"

"Face cuts."

"Cuts?"

Em'Dor pointed to the scars on her face. "Make pretty. Show she woman."

"She wants this?"

"Yes," Em'Dor said with a smile. "Show she brave."

"Boys cut younger?"

"Yes, boys cut when father says. Two, three, four summers. When morning star is high."

Oh my God, Cassie thought, holding Ka'Tor closer. *Does that mean that Ka'Chull is going to disfigure Ka'Tor's face one day?*

"If I not want?" Cassie asked.

Em'Dor frowned as if the question puzzled her. "Father say. Not mother."

"That's absolutely disgusting, horrible," Cassie muttered in English. *How can they think such a thing is normal? How did such a thing even get started?*

"Hah, mad talk. Not do cuts in your tribe?" Em'Dor asked, her fingers touching Cassie's cheeks, smooth apart from that one tiny scar.

"No, never," Cassie gasped, looking closer at Em'Dor's scarring, wondering how much it had hurt. *I've never even had my ears pierced.*

"Ka'See tribe strange," Em'Dor concluded, stroking her daughter's hair.

The tribe formed a circle in the open area before the cave entrance. At the centre facing eastwards to where the sun would soon rise sat Em'Lo. Waiting patiently with eyes closed, she was perched on a boulder, naked. Cassie was certain she could see Em'Lo's hands shake. Beside her stood her parents, Ka'Gar and El'Ra. Ka'Gar's hands held two fine stone tools: one pointed, the other a short blade. El'Kek approached El'Ra, the former's hands cupping a bowl containing a sticky grey paste.

One by one, the adults approached Em'Lo's parents and touched both the stone tools and the bowl as if blessing them in some manner. Em'Dor encouraged Cassie to do the same.

"What I say?" Cassie asked.

"Wish her good life. Do mad talk if want."

Cassie muttered, "Hope it doesn't hurt," as she touched the stone tools with a single finger. She did the same to the bowl of paste. It was the same concoction that had been applied to Ko'Lak after the bear attack.

Not that it did any good.

Standing a few feet away from all three was Em'Kell's partner Pe'Kat. At forty-nine summers he was the eldest in the tribe.

Forty-nine, yet he looks as old as Grandad, Cassie thought and then sighed. *Oh, Grandad. Will I ever see you again?*

Pe'Kat was watching the morning star as if waiting for the right moment. After several minutes he took a deep breath and began an intonation deep in his throat that rose in pitch until it cut off suddenly. Then he repeated the sequence and the tribe took up the sound, humming with the men pitching their voices an octave lower than the women. The sound filled the open space between the cave entrance and the trees. It was unearthly but impulsive and Cassie found herself joining in as if she had no choice.

After what seemed to be several minutes, Pe'Kat raised one hand just as the first rays of the sun poked over the horizon and the drone halted. Everyone, including all the children and even the babies, fell completely silent. Only a light breeze whistling between the trees broke a stillness that even the birds feared to intrude upon.

All eyes were on Em'Lo whose own eyes opened. Cassie could see that the girl looked scared but she was also smiling as if happy that this mutilation was about to be inflicted upon her.

Ka'Gar moved closer to his daughter and, taking the pointed tool in his hand, he placed it against Em'Lo's left cheek. The girl scrunched up her eyes in anticipation. A sharp downward thrust and the point pierced her skin, burying itself at least a centimetre within the flesh. Em'Lo barely flinched. Cassie, suppressing a gasp, bit her tongue as blood oozed from the wound on Em'Lo's face. Ka'Gar made two more incisions in the cheek so that the three cuts were arranged in a horizontal line. The blood dribbled down Em'Lo's face to form droplets under her jawline that splashed over her bare chest. Then Ka'Gar moved across to Em'Lo's other cheek to replicate the pattern.

Oh my God, Cassie thought, her heart pumping wildly in her chest. Cradled in her arms, Ka'Tor had gone back to sleep. *How can she sit there completely silent?*

Then Ka'Gar took the blade and cut a curve between the first and third incisions on the right cheek so that it arced over the middle incision. He repeated the procedure to cut a line under that incision. The result resembled an eye, the blood flowing from it like tears. He moved back to the left cheek and the pattern was repeated there.

Cassie tried to divert her eyes but couldn't tear her gaze from the horror of what she was watching. As the blood pumped down both sides of Em'Lo's face, tears fell from Cassie's own eyes. *It's so barbaric. Poor girl. How can they do this to their own daughter? Why does she even want it?*

Next Ka'Gar took the pointed tool and pierced seven small equidistant points across Em'Lo's forehead an inch above her eyebrows, the centre one directly above her nose. Each oozed blood which ran to mix with that still dripping from her cheeks. Then he stood back and Pe'Kat stepped forwards to examine the lacerations. After the inspection was complete, he raised both hands and cried out something meaningless.

Pe'Kat returned to his original position and beckoned to El'Ra. She scooped some of the paste from the bowl and smeared it across the wounds on her daughter's face.

Em'Lo's eyes watered and her lips trembled as the paste was massaged into the cuts. Her fingers gripped each other so tightly that the tendons along the backs of her hands were raised high. But she didn't utter a sound.

Em'Kell passed a bowl of water to Pe'Kat as Ka'Gar and El'Ra moved away from their daughter. Pe'Kat stepped forward again and gently rinsed the loose paste from the girl's face, exposing the damage to her previously unblemished skin. The cuts were no longer gushing blood, the paste packed into them having reduced the flow to mere seepage. Passing the empty water bowl back to Em'Kell he retrieved the paste bowl and the stone implements from Em'Lo's parents. These he also passed to Em'Kell, who returned the paste to El'Kek.

Pe'Kat raised his hands and intoned another meaningless incantation.

Is that a song or some even more ancient language that no one speaks anymore?

The intonation stopped and Pe'Kat bowed to the girl.

Ka'Gar and El'Ra stood either side of Em'Lo and, each holding one of her hands, beckoned her to stand. She did so, unsteadily.

They led her down the forest path, with the rest of the tribe following, until they reached the bathing area.

"What is stuff in bowl?" Cassie whispered to Em'Dor.

"Takes hurt away," came Em'Dor's reply as she fingered her scars with her free hand. "Makes marks stay, big, lumpy. Not fade."

Oh my goodness,

"You will do to El'Tesh if she wants?"

"Yes."

Em'Lo was washed clean of the blood that had run in rivulets down her body. Afterwards, she stepped unaided from the water, her mouth and eyes beaming as her fingers tenderly explored the lacerations.

She must be in agony. But she looks so proud of what's just been inflicted upon her. At least they don't cut anything else, Cassie thought, remembering the TV programme she had watched about FGM when she was fifteen.

Several of the men stepped towards Em'Lo. Amongst them were Ka'Chull, Ka'Thon and others who already had partners. Even Em'Dor's partner, Pi'Tut joined them and Cassie noted how Em'Dor's eyes narrowed slightly at this. Each held his right arm out towards Em'Lo whilst patting his chest with his left hand.

"What they do?" Cassie whispered.

"She choose first man to break her," Em'Dor replied.

"Huh? What if choose Pi'Tut?"

Em'Dor shrugged. "Is possible. But I kill him," she said with a chuckle that made Cassie wonder how much she was kidding.

Em'Lo smiled at Ka'Char who was currently without a partner. Still naked, she stepped up to him and let him enfold her in his arms. A great cheer went up and Ka'Char grinned at everyone around.

After a few more celebrations the whole party returned to the cave and set about their normal business. Cassie was tasked, once again, with mashing up ash to convert into soap but her mind was far from on the job.

All she could picture in her mind was the blood running down Em'Lo's face.

How can I stop them from doing this to Ka'Tor?

Just before sunset, Ka'Char took Em'Lo's hand and led her to the edge of the forest. Ka'Gar and two other men, all armed with spears stood about ten yards to the couple's left. An equal distance to their right stood Ka'Thon and two others, similarly armed. Upon some unspoken signal, all eight slid into the forest.

"What happen?" Cassie asked Em'Dor, as they worked with Em'Jex and Em'Kell to cook the communal evening meal.

"Men protect Ka'Char and Em'Lo against bears, wolves," Em'Dor said.

Several minutes later Cassie froze as she heard Em'Lo scream. Then the scream came again but turned immediately into a giggle.

"Em'Lo now proper woman," Em'Jex laughed. Em'Kell joined in the laughter but Cassie only shivered.

Thank God I don't remember it happening to me.

Boy Scars

A little over a week later Cassie groaned when she awoke to find the early morning sequence was about to be repeated. But this time it wasn't a willing but nervous girl of twelve being subjected to the knife, it was the turn of Zo'Mar, one of those she'd wet-nursed in addition to El'Tesh and Ka'Tor.

He was barely over two years of age.

As before, the tribe rose before sunrise and, with the point of light of the morning star Venus still prominent in the sky, the tribe assembled outside to encircle the new victim and his parents. As Zo'Mar's mother, Em'Pell, had died giving him life, it was up to Gu'Tun to do the paste duties as she and his father, Ko'Tek, had become partners not long after Em'Pell's death.

Pe'Kat, presiding over the proceedings as before, intoned the same utterances again. This time, seeing the fear lacing Zo'Mar's darting eyes, Cassie refused to participate, keeping her mouth clamped tight while those around her joined in with the second round.

Then the torture began.

Unlike Em'Lo's mute acceptance of the blades cutting into her flesh, the boy screamed while Ka'Gar guided the inexpert hands of Zo'Mar's father, Ko'Tek, into puncturing his son's face. The boy kicked and struggled so much that Ka'Chull and his brother Pa'Tay stepped forwards to help restrain the boy.

Cassie flinched as each scream escaped Zo'Mar's mouth and she had to look away, unable to witness it. Beside her, Em'Jex tutted and chuckled at Cassie's squeamishness. But it was more than just the bloodletting in front of her that she was experiencing. Her mind was, once again, unable to dispel the images of the field of butchered bodies from Robert Kett's last battle. That, along with the screams battering her eardrums, was making her extremely nauseous.

How can they do this? Em'Lo asked for it to be done – Zo'Mar doesn't have any choice. Oh God, this mustn't be done to Ka'Tor.

At one particularly loud screech, Cassie glanced up to see Zo'Mar's face and chest drenched in blood.

They'll kill him, surely, her thoughts shouted.

As another piercing scream left the boy's mouth, it all became too much for Cassie to bear. She turned and ran out of the circle. Reaching a patch of grass she fell to her knees and threw up.

She heard several in the crowd laugh at her exit and she heard Za'Lak's jibe of, "Pale face, sky-eyes tribe weak."

Fucking primitive morons, she thought, as she spat out the last of the partly digested remnants of the previous evening's meal. Someone stood over her, placing a hand on her shoulder and Cassie glanced up to see Em'Dor's face.

"Why?" Cassie gasped, bursting into tears.

"Not do in your tribe so not understand," Em'Dor whispered.

No, I don't bloody well understand. How can I?

It was only when Zo'Mar's screams had reduced to grizzles that Cassie allowed Em'Dor to help her up. By this point, Gu'Tun had almost finished applying the paste to the boy's face and its anaesthetic properties must have been starting to numb his pain.

The ritual over, apart from the body cleansing, the tribe began to move down to the river. Cassie refused to accompany them and watched as Em'Dor took Ka'Tor's hand and, along with El'Tesh in her other arm, followed the rest of the tribe.

Cassie, still crying, returned alone to the empty cave.

One day they're going to do the same to Ka'Tor.

"I've really got to get away from this place," she told herself. "If I can, I'll take Ka'Tor with me so he won't have to go through it."

She shut her eyes and, for the first time in several months, tried to teleport.

Even if I don't travel in time, I might be able to take us somewhere less barbaric. There must be other tribes around that don't do this, surely.

She concentrated as hard as she could, trying to replicate what she'd managed behind the shed in Erin's garden. But, no matter how much she strained, it didn't even begin to start.

"Damn and fuck it," she screamed out loud. With the rest of the tribe hidden by the trees, her shout merely disturbed several birds in the nearby branches.

Beyond the clearing, most of the trees in view were pines, with the occasional bush breaking up the monotony of the uniformly vertical trunks.

One bush stood taller than those nearby and, even at this distance, she could see the distinct curls in the edges of its leaves. It wasn't a bush, it was a sapling spreading its branches on its way to becoming a tree.

It's an oak. What's an oak doing in a pine forest?

Another memory returned and she felt her mind travel back to when she had encountered a far more impressive member of the same species.

Oh, what I'd do right now to be back there.

Breaking The Timeline

The Oak of Reformation

Cassie, remaining invisible, materialised close to where that water tower stood in her time. When Kett's ghost had described his Oak of Reformation, she'd tried to imagine how it would have looked.

Now she knew.

She'd appeared at night to lessen the chances of anyone seeing her pop out of thin air but, even at just gone ten the encampment thronged with people. Thousands possibly, given the hundreds of fires that dotted the hillside.

Towards the west were more lights – the fainter ones possibly candles in windows, the larger ones, fires. They showed where the city of Norwich lay. In the dark, she could make out little of its layout and size.

Further up the hill was the great tree itself – the pictures she'd seen on the Internet hadn't done it justice. In her mind, she heard Kett saying, "It was just a large tree though we'd built it up into a shelter, and a meeting place."

No kidding, she thought as her eyes took in the sight. The tree itself was large enough but, around its base, poles had been erected to enclose the entire circumference of the trunk in what appeared to be a huge tent. Beyond the tent, the tree was ringed with fires that painted the underside of its canopy with a dancing display of red, orange and yellow. Visible across much of Norwich, it must have been an intimidating sight to behold for those within the city.

There was movement close to one side of the tent. Cassie willed herself nearer to observe serving women of all ages pass a guard who was holding a tent doorway open for them. Those entering were carrying plates of food and tankards of drink. Those leaving with the empty cups, tankards and plates, traipsed back down towards a row of makeshift tables. There, drink was being poured into tankards and further meals were being prepared.

Many of the women were attired in clothing similar to her own.

My ticket in, I reckon... if I dare.

Apart from a few whose hair was braided, the style worn by the women who were bare-headed was predominantly straight, though far from neat. Cassie ran her hands through her hair several times, ruffling it up, to make it resemble those she observed.

Still invisible to any onlookers, she walked down the hill until she found a position south of the camp where the crowd was sparse and the fires more widely spaced. By the twentieth century, this area would be lined with terraced houses adorning the slope down towards the river and the railway station. Here, it was a cross between open heathland and the occasional stand of trees.

I wonder if it's like this all the way out to Mousehold Heath?

Cassie discarded her invisibility under the cover of one of the larger trees. The atmosphere became saturated with odours, barely detectable while she had been hidden. Burning wood was mixed with a cornucopia of scents from the food that was being cooked, making her mouth water.

How many hours since I last ate something? She tried to figure that out as she walked back up the hill towards the greatest concentration of people. Around her, there were men, women and even a good number of children. None of them took much notice of her other than the occasional glance. With so many attired in similar clothing, that wasn't surprising. However, she prayed that none would pay too much attention to her modern, plastic-soled boots, which might have given the game away. But, like those worn by the other women, her dress reached almost to the ground.

The higher up the hill she progressed, the more industrial the area became. There were horses being tended, watered and fed and, in one case, being shod. She passed areas where weapons such as swords, pikes and spears were being built, repaired and sharpened. Carts and wagons, hauled by both beasts and men, being manoeuvred between the makeshift tents and temporary wicker abodes, imbued the camp with the sensation of constant movement. In amongst all of this, sheep, pigs and cattle were being herded, driven, corralled, slaughtered, gutted, cooked and prepared. Boiling pots, from quite small to the size of cauldrons, were stuffed with vegetables, skinned rabbits and plucked chickens. The cooked results were ladled out to those who needed sustenance as well as being taken to the trestles she saw earlier. The clamour arising made

Cassie wonder how people would manage to sleep and prepare for the battles that she knew must be coming.

Drawn by the aroma she drifted towards the tables arranged between the main part of the camp and Kett's oak. Most were surrounded by those awaiting their share of what was on offer. Each was handed a plate of steaming food along with a tankard of drink. Wanting to avoid the crowded tables, she picked one of the smaller trestles to one side and held her approach back until only three people remained to be served.

To reach it she had to pass close by a couple of men. Each held a large tankard from which they sipped. As she passed them, they turned to watch her, which made her feel distinctly uncomfortable.

Have they noticed anything odd about me?

Then the nearest reached out and grabbed her bottom, giving it a powerful pinch. She shrieked.

"Hah, neece," the man roared, obviously drunk.

Cassie spun around and faced both of them. "Fuck off, you lecherous bastards," she screamed.

"Tow feisty far ya, Fulke?" the man's companion laughed, adding. "Gud mate on them bones, thow."

The first man made another lunge for her but he was slow with drink. She evaded him and ran for the table as both men laughed at her.

"Trouble, he is, that Fulke," said an older woman filling tankards, as Cassie approached. "Thow his mate's good."

"Huh?"

"Butchery's one of his trads," the woman added. "That's his rawsting there." Cassie's eyes followed where the woman's finger pointed. Downhill, there were several carcasses being spit-roasted over open fires. Children were engaged in turning the spits to keep the cooking even.

Oh, did she mean meat – and not mate? Their English is all spoken wrong.

"Um," Cassie started, not knowing what to say and afraid that anything she did say might sound wrong.

"Hongry?" the woman said.

Cassie nodded in reply. *It's like they're using the wrong vowels or something.*

The woman grabbed a bent tin plate from a stack and piled it high with meat and vegetables. She slid the plate towards Cassie before pouring something into a tankard to accompany it.

Cassie nodded her thanks while her eyes searched in vain for cutlery. She glanced around at others nearby who were still eating – some were using their fingers while others skewered the food from the plates to their mouths using knives, daggers and even what appeared to be whittled wooden sticks.

Fingers it is, then.

Avoiding the drunken pair who had accosted her earlier she angled away from the crowded areas and sat down with her back against a tree. Her vantage point kept her relatively hidden yet afforded a good view of the Oak of Reformation and the occasional human traffic that flowed to and from it.

A Wolf in Fox's Clothing

The meal was quite filling though it lacked potatoes. Cassie wondered why they weren't included.

Haven't potatoes been invented yet?

Whilst eating, she continued to observe the tree. A few of the men coming and going seemed to be under guard or were being escorted. Cassie couldn't determine whether or not it was for their own safety or everyone else's. Their clothing was of a higher quality than those worn by the general crowd.

She put the tankard to her lips but stopped, sniffing. Some sort of ale or beer, she decided, though wasn't sure. While it helped to wash down the meal, it was not a taste with which she was familiar. Its flavour was slightly bitter and the odour pungent. But there hadn't been any alternative. She had looked around for water but a nagging suspicion at the back of her mind – possibly originating from a long-forgotten school history lesson – suggested that plain water wasn't safe to drink. She knew the River Wensum flowed close by but then thought about sixteenth-century plumbing and sanitation.

I bet hygiene isn't even a proper word yet, she thought, contemplating what might be in the river water. *Ugh. Raw sewage, and probably worse.*

Cassie shuddered at the thought of the diseases that might be lurking around. *Could be plague or something even worse. I'd better be careful. Good job we don't have things like that back in my time.*

So, she persisted with the ale or whatever it was. The taste grew on her but so did its effects.

Damn, I'm just not set up for alcohol, she thought, thinking of Erin. But that only reminded her of Jason and the party. She felt her anger rise yet again.

"It's his fault I'm here," she spat. Then she wondered how true that might be.

She drained the tankard and, as she stood, realised she was more than a little tipsy. But the traffic between the tree and the rest of the camp had reduced to almost nothing.

With the camp settling down for the night she thought, *Better do something before everyone goes to bed.*

Picking up the plate and tankard, Cassie returned to the table finding the same woman still tending it. The stall's clientele had reduced to a solitary child who was helping himself to scraps.

"Yo," the woman called, nodding at Cassie as she took the plate off her.

"Huh?"

"Yo mard? Server? Yah?"

Cassie nodded, as it seemed simplest that she should agree to whatever the woman said, whether or not she understood it.

"Maw ahl fer Kett an' them," she said – or at least that's what Cassie thought she said. She could still make little sense of the language that seemed several steps removed from the English she'd grown up with. But the woman had distinctly mentioned Kett's name.

Four full tankards were pushed towards her and she managed to pick them all up by grabbing two handles per hand.

"Where?" she asked, not daring to use more words than necessary in case she was misunderstood.

"Tray," the woman said, nodding in the direction of the Oak of Reformation. *Good. I hope.*

"Donnut dally, girl."

Cassie nodded and tottered off towards the oak, trying not to spill too much.

The ale, slopping over the rims of the tankards, smelt even stronger than what she'd drunk with her meal. By the time she'd reached the tree her hands were sticky and dripping.

"Kett," she said to the guard, nodding at what she held.

Coming from the curtain behind him she heard agitated voices. His eyes gave her the once over and then he lifted the curtain. Ducking under his arm, she entered.

Inside, the air was thick with smoke and her first thought was that they were smoking tobacco. But the odour was more like wood. Through the haze, she could make out several metal braziers from which smoke and flames issued. A central table, at which eight people sat, was surrounded by more than a dozen standing. To one side the main trunk of the oak could be made out through the smoke. Its diameter exceeded Cassie's height and, around its base, was a wooden platform about a foot high upon which several more men sat.

She recognised none of them until the man whose back was to her turned his head in her direction. She gulped seeing Robert Kett's profile. But this version of Kett was no ghost – he was very much alive and even older in the face than his ghostly twenty-first century incarnation.

"Aboat time," he muttered, snatching one of the tankards from her grip causing the other in that hand to slosh. She deposited the remaining three on the table, trying to avoid any further spillage. Several sheets of paper were scattered across the table, which was inadequately illuminated by three candles.

"Maw," one of the others at the table demanded. She glanced from the new speaker to Kett noting a resemblance between the two.

His brother? Can't remember his name.

"And fawd," Robert Kett added.

Cassie nodded and was about to leave when Kett grabbed her arm.

"Your face…" he started.

Cassie gasped as he pulled her closer.

"Do I know yo?"

Cassie shook her head. *Not yet you don't.. Or is something else going on?*

"I like ya haw," Kett said, his eyes examining her hair.

Cassie had a sense of déjà vu and remembered ghostly Kett saying, "It reminds me of a serving wench back when I was alive. Hers was shorter."

Then she shuddered, remembering another of ghostly Kett's statements: *Time messes up around you.*

"Lave the wench, brother. Finish the grevaunces."

Kett's brother was pointing to some hand-written documents before one of the others seated at the table.

The man who was writing held a quill pen wet with ink. Cassie, still held in Kett's grip, stared at the paper. Much of the writing was indecipherable to her eyes.

"We prah that it be not lawful to lords of any manor to purchase lands," the man intoned, his finger tracing the words of the last entry on the paper.

Cassie squinted at it. From what she could make out, the words appeared to be: 'We pray that it be not lawfull to the lordes of eny mannor to purchase londes.'

Their spelling is as good as their pronunciation. Georgia would feel right at home here.

"Freely. Purchase lands freely," said Kett's brother.

Kett and several of the others nodded their agreement. The man with the quill repeated 'freely' and added 'frely' after 'londes'.

"Fetch those drinks, gairl," Kett said, releasing Cassie's arm. He and the others returned their attention to the writing.

Forgotten for the moment, Cassie took the opportunity to slip outside. Away from the tree she rubbed the smoke from her eyes and exhaled loudly. She was shaking, and questions buzzed through her mind.

Am I actually going to do this? Was his ghost right? Can I make the future a better place? What on earth was that writing all about? Did he really recognise me in some way?

Her eyes hunted the darkness for the trestle table where the woman was still pouring drinks. *There it is.*

"Want more," Cassie said nodding back towards the tree, hoping her intonation was more or less correct. "Food, too."

"As likely he do," the woman tutted. "Yo not from these parts? Foreign you sound. Southern?"

Cassie nodded. *What a difference a few hundred years makes. But I think I'm beginning to figure it out – ignore the vowels, listen to the shape.*

"Here." The woman slid two more tankards across the table towards Cassie and followed them with two more. "We'll bring his midnight supper soon, tell him."

Cassie nodded scooping up the tankards before she headed back to the tree.

The man guarding the door passed her through and she found herself in Kett's presence for a second time.

"Dinner soon," she said.

Kett's eyes scanned her yet again.

"Where are you from?" he demanded.

"Um, south."

"Could be," he said.

"Leave the wench, Kett," came another voice.

"Aye, preacher," said another. "We have far more of import to complete."

"Um, Mister Kett?" Cassie said, hesitating.

"What?" came Kett's response.

"Er, don't believe the rhyme."

"Rhyme?" Kett said, frowning.

"The one about Dussindale."

"Dussendale?"

"Yeah, um, yes."

"It is said that it shows us victorious," came another voice.

"No," Cassie said, shaking her head, "it doesn't."

Kett raised his eyebrows.

"It, er, it predicts your defeat," Cassie said, conscious of all the eyes upon her.

"What? How came you by such knowledge?" Kett demanded.

"I, er, visions of the future," she said, pointing at her head.

"Visions?"

Cassie nodded as Kett grabbed her arm.

"Prove it, girl."

Oh shit, how can I do that?

"Um, I-I've seen what happens after you lose. Thousands dead. Three thousand. I-I saw all the blood." Cassie felt her whole body shake.

"Saw? Things in the past?"

"You lose. Please believe me. Stay up here. Don't… um… break the camp."

"Robert," came his brother's voice. "Don't listen to nonsense."

"It may be such, William," Kett said, "but with no victory warranted, I'd hear more from this…"

Cassie heard several of the others whisper 'witch' and 'witchcraft'. She mumbled, "I'm not a witch. Please believe me."

One of the men recited the rhyme, "The country knuffs. Hob, Dick, and Hick, With clubs and clouted shoon, Shall fill up Dussendale, With slaughtered bodies soon."

"Yes, that's the one."

"We will slaughter them."

"No, it fills with your bodies – I-I've seen it." She closed her eyes as the sight that had greeted her upon her arrival swam across her mind's eye.

"You shake, girl," Kett said. "Is it because you lie?"

"No, but if you believe the rhyme then Warwick will win."

"Warwick? The Earl?"

"I think so."

"So, he is the one they will send."

"Not at first," Cassie said, trying to remember the names of the others, and of the one who got killed. But, at that moment, names eluded her.

"When?"

"I-I can't remember but the final battle is August the twenty-seventh."

"Five weeks hence? It lasts 'til then?" Robert Kett asked.

"Do we take Norwich?" said William Kett, now obviously listening to Cassie's 'nonsense'.

"Yes," she said, trying to remember the details of the play. "But Warwick will come and take it back."

"With how many men?"

Oh hell, I can't remember. Was it ten thousand? Or am I getting it mixed up with that Grand Old Duke of York rhyme?

"Nine, ten thousand – maybe more," she whispered.

"We are twenty thousand, and more come every day."

"Not enough," Cassie said, her voice almost cracking.

"And what of us?" William demanded.

Cassie's eyes fell and she shook her head.

"They hang you. Both you and your brother," she said. "Sorry, but it *will* happen."

"She lies," said one man, striding forward and drawing his sword. "I say cut her throat now before we fall under her spell."

"No, please," Cassie said watching the sword's point circle inches from her nose. She felt herself wanting to teleport away. *Don't jump,* she told herself. *I've got to resist it.*

"Desist. Put that away," Robert Kett snapped and then turned to face Cassie. "What is your name, girl?"

"Erm."

"Speak your name," Kett shouted.

"Ca–er… Kay," Cassie blurted. *Why did I say that?*

"Kay what?"

"F-Wolf. Kay Wolf." *Damn it – totally lame – was that all I could come up with? I should have had a proper plan.*

"Wolf," Kett said. "I will remember you, Kay Wolf. Now go, but not far. I would talk more of this on the morrow. You will inform us of how you have knowledge of such things."

"Pah, we wast time," said one of the other men at the table. His fist thumped the wood before him. "The grevaunces must be completed."

Proof

Cassie ran for the shadows of a lesser tree to hide her departure. Once out of sight she teleported home, or at least to the place where the house she lived in would exist several hundred years in the future. It had been the first location she'd thought of.

"I need another pee after all that," she muttered. "Damn their ale."

Afterwards, she moved forwards in time to just before dawn the following day. She materialised on rough ground that had possibly been used for crops at one point but seemed to have reverted to wilderness. Towards the north, the land sloped away and she tried to imagine it covered with the houses of her neighbourhood. Her home felt more remote than when she'd first arrived.

I'll be back there soon enough, she thought, trying to reassure herself, but couldn't help adding, *I hope.*

Shaking, she sat down with far too many thoughts rushing through her head.

Kay Wolf? What on earth did I call myself that for? Would telling him my real name have made any difference?

Did he believe me? Was that enough? It didn't feel like it.

How can I make sure?

But, at the back of her mind, she already knew how she could test whether or not it had worked.

"Okay, I need to do this now before I run all the way back to 2019," she muttered, trying to instil some courage into herself. She shut her eyes whispering, "Twenty-seventh of August. Before the battle. Dawn."

Arriving on the hill overlooking the city walls – the place she'd hopped to after fleeing the scenes of blood – she detected a hint of smoke in the air. Towards the south-east there were several plumes of smoke rising from the higher ground.

Oh, no. Are they burning the camp? I've failed. No, I have to make sure.

She returned her attention to the city wall, her eyes scanning the structure as the first light of dawn rose in the east. Between two of the gates a small copse, partly in shadow, held the promise of suitable shelter. She hopped across and, after determining she was alone, crouched down behind a thick bush. Only then did she fully materialise to avoid the effort of holding herself invisible.

Peering between the leaves and branches she saw that the incline before her appeared devoid of people, dead or alive.

"Right," she whispered, hoping that mouthing the plan she had just thought up might be enough to make it work. "Go forward an hour or two at a time. If the battle happens here then I've failed. I don't need to go all the way to the end of the battle. I don't need to see what I saw before."

But she couldn't prevent those images flashing across her mind once again.

No. I've got to stop that from happening.

She took a deep breath and held it – she didn't need to for travelling, but she felt she had to in preparation for what she might be about to see. Then she hopped one hour future-wards keeping herself invisible.

On the hill, she could see people – plenty of people.

Oh hell, they're assembling for the battle.

Another hour on showed the hill thick with a bustling crowd, some on horseback. Each of them was armed with weapons: pikes, swords, long knives and other unidentifiable implements, some of which appeared more suitable for farming than warfare. More smoke was rising from where the camp had been.

Another two hours on, the battle was well under way.

Enough – I've failed. Back to the camp.

She travelled back in time.

As the sun rose on the sixteenth of July, Cassie materialised on the southern edge of the camp between some trees that provided more than adequate cover. She flashed forwards until it was around ten o'clock by which time the early morning sun had been replaced by clouds. Then, as she had done the previous night, she walked up the hill towards the Oak of Reformation. Once again the camp was a hive of industry though the number of people around seemed reduced.

Probably still sleeping.

But it wasn't the only thing she noticed. In the daylight, she marvelled at how muted the colours were compared to those of her time, something she hadn't noticed in the darkness of the previous evening. While the greens, browns and oranges of the foliage were no different, it was in the man-made shades where the contrast could be detected. The clothes the people wore, the materials of their tents as well as the rare painted decorations on the wagons and horse bridles were markedly different. The vibrancy of twenty-first century colours was absent – instead, the greens, blues, yellows and reds were distinctly muddy by comparison.

If the colours were muted, the same couldn't be said for the smells. The air was saturated with the odours of smoke and stale ale, coupled with that of the multitude of animals that shared the camp with the rebels. Alongside all this, the smell of fresh cooking was growing but Cassie wrinkled her nose.

I'm still full from last night's dinner, which feels like only a couple of hours ago. Then she stopped, a frown passing across her face. *Damn, it really was only two hours ago. I know it's ten in the morning here but I have no idea of how much time has passed for me since I left home. A few hours or more than a day?*

Her thoughts returned to the year before and Kay telling her she had no idea of her own age. *I understand that now. I may have a built-in calendar but I have no way of measuring my own personal time.*

She located the trestle table from the previous night, but it was bare. Also absent was the woman who'd been serving the meals and ale.

Amongst the other tables and makeshift tents, there was only the occasional sign of movement. Finally, she came across another area where drink was being served from a trestle table. Again, it was ale.

Is that all these people ever drank?

A tankard was pushed towards her as she approached.

As she picked it up and was about to take a sip, she heard, "Ah, the wolf girl."

She turned to see one of the men who had been with Kett at the tree. He was amongst a small crowd who were already copiously swilling ale. At least none of them appeared to be the one who'd threatened to cut her throat last night.

"Kett told us to watch for you. Go to the tree," the man said.

"What? Right now?"

"Now."

Cassie nodded and, tankard in hand, sipped from it as she walked slowly up to the tree.

This time there was no guard outside.

Security's crap, she thought to herself as she pushed the tent curtain aside.

The interior still smelt of smoke, though the braziers and candles were no longer lit. But there were enough gaps between the sheets of tenting material to allow light in from outside.

On the table the hand-written papers sat in an untidy pile, the quill set down alongside, a blob of ink staining the table below its nib. Of Kett, there was no sign. Cassie peered at the writing on the top sheet trying to make out the words but the cursive script was almost undecipherable to her eyes. She thought she could make out 'pray your grace to' possibly followed by 'give' though it appeared to be spelt as 'gyve'. The word after that looked like it started with 'lj' or maybe 'ly' but the rest of it didn't make any sense. There were two more slightly shorter passages after the one she was attempting to read but underneath those, squeezed onto the bottom of the page, came what appeared to be signatures against the printed names of 'Rob't Kett', 'Thomas Cod' and 'Thomas Aldryche.'

"You can read?"

The voice made Cassie jump and she almost dropped her ale. She turned around to see Kett standing just inside the curtain.

"Uh, yes," she said, taking a deep gulp of ale. "But this isn't easy."

"The manner and accent in which you speak is unknown to me. What town birthed you, Kay Wolf?"

"Um." *Come on, he wants an answer. They said I sounded southern.* "South-er Southampton."

"Could be. But I feel you lie."

"Sorry, but I need to convince you about the rhyme."

"Why would you do that? To save me?"

Cassie swallowed another mouthful. *I need it. This damn time travelling is going to turn me into an alcoholic.* "I told you. If you believe the rhyme, you will lose."

"Prove it."

How can I do that? It's not like I can get him to time travel to see his own future, can I?

Then she frowned. *Wait, yes I can. I did it for Kay after Laurence burned her. I rescued her, carried her home and then took her to 2000. All I need is physical contact – I hope.*

She looked at Kett.

"Can you?" he said.

"Yes, I can. If you let me," she said, stepping closer to Kett.

He stared directly into her eyes for a moment and she locked her gaze upon his, willing herself not to break contact.

"Do it, then," he said.

She downed another gulp of ale before setting the tankard down on the table. "Do you want to see the battle for yourself?"

"The one you say is to come five weeks hence?"

"Yes."

"You said it was a vision."

It's a bloody vision, all right. I can't get it out of my head.

"I think I can let you see it," she said, standing on tiptoe but failing to approach his height.

Kett looked down at the tankard and laughed. "And how much do we quaff before we see it?"

"None," she said, grabbing his hand. *Here we go.*

Kett shouted in surprise as Cassie whisked him away from the sixteenth of July to reappear in the same spot from which she'd viewed the hill earlier. To avoid her earlier self she aimed for noon. Kett snatched his hand from hers and was wailing almost like a baby, his eyes wide with fear.

"Quiet," she hissed to him. "They mustn't see us."

But there seemed little chance of that. From barely thirty yards away came the noise of battle – men shouting and screaming, horses galloping, and the clash of sword and pike. A raucous cacophony that was a solid onslaught on the ears.

No, Cassie thought, *they're definitely too preoccupied to take much notice of us.*

"Mustn't see us?" Kett said, his voice quivering as hers had done in his presence last night. "This is no vision, then?"

Cassie saw his eyes constantly darting from one part of the battle to another. Already, the scent of spilled blood was making her nauseous.

"Not in the way you think of them," she said, swallowing and trying not to gag.

"We are really here?"

"Yes."

"How?"

"Don't ask – you don't want to know."

"But who is winning? I cannot tell."

Cassie remembered his ghostly incarnation saying, "It started hours before noon and we were evenly matched for much of it."

"No one. Not at this stage, anyway. But, brace yourself. I'll show you the end of the battle."

Shit, I really didn't want to see this again.

Gritting her teeth, she grabbed his hand a second time and, deliberately turning her back to the battle, pushed forward once again. The sun shifted position in the sky and it was no longer noon – Cassie had aimed for seven in the evening.

"God's teeth," Kett moaned. "Kay Wolf, what have we done?"

Keeping her eyes focused on the bricks and stones of the city's wall, Cassie's mind pictured the scene that greeted Kett's eyes. *I don't dare turn around to see it again.* She stole a glance at his face. He was as pale as his twenty-first century ghost. He swallowed as if trying to prevent himself from throwing up.

Looks like you don't have the stomach for it, either, she thought, though she just said, "Seen enough?"

Kett grimaced and nodded.

"Hold it in until we get back," she said, hoping she could do the same.

A moment later they were back at the tree, arriving only seconds after they had departed.

Cassie grabbed the tankard and chugged several mouthfuls until Kett snatched it from her hand to drain the rest. He chucked the empty vessel away across the tent with a growl.

"What are you?" he spat, stepping backwards and away from her whilst wiping his lips. "Witch, angel or death?"

"Death? No, I'm trying to save you from a stupid wasted death."

He turned away from her.

"We were there," he whispered, staring into emptiness. "You showed me times to come."

"You asked me to prove it. It was the only way."

Then he swung back to face her. "Show me what happens if I don't fire the camp, if I make them come for us here."

"I-I don't think I can."

"What? Why?"

"Because it hasn't happened yet. What you saw was the future as it currently stands. Maybe once you've done something to change it, we will be on a different timeline, or something like that. Oh, I don't know, maybe an alternate reality will kick in so that the future gets flipped into something different. Damn, that isn't what I meant to say, either. I don't think I can explain it properly. It might as well be quantum physics for all I understand it."

"Your words are strange and I know not what many of them mean," he muttered. "But I have seen your power. No, I have felt your power, Kay Wolf."

Kett fell silent.

"So?" Cassie asked.

"What?"

"Do you understand what I've shown you?"

Kett's eyes took on a faraway look while he pondered the question.

"Yes," he said, eventually, his eyes even more haunted than when he had viewed the ending of the battle. "We will not fire the camp. We will hold this summit and make Warwick pay for every inch."

"Thank goodness," Cassie sighed, conscious of Kett's eyes upon her.

"Your sound of relief tells me that your concern for me rings true," he said, his hand at his throat. "They will hang me by the neck if I fail?"

"They will wrap you in chains and dangle you from the castle until you die."

"You've seen this also?"

"Not exactly – I didn't see them hang you up. But I've seen you in chains. You've been hanging there for centuries – waving at me for years."

"Years? Centuries? At Norwich Castle? Waving?"

"Yes," Cassie said, nodding. "Your ghost. Your long-dead ghost."

"Where are you from, Kay Wolf? No lies."

Cassie sighed, thinking, *Is he ready for this?*

"Here. Norwich," she whispered.

"Not Southampton, then?"

"No, you, er, figured that one out for yourself."

"But your words, the way you speak. They are strange to my ears. You are, if

I can speak of so odd a thing myself, not of this time?"

"Yes," Cassie said. She watched Kett's eyes closely as she added, "I was born in the year two thousand and one."

Kett was silent, mouth open, as if he was trying to calculate the number of years between now and Cassie's time.

"You are of the distant future?" he finally said.

"Yes. I can travel in time."

"And carry others there also? As you did me?"

"Yes."

Kett stared at Cassie for a moment longer. Then, with a grunt, he turned on his heel to leave, only to stop at the exit.

"You are, then, my guarantee of success?"

Cassie thought for a moment before whispering, "I suppose I could be."

"Good enough. It is more than I dared hope."

History Update

Kett left the tree and, as soon as the tent curtain had fallen, Cassie whisked herself away back to where her house would one day stand. Upon arriving she sank to her knees. She felt weak and her whole body was shaking.

Did I do it? Dare I go and check?

Instead, she just sat there unable to do anything.

But what if I've done something wrong? What if I've made things worse and wrecked the future? If I have then could I undo it?

"Damn it," she spat. "I wish the device was here. Or Kay. Oh, I could definitely do with another drink."

She came to a decision and flitted forwards to the twenty-seventh of August, to the same place she'd taken Kett but arriving several minutes past noon. Where the battle had taken place was now almost empty – more importantly, the fields and heathland were devoid of blood and carnage.

But, before Cassie could sigh with relief, she realised she could still hear something. From the east came the distant clash of swords and the shouting of men. She teleported to what, in her time, would be the bottom of Kett's Hill. Remaining invisible, she sought out a clump of bushes before fully materialising. Some way to her right men in various uniforms were attempting to ascend the hill leading to Kett's Heights. But they were being beaten back as volleys of arrows dropped from above to cut them down. To her left, in between the trees, she could make out more men trying to take Saint James's Hill – they were meeting with a similar lack of success.

I must be right where the roundabout will be, she thought. In front of her, a trackway ascended the hill, a precursor to the road that would one day be built in its place and named after Kett himself.

Swivelling around she faced back along a similar track. A troop of soldiers were running along it towards where she was hidden.

Barrack Street, she thought. *Oh, and there's the Cow Tower.*

Looking far more resplendent than the ruins she remembered, for some reason it didn't induce the same fear in her that it would in her time.

Well, that's a relief. I wonder why?

With the soldiers getting closer and, not wanting to see more death and injury, Cassie hopped back to the camp.

When? Oh, how about the first of August – not a date I'm likely to forget, she thought. *Early evening – six-ish.*

Planning to hold herself invisible until the coast was clear, she was surprised to see few people about. Compared to the crowds previously, the place was almost deserted.

What's happened? Have they all been killed or something?

But, of the few people she could see, it was plain that they were wearing smiles and greeted each other cheerfully. From the direction of Norwich itself, Cassie could hear a commotion. It wasn't the noise of battle, but more like a raucous party. There were also several columns of smoke rising from the city.

Still invisible she crept close to a table where several men and women loitered, cups, mugs and tankards of drink in their hands.

Damn, this makes me even thirstier.

While she couldn't make out everything they said – though she was getting better at understanding the accent – it became obvious that the rebels had been victorious in a battle and that many of them were now down within the city walls, celebrating the event.

She glanced up towards the Oak noticing that it was, as before, surrounded by fires. There appeared to be movement within the tent. *Maybe I can find out what happened from Kett himself.*

Teleporting straight inside it but remaining invisible, she saw two men seated at the table. One of them she recognised as Kett's brother, William. The other was new to her. But Robert Kett wasn't present.

"Both you and your brother have made an enemy of Lord Northampton, without a doubt," said the man, a smile on his lips. He had a bloody rag of a bandage wrapped around one hand and, before him on the table, was a sword that exhibited several notches along its blade. As he talked he examined the damage to the weapon.

"Yes," William replied and, with a laugh, added, "I hear the Marquis flew like a scared bird once he'd lost the market."

"Yet he sought of you to have your brother yield? And you agreed?"

"I did offer that to the Marquis when we spoke, indeed, but even as Northampton instructed me, I learned that he had few soldiers and Robert had many. Robert's victory was as good as assured."

"Ah, you have the art of deception. It has proved useful," the man said, his grin wider.

William Kett nodded and then pointed at the other's hand, "Your wound is not painful?"

"No more than a deep scratch," said the man. "After Holme Street had been taken I hasted to the market to see Northampton take flight. Your brother was a tempest."

"Aye, we had good fortune with us today. Robert had the fire in him and, so I hear, did your troops."

The man nodded but then sighed, "Fires, yes. A choice word. It wasn't the plan to burn Holme Street."

"No, but the men need to celebrate their victory."

"A pity about young Sheffield, though."

Oh yes, Sheffield. That's the one who surrendered but got killed.

"Aye, indeed. Might even have negotiated for us," William said with a shake of his head. "At the Great Hospital itself, wasn't it?"

Do they mean the old N and N where Kay cut Laurence's head off?

The other man nodded. "Killed by that butcher, Fulke, after Sheffield had been dismounted. Didn't see it myself as I'd already left but those with him all declared it was he and Fulke didn't deny it. Clubbed Sheffield about the head all while he tried to surrender. Ah, what are we to do with him?"

Fulke? Wasn't that the name of the letch who grabbed my bum earlier? I owe him a damn good kicking, just like I did to Jason.

"For all that his carcasses feed us, that uncouth swine-butcher treads dangerously," William said with a slow nod. "I hear he also mistook another for Knevet, clubbing him to death likewise."

"Aye, a doorkeeper for Christ's Church. Wolvaston, his name was."

William shook his head. "Another unnecessary loss."

"Fulke is ever too ready with his club and, I have come to understand, he joined in the sacking and burning of Holme Street. He is a butcher in more than a singular manner."

"We will watch him," William agreed.

So will I, Cassie thought. *So will I.*

"He must not be allowed to make such mistakes again," the other man said. "Sheffield was far more valuable to us alive. At the least, he would have gained us a tidy ransom."

"Agreed," William sighed. "And it would have shown that we have mercy, even if Northampton's troops didn't."

Bit late for Sheffield now, Cassie thought.

Or is it? Could I go back and save him as well? Dare I? What changes would it make? Well, they won't be having this conversation for a start. How dangerous would it be to try? Oh, sod it. I've already got Kett to change his mind about the final battle so... in for a penny... but damn it, I really need that drink.

Cassie popped back out of the tent and, seeking a place where there were few people about, materialised on the eastern side of the encampment. Then she walked back towards the main part of the camp, her eyes and ears open for sight or mention of Fulke. She spotted a table serving ale – its current clientele being two women and four men. Cassie strode up to it selecting the largest, most clean-looking tankard.

"Bit strong for yer, girlie?" chuckled the man who appeared to be in charge of serving.

"Fill it up," Cassie snarled back.

Behind her, she heard a whisper from one of the men, "The wolf girl – back again."

My reputation is obviously spreading.

The man serving the drinks heard the whisper as well and, with a somewhat changed expression on his face, filled the tankard to the brim.

Cassie grabbed it and swigged several mouthfuls down.

I'm really getting the taste of this stuff. Hah, wouldn't that just wipe the smile off Jason's face if I could drink him under the table… Shit, why did I have to think of that bastard again?

Thoughts of Jason were enough to make her take several more gulps. Already, the tankard was half empty.

Woo, I'm going to regret this in the morning… whenever that might be.

"Kett looks for you," said one of the women behind her.

"Yeah?" Cassie said as she turned to look at the speaker. Behind the woman, she could see the cathedral's spire towering over everything else. Some distance to its right several rooftops were ablaze. She took a couple of steps towards the woman, who flinched under Cassie's gaze. After swallowing another mouthful, she said, "I let him see me when *I* want, not when *he* wants."

Her retort seemed to unnerve them.

"Where is he?" she demanded.

The woman pointed towards Norwich.

"Duh. Where exactly?"

The woman looked confused as if she didn't understand the question.

Cassie sighed. "Where is Kett right now? What street?"

The woman looked at her companions and shook her head.

I should have brought him a spare mobile phone so we could keep in contact, she thought. *No, you idiot – wouldn't work – no mobile networks – damn, not thinking straight.*

"Okay, I'll look for him myself. How about Tombland? Does that exist yet?"

"You speak strange, wolf girl," one of the men said.

"Yeah, I do that," Cassie said, finishing off the ale.

"Kett may be at Tombland or at the market square or the hall beside it," the man continued.

"Where are those fires burning? Bishopgate?"

"Holme Street – the Great Hospital. Beyond the gate."

"Looks like Bishopgate to me. That's where the hospital is?"

Several of them nodded. *Ah, do I want to go there? It's not far from Cow Tower and Lollards Pit. But they don't appear to affect me here like they do back home.*

"I'll try Tombland."

All six were staring at her as if wondering what she was. *I was going to get out of sight before hopping but they're looking at me as if I'm some sort of weirdo or witch or something. Well, this will give them something to talk about.*

She turned invisible at the same time as dropping the empty tankard. The two women screamed and one of the men drew his sword, aiming its point at the tankard as it rolled across the ground.

"Yeah, that's it, attack that dangerous tankard," she hissed as she moved behind the man. Still invisible, she darted backwards as the man spun around to find no one there. He waved his sword around in confusion.

"Bye," she shouted and teleported from the camp to Tombland alley.

Saving Lord Sheffield

As was becoming habit, Cassie held herself invisible upon arrival but seeing no one around, materialised fully.

Oh, this is where me and Kay met that Grey Lady ghost.

She looked back towards the church wondering if the ghost would appear but she couldn't remember what year the girl had died in the plague.

Maybe it hasn't happened yet or her ghost was just part of the portals stuff.

She left the alleyway.

Well, I can see it's Tombland but, oh my goodness, things are so different.

To her left, the Maids Head Hotel failed to resemble its twenty-first century counterpart.

Picking her way across the cobblestones, she tried to avoid stepping in what at first appeared to be mud. It wasn't mud.

Ugh, no wonder this era stinks of shit.

She heard running footsteps from behind her and a small group of people hurried from the direction of Palace Street.

"Where's Kett?" Cassie called.

One of the women burst into tears.

"Curse him," a man shouted. "His ruffians torched our house. May he hang for what he's done today. You also, should you be of his rebels."

"He probably will, unless I've fixed things right," she shouted at their backs.

So, not everyone here was on his side. Maybe I'd better find that hospital after all – there's nothing here.

Hopping to Bishopsgate, she secreted herself in the shadow of a wall near yet another church to check for onlookers. There were no onlookers – just plenty of carnage. While the burning cottages caught Cassie's eye first, it was the bodies of men, women and even children lying where they had been cut down that made her cry out. She ran in the direction of the Adam and Eve pub. Two injured horses, with arrows protruding from their flanks, lay in a ditch. Disgusted at the sight of the injured animals, she hurried on keeping the distant cathedral to her left. Her legs shook, and not just from the amount of ale she'd consumed.

Turning a corner she almost bumped into a man carrying a limp child in his arms. Her dead face was a pallid grey.

Oh hell, I wasn't prepared for all this. Did I do the right thing? Would this have happened anyway?

"Sorry," she said to him.

The man spat at her feet before continuing on his way.

Ugh. How did he realise I was with the rebels? Sod it, I need another drink just to deal with this.

She approached the Adam and Eve. To her amazement, the building itself was hardly changed from how it appeared in her time. There was a rowdy crowd – rebels she presumed – outside it, laughing, shouting and drinking. The serving girls, darting between them, looked harassed and scared. Cassie followed one who was carrying a tray of filled tankards. The girl placed it on a table occupied by several rebels, before running away.

Cassie strutted up to the table and grabbed a tankard before anyone else could.

"Hey, that's mine," one man shouted.

Cassie swigged a large mouthful and said, "You can have it back if you tell me where Lord Sheffield was killed."

"Why? Ya come to kiss his pretty dead face?" another one said, laughing.

"Come here, girly. If it's a kiss ya wish," another leered.

"Where?" she shouted, slamming the tankard down on the table, spilling half its remaining contents.

"Yah, girly. Roundabouts here or over there. Where's Fulke? Ah there. Hey Fulke – where'd you nobble that posh lord? A wench demands it of thee."

A figure turned to face her and Cassie recognised the letch who had attempted to molest her a few hours earlier on. Only, for him, it would have been about two weeks previously. Would he remember her?

"Wassat?" Fulke slurred.

Totally drunk. Not that I'm anywhere near sober myself. Wouldn't have the nerve to face this lot if I wasn't.

"Sheffield. Where did you kill him?" she shouted.

"Huh?"

"Sheffield, you moron, where?"

"Yah, hit with me club, ah did."

"Yes, where?"

Fulke shrugged, looking about him as if trying to figure out where he was. Then he pointed back towards the church.

"Grett 'osp'tal," he drawled. "Onna road down there. Fell off his 'orse, he did. Hit him with me... what? Hey, where did she—?"

Cassie had turned invisible and hopped back along the road while simultaneously moving back in time.

Oh, is that him?

Before her, a small crowd of people, Fulke amongst them, stood around an armoured man on the ground. Keeping herself invisible, she approached them.

"He was surrendering," another man said to Fulke.

"What? He just took off his helmet. So I hit him."

"Killed him, I'd contend."

"Nah, just a light tap it was," Fulke countered, looking down at the blood-covered head of the fallen lord.

I need to go back to before this happened.

Popping back a full hour, Cassie appeared right in the middle of a battle.

Youch, too close.

She teleported further up the road and back another hour. Here, the battle was far less intense. She crept forwards several minutes at a time until she was aware of horses' hooves rattling along the road from the direction of the city centre. Several men in polished armour rode at the head of the cavalry and launched themselves at the rebels.

At first, the rebels were scattered by the cavalry charges but many circled back and slashed at the horses' legs and flanks whilst trying to avoid the swords of the riders. Many of the slower rebels were cut down and Cassie initially thought they didn't stand a chance. Then a volley of arrows coming from the direction of the Great Hospital took down three of the horsemen and the rest scattered in all directions, attacking anyone in their path, rebel or not.

Hell, I'm watching people kill each other again, Cassie thought. But, this time, she felt more than a little disconnected and merely swallowed, adding to herself, *The ale helps – if 'helps' is the right word – numbs it, more like.*

Cassie struggled to identify which of those in armour might be Lord Sheffield. But, after a few minutes, she spotted one who appeared more courageous than the others and led the horsemen into one attack after another.

Sheffield, Cassie thought. *It's got to be.*

She watched as the man pushed through into a thick wedge of the rebels, slashing indiscriminately. It was close to where she'd seen him lying dead.

There's too many for him.

Sheffield circled his horse, possibly realising for the first time that he was surrounded. Both himself and his steed were being attacked on all sides by rebels armed with pikes and swords. As the horse's legs buckled Sheffield swung his sword around to confront the attackers. Cassie gasped as the horse started to fall and Sheffield's sword was knocked from his hand. He was thrown from his saddle to slide head first into a ditch that ran alongside the road. His horse, lamed and bleeding, collapsed next to him.

From a safe distance, Cassie watched Sheffield haul himself to his feet with a clanking of his armour. Standing, he was at least six inches taller than any of the half dozen rebels who began encircling him, though keeping a safe distance. Seeing them shouting and brandishing their weapons, Sheffield raised his hands.

"I am Edmund Sheffield, Lord Sheffield," he shouted. "Spare me and you will be rewarded."

One of the rebels shouted, "Prisoner."

Sheffield nodded at this and slowly removed his helmet and face protection ready to surrender. One of the rebels dashed forward and retrieved Sheffield's discarded sword. He held it up high while discarding the crude hunk of metal that he had previously utilised.

Now that is a handsome guy, Cassie thought, remembering how they'd asked her if she wanted to kiss his 'pretty dead face.' *Oh no, here it comes.*

Fulke, standing directly behind the young lord, swung his club at the back of Sheffield's unprotected head. The man tumbled down face forward to lie still.

Cassie felt sick.

Some of the crowd laughed but others immediately saw the enormity of what Fulke had done. Some shouted at him while others rushed forward to help the fallen lord. But Sheffield didn't move.

Okay, if I'm going to do something I need to do it now.

Cassie moved back in time to the point just before Sheffield removed his helmet. She materialised right behind Fulke, remaining invisible. As Fulke prepared to swing his club she tried to grab it while still invisible, but it was like grasping air and the club again connected with its target.

Oh, I need to be fully here and visible to do this.

Cassie moved back thirty seconds and, this time, fully materialised behind Fulke. She caught the club as it began to swing and, unable to complete the action, Fulke swivelled around to face her.

"No," Cassie shouted. "He's surrendering."

Fulke growled and swung the club at Sheffield who, sensing the commotion behind him, had started turning. The blow caught him across the face and Cassie heard the crunch as Sheffield's nose was flattened. The man let out an anguished yell and fell to his knees, alive but badly injured.

"Fuck it," Cassie screamed. "I said no."

This time she moved back a full minute and materialised right in front of Fulke. As she did so several thoughts passed across her mind, *Am I creating completely new timelines here? What happened to the previous ones? How can I still remember them if they've been replaced?*

There were screams as the other rebels saw her appear from nowhere and then Cassie experienced something even weirder. Seven copies of herself appeared encircling Fulke, all armed with clubs identical to the one held in the butcher's hands. The effect on the other rebels was instantaneous and, apart from Fulke and Sheffield himself, they ran in all directions. Seeing Fulke hesitate she stepped forwards and wrenched his club out of his hands. All the other versions of herself used their clubs on him in turn starting from the one directly to her left. The copies of Cassie hit him on his arms, his torso and his legs, though not hard enough to inflict any major injuries. The man fell to his knees, a look of total bewilderment upon his face. Then the copies of herself winked out of existence apart from the one to her right.

That Cassie looked at her and said, "Right, now you've seen it – go and be all of us, one at a time."

"Oh, I see," Cassie said. *Just like when I appeared behind Jason – but this time I do it lots of times.* Then she hopped a couple of feet to her left and fifteen seconds into the past and hit Fulke on the arm with his own club. She repeated the action six more times always aiming the club at a different piece of his anatomy. Finally, with Fulke on his knees, she stood facing her earliest self and gave her the instructions, watching that version wink out of existence.

She walked round to face Fulke.

"That'll teach you, ya murd'ring bastard," she spat and, just as she had done to Jason, kicked him hard in the groin, smiling as he fell face down. "And that's for grabbing my arse."

"What manner of...?" Lord Sheffield whispered, unable to complete the sentence.

"I just slaved, er, saved your life," Cassie slurred, trying to study the man's face. "This bastard was going to club you to death. In another timeline, he did just that. Better a prisoner than a corpse. Yes?" *Damn, he'd be worth staying back in this time for – and I thought Jason was handsome.*

"Aye, my lady," Sheffield agreed, his face white as if he was afraid to voice any opposition. "Both myself and, I'm sure, my wife, son and daughters are indebted to you, whoever... or whatever you are."

Bugger, he's already married. Just my sodding luck.

But Sheffield was speaking again, "You may have saved me for this moment but, what now? Yon rebels appear not to approve of your actions."

Cassie looked at the crowd who were plucking up the courage to return. They looked far from friendly and she could hear mutterings of 'witchcraft.' Some of Sheffield's cavalry, oblivious to the events of the last few moments, still battled the rebels but were beginning to fall back given the number of rebel reinforcements that were arriving.

"I need to get you back to Kett," Cassie said, adding, "in one piece."

"How?"

"Right, hold my hand. We'll take the short cut and I suspect both of us will need a stiff drink after this."

Giving him no time to refuse, she grabbed his hand and, before the rebels could rush them, they were gone.

"How on God's Earth–?" Sheffield shouted as Cassie materialised them at the eastern edge of the camp, and several hours after the events on Bishopgate or, as she now knew it was called in these times, Holme Street. He wrested his hand out of her grip and stared around at his new surroundings.

"Right, shut up and follow me," she ordered, as she headed for the Oak of Reformation.

"This is the rebel camp?" he gasped.

"Yeah, I dunno where Kett is – but I do know where his brother is right now," she said pointing at the tree.

"The oak itself," Sheffield said, as they walked towards it. "Parr wants it burned to the ground."

"What? Who's Parr?"

"The Marquis of Northampton."

"Ah. People here have too many titles – I can't keep tabs on them all."

"Tabs? You are beyond me, witch girl. Your words are wrong. You work magics unknown to normal men. I warrant that I am more terrified of you than anyone I have ever faced fully armed."

"Yeah, good, probably. I'm not a witch."

They approached the tree.

"Keep quiet – I want to listen to what they're saying before we go in."

"Why?"

"You'll see."

Cassie listened at the flap that substituted as a door and heard a voice say, "…art of deception. It has proved useful."

Then came William Kett's voice. "Your wound is not painful?"

"No more than a deep scratch," the first voice replied. "After Holme Street had been taken I hasted to the market to see Northampton take flight. Your brother was a tempest."

"Aye, we had good fortune with us today. Robert had the fire in him and, so I hear, did your troops."

"Fires, yes. A choice word. It wasn't the plan to burn Holme Street."

"No, but the men need to celebrate their victory."

"A pity about young Sheffield, though."

"Aye, indeed. Might even have negotiated for us. At the Great Hospital itself, wasn't it?"

Cassie pulled the curtain aside and strode in with Sheffield at her heels.

"Evening all," she announced. "Surprise. Sheffield's not quite as dead as you thought."

Summer Holiday

Death Wish

Autumn was replaced by winter and, in turn, with the last snowfalls only a memory, the spring had begun to awaken the land. With it came renewed thoughts that Cassie should hunt for somewhere where Ka'Tor could grow up safely without the threat of permanent scarring.

Stupid damned rituals, Cassie thought. At least, the morning star was no longer in the sky, which apparently meant that scarring couldn't take place. She shuddered thinking back to Zo'Mar's scarring. It had taken the boy weeks to recover – at one point the swelling on his right cheek had gone septic. Cassie had thought he might die from it and the miserable Za'Lak had even accused Cassie of bewitching the boy. His partner, El'Kek, had resorted to lancing it with a wooden, fire-hardened spike similar to the needles used for sewing. The boy had recovered but his scars were worse on that side of his face due to the infection.

It was a few days before Ka'Tor's second birthday. Leaner and taller than other children of a similar age, he could outrun many of his contemporaries and several of the older adults as well. He was also at the stage of constantly asking annoying questions. Cassie always tried to get Em'Dor to answer them, where possible – especially the weird ones – he had plenty of those. Sometimes even Em'Dor was perplexed over what he was asking.

"Why some trees sleep?" was a recent one.

"Trees not sleep, not like people," she'd replied while nursing her new daughter. Oh'Sep had been born not long after the winter solstice.

"That one sleep," he countered, pointing to an oak currently barren of leaves.

"Yes," she said. "In cold, some trees lose leaves."

"Why?"

"Is what is," she replied, which had made Ka'Tor frown.

"Why?" he repeated.

"Spirit in trees decide," she said. "Spirits know, men don't."

"What is spirit?"

"Alive but you can't see."

"Why?"

"Is what spirits are. Mustn't make spirits angry. Spirits shout bad."

"What they say?"

Em'Dor frowned. "Ask Pe'Kat, Za'Lak. They talk spirits. Spirits talk they."

Ah, like high priests, Cassie thought. *Is this how religion starts?*

"Spirit talk in head," he replied, pointing to his ear.

"One day," Em'Dor said.

"No, spirit talk now."

This time it was Cassie's turn to frown. *Imaginary friend?*

A few days later he'd asked, "What is ------?"

But the word he'd used wasn't in the language of the tribe.

"Mad talk," Em'Dor had laughed. "Like Ka'See."

But a shiver had run down Cassie's spine – the sound he'd made shouldn't have been possible using the human larynx. But, she was almost certain she'd heard something similar.

One morning, several weeks after his birthday, Ka'Tor was nowhere to be found.

Damn kid's run away again, Cassie groaned. She hauled herself from her bed, automatically picking up her spear as she got to her feet. The day was cold and there had been an overnight frost.

"Ka'Tor?" she shouted, waking a few of the others. She pulled her coat on and ran outside. The fire, while still burning, was quite low and she saw Ti'Pik returning with an armful of logs to build it up. Ka'Tor must have slipped away while he had gone to get the wood.

"See Ka'Tor?" she asked him.

"No," he said, looking around. He pointed to the ground. "Tracks."

Cassie spotted where child-sized footprints had trampled the patchy grass. She inspected it, noting how some of it lacked the icy frosting.

Heading east yet again.

"Tell others where I gone," she said.

"Want help?"

"If not back soon."

Breaking into a run, her eyes picked out the telltale signs where Ka'Tor had pushed through into the forest. It was not an area that she'd often been to, as the stony ground wasn't the best for roots and tubers.

Little sod never feels the cold. In her mind's eye, she could picture him dashing between the trees completely naked. *Thank goodness the bears are still hibernating, I hope.*

She traced Ka'Tor's tracks to the stream. Here the water, while a lot shallower, was colder and more violent in its descent, tumbling over rocks as it rushed on its journey towards the sea. Cassie's eyes spotted where Ka'Tor's feet had padded out on the far bank. She winced as she edged across the icy torrent that barely came up to her knees.

Once on the far side, she broke into a run following the tiny clues.

At least he's not making any attempt to hide his route. I'm still nowhere as good at this as proper hunters.

The track curved to a more north-easterly direction where the land sloped upwards before levelling off prior to dropping into the next valley. As she ascended she saw him leaning against a tree staring off towards the rising sun.

As quietly as she could, she shrunk the distance between them, creeping up until she was only yards from his back.

They both saw the boar at the same time – it was nuzzling its way down from higher ground to her left. Cassie gasped as Ka'Tor squealed and ran off, disappearing from view over the ridge, the boar following.

Shit, shit, shit, Cassie's mind screamed. Grasping her spear firmly, she hurtled after the two of them, unconcerned for her own safety.

She pumped her legs as Ka'Tor's screams echoed through the trees. Then she saw him, his back against a tree as the boar approached him. Hearing her coming from behind, the boar slowed, as if uncertain which path to take. As Cassie closed upon it she could see it wasn't fully grown but wasn't juvenile enough to suggest that the rest of its family might still be around.

Please let it be on its own.

"Get away from my son," she screamed, levelling her spear at it, gripping it in both hands. She knew her ability to aim accurately still wasn't up to the task. Without thinking of what might go wrong, she rushed closer.

The boar turned towards Ka'Tor, who screamed even louder. Cassie shouted as well, causing the animal to hesitate. Facing two screaming humans must have been too much for it to contemplate. Instead, it loped off down the slope.

Cassie ran to grab Ka'Tor who was yowling by this point.

"You stupid bloody kid," she shouted in English, picking him up. "Why the fuck do you have to keep running off like that? You got a death wish?"

This just resulted in Ka'Tor crying even louder and kicking his feet into her ribcage. Roughly, she put him down, grabbed his wrist and started dragging him back in the direction of the cave.

He tried to pull in the opposite direction, screaming, "There. Spirit talk."

"No," Cassie shouted, yanking his arm. "Home. Now."

Damn your stupid spirits. I shouldn't have let Em'Dor talk to him about them.

They hadn't gone far when she heard voices and, moments later, saw Ka'Chull and Ka'Thon approaching, both doubly armed with spears. Behind them came Ka'Char and Pa'Tay, the latter looking as sullen as ever.

Ka'Tor broke free from Cassie's grip and ran to his father, who picked him up. Ka'Tor's crying was replaced with chuckles.

Damn the fucking kid, Cassie thought, fuming.

"Any hurt?" Ka'Thon asked her.

"No, but young boar there – not far."

"Ah, see tracks," he grinned. "Go with Ka'Chull to cave."

You don't have to tell me twice.

"Ka'Char, Pa'Tay," Ka'Thon said, "we hunt."

"Ka'Tor. What I do?" she asked Em'Kell as they sat eating their breakfast.

Em'Kell wobbled her head. "Not know," she muttered. "Boy is touched with spirit and run like wind."

"In night, we double men at cave fire," Pe'Kat said, sitting beside his partner, Em'Kell. They were all watching Ka'Tor who, along with Em'Sell and Em'Tull, were being looked after by El'Pak. "Ka'Tor not easy escape then," Pe'Kat added.

I hope, Cassie thought.

As she helped clear away the remains of the breakfast, she heard a commotion. Ka'Thon, Pa'Tay and Ka'Char emerged from the forest with the speared boar being carried between them.

Bloody thing deserved it, she thought, and then felt guilty. If Ka'Tor hadn't run away and she hadn't told the others about it, it would still be alive.

Choked Up

As the summer solstice approached, the tribe were finishing off a meal of roasted boar, along with various root vegetables and mushrooms. Ti'Pik stood up and, with his hand upon his daughter's shoulder, said, "Ge'Tal mate-meet. When?"

Ge'Tal's face noticeably flushed red but she was also smiling. With Ko'Lak's passing, there were no longer any boys of suitable age within the tribe.

Pe'Kat stood and, in between chewing the meat off a cooked bone, responded, "Soon. River, lake, forest – where? Take what? Trade?"

There were several murmurs of agreement and some repeated Pe'Kat's words.

"What mean – river, lake, forest?" Cassie whispered to Em'Dor who was sitting beside her just outside the entrance. The girl simultaneously ate and nursed Oh'Sep. In front of the two of them Ka'Tor and El'Tesh peeled cooked meat off the ribs they held in their hands and shovelled the food into their mouths. Ka'Tor, now nearly four months past his second birthday, seemed twice the size of El'Tesh, whose slight frame echoed her mother's petite body.

"He ask which places and tribes," Em'Dor replied. "Tribes all places – many rivers, many lakes, many forests."

"What they call us?"

"Mountain, forest. Many names."

Well, that's rather confusing. Just how many tribes are there around here?

"How far?"

"One, three, four days. Different tribes, different fars."

"Safe journey?"

Em'Dor shrugged. "Never safe. Always danger – bear, pig, rat, snake. Also if bad thing – fall on rock – hurt. But is normal."

Yeah, this is not exactly a safe world, I know that now. At least Ka'Tor hasn't attempted to run away anymore.

"You been journey?" Cassie asked.

"Two – mate-meet river tribe when twelve summers. Not find mate. Then with Ti'Pik, Ka'Thon, Em'Kell and Pi'Tut when he mate-meet to lake tribe."

"Oh, before you-he?"

"Yes."

"He not meet mate?"

Em'Dor chuckled. "Not in tribe. On way back."

"Who?"

Em'Dor grinned, "Me. We mate."

Cassie frowned. "Why not before?"

"Didn't like before. Then did."

"You-he not always same bed?"

The girl shrugged again.

"He snore," she said, wearing an expression that hinted that there was more to it than that.

Definitely not a match made in heaven. Still, it's far more than I've ever managed, Cassie thought, as Jason's face passed across her mind's eye. But Jason's features changed and were replaced by that of a tall handsome man dressed in armour. For a moment she couldn't figure out who he was.

"You mad face?" Em'Dor said, peering at Cassie, her head tilted to one side.

"Oh, Sheffield," Cassie gasped as recognition dawned, and then, as if a dam had burst, another raft of memories became accessible. "Ah, now I remember saving Lord Sheffield from Fulke. It's all come back."

"Mad talk," Em'Dor said. "You remember your tribe?"

"Yes," Cassie whispered, knowing she could never fully explain what had just popped into her head. Then she frowned. *I remember saving him, but then what?*

Recalling nothing more, she turned her attention back to eating.

A short distance away, Pe'Kat was giving his blessing to Ge'Tal's mate-meet journey. "Leave after another moon," he said, adding, "Ka'Thon, you lead?"

Ka'Thon stood and said he would.

"Choose," Pe'Kat said, his arm sweeping out in an arc taking in the rest of the tribe. Then he sat back down and popped a large chunk of meat into his mouth and began chewing.

Now there's a man who has no problem with delegation.

Ka'Thon wobbled his head in acknowledgement as he scanned the faces of the adults. That Ti'Pik would be accompanying his daughter was assumed, so Ka'Thon asked for volunteers to make up the full party. His partner, El'Po was the first and Em'Jex agreed to mind their son, Te'Set, while they were gone.

Cassie had the urge to join them, to find out more about these other tribes she'd barely heard mentioned.

What is the rest of this world like? I've never been away from here since I arrived. Should I volunteer? Would they accept me? If I go, then maybe I can find somewhere to raise Ka'Tor where they don't cut faces. She looked at him. *He's only two. Dare I leave him? What if he runs away again?*

A slapping noise made her look up. Ka'Thon was patting Pe'Kat's back as the latter was coughing and pointing at his throat.

Something's gone the wrong way, Cassie thought, expecting him to bring up the obstruction any moment. Then she frowned. The older man had struggled to his feet, gasping. He was having trouble breathing.

Several of the tribe, including Ka'Chull, Za'Lak and Ka'Gar, rushed to assist Ka'Thon's attempts in dislodging whatever was in Pe'Kat's throat, but none of their efforts were working.

He's choking, Cassie realised. *Hitting him on his back isn't enough.*

Her mind went back to that first aid course she'd done with Georgia. They'd been taught the Heimlich manoeuvre using a dummy designed for that purpose.

Oh my God, can I remember how to do it?

She sprung to her feet and ran across. Upon reaching Pe'Kat, whose eyes were staring wildly, she moved behind him. The olive skin of his neck was starting to change to something more akin to grey.

"Out way," she shouted at those crowding him. When they didn't move she screamed, "Out way, now."

This time they moved. Standing directly behind Pe'Kat, she put her arms around his waist with her hands gripping each other and her fists against his stomach just below his ribcage.

She braced herself and yanked hard as if she was trying to lift him, but he continued choking. Za'Lak tried to pull her away. She screamed, "No," at him.

Taking a deep breath, she tried again using even more force. Pe'Kat let out a scream as something flew from his mouth. Releasing her grip, she guided him safely to the ground. His breathing was fast but he had stopped choking.

After a few minutes his breathing had returned to normal and he reached out and picked up the large piece of gristly meat that had been the source of the trauma. He chucked it out of the cave entrance and then hugged Cassie, a large smile spreading across his face.

Ka'Thon sat down with them and said, "Sister, Oh'Lar, choked, many summers past. Hit back lots. Not save – dead. Ka'See teach how save?"

Conscious of the number of eyes upon her, Cassie nodded. "Ka'See teach," she said. A cheer reverberated around the cave apart from Za'Lak, who grunted and stalked off.

After they'd all finished the meal, she spent a while showing others how to grip and tug upwards to force a blockage out of the windpipe.

This is probably too soon after eating, but what the hell. Some of them seemed to be rather over-enthusiastic in applying their newly learned skill. *I just hope they don't end up breaking each other's ribs.*

As the sun began to set, Ka'Thon announced those who would be accompanying Ge'Tal on her mate-meet, but then added, "Two more – six best."

Ja'Mutt, who was El'Po's brother, waved his hand after his partner, El'Pak nodded approval.

"One more," Ka'Thon said, but he was looking at Cassie as he said it. When she didn't respond he said, "Ka'See?"

"Me?" she said, almost nervously.

"Ka'See teach more," Ka'Thon said, glancing at Pe'Kat, who nodded approval.

"Oh," Cassie said as her eyes fell on her son who was chasing El'Tesh just outside the cave entrance.

"Ka'Tor with me," Em'Dor said. "You go."

"Okay," Cassie said, at which Em'Dor grinned. Cassie stared hard at her son, saying, "Keep home. No run away."

"Mate-meet for Ka'See?" said Gu'Tun.

"About time," said Ko'Tek. His laugh was taken up by several others.

Oh shit! Okay, why not? Maybe it's time to find out more about this world – especially if I've got to live here for the rest of my life. I've never had much luck in the twenty-first century or even in 1549. Maybe, back in this time, if it is the past, could there really be someone here for me?

"Yes," Cassie said. "Ka'See go journey."

Downhill

"Look after Ka'Tor good?" Cassie said, handing her son over to Em'Dor. The boy, laughing, ran across to where El'Tesh was splashing in the pool. Fearless, he jumped straight in and wrestled with her.

Em'Dor, sitting on the edge of the pool nursing Oh'Sep, tutted but smiled. "He safe. El'Tesh not safe from Ka'Tor."

Cassie couldn't help but agree. The boy was still a handful and far more boisterous than other children. Always getting into scrapes and arguments with others, it seemed that barely a day went past without him causing at least one upset. She thought that it would be a relief to get away from him for a few days. But there were still a couple of worries on her mind.

"No cut face," Cassie stressed.

"Not time. Star not in morning," Em'Dor said peering at the sky just above the horizon. "Many moons before next star."

Yeah, I know, Cassie thought. *But I don't trust Ka'Chull not to try.*

"Keep guard at night. Not let Ka'Tor out."

Em'Dor nodded. "All guard," she said.

Cassie was nervous as she had never been separated from Ka'Tor for anything more than a few hours before. That wasn't her only fear – leaving the tribe's home for the first time made her just as apprehensive.

As she returned to the clearing before the cave mouth, she thought over the preparations she'd made for the journey. She'd put Ka'Jat in charge of updating her calendar while she was away. She'd also spent the last three weeks accompanying tribe members on increasingly longer excursions into the nearby terrain. Despite her reservations about killing wild animals, she had begun learning how to hunt, though she had yet to make anything resembling a kill. In the first year after Ka'Tor's birth, she had mainly gone foraging with the women and younger men. But during the second year, she had learned how to use both her spear and a sling along with tracking prey, determining not only how many there were but their probable ages. She had also engaged in mock battles to acquire the skills of hand-to-hand fighting.

Over the past few weeks, she'd honed all of those skills to her best ability. While she still fell far short in many respects, she would be able to handle dangerous situations with far more confidence.

It just might mean the difference between life and death, she thought, remembering Ko'Lak and the boar that had stalked Ka'Tor. *Maybe I could give Georgia a run for her money, if I ever get the chance to see her again.*

Ti'Pik beckoned her across to where the trade party were assembling. *Well, it's not as if I'll be on my own but it's still damned scary leaving this place.*

Cassie picked up her stone knives and spears, and joined Ge'Tal and Ti'Pik, who were assembling their packs. Ge'Tal flashed Cassie a brief nervous smile while Ti'Pik handed Cassie her multi-purpose backpack.

Several days ago he had instructed her in its use. It was constructed from folded animal skin, laced together with leather straps threaded through various holes that would enable her to carry it. But, that wasn't its only purpose. Unfolded, the skin was nearly as long as she was tall and was large enough to wrap around her. Threading the straps through the holes in a different manner enabled it to be converted into either a cloak with a broad collar and also into something that resembled a sleeping bag. Ti'Pik had explained that she would need to find something soft – such as moss or dried grass and leaves – on which to place the skin to enable her to sleep comfortably. Cassie had been astounded at the ingenuity that had gone into the design.

Ti'Pik helped her pack it with food – meat and vegetables, both separately contained within carved wooden bowls to keep the worst of the flies and heat off – along with flint knives and carved sticks for trading. Cassie added a couple of her knives to its weight but opted to carry her spears so she would have them ready at the first hint of trouble.

I just don't want to have to use them to hunt for food.

Ja'Mutt and El'Po walked out of the cave similarly attired. El'Po also carried a bundle of small spears that were attached to her belt. Some were flint-tipped, while others were just wood but their tips had been hardened in fire. In addition, she carried a collection of stone knives whose blades were specialised for the construction of such spears. Ja'Mutt had his own array of tools and weapons, including an expertly chipped stone axe whose head was tied and glued to a wooden handle. He had promised Cassie that he would teach her how to make one for herself after they returned from the trip.

As they made their last checks, securing the packs on their backs and making sure the straps were comfortable, Pe'Kat, Ka'Chull and El'Pak approached them.

"Good journey," Pe'Kat said while El'Pak embraced Ja'Mutt. Ka'Chull stood to one side.

"No cut Ka'Tor," Cassie said to him, pointing to her cheek, her finger resting on the scar.

He grinned and then laughed, dismissing Cassie's request.

"No star, no cut," he said, still grinning even with the tip of her spear touching his chest.

I still don't trust him.

The rest of the tribe who were present surrounded them and Pe'Kat raised his arms. He began to sing that song she had first heard two years previously.

Off we go then, Cassie thought, as Ka'Thon led them towards the trees.

Following the stream that alternatively meandered or rushed down the mountain, by mid-morning they had left the tribe's normal foraging ground far behind. The tall, straight pines had begun to be replaced by deciduous varieties with which Cassie was more familiar, even if she had no idea what species most of them were. Apart from the occasional beech and oak, whose leaves she recognised, the rest remained nameless.

The temperature was also beginning to rise the lower they descended, though Ka'Thon seemed to be in no hurry and the pace was far from strenuous.

Good job. This pack is not exactly light.

Glancing behind, she saw the path they'd already trodden snake its way up the incline. *I bet the return journey is going to be a lot harder.*

Beneath her bare feet, the pathway was smooth, an indication it had been used quite regularly as a route for many years. Occasionally, the path would fork and Ka'Thon would stop and consult with Ja'Mutt or inspect a particular tree. After rubbing his chin, he would then decide upon the best direction to take.

Is he remembering the route from when he was here before or working it out fresh? It's not as if there are any road signs. Well, not ones I can read.

The long summer morning grew old and, as the sun passed its zenith, the path they were following ran directly beside the stream. Joined by several tributaries, some of which they'd had to wade through, the combined channel was far wider and deeper. Ka'Thon picked a clearing beside which the torrent wasn't quite so manic and they stopped for their first rest.

Ka'Thon was at the water's edge peering into its depths.

"Fish," he announced. Ge'Tal squealed her delight, and both she and El'Po immediately stripped off their backpacks and clothes, and dived in. Ka'Thon and Ja'Mutt joined them, each armed with wooden-tipped spears.

While they fished, Cassie rested watching T'Pik as he extracted a small stringed bow from his pack along with two pieces of carved, shaped wood. The first was a circular disc, about a hand's width in diameter. She could see that it had an indentation in the centre of one side.

Reminds me of another disc.

The other piece was several inches long but no more than three wide. It exhibited charring at a notch cut into it towards one end. All of these he placed on the ground beside each other. Retrieving a spindle of wood from his pack, he placed it alongside the others. It was also charred at one end,

Standing, T'Pik scanned their immediate surroundings, spotted something and walked back along the path. Cassie examined the wooden pieces.

I'm sure I've seen something like this before. But where?

T'Pik returned with an armful of dry leaves and twigs. Seeing Cassie's interest in what he was doing he beckoned her across.

"Not know this?" he asked.

"No," Cassie said. *Or do I?*

"Watch, learn," he said as he picked up the bowstring and spindle, looping the string of the former around the latter. He then positioned the charred end of the spindle into the similarly charred notch of the piece of wood that he held fast under one foot. The spindle was clamped between that and the disc held in one of his hands. His other hand moved the bow back and forth causing the spindle to rotate between the two pieces of wood. After no more than a minute she could see wisps of smoke being emitted between the spindle and the notch.

Oh, he's making fire. Now I remember. I watched someone doing this on YouTube a few years ago.

"Put leaves on," T'Pik said. Cassie nodded and positioned some of the dry tinder around the spindle. T'Pik continued for a few more seconds before removing the bow and spindle. He lifted the smoking pile to his face and blew on it gently. Cassie squealed in delight as the first tiny flames flickered into life.

T'Pik lowered the smouldering clump to the ground, adding more leaves and dry twigs to it to carefully nurture it into a proper fire.

Cassie tried to remember if she'd seen anyone else starting a fire like this back at the cave but she couldn't. *Probably no need. That fire at the entrance is never allowed to go out.*

Their attention was diverted by a shriek from El'Po who flung a stunned fish onto the bank. A few seconds later Ja'Mutt shouted and waved a second speared fish above his head. Both fish were nearly a foot in length.

Ti'Pik found some sturdier Y-shaped twigs which he stuck into the ground on either side of the fire to form a cooking support frame. Then he located a straight length and whittled a point at one end. He had barely impaled the two fish on the stick when Ge'Tal caught a third. She was about to return to the deeper water but Ka'Thon raised a hand for her to stop.

"Enough for us. Never take more than need," he instructed. Ge'Tal nodded and hauled herself back onto dry land.

Wise words. My world is far too greedy. If it wasn't for the threat of Ka'Tor being scarred, then maybe having to live here for the rest of my life might not be quite so bad. But she shuddered at the thought of having to kill the fish herself.

While the fish were being cooked, Cassie and T'Pik extracted some of the pre-prepared food from the backpacks to accompany it. Those who had been fishing lay naked on the bank drying off in the sun.

I'm still not quite as unselfconscious as them. She looked down at her almost bare chest. *These bras I made don't hide a lot – but that wasn't the point.*

While several other women had taken to copying the crude halters that Cassie had concocted nearly two years previously, they had never been a total success. Because they were sometimes more trouble than they were worth, even Cassie had a habit of going around topless. But here, the constant jolting of footstep after footstep as they descended, meant that the bra cushioned the worst of the movement, making the journey just that little less uncomfortable.

After the meal was finished, T'Pik dismantled the cooking frame. He put the fire out, scattering the ashes until there was little evidence that they had ever halted there.

Soon they were tramping downwards yet again and the temperature had risen further. Having spent more than three years becoming acclimatised to a higher altitude and its accompanying cold, Cassie was beginning to suffer the opposite, with the sweat running down her brow, arms, cleavage and, most uncomfortably, down her back under the weighty backpack. As they were still walking beside the river – for it could no longer be called a stream – she would occasionally splash her feet in the water. Enjoying the cool currents flowing over her calves, it also enabled her body to dissipate the excess heat for a while.

Every so often they would take a detour to hunt down roots, tubers and mushrooms. Even if they didn't eat them there and then, they were, she was told, good for presenting to their hosts as an additional courtesy in exchange for being fed after they'd arrived. They found a few mushrooms and these were added to the backpacks.

As they descended, Cassie became aware that the land was flattening out and they were entering a broad valley. Increasingly, there were breaks in the trees that grew more spacious the further they went. They continued until the sun wasn't far from grazing the distant mountain tops in the west behind them, where the peaks could occasionally be seen poking above the forest. Seeing the sun's position, Cassie realised that their route had changed from southerly to something more easterly. She also wondered about just what sort of distance they had covered. It had probably been the best part of fifteen hours since they'd left their cave.

Ka'Thon stopped and pointed into the distance ahead of them.

"Valley Tribe," he announced.

Cassie stared ahead along the route but couldn't see anything resembling any place where a tribe might live. To their left, the river had been joined by several more tributaries descending from the hills to the north and was now as wide as the River Wensum that flowed through the heart of Norwich. Being unrestricted by buildings and engineered banks, this river appeared far shallower than that of Cassie's home city.

Looks a lot cleaner, too, she thought, peering into its waters as the ripples lapped around her ankles. Her eyes scoured the water and the banks.

No litter or pollution. If the whole world is like this then this must be the past.

To their right, the southern valley walls sloped more gently up to the distant heights than those across the river on their left. But, her eyes spotted something up ahead, though, as yet, it was still mostly obscured by the trees. It was an outcropping of rock rising from the floor of the valley.

By the time it took them to reach the first of the rocks the sun had all but disappeared behind the mountains and twilight was falling.

Ka'Thon halted and put his hands to his mouth and bellowed out a call.

Blimey, that wouldn't have been out of place in a Tarzan film.

A few seconds later the call was echoed from a distance and Ka'Thon repeated it with an additional 'whoop' at the end.

He turned to the others grinning.

"Ki'Dek," he said.

"Who?" Cassie asked Ge'Tal.

"Ka'Thon brother," Ge'Tal replied. "He come meet."

Minutes later three men, each armed with spears, came running towards them from the direction of the outcrop. Ka'Thon raced to meet them. The rest of the party, exhausted from the journey, followed at a more respectable pace.

Valley

The Valley Tribe occupied a series of smaller caves dotted around the rocky outcrop. Up close, Cassie could see that the formation wasn't a single large rock but a series of massive boulders set in a hill that jutted out from the slope that led up to the southern mountain range. Turf grew anywhere it could and bound the earth to the boulders.

Maybe glaciers dumped them here, she thought, trying to remember school geography lessons.

With the falling of dusk, the party were invited to join the family of tribe elder, Ti'Fet. He would not only provide their evening meal but also sleeping arrangements for the night. T'Pik accepted for the party but Ka'Thon and El'Po excused themselves and accompanied Ki'Dek to another nearby cave.

"Family," Ti'Pik explained.

Cassie compared the sizes of the caves in the immediate vicinity. This was one of the larger ones, though it was dwarfed by her tribe's cave. Fires burning before each entrance enclosed the outcrop in a semicircle of flames.

Reminds me of the fires around the Oak of Reformation.

At each of the fires, food of all varieties was being prepared and cooked. The mix of aromas was making her extremely hungry, especially after the effort of the journey. She sat with Ja'Mutt, Ti'Pik and Ge'Tal along with Ti'Fet and his family. He appeared to have two wives and multiple offspring whose names she forgot as soon as she was told them. But her mind couldn't concentrate on names when the food was causing her nose to work overtime.

I could eat a horse, she thought, watching the carcasses dripping their juices into various fires. *Looking at their size, some of them might actually be horse.*

Once the meats and vegetables were ready there were exchanges between the nearby caves so that everyone could share in all that had been prepared. By this time Cassie was drooling with anticipation and tucked in with gusto once a huge wooden plate was finally presented to her.

But there were constant interruptions. Whilst she was eating she was introduced to a stream of new faces arriving from the other caves. Many of them marvelled at her pale skin and blue eyes. Some of the children shrunk away from her and she felt growing embarrassment at being under such scrutiny.

I feel like some kind of circus freak put on display.

As each arrived she was told their names and family relationships by parentage and partnership, which she forgot as soon as the next was presented.

I'll be lucky to remember any of them by morning.

Like her tribe, their names were all very similar – each two syllables long and separated by a short break into which was sometimes inserted a *click* sound. Familiarity had strengthened the names of those within her tribe, but learning dozens of new names in a single evening was impossible. They were all so similar, especially as some of the names appeared to be composed of two separate yet familiar parts.

Cassie wondered what would have happened if she'd had more than two syllables in her name – would they have been able to handle the idea? She recalled how surprised they'd been when she'd insisted that her name was Cassie – or Ka'See as they pronounced it – declaring it to be a man's name. She'd later realised that only men – such as Ka'Chull, Ka'Thon, Ka'Gar and, of course, Ka'Tor – possessed initial syllables containing the hard 'Ka' sound.

These people had no written language and no concept of how sounds could be written down. Women possessed names that mostly started with rounder sounds such as 'Em', 'El' and 'Oh' though the sharper 'G' was also common in names such as Ge'Tal and Gu'Tun. She pondered on how the names had evolved. There didn't seem to be any equivalent to family names and, when relationships were described, it was just a case of naming the parents.

The Valley Tribe, whose numbers were at least double that of her tribe, followed the same naming customs, though she'd heard at least one new prefix when a woman called Ah'Ness was introduced along with her partner Pe'Sol.

Good job they weren't combined the other way around, Cassie thought, trying not to snigger. *Well, at least there are two I might not have too much trouble remembering – if I can actually recognise what they look like by the time morning arrives. Glad they're not in my tribe – I would never be able to keep a straight face.*

She chuckled to herself and then realised she was now thinking in terms of *my tribe* instead of just *the* tribe.

Maybe they really are going to be my tribe for the rest of my life, she thought, *unless they threaten to cut Ka'Tor's face.*

The meal ended and the flow of newcomers ebbed. A more familiar face appeared before her and she shouted, "Ge'Tek," recognising the girl who had left her tribe two years previously. Cassie jumped up and embraced her before stepping back to look at her properly.

"Baby," Cassie said, seeing how pronounced Ge'Tek's belly was.

"Baby two," Ge'Tek replied, pointing behind her to a man carrying a child, aged not more than a year. They were accompanied by Ge'Tek's parents, Ka'Thon and El'Po, who looked on in awe at their grandchild.

"Oh'Fey, Zu'Mak," Ge'Tek said. Cassie's knowledge about names meant that Oh'Fey was the female child and Zu'Mak had to be Ge'Tek's partner.

Well, at least she's found her man – can't say any of the men here strike me as being partner material. Most of them seem rather afraid of me. Yeah, probably think I'm too repulsive or something.

Cassie sighed.

"What?" Ge'Tek asked.

Cassie smiled. "Good man. You lucky."

"Yes. Good hunter, strong," Ge'Tek agreed, rubbing her stomach. "Make good babies."

Cassie nodded.

"You have man?" Ge'Tek said.

Cassie looked away.

"Ah, poor Ka'See. Too pale and ugly for men."

Don't rub it in, thanks.

After the short summer night, Cassie wasn't the only one reluctant to rise the following morning. She was extremely tired and ached from the previous day's journey. The sun was several hours risen by the time she joined Ge'Tal, Ja'Mutt and Ti'Pik for the morning meal.

Ti'Fet was presiding over a special breakfast of cold meat – the previous evening's leftovers. It wasn't the meal itself that made the breakfast special, it was more the fact that it was dominated by young men. In addition to two of Ti'Fet's sons, there were more than a dozen from other families. Ti'Fet introduced Ge'Tal to each, describing their attributes and achievements to her in minute detail.

Oh, I see – a meaty breakfast for a meat market.

One of the young men, who couldn't have been much older than Ge'Tal's twelve years, kept stealing glances at Cassie as she sat on one side nibbling at the leftovers. The boy's skin was blotchy, exhibiting several patches where the skin was lighter than normal. He was quite skinny with one leg that seemed to be shorter and possibly malformed. Ti'Fet introduced him as Ka'Lam, of thirteen summers, and that, despite his appearance and his inability to run and hunt, he was very talented when it came to flint knapping and making weapons. Ti'Fet went on to explain that many of the beasts that had roasted over the fires the previous evening had been felled by spear tips fashioned by the young man.

Ge'Tal smiled at the boy but her gaze quickly slid on to the next candidate. Her eyes lingered on the tall, grinning boy whose muscular body was obviously more pleasing to her. Cassie's eyes caught Ka'Lam returning his gaze to her once he'd been passed over.

Poor kid. Welcome to freak city. Pity he's too young, as his face is a lot narrower than anyone else's here apart from mine. He's almost attractive. But only almost.

After breakfast had finished Ti'Fet offered to house Ge'Tal should she wish to prolong her stay. Given the number of candidates on hand, Cassie knew that Ge'Tal would be wise to spend as much time as possible getting to know the boys of the tribe properly to see if any were potential partner material. Ti'Pik glanced across to his daughter and she nodded agreement. If nothing worked out for her then she could return at a later date when another trade journey was made by either of their tribes. Or she could join a different trade party to one of the other tribes in the area.

Cassie spent the rest of the day with Ge'Tek and T'Pik, being given a tour of the families and caves by one of Ti'Fet's wives, Oh'Pell. On T'Pik's urging, Cassie had endeavoured to teach some of them the Heimlich manoeuvre but they seemed less interested in learning the technique than staring at her pale skin and fondling her hair.

Well, it's obvious none of them have ever come across anyone even remotely like 'circus freak' me. Is that more evidence that this is definitely the past? In that case, just how far back am I if people like me either haven't evolved yet or reached this area, wherever it is?

The only family interested in the Heimlich manoeuvre were Ka'Thon's parents. They lamented that if they'd known of the technique several years previously, then they might not have lost Ka'Thon and Ki'Dek's sister, Oh'Lar.

Before she departed their cave they presented her with a leather scabbard containing a long knife. Extracting it from its sheath, she marvelled at the blade, which was almost jet-black and glassy in texture. It caught and reflected the sun's light as she turned it this way and that, examining its construction. The word 'obsidian' came to her mind, though she wasn't sure if this was correct, unable to recall how such a stone was formed. The edge of the blade was so keen that she was almost afraid to touch it in case it sliced her skin. Embedded in a wooden handle, the black rock was secured in place by dozens of windings of a far finer type of twine than she had seen anywhere else in this world.

Ka'Thon explained that his father had obtained the knife on one of his journeys and then given it to Oh'Lar upon his return, teaching her how to use it for hunting or to defend herself should the need arise. It looked a formidable weapon and one that would do a lot of damage if used correctly, given the length and sharpness of the blade. Ka'Thon thought it appropriate that Cassie should have it and explained how it had come from the Water Tribe who lived either on the coast of a sea or on a large river – there didn't seem to be any differentiation between the two in the tribal language.

Cassie thanked Ka'Thon's parents profusely.

Over the following two days, as the members of the Valley Tribe got used to seeing Cassie around, several of them asked about the bra she wore. Avoiding any hint that it was partly due to modesty, she explained how it made walking and running more comfortable for those who, like herself, were relatively well endowed. She looked down at her chest, remembering how Jason had ogled her breasts when she'd worn that low-cut dress for Erin's party.

He'd be even more impressed by them now. At least they're a bit smaller than after I gave birth. Running was definitely out of the question back then.

Several of the women asked how to construct the bras, so she gave lessons on that as well. Before the third day had reached nightfall, several of the larger

Valley Tribe women had made their own and were proudly exhibiting them.

On the fourth day, as Cassie moved around the complex of caves, she became conscious that she was being followed, noticing that Ka'Lam often seemed to be nearby. Walking between two caves and hearing footsteps behind she stopped and swirled around, coming face to face with him.

"Why follow?" she demanded.

He flinched and his face fell, embarrassment flashing across it.

"Sorry, not want scare you," she said, seeing his reaction.

"K-Ka'See," he stuttered. "You different. I different. Ge'Tal not want partner me. No girl partner Ka'Lam. Bent. Slow... Ugly. I-I hear Ka'See no partner."

Oh, you poor thing. Maybe if he'd been a bit older... but no. Anyway, by the standards of these people, I'm almost old enough to be his mother. Not that I can figure out how old I am – probably around twenty-one by now. Who can tell?

"You find someone one day. Ka'See more than twenty-one summers. You thirteen. Not good match."

The boy sighed.

"Any no-partner girls in Mountain Forest Tribe?" he asked, using the Valley Tribe's name for her tribe.

Cassie shook her head. The only unpartnered girls were El'Tesh who was merely four, along with Em'Sell and Em'Tull who were both even younger.

"No," she said. "You find partner in other tribes?"

Ka'Lam pointed to his lame leg. "No journey," he said. "Slow. Pain."

Cassie patted him on his shoulder. "When Ka'Lam seventeen summers and still no partner, ask Ka'See again."

He brightened at that.

"Yes. Seventeen. Four summers. Ka'Lam ask – good partner for Ka'See."

That wasn't a promise. Oh, I just wanted to give you a bit of hope, that's all. Me and my big mouth.

By the evening of the seventh full day, the remaining trading had been completed. With Ge'Tal confirming that she would remain behind, Ti'Pik announced that they would begin the return journey early the next morning.

As she was packing things ready for the trip Cassie attached her obsidian knife to her new leather belt. The belt was one of the other items she had picked up in exchange for explaining how to make bras and also how to count days and determine when the winter and summer solstices were due.

It's good these people value knowledge as well as physical items, otherwise I might not have had anything much to barter with.

Uphill

In the false dawn, after numerous hugs and farewells, Ka'Thon led the reduced party back along the pathway. He told them they would spend one night in the forest as the climb into the mountains would take far longer than the trip down.

"Know good sleep places," he said, grinning when Cassie looked worried about not reaching their home cave before nightfall.

Each of their packs was laden, filled with fresh food and new goods. Long knives like Cassie's own, though made of flint, were secured to each of their belts. The technique for knapping such knives from a newly discovered cache of flint had been another recent addition to the Valley Tribe's knowledge. A year previously, a younger man from a visiting delegation had stayed to partner with a daughter of Ti'Fet's sister. Like his father, the newcomer had been skilled in the technique, which he taught to others in the Valley Tribe.

By mid-morning, they had left the broader valley and were climbing the foothills. Here, their rate of progress dropped significantly. The deceptively shallow incline was already slowing the party down. They were having to take longer and more frequent breaks just to have the energy to tackle the next stage.

"Nearly there yet?" Cassie asked as the incline became steeper. But she knew they weren't, for the river that ran to their right was still more than three times the width of the stream that ran past their cave.

Ka'Thon laughed. "Not even half."

Cassie sighed and continued trudging behind Ka'Thon and El'Po who were currently in the lead. Behind her, Ti'Pik and Ja'Mutt brought up the rear.

The afternoon wore on and Cassie's legs were demanding a halt but Ka'Thon seemed to be in a hurry. Late afternoon turned into early evening and Ka'Thon was looking worried until they entered a small clearing. Ringed by trees save one side where a stream rushed to join the main river, it hadn't been on their original path as Cassie didn't recognise it from their descent.

They set up camp in the centre of the clearing, with Ti'Pik and Cassie on fire-starting duties while the other three went fishing. Cassie collected an armful of dry tinder for Ti'Pik but he indicated that what she brought back wasn't sufficient. She understood why when, after he'd got the initial fire blazing in the centre of the clearing, he set up six more in a circle each halfway between the central fire and the edge of the woods.

"More wood. Burn all night," he said leading her back under the trees where they searched out the driest twigs and small branches. Once each of the fires had enough to keep it burning, they sought out more, piling up the reserves to last throughout the night, keeping the softer leaves to use under their bedding.

Oh yes, keeps the wild animals away. We will be sleeping near the large fire within the circle of smaller fires for protection.

She looked up at the sky, which was starting to darken.

I've never actually slept out under the stars before. Good job the night will be pretty short. It must already be past nine.

Before dusk fell, Ka'Thon, El'Po and Ja'Mutt returned with a dozen small fish, which they cooked over the central fire.

Accompanying the fish they had an assortment of dried meats, mushrooms and tubers that could be eaten either with or without cooking. El'Po's pack also held a surprise as she unwrapped a bag made from goat skin that contained a chunk of raw meat – a thigh stripped of fur – that Ka'Thon's parents had gifted them for the journey. Cassie wondered what animal it had once belonged to. This was speared and dangled over the central fire where its cooked juices spattered and mixed with those dripping from the fish.

The stars were coming out as they ate their meal. None of the constellations were recognisable as anything she remembered from her own time.

Oh, I wish I knew what year this was. Will I ever find out?

"Take turn guarding," Ka'Thon said as they cleared away the remains of the meal, throwing the unwanted leftovers into the stream so that it would carry the scent away from them. Ka'Thon proposed taking the first watch, with Ja'Mutt second. Explaining to Cassie that she would follow Ja'Mutt, he pointed out the stars that would be at the zenith when she would be woken. Next, he got her to recognise one star in particular that needed to be directly overhead to signal the end of her watch when she was to awaken El'Po.

"You watch before?" he said.

"No. What I look for?"

"Danger," he said, and then left her to bed down.

Well, that's definitely confidence building, she thought with a shiver.

Cassie was in the middle of a dream about school when she was shaken awake by Ja'Mutt. Much to her surprise, she had fallen asleep quite quickly after making up the temporary bed from the unfolded skin of the backpack. It was similar to using a sleeping bag except for being less padded. The dried leaves over which it was spread were less than comfortable but Cassie had been extremely tired after all the travelling, so sleep had come easily.

Ja'Mutt retired to his bed a short distance away and Cassie hauled herself upright to a sitting position, still inside her makeshift bed, rubbing her eyes. She started scanning the night but everything outside the glow from the ring of fires was lost in the darkness. Every so often a bat flew overhead, picking off moths that were mesmerised by the flames. In the distance, she could hear the occasional cry from a wild animal – probably some kind of deer. Closer, but still out of sight in the blackness that surrounded them, she detected the sounds of small, nocturnal animals rummaging in the undergrowth.

Several times she nearly dropped off again and so got out of the skin and made a circuit of the camp, replenishing the fires as Ti'Pik had instructed. While the stockpile of branches, twigs and leaves was noticeably shrinking, there would still be ample to last until dawn broke.

Sitting near the central fire, she poked it with a branch every few minutes hoping to re-energise the flames and prevent the night from closing in on her. Something howled further down the slope, which made her jump. Her hand moved to the obsidian knife at her side. But the noise wasn't repeated and she tried to relax, wishing she had a watch to tell the time properly.

The constellations crawled across the sky. She picked out the star Ka'Thon had emphasised but, for what seemed like ages, it remained obstinately to one side of what she perceived to be the zenith.

How can I tell when it's directly overhead?

An idea made her seek out a dumbbell-shaped stone of around three inches in length. Plucking a long length of grass from nearby, she tied the stone to one end. Then she lay on her back and held the stone above her face by the grass using it like a plumb line. She remembered her grandad using something similar to mark a vertical line on a wall before hanging wallpaper. If the star was obscured by her fingers holding the grass then, she figured, if her fingers were also obscured by the stone then the star would be directly overhead. However, because the star wouldn't ever be ninety degrees above her head, the stone would never obscure her fingers, but she could roughly estimate when it had passed its zenith. In the end, she waited until she was sure it was well past that point before, with relief, she approached El'Po and gently shook her awake.

El'Po groaned but nodded for Cassie to return to her bed. Seconds after she'd slid back into the skin, she was asleep.

Shouting awoke Cassie. Her eyes sprang open in alarm, hoping it was nothing more than a vivid dream. But the noise continued and she sat up trying to make sense of everything. It was still quite dark though a glow in the east indicated impending sunrise. She made out Ka'Thon and Ja'Mutt running towards her, each brandishing a spear and shouting.

Behind her, a scream from El'Po made her hand reach for the knife. As she turned to face whatever had awoken them, she slid it from its sheath.

Cassie's scream joined that of El'Po as her eyes locked on those of the huge animal bounding towards her. The grey and brown of its coat, coloured umber in the light from the campfires, rippled as each leap brought it closer. But it was the teeth, bared and dripping with saliva, that held her eyes as the beast closed the gap between them.

Wolf.

Time Screwed

Conversations and Speeches

"Wolf girl," William Kett shouted.

His companion gasped, the man's eyes passing from Cassie to Sheffield.

"Lord Sheffield? But you were slain-" He stopped mid-word, a look of confusion crossing his face. "No, it's as if I dreamed of being told so. Now I remember no such thing for real. Things I thought true are no longer as I recall. What transpires?"

Then the man's eyes focused on Cassie. "Wolf girl. You bewitch us."

Have I done the right thing? It's like they're seeing timelines being rewritten right in front of their eyes.

The man grabbed his sword from the table but acted as if he wasn't sure it would be of any use. Beside him, William Kett, staring at the two of them, looked incapable of forming any further coherent words.

"Yeah, whatever," Cassie said, ready to teleport away if the sword threatened to come closer. "Look, Sheffield should have died – but I rescued him. Just don't let Fulke or any of your other idiots get at him. Now, I've got to go."

I need to see if it's made any difference – to see if Robert Kett does finally win.

Leaving Lord Sheffield for William Kett to deal with, Cassie teleported out to one of the trestle tables serving ale. A woman was filling tankards and Cassie materialised for a merest second to snatch one, not caring if anyone noticed.

Jumping to Tombland Alley she pushed forwards to the early morning of the twenty-seventh of August. Checking at half-hour intervals she tried to determine the outcome of her earlier actions. Staying invisible, she witnessed skirmishes between rebels and troops with increasing frequency as the day wore on. In the original timeline, these rebels would have been fighting outside the city walls, dying in their thousands under the advances of Warwick's soldiers. But now they were battling on the city streets, and it was Warwick's troops who were having the harder time of it. By late afternoon, the road was clear of fighting and cheering could be heard from the direction of the market.

On Gentleman's Walk, next to a building that would one day be replaced by Lloyds Bank, Cassie arrived to find few of the buildings familiar to her. Only the Guildhall to one side and the St Peter Mancroft church to the other were recognisable. The market square itself was half the size of its twenty-first century incarnation and it was bordered to the west by buildings that were long demolished by her time.

But, it was the crowds that thronged the square itself that grabbed her attention. Devoid of the temporary market stalls, the area was packed with thousands of people celebrating. They looked like rebels but she wasn't certain. The centre of the action was close to the corner nearest the Guildhall.

I need a better view.

A second later, she was on the Guildhall roof.

She crouched behind the battlements and discarded her invisibility. As she did so, the smell of the place hit her nose – rotten fruit and vegetables mixed with the odour of raw sewage and stale ale.

Oh my God. I bet it smells even worse down at their level.

She drowned some of it out with a gulp from the tankard.

Peering down upon the heads of the crowd, she spotted a raised wooden platform erected about thirty feet from the building. Upon it stood several men, and they were being joined by another.

Kett, Cassie realised, *he's won.*

Robert Kett stepped to the front of the platform, holding up the ragged remains of a banner. Upon it was emblazoned a coat of arms. A roar erupted from the crowd as he tore it in half and flung the tatters over their heads.

Cassie looked at the windows of the buildings overlooking the square, spotting scared faces of people who were far from celebrating.

Ah, obviously not rebels.

Robert Kett beckoned for silence and, as the noise level decreased, he spoke.

"Warwick has fled, his troops dispersed. The battle is fought and won."

Kett waited for the cheering to subside before he continued. "The city is ours but the war may not be over."

Well, that's quietened them down a bit.

"But, we hold valuable bargaining assets. See."

A man, whose hands were tied behind his back, was ushered to the front of the platform. The cheering recommenced.

"Oh," Cassie gasped. "Sheffield."

But Sheffield didn't appear to be injured. Conversely, he might have even been smiling though, from that distance, she couldn't be sure.

"Thank you, Kay Wolf," Kett shouted. "It is known that you move where you will, unhindered by the physical laws to which mortal men must adhere. I know not whether you are present this day but, should you be, then hear this. You have been my token of luck and good fortune. Certain I am that I would not be standing here had you not diverted my intended route through this day. Nor would our new friend, Lord Sheffield, still be breathing. He, too, owes his life to the Wolf Girl as do many of you here."

His voice dropped. "I saw your fate, which was to be butchered beyond the northern gates of this city. Because of the Wolf Girl it didn't come to pass. Like Lord Sheffield, who will eventually return home to his wife and children, thanks to her, you also will return alive to your families."

Another cheer rose from the crowd and Cassie heard shouts of 'Wolf Girl' coming from below, though those at the windows did not join in.

Once it was possible to speak, Kett continued. "Edmund Sheffield has listened to our claims and studied our petitions, and now he knows how unjustly we have been accused and served. For the release of his chains, he has agreed to argue those petitions on our behalf with the King himself – God bless his majesty – and beg for the restoration to common ownership of those lands so wrongly enclosed from us."

That part brought thunderous applause.

Wow, I hope the king listens, Cassie thought, downing more ale. *This could really bring in a better future.*

Cassie spotted a small group of people near the northeastern corner, standing apart from the main crowd. Although they joined in the cheering, they did so with little enthusiasm. One of them glanced up in her direction.

Fulke, she gasped, *so he survived this as well.*

The man stepped closer to get a better view, but Cassie could see that he moved with a limp. *Serves him right.*

Fulke shaded his eyes. With the sun setting behind her, maybe he wasn't certain his eyes were seeing what he thought they might be. Cassie ducked down, hiding herself completely.

"Wolf Girl, join us," Kett shouted. "This victory is as much yours as it is mine. I will later retire to the Adam and Eve – join me there if you fear to show yourself here. Though I doubt you know what fear is – given you can walk through time as others walk through doors."

Oh, don't worry, I know exactly what fear is. No, I daren't go down there, too many people, especially with Fulke and his mates around. Anyway, I've done enough. Maybe too much. At least Kett has got his chance. Maybe the future has, too.

Below her, the crowd continued to cheer. Many of the people held up swaying tankards that spilled as much as they managed to swig into their mouths. Cassie downed the last drop from her own.

Well, I think I've certainly had my fill of their ale, she thought. *Hell, I'm exhausted, drunk and hungry. If this hasn't worked then I'm definitely not coming back for a second go.*

"Time to go home," she whispered. She looked down at herself. "Ah, nearly forgot – I'd better change back into my normal clothes."

Missing

Cassie returned to the fifteenth of July, materialising in the upstairs room of the cottage. It was around seven-thirty in the morning, several minutes after she'd originally left. It seemed like days ago but probably wasn't more than a few hours.

Opening the wardrobe door she retrieved her jacket, jeans and top, laying them out on the slats of the bed. She peeled the heavy dress off and started putting on her proper clothes.

Oh, that's so much more comfortable. Goodbye Wolf Girl. Back to being twenty-first century Cassie again. Better return these clothes like I said I would.

She was about to gather them up when she frowned.

Something's not right – I'm missing something.

Reaching into one of the jacket's inside pockets, her fingers located her house keys in their usual place. But, aside from the keys, a couple of tissues and a half-empty pack of chewing gum, nothing else was present.

"Shit – where's the disc gone?"

She checked all the other pockets in the jacket and those in her jeans without success. "I remember hearing it hit the wardrobe floor," she said. "Maybe it fell out inside that."

Searching there also drew a blank. She examined the floor of the wardrobe – there were small gaps in its construction, but none large enough for something the size of the disc to drop through.

Investigating underneath the bed, she thought, *It can't have fallen out when I picked the jacket up. I would've heard it hit the floor. Where the fuck is it?*

Cassie extended her search, shifting several items of furniture in case the disc had rolled underneath. There was no evidence of it.

"Okay, be rational," she told herself, trying to suppress impending panic. "All I need to do is go back to before I first arrived and then watch myself put the jacket in the wardrobe. Then, when that me leaves, I can check the jacket for the disc. Simple."

She moved back in time to just gone seven. Keeping invisible, she stood motionless further down the hallway. She had to wait about three minutes and then a few more for previous Cassie to size up the room and stash the clothes.

Right, there it goes into the wardrobe, she thought, hearing the satisfying clunk of the disc hitting the wardrobe floor. She crept up to the doorway.

"Now where?" said previous Cassie.

That was definitely spooky, Cassie thought as the floorboard creaked.

"Who's there? Damn it, now I'm spooking myself," her earlier self said. "Right. So where do I go? And what do I do?"

The Oak of Reformation, Cassie thought a second before earlier Cassie said the same thing and disappeared.

She rushed into the room and opened the wardrobe. "Right, let's get that disc. Yeah, if I grab it now then it explains why it wasn't there when I first got the jacket out of the wardrobe."

She picked up the jacket. Keys, chewing gum, tissues – but no disc.

"It *has* to be here," she cried. "I was watching the whole time."

She dropped the jacket back in. As it hit the floor of the wardrobe, she heard only the lighter jangle of her house keys.

"This is impossible. Now what do I do?"

Oh God, I'm so tired. I just want to be back home and in my own bed. Maybe that's the answer. Go home, sleep it off, come back when I'm more awake. And more sober, as well.

"To hell with it," she sighed. "2019, here we come."

Anonymous

Cassie shut her eyes and, as the process started, whispered, "2019. February the twenty-fourth. Dinner time."

Moving a few days at a time, as she had been doing in 1549, was almost instantaneous, but travelling nearly five hundred years when tired took a lot longer. It was also far harder.

As she passed the year 1900 the effort it was taking was making her dizzy.

Got to keep going, she told herself. *Only a few more decades.*

Finally, she passed 2018 and, slowing down, moved from where that cottage had been to her own house. She decided to reappear in her bedroom, hoping her grandad wasn't in there doing something like making the bed.

Exhausted, she didn't bother remaining invisible and materialised fully.

And froze, mouth open.

The room had changed. It was still the same shape, with the door and window in identical places, but the decor couldn't have been more different. The bed, a single and not the double she'd inherited from her mother, was positioned the other way around.

There was a scream behind her and she spun around to see a girl out in the hallway whose scared expression reflected her own.

Wrong house, it must be.

"Sorry," she said and teleported down onto the street outside, this time remaining invisible. She could see that it was her own house, but the paintwork on the exterior wasn't quite the same and the garden held different plants and was far from the untidy mess she remembered.

"What's going on?" she whispered to herself. "Where's Grandad? What's happened to my room?"

She concentrated and her calendar confirmed the date was correct.

Could the changes have meant we moved somewhere else? But when? My mum was born in this place.

Taking a deep breath, she teleported back to 1978, the year her mother would have been two years old, and re-entered the house, remaining invisible. Finding it empty of people, she explored each room – the décor and furniture in each was unfamiliar. In addition, they contained photos of people whose faces were unknown to her.

Oh my God, what have I done? Have I erased myself from history or something? Or do we live somewhere else? How can I find out? If only I knew someone I could ask. Wait. Georgia lives not far. Will she still be there? Please let her be there.

She returned to 2019 but diverted to Georgia's house, materialising close by when the coast was clear.

I've already scared one girl – better not make a habit of it.

Cassie was relieved to see that Georgia's home looked as it had always done. The front garden was as neatly arranged as normal and, despite the month, had flowers in the form of snowdrops already in bloom. Cassie rang the bell and, seconds later, heard Georgia's voice call from inside, "Won't be a mo' – just getting me jacket."

Ten seconds later the door started opening and Georgia said, "Hi, Ja–" and stopped.

"Georgia," Cassie gasped. "Oh, thank goodness you're still here."

"Huh? Sorry, do I know you?" Georgia said, frowning.

"It's me. Cassie."

Georgia's expression of confusion looked genuine.

"Oh, my God," Cassie whispered. "It's affecting you as well."

"Who are you?"

"Cassie. Cassie Fox. Don't you remember me at all?"

"Sorry, no. Pretty certain I've never met you before in my life. I thought it was my boyfriend at the door."

"Mark?"

"Who? Look, I don't know who you think I am but you've got the wrong person or address or something. Anyway, I've got somewhere else to be. Like, right now."

There was a noise behind Cassie as a car drew up and stopped at the gate. Cassie immediately recognised Jason getting out of the passenger side. She was about to start cursing at him when she realised he looked odd. His hair was slightly longer and styled differently. The expression on his face was also softer. Not only that but he wasn't sporting sunglasses and, to Cassie's surprise, he was wearing a proper suit and was also clean-shaven.

"Jason?" Cassie said, nervously.

"Yes?" Jason frowned. "Do I know you? Friend of yours is she, Georgie?"

Georgie? She's never been called that.

Georgia shook her head. "Seems to know us, though."

Then the driver got out of the car and said, "Another friend?"

"No, Dad," Jason replied. "No idea who she is."

Seeing the driver properly for the first time, Cassie gasped and couldn't suppress the scream that erupted from her lips. She didn't recognise the man's face at all but it was as if some unimaginable terror had crawled inside her head and turned her legs to jelly. Her vision was filled with images of flames engulfing her and the sensation of being crushed by the pressure of dead and dying bodies surrounding her on all sides.

The urge to escape became overwhelming and, with her mouth still making unrecognisable noises, she couldn't prevent herself from fading away as some sort of self-preserving teleport was initiated. Before she'd completely departed, she heard Georgia's accompanying scream along with shouts from Jason and the terrifying man he'd called Dad.

Then, she was zipping back in time with no control over it.

Stop, stop stop.

It took several seconds but she managed to halt the process and found herself on what looked like Mousehold Heath. Not far away, there were several open gravel pits. It took her a few moments to realise she hadn't moved in space at all, but only in time. Her calendar told her it was 1927, long before the housing estate had been built. Some distance to her left was what might have been Norwich prison.

She sunk to the stony ground and sobbed.

Oh, why did I ever listen to Kett? Why did I break my promise and go back in time? I've wrecked everything. I've wiped my own family out of existence. I've killed my mum and grandad. Does that mean I was never born in the first place? How come I'm still here if I was never born? I've got to change it all back – but how?

Wait. The disc. Emergency. This is definitely an emergency.

She reached into the inside pocket of her jacket, and then screamed, "Fuck, fuck, fuck, FUCK!"

It's gone. What the shitting fuck do I do now?

She groaned as she realised what she had to do.

"I've got to go back and, if I can't find the disc, I've got to somehow undo everything I messed with. Put it all back as it was."

Shaking, she shut her eyes.

"If it's at all possible," she whispered.

Hunters

Blade, Claw and Tooth

Cassie ran, but the crunch of the wolf's paws on the ground brought it closer by the second. She couldn't run fast enough.

Hearing it right behind her, she spun around. Her knife held out in front of her looked as much use as a toothpick against an elephant. Up close the animal was huge, far larger than any dog she'd ever encountered.

She screamed as the wolf launched itself. Its body slammed into her, the impact cutting off her scream, the momentum hurling them both to the ground. Flat on her back, with her breath knocked from her lungs, she hardly noticed the pain at the back of her head due to the agony that rippled up her left leg. The wolf's jaws were inches from her nose, its spittle spattering her face.

I'm as good as dead.

The beast opened its jaws but, instead of going for her throat as she expected, it raised its head and howled as if in pain. Trapped beneath it, Cassie felt sticky warmth running over her right hand, in which she still gripped her knife.

The wolf's body shifted and shuddered as two spears punctured its side simultaneously. It let out an ear-piercing screech and lowered its head, jaws open to attack the nearest thing that might be the cause of all its pain – Cassie.

She wrenched her left hand free and, burying her fingers in the fur of the wolf's neck, tried to push its head away from her face. Despite its injuries, the wolf was far too strong and the jaws were inching closer.

A hand wielding a knife cut across Cassie's view. The knife punctured the wolf's right eye, burying itself deep into its skull. Leaving his knife where it was, Ka'Thon threw his arms around the beast's head to drag its jaws away from her.

Cassie felt the wolf on top of her shudder several times as Ka'Thon fought its last efforts. Its body fell limp, its weight pinning her down, crushing out what little air remained in her lungs.

Ka'Thon and Ja'Mutt pulled their spears from the wolf's body and rolled it from on top of her. She felt bruised all over and could do nothing other than lay there, gasping. Ka'Thon removed his knife from the wolf's eye and then slashed its throat to make sure it was really dead.

Then, with one man on either side of her, they tried to help to sit up.

"Ow, no," Cassie screamed.

El'Po, rushing over to help, said, "Not move. Me check."

"Leg," Cassie whispered, raising her left hand a fraction to point to where most of the pain was located, and then added, "Head."

El'Po examined Cassie in minute detail, her hands exploring Cassie's entire body to complete her examination.

"Cut head," El'Po announced. "Claws cut legs – one deep – bad. Bones good. Wash cuts then paste."

She slowly inched Cassie up into a sitting position, which caused her to wince as her damaged flesh was made to move.

"Dead?" Cassie asked, seeing the wolf's body lying still only feet away. Both Ka'Thon and Ja'Mutt were examining it.

Ka'Thon pulled Cassie's knife from the wolf's stomach and, holding it up, grinned. "Ka'See kill wolf first."

So, I did kill an animal – but it was either that or be killed. No choice.

Feeling the back of her head, her hand came away bloody, but then she realised she'd used the hand that had been holding the knife. Using her other hand she figured out that she'd suffered a couple of minor cuts from her head hitting the stones. Her thick, tangled hair had prevented further injury. But something nagged at her about having already suffered a head injury.

She examined her leg, feeling nauseous as she saw the two long bloody lines, about an inch and a half apart where the wolf's claws had raked her thigh.

"Get water. Wash," El'Po said, running off to the stream. Ka'Thon accompanied her while Ja'Mutt was joined by Ti'Pik as they hung the wolf's carcass from a tree by its back legs, letting its blood seep into the ground.

In the east, the first glimmers of dawn appeared as El'Po returned and rinsed Cassie's injuries, which made her whimper in pain. Then El'Po retrieved a pouch from her pack and mixed the contents with water in a shallow wooden bowl. Cassie recognised the grey paste as that which had been rubbed into the faces of those who had been scarred. She gasped as it was applied, though she was grateful minutes later when the pain began to subside to a dull throbbing. El'Po finished by tying strips of skin around the injured leg to protect it.

After the sun had fully risen, Cassie attempted to stand with El'Po's help but could merely hobble. Walking aggravated her dizziness, bringing on bouts of double vision, which she had trouble explaining. With relief, she sat on her makeshift bed, glad to get the weight off her injured leg.

Oh God, am I going to be able to carry on walking? Will we be able to get back before another nightfall if I can't walk? I don't want to be a burden.

Ti'Pik prepared breakfast. Despite having carved several large hunks of meat from the dead wolf, he used none of that for the immediate meal. Instead, the wolf meat was wrapped up and set aside to be added to their packs for the journey home. Cassie questioned El'Po about that as they ate dried meat and roots supplied by the Valley Tribe.

"Wolf meat long cook," El'Po said. "Days soak in juices. Better eating. If wolf eat bad meat, we eat wolf quick, not taste good, we sick."

"Oh," Cassie said, not sure she fully understood it. But she recalled that wolf meat had occasionally been eaten by the tribe, though it was often from cubs. Even then, it wouldn't be used immediately.

After breakfast, Ja'Mutt and Ka'Thon removed the pelt from the wolf in one piece and the latter also spent a while removing some of the beast's teeth, collecting them into a pouch. Then he took both his own and Cassie's knife down to the stream to wash them. As he returned the coal-black blade to Cassie he said, "Good knife. Ka'See use well."

She didn't know how to respond to that.

Ti'Pik helped Cassie reassemble her bed back into a backpack and, by mid-morning, they resumed their journey.

Within half an hour it was obvious that Cassie's ability to travel was severely impaired. Already, their rate of progress was less than half that of the previous day. Cassie was reduced to hopping or leaning on one of the others as the group crawled along. Her pack was redistributed as she was no longer capable of carrying such a load.

While that helped, by midday the pain had become excruciating and Cassie collapsed. Seeing fresh blood seeping from the injury, El'Po unbandaged the wounds. Cassie cried out as it was peeled away and blood flowed from the cuts. El'Po applied some more of the paste but she was running out of the stuff. Another application would use the last of it.

"Need a... a..." Cassie said as El'Po rebound the wounds, but there was no word in their language that meant 'crutch.' The three men wore worried expressions. Ja'Mutt shook his head while the others looked away from Cassie.

They're not thinking of abandoning me, are they? Is that what they do?

She shivered as the term 'mercy killing' crept into her mind. *No, please no. I need them to understand.*

"Crutch," she shouted, using the English word. Seeing some dusty ground nearby, she dragged herself over to it. With one finger she drew the shape of a simple crutch in the dust like a capital T with a short protrusion – the hand grip – sticking out from the upright. The others just looked confused. She tried to draw a representation of herself on one leg being supported by the crutch.

Have they never seen drawings before? Am I going to be abandoned just because they can't understand a simple diagram?

She thought back to the unadorned walls of the tribe's cave – it was bare of painted handprints and representations of animals and people. The only thing on it was her calendar and only Ka'Jat understood that. None of the caves of the Valley Tribe had had any decoration, either. The only form of art expressed by them was what they did to their faces.

When were the first cave paintings made? No idea. I need to try a different tack.

She asked them to locate a tree branch that shape. After several false starts, Ka'Thon located a young tree that had a branch that might fit the requirements. He chopped it from the tree using his axe. Cassie examined it, noting the smaller branch in roughly the correct position for a hand grip. She instructed him to trim the top bar of the 'T' down and remove some excess length from the grip. Demanding some of the wolf pelt, she wrapped one strip around the top as protection for her armpit. A second strip she attached to the hand grip.

With Ti'Pik's help, she got back on her feet and positioned the crude crutch under her shoulder. It was slightly too long.

"Chop bottom, this much," she said. Leaning on El'Po she watched as Ka'Thon used his axe to hack about three inches off the bottom.

She tried walking with it. Holding her injured leg off the ground took some practice but she found she could cover more ground than before.

"Ka'See tribe make magic things," El'Po said, watching in amazement.

Yeah, bloody wish I didn't need to.

So, with Cassie insisting that she carry her backpack at least half full, they continued for another half an hour until Ka'Thon called a halt for lunch.

By mid-afternoon, deciduous trees had given way to pines and the air was noticeably cooler. Driving herself to keep up the pace, Cassie was sweating profusely and was beyond exhausted. But, she was determined to continue until they reached the sanctuary of the cave.

By late afternoon, the others had relieved her of her backpack, though she kept her obsidian knife in its sheath at her side. Passing through a clearing, Cassie observed the sun scraping the mountains to the west. But she recognised the location. She'd often foraged here with the other women of the tribe.

Nearly home – got to keep going. With her eyes set on the ground in front of her, her vision kept fogging over but she kept pushing herself. *Not far now.*

She heard voices up ahead. *That was Em'Jex, surely.*

The sound of running feet made her look up. Her good foot caught on a tree stump and she tripped. Making little more than a whimper, she fell forwards, grazing her arm as it automatically raised to protect her face.

Need to sleep. Can't take another...

Her eyes closed. The last thing she remembered hearing was Ka'Thon and El'Po both shouting for assistance.

Wolf Girl Necklace

Wolves dominated Cassie's dreams. In some, she was the wolf searching for the missing disc. In others, she was fighting and killing the animals while people she knew looked on. Tribe members as well as Georgia and her grandad refused to recognise her while wolves clawed at her legs. The wolves she killed were replaced by dozens more, some on fire, others partly skinned. One stopped in front of her and growled, "Stay dangerous, Cassie Fox."

Perception shifted and she was no longer asleep. Her body felt like a battlefield, her head throbbing, her left leg on fire. She kept her eyes shut until she realised someone was washing her face.

Blinking a few times, her eyes focused upon Em'Lo sitting beside her, dabbing at her face with a damp piece of animal skin. Around her were the familiar walls and arched ceiling of the cave.

"Oh, we made it," she whispered, relieved, as the images of fire faded from her vision. The pain lessened, too.

"Ka'See wake," Em'Lo shouted.

Suddenly she was surrounded. Em'Dor, Em'Jex, Ka'Jat, Ka'Tor and even Ka'Chull crowded around the bed.

"Ka-kass," Ka'Tor shouted, a smile spreading across a face whose cheeks were, she was relieved to note, still free of scarring.

El'Po pushed them all aside and called her mother, El'Kek, across. Her father, Za'Lak glared at both his partner and daughter but finally allowed El'Kek to attend Cassie. El'Kek placed her palm on Cassie's brow.

Is she checking my temperature? What's happened to me?

She tried to sit up but her head spun and she felt nauseous. El'Kek forced her down, ordering, "Rest."

Then she remembered the wolf, though her memories were mixed with the dreams of being a wolf herself.

Wolf girl, she thought. *Oh, that's what they called me in Robert Kett's time.*

Memories of the missing disc returned but she remembered the button being pressed as well. *I must have found it again. But when? Everything is all so mixed up. Am I going mad?*

She realised it was daylight outside the cave. *I must have slept all night.*

She asked, "How long sleep?"

"Four day," Em'Dor said.

"Huh? Four?"

"Yes, afraid Ka'See not wake ever."

El'Po explained. "Dead wolf put bad spirit in Ka'See. Ka'See burn like fire for two day. Ka'See fight spirit like Ka'See fight wolf with knife. Ka'See win. Wolf lose. Bad spirit gone. Ka'See come back."

Cassie mulled over what that might actually mean. Burning like fire sounded like she'd had a fever. Her forehead was hot and clammy.

Okay, so in other words, I probably got some sort of infection and fever from the injuries. Damn, my leg really hurts.

She reached down to her leg with her left hand. Similar in feel to her forehead, it was also tender and swollen, but she couldn't reach far enough without either sitting up or rolling over. At that moment, she didn't have the strength to do either.

"Show me leg," she said.

El'Kek pulled the cover down and assisted Cassie in raising her head enough to see the injuries for herself. Cassie gulped seeing the two long rakes down her thigh, each around eight inches in length. One was healing nicely but the flesh around the deeper cut was red, puffy and oozing yellow pus.

Oh, abso-bloody-lutely fantastic, she groaned.

But, she knew it could have been far worse. She was lucky to have escaped with her life.

Bed-bound for several days, Cassie was relieved when the last of the pus drained away and the deeper cut began scabbing over properly. The shallower injury was now a line whose diminishing red glow looked healthier every day.

One morning Ka'Thon came to her bedside and presented her with a small pouch. Inside, she found several of the teeth he'd pulled from the wolf's jaws, now washed clean. Squeamish at first she plucked up the courage to examine them: two were canines, almost three inches long, while the rest were a mixture of incisors and molars – nearly twenty in total.

Cassie looked at him, quizzically. "What for?"

He pulled out one of his knives from the sheath at his belt, the one he'd plunged into the wolf's eye. He pointed to where a groove had been cut into the handle. Inserted into it, and glued in place with tree resin, were four teeth, one canine and three incisors.

"Spirit of wolf in knife. Kill better. Ja'Mutt put teeth in knife. You want?"

Cassie retrieved the obsidian knife from beside her bed. She looked at the fine windings of twine that helped to keep the blade in place on the wooden handle. There wasn't room to make a groove without cutting into them. Ka'Thon's expression suggested he was coming to the same conclusion.

"No," she said, having a better idea. *These people never wear anything ornamental.* "Make holes in bigger teeth? Here at end."

"Teeth hard."

"Yes. Bow drill. Like use to make fire?"

Ka'Thon frowned for a moment, then his eyebrows rose as he understood what she meant. "Need sharp flint. What for? More magic from Ka'See tribe?"

Cassie nodded and grinned. *Yes, maybe.*

The next day Ka'Thon returned with something similar to the tool that Ti'Pik had used for fire making. Embedded into the rod was a slender sliver of flint – a crude drill. He produced a larger chunk of flat wood that had a v-shaped groove cut into one side with a knife – the width and depth of the groove varied along its length. He then took one of the molar teeth and pushed it into the groove at a point where the wood gripped it lightly, tapping it further down with a large pebble to hold it fast. He positioned the drill over the tooth and started drilling.

Cassie knew what was going to happen and watched the flint skid off the tooth's enamel, only making the lightest of scratches.

It needs some sort of guide hole.

She got Ka'Thon to cut out a strip of flat wood nearly two feet long, about two inches wide and just under half an inch thick. Once he returned with it she got him to drill a hole into the middle of that first, which he achieved after several minutes. Then she indicated how the new hole needed to be positioned over the tooth to prevent sideways movement of the drill. She wasn't sure how to keep the guide from moving but Ka'Thon solved that himself by placing one foot on each side. He then attempted to drill the tooth once again, making a reasonable start before the flint shattered.

Undeterred, he spent a couple of hours knapping several new drills of varying thicknesses and strengths. Over the rest of the day, he managed to drill five teeth, though two of the smaller ones had shattered in the process.

The fading light halted further progress and Ka'Thon left the drill components with her.

The following morning, and with assistance from El'Po, Cassie struggled to her feet. Her leg was still painful, but she forced herself to take a few steps, promising herself to attempt a few more each day.

After breakfast and with Ka'Thon away hunting, Cassie felt well enough to attempt some drilling herself. She couldn't use both feet to hold the guide steady but, instead, used her right foot as Ka'Thon had done, but sat directly on the other end. It was slow going but, by the end of the day, she had eleven drilled wolf teeth. After locating some suitable twine she threaded the teeth onto it, tying knots before and after each tooth to keep them evenly spaced.

Just like the one I wore at the party. No fake plastic – this is a real tooth necklace.

She hung it around her neck.

The others were perplexed, asking why she wanted to adorn herself in such a manner. After a moment, Cassie adapted what Ka'Thon had said about the teeth embedded in the knives.

"Spirit of wolf in teeth," she said. "Wolf spirit know Ka'See fight it, kill it, own it. Spirit now help Ka'See fight, walk, run fast again."

They seemed to accept this explanation at face value.

I really am a wolf girl, now.

Within a few days, others wanted to try something similar. Given a lack of further wolf teeth, other objects were pressed into service. Small pebbles from the stream with naturally worn holes were one source, while others sought out larger feathers shed by birds. Em'Dor discovered that discarded shells of freshwater clams could be a reasonable substitute. They had been harvested for food from a larger pool miles downstream. Even Ka'Tor collected striped snail shells and demanded that Cassie make him a necklace from them. However, attempting to drill or punch holes in their delicate shells destroyed many of them. Finally, she had enough for him to be satisfied.

Three days later he lost the entire necklace when he went swimming.

He's too damned good at losing things, Cassie thought. *Especially himself.*

The Hunt for Ka'Tor

Four weeks later, Cassie replaced the crutch with a walking stick she made for herself. With that, she was able to get around the cave and the cleared area beyond its entrance, albeit slowly. The wolf's claws had torn the muscle in her thigh and there was little she could do to speed up the healing process.

With her calendar suggesting that September was imminent, the weather was still warm enough to enable her to alternatively relax as well as exercise her leg in the pool by swimming. A trip to the pool became a much-needed daily pastime. Whilst bathing she would also keep watch over Ka'Tor, El'Tesh and any other young child foisted upon her by their mothers while they went foraging.

She didn't mind. The others realised that, despite any assumed assistance from her necklace, she wouldn't be able to provide much physical help for a while. Any task that required walking any distance or carrying heavy objects, such as chopped logs, was beyond her current capability.

If I don't watch it I'll be getting back to my old flabby self.

Another week passed before she dared venture further down the path to the spot where the stream was wide and deep. Once in the water, she was able to swim as strongly as she'd managed before the injury. Out of the water, she couldn't walk more than a few hundred feet without pain and tiredness setting in.

One morning, while in charge of several of the younger children at the pool, Ka'Tor got into a fight with Em'Sell. The daughter of El'Pak and Ja'Mutt was about a year older than Ka'Tor. Cassie didn't see what had started it but observed Ka'Tor pushing Em'Sell over. The girl got up and slapped Ka'Tor across the face.

"Em'Sell, Ka'Tor. No," Cassie shouted.

They ignored her. Em'Sell kicked Ka'Tor but he sprung away and retaliated by throwing stones at her. Cassie shouted as Em'Sell picked up a larger stone that had landed near her feet and slung it back at him. It caught him on the arm, drawing blood. He squealed and took to his heels.

"Bloody kids," Cassie screamed in English, as she struggled from the pool.

With Ka'Tor disappearing off into the trees Em'Sell went to follow him. Cassie's bark of, "Stop now," was finally enough to halt her.

Shouting for Ka'Tor to return, all she heard was the sound of his feet crashing through the foliage, before distance hid them from her ears.

"Damn him," she muttered, rubbing her leg. *There's no way I can follow.*

Grabbing her walking stick, she herded the other children back up to the cave. By the time they'd reached the clearing, her leg muscle was burning.

"Ka'Tor run away," Cassie shouted once she was close enough.

Only Ka'Jat and Ja'Mutt were near the entrance, though Gu'Tun appeared from inside seconds later.

"Which way?" Ja'Mutt asked.

"There," Cassie gasped, pointing towards the east. He always ran in that direction. "Went from pool," she added.

"I look," Ja'Mutt said. After returning to the cave to arm himself with spears and knives, which he attached to his belt, he ordered Ka'Jat to find others to help him track the boy. Then he ran towards the pool to pick up Ka'Tor's tracks.

Gu'Tun ushered the children into the cave entrance while Ka'Jat ran off towards the path near the stream. As he entered the forest she could hear him calling, "Ka'Chull, Ka'Char, Pi'Tut."

Cassie lowered herself to the ground next to the fire. There was a stack of branches and logs nearby ready to be put on it. "I look after fire," she said.

Gu'Tun nodded and attended to the needs of the children.

Cassie winced as the pain in her leg slowly subsided. Her eyes scanned the tree line as she watched for signs that Ja'Mutt had located her son. But the minutes dragged on without either of them appearing.

Sometime later, Ka'Jat returned with Ka'Char beside him.

"Ka'Chull, Pi'Tut hunt Ka'Tor," Ka'Jat announced as they approached.

"Not found?" she asked.

"No," Ka'Char replied. "He fast. Like magic wind."

As the day wore on and there was still no sign of Ka'Tor, Cassie began to fret.

What's taking them so long to find him? Has he been injured? Or killed by bears or wolves? That bloody kid will drive me to the grave.

Every time she heard voices in the forest her hopes were raised. But it was usually the return of one of the foraging or hunting parties. When Em'Dor's group ascended the incline to the cave entrance she took one look at Cassie's face, glanced around, and said, "Ka'Tor? Run?"

Cassie nodded her head and Em'Dor sat down with her and wrapped her arms around Cassie's shoulders. Em'Lo joined them to cuddle her as well.

Men will be the death of me, Cassie thought, as tears ran down her face. The situation reminded her of Holly, Megan and Erin comforting her at the latter's party. *I sometimes wish I'd been born lesbian or something.*

A hunting party consisting of Ko'Tek, Ka'Thon and Za'Lak returned with a deer and a young boar to add to their food stocks. Ka'Thon, hearing the news about Ka'Tor expressed concern but Za'Lak, as usual, treated Cassie with contempt and muttered that he hoped her troublesome brat had been eaten by bears. El'Po, upon hearing this, reprimanded her father, but he ignored her.

As evening approached, Cassie had run out of practical diversions. She'd helped Em'Jex with preparing some of the roots and other vegetables gathered that morning. But she was conscious that it was getting towards the time for the main evening meal and her son was still missing.

Hearing voices from the eastern side of the clearing, Cassie grabbed her walking stick and hobbled awkwardly until Em'Dor caught up with her and helped her along.

Figures burst from the forest – two men, Ka'Chull and Pi'Tut, and, yes, there was her son between them.

"Ka'Tor," she shouted.

Ka'Tor came running towards her, arms outstretched. She dropped her walking stick to snatch him up into her arms. Tears of relief fell from her eyes.

"He hide," Pi'Tut said. "We go past, he go new way. Hide. We miss."

"He go to place where trees fall over," Ka'Chull said, grinning.

"Run fast as deer," Pi'Tut added. "Faster. Magic."

"Spirit call," Ka'Tor told her.

"Where spirit?" Cassie asked.

"In head. All place," Ka'Tor said grinning and waving his arms around.

"What is spirit?"

Ka'Tor frowned as if he was waiting for an answer to arrive.

"Thing," he finally replied.

Undo Unavailable

Maps and a Mountain Stream

"Yaaah," Cassie gasped, materialising at the deserted cottage. The effort of racing back to 1549 had left her hyperventilating. On the bed were the clothes she'd previously discarded.

With her shout still echoing around the rooms, she stood still for a moment listening for other sounds. Certain she was alone, she sat down on the edge of the bed and sobbed, unable to stop herself.

For several minutes her mind skittered over the enormity of what her actions had caused. *I've changed so much history, I don't know where to start. Oh, my God, how can I put it all back as it was?*

She tried to concentrate on what she'd need to do, but her exhaustion didn't result in any coherent answers.

"Damn it, I need to sleep," she sobbed.

Spotting the rolled-up mattress on top of the large wardrobe, she hauled it down. Whatever it was filled with felt soft but a bit lumpy and uneven in places.

"At least it's not damp," she muttered, remembering she hadn't wanted to experience sleeping on it. "No choice, now."

The string tied around it was coarse and she couldn't undo any of the knots. Reaching into her jacket she pulled out her house keys and used the front-door key as a substitute saw to hack through the string. After a minute it pinged apart and she unrolled the mattress. Chucking the sixteenth-century clothes on the floor, she positioned the mattress on the bed slats. Lying down on it caused a puff of dust to rise, which was followed by a musty aroma.

Exhausted, Cassie was beyond caring and a few minutes later, still dressed in her twenty-first century clothing, she was snoring.

Cassie awoke with a start, forgetting where she was. She looked around in confusion until she remembered the most recent events.

Her head still rung from a nightmare in which Jason's father was invading her skull just like Laurence had done on her great-grandfather's bus.

She sat up and groaned, conscious of the hangover that was causing her temples to throb. Her mind skittered over the problems she had to undo, but she still had no idea how to go about rectifying the damage.

"Have I got to try and prevent my earlier self doing what I did? Won't that be changing my own timeline or something? If I manage to do that then what happens to the me here and now? Will I wink out of existence or something?"

She hauled herself off the bed and tried to stand.

"But didn't I already do that when I changed the timeline around Lord Sheffield? Oh, hell, why did I let Kett talk me into this?"

The sun tried its best to shine through the grime on the single tiny window. The shadows it cast were not the same as when she'd first entered the room.

"Still can't think. Damned ale," she said, rubbing her eyes.

Cassie concentrated and, via her built-in calendar, concluded that the local time was just gone half three in the afternoon.

"Feels more like midnight," she muttered. "And I'm thirsty and hungry. How long has it been since I last ate?"

She tried to work it out, but couldn't. "Wish I'd brought my phone along so I could see what my own personal time was. Or maybe a watch."

Then she remembered Kay talking about watches and how they always broke after going through a few portals.

"Yeah, but that was portals – not teleportation. Oh, my God, does my head hurt. There's no way I can concentrate on putting things back with it thumping like this. I need a drink – but definitely not ale."

She squeezed past a chest of drawers to stare out the window. The glass was so covered in dirt that she could barely see through it.

"Where can I get some fresh water? It's not as if we have any mountain streams around here. And I don't trust the water in the normal rivers."

No, maybe I can go to a mountain instead.

She teleported outside the cottage not even bothering to check if anyone was around. The late afternoon sun was bright and warm on her skin.

Where's the nearest mountain? Wales? Scotland? How high are the peaks in the

Peak District?

"Hell, my knowledge of my own country is absolutely pathetic. And all this just for a drink of unpolluted water."

She shaded her eyes from the sun and thought, *Wales. I vaguely remember going there on holiday with Mum and Grandad. When was that? I couldn't have been more than about five or six. Wasn't there a little railway or something going up a mountain? How can I find it if I don't know where it is?*

"Wait. The map – can I still see the map inside my head? Or was that just connected to the portals?"

Shutting her eyes, she tried to recall how to bring the map up. At first, nothing happened but then she became aware of the shape of the cottage as a grey shadow against a dark background. The building grew to become more substantial. Around and beyond it, trees appeared like gossamer tangled webs that stretched into the distance. She turned westwards and tried to locate mountains – but the Norfolk landscape was flat for miles.

She tried to bridge the distance by flying over it. Perspective shook and it was as if the tens and then hundreds of miles had become condensed. Just as she had done when she'd sought out the portal in that tower at Pinebanks, she was flying over a shadowy model of the landscape. Below her were foothills and, ahead, rose the mountains of Wales.

A line of mist tumbling down the flanks of one caught her eye. Desperate for a closer look, she was wrenched bodily from Norfolk to find herself standing physically on the mountainside. Between patchy grass and bare stones, a stream hurtled towards the lower slopes. The transition of exchanging the warmth of a summer sun with the equally sunny, but far colder heights, induced shivering.

"I'm going to freeze if I stay here too long."

Kneeling, she dipped her hands in the icy water, cupping a handful to her lips. It was delicious.

By the time she'd repeated the action twice more, her teeth were chattering. She teleported back to Norfolk.

"Woah," she gasped, materialising beside the cottage. "That was something else, but I'm still hungry."

Dinner for Two

Facing north towards Norwich, Cassie conjured up the map again. Identifying the mound upon which the castle sat, she scanned to its east detecting the activity in Kett's camp. The cooking fires flickering in lighter grey reinforced thoughts of food so intensely that, suddenly, she was there.

Appearing in the afternoon light in her twenty-first century clothes elicited screams from a crowd of people. Immediately turning invisible caused them to scatter in all directions, and the shouting increased in intensity.

Shit, what am I doing? Am I losing control over it?

But that moment of visibility had allowed the cooking scents to reach her senses and she felt even hungrier.

Better try again later.

She moved forwards in time but, even close to nightfall there were still too many people around.

Another hour, maybe, she thought, moving forwards but, at ten o'clock, she hit something. *Woah, what happened there? I can't go forwards. Something's stopping me. Can I go back in time?*

There were no issues moving back to just before the midnight of the day before. Hunting around, she spotted a few tables from which meals were still being served. She approached the least crowded, materialised and grabbed a full plate before anyone noticed her clothing.

Materialising back inside the cottage a second after she'd left, she sat on the bed and, lacking cutlery, shovelled the food into her mouth with her fingers. It was a mixture of beef and stewed vegetables. *Still no potatoes.* A few minutes later, as she licked the metal plate clean, she knew it was nowhere near enough.

Need more. Glancing at the sixteenth-century clothes on the floor, she thought, *Don't need to change – I can stay invisible.*

Returning to the camp an hour before her previous visit, she picked a table further east that was laden. There were also around a dozen tankards of ale waiting to be drunk. Forgetting she was still invisible, she grabbed at a plate, her fingers sinking through the plate, its contents as well as the table.

Whoops – I could feel it but not pick it up properly. I forgot I need to be fully visible to grab things. Like when I tried to stop Fulke's club hitting Sheffield. Weird, the ground feels solid enough under my feet, though.

To Cassie's frustration, more people arrived and helped themselves to much of what remained on the table. As soon as they turned their backs, Cassie became visible, grabbed one of the last two plates and, on the spur of the moment, a full tankard as well. Then she was back at the cottage.

Chicken or turkey, I reckon – definitely not beef, she thought.

After polishing off half of it she raised the tankard to her lips.

"Ugh. No," she groaned as the smell of the fermentation hit her nostrils. "Wait – I know…"

Teleporting back to the welsh mountain stream, she tipped the contents of the tankard out onto the ground before refilling it with water and returning.

"Ah, that's much better," she said, after taking a sip, though the odour of the ale still hung around the tankard. She finished off the second meal and drained the rest of the water before it had a chance to warm up.

With the meal finished, she could no longer put off the reason for her return.

"So, how on Earth do I undo everything?"

She rubbed her stomach, procrastinating. "Not doing anything on a full belly. I need a proper plan."

Covered in one of the musty blankets, Cassie lay in bed for over an hour trying to figure out the best way of undoing all that she had done. But nothing concrete occurred to her no matter how hard she tried.

"My family are depending on this," she told herself. "I've got to get it right."

Think, you idiot, think. The last thing I did of any significance was save Lord Sheffield. Does that mean I've got to go back and change things so that Fulke's butchery will succeed once again? Oh, poor man, poor Edmund. I'll be taking away his chance of a longer life to save the lives of my own family. Is that fair?

"Sod it," she grunted.

I'd just be putting it back as it should have been. That can't be wrong, can it? But I've got no real plan on how to do this.

"Damn it, I can't just sit here doing nothing – I've got to try something."

She jumped off the bed and stripped off her modern clothes, donning the stolen garments in their place.

"At least I shouldn't scare people this time. Okay right, let's do this. When did Sheffield originally die?" Cassie's mind dredged up August the first. "Oh yeah, that date again. But what time? I should have taken notes."

Cassie teleported to Bishopsgate in the early afternoon of the first day of August. She held herself invisible, appearing about seventy-five yards from where she remembered Sheffield standing when he'd been cut down. There were signs of the battle but it was still too early, and Sheffield's injured horse was not in the ditch beside the road.

Her built-in calendar told her it was around two o'clock so she moved forwards in ten-minute increments. At just gone two-fifty she was zapped forwards by twenty minutes. Sheffield's horse lay dead but neither Sheffield nor Fulke could be seen and the battle had moved nearer to the Cathedral.

What the hell happened there? How did I miss everything?

She tried to go back to witness her saving of Sheffield but was pushed back to around two-fifty instead.

Still invisible, she watched Sheffield's cavalry ride in from the direction of Palace Plain but, before he'd engaged the rebels, she was pushed forwards once more to around fourteen minutes past three.

Several more times she tried to place herself within that twenty-minute window without success.

Shit. I can't get at it – what the hell's happening? Something's stopping me every time. It's as if time itself is cutting me off from my previous changes, preventing me from changing things back to how they should be. This is getting worse by the second. Oh fuck, fuck fuck – what on Earth do I do now?

Domes

Cassie hopped back to July and the cottage, and tried to think things through.

"This is July the fifteenth," she said, consulting her calendar. An idea pinged into her head. "Can I go to the same date and time in some other location? Better not try it here in the cottage in case someone else turns up."

She hopped to the woods where she'd first tried the clothes on. Then she moved forwards until she reached ten minutes to three on the first of August.

And waited in real time.

The time crawled to the top of the hour and then a minute past.

"So, it depends on the location," she said, frowning. "I wonder…"

Calling up the map, the buildings were once again isolated dark shadows against a grey background. In between them, the wispy ghosts of trees filled the gaps. Concentrating on Norwich itself, she flew above the map to see the city and the solid walls surrounding it on its southern and western sides. The mound of the castle and the spire of the cathedral rose high above the houses and the towers of the many churches that clustered around the centre.

Then, within the monochrome display of the map, something coloured green caught her eye before it winked out.

"What the hell was that?"

The portals had been like coloured points of light but this was different. Larger than a single point, it had been where she'd rescued Sheffield. But it was no longer there. She checked the time: fifteen minutes past three.

I need to replay that last bit – just the last two minutes. How can I make it… oh, it's doing it.

Amazed at her new, unexpected skill, she watched the map slide two minutes back in time – she could sense that the time displayed within the map was thirteen minutes past three while, in her reality, it was now sixteen minutes past.

But her eyes caught the anomaly.

"I was right. There's something like a dome over where I rescued Sheffield."

It was around eighty feet in diameter and forty high. She thought it might be spherical with half of it hidden underground. But it wasn't green – viewed in normal time, it was more like it lacked any colour at all. She moved the map back several more minutes and could see that, when viewed in 'fast forward' or 'reverse', the dome took on a green tinge – the faster she made the map time go – the greener it appeared. She whizzed the map time back to before it appeared and then moved forwards again in slow motion. The dome didn't fade in slowly – one moment it wasn't there, the next it was. She confirmed it disappeared just as suddenly.

Moving back to when it first appeared, she continued watching at normal speed. Around the dome were pale wispy forms that flitted here and there above the ground. Some were larger than others and, often, one would fade from view. It took a few seconds before she realised what they were.

These aren't ghosts. They're the map's representations of live people. Are the larger ones horses?

She approached until she was right above the moving forms.

It's like watching ghosts fighting. One fell to the ground and faded from view. *Or dead people,* she thought, with a shudder, realising the person had just died in battle. An unwelcome flash of the blood bath outside Magdalen Gates flitted across her mind.

Need to ignore them. Got to concentrate on investigating the dome.

She floated in front of it, even while she knew she was still standing miles away in that woodland. Reaching out her hand, she was surprised as her fingers passed through the dome's wall without resistance. But the dome winked out of existence as she went to move inside it.

Three-fifteen again. She willed the map back to five minutes to three and let it move forwards again in real time, floating inside where the dome would appear. Suddenly she was inside it – the light dimmed and turned green – *that* green. The inside walls flowed and shimmered, a mottled mixture identical to that in her dream when she'd been asleep inside Saint Augustine's swimming pool.

Does this mean the device has done this? But where is it? Is it here?

She tried to call out to it with her mind – but there was no response.

All around her moved the wispy forms of the people. Here within the dome, they looked more substantial and human. Occasionally, one seemed to flow right through another, and even right through her, just as Kett had done when he'd cooled her off at the castle. But, these caused no drop in temperature. Cassie tried to figure out what was going on.

At the dome's centre, she saw a large horse-like shape collapse and a smaller human shape detach itself to stand upright.

Sheffield.

The number of human forms around him grew dense as if several things were happening simultaneously. She lost Sheffield's form in the confusion.

Moving the map back a minute, she concentrated on a human form close to Sheffield. *Fulke.*

But his form split into several and another slightly greener form also appeared multiple times. It interacted with some of the Fulke-forms and that of Sheffield as well.

Me, Cassie realised. *I think I must be watching all the different timelines taking place at the same time. Everything's overlapped. How is that even possible?*

It all became a bit much for her. She closed the map down, finding herself still in that small wood. She sat down on a fallen tree trunk.

"So, was the dome the thing that was preventing me getting in to change things back? But, it didn't prevent me seeing it within the map."

Then she remembered, when she'd gone to grab the food, she'd tried to move forwards to the evening and had been prevented from doing so.

Another dome?

She called up the map, setting it to the date she'd first arrived. Then with it playing back, she floated above it, watching to see if any other domes appeared.

They did. Moving the map back and forth quickly she found she could sometimes spot a quick flash of green if she happened to be looking in the right direction. It took several attempts to run through the forty-five days between the fifteenth of July and the twenty-seventh of August. Then she realised she only needed to concentrate on the dates when she'd interfered with history.

There were six. The earliest was small and only existed for a few seconds when she'd first arrived and seen the field of dead bodies. The dome had covered both herself and the soldier who had spotted her and called her a witch. The second was at the house where she'd stolen the clothes from the girl. There, the dome covered the entire house for the two minutes it had taken for her to enter and then take the clothes.

The third dome was huge, covering a large area of the Kett's campsite, and was in place for nearly two hours, starting from just before she materialised and Fulke grabbed her bottom and ending several minutes after she'd left the Oak of Reformation for the second time that night. It then reappeared the following day, centred again upon the tree, but far smaller in size and lasting less than ten minutes. This was when Kett had discovered her reading the grievances and she had taken him to witness the battle. The next was where Sheffield was dismounted and the final one was the few seconds on the twenty-seventh of August where Kett had seen for himself the outcome of the original battle.

Anger is an Energy

Cassie shut the map down and opened her eyes, surprised to find the shadows lengthened.

"Oh, my God. How long was I in the map?"

She checked – the time was nearly eight – several hours.

Teleporting back to the cottage and July, she tried to work out what had caused the domes to appear. But, she knew what they signified.

"They're preventing me from going back and fixing things," she said, sitting on the edge of the bed, unable to stop the tears running down her cheeks.

And I know what that means. It means I'm never going to see my friends and family ever again. My family no longer exist and my friends don't know who I am.

"Fuck it," she screamed. "Fuck Kett and everything. Why the fuck didn't I stay where I belonged?"

She howled her eyes out for several minutes. As the howls turned into whimpers, a growing urge that started with a niggle and developed into anger and then into a full rage came to dominate all her emotions.

She sat up.

"Someone's going to pay for this," she hissed. "If I can't put things back as they were one way, then I'll have to find another way. There are still plenty of times when I'm not restricted. I've got to stop his victory any way I can."

An idea formed in her head and, a second later, she was gone.

Cassie approached the Adam and Eve pub. It thronged with rebels celebrating their victory. Flaming braziers and torches illuminated the night.

"Well, he did invite me to come along," Cassie muttered, remembering Kett's speech in the marketplace of the evening of August the twenty-seventh. It was now nearing midnight that same day.

She barged her way past many who were worse for wear, looking for anyone who might still be capable of coherent speech. The stink of ale and worse was all that greeted her.

"Where's Kett?" she shouted.

Whispers of 'Wolf girl' came from the crowd and one of the serving girls pointed towards the pub entrance before hurrying away.

Cassie pushed past more people, aware that their eyes, at least the eyes of those that weren't completely addled with drink, were upon her.

Nearing the door she flinched feeling a hand upon her shoulder.

"Not in there, Wolf Girl," a voice close to her ear said. "I know where he is."

She slapped the hand away and spun around to see a man smiling. It wasn't a face she recognised. She took two steps back but the man raised his hands indicating he meant her no harm.

"Where?" she hissed.

"Round the back. Come. This way. He's been waiting for you."

"He'd better be," she snapped.

"Follow," the man said.

She was led around the side of the pub, away from both the crowd and the light. A couple of men, apparently drunk, staggered arm in arm behind her.

Leaning against a tree in what, in her time, would be a floodlit car park was a huddle of figures. Now, the only light came from the crescent of the moon, plus what little filtered around the corner from the main merriment. Under the tree, the faces of the men there were hidden. The man she'd followed beckoned her to come closer. She did, warily.

"Ah, Wolf Girl," said a voice. Cassie didn't recognise it until the man stepped forward allowing the pale moonlight to illuminate his face.

"Fulke," she said, stepping backwards, only aware at the last moment that someone was behind her.

"Now," Fulke shouted.

She started to teleport away but she was too slow. The blow to her head rendered her unconscious.

Flight

Winter Hunter

It took Cassie's leg another two months before it was healed enough for her to join the foraging parties. The scars, while still visible, no longer pulled on the skin around them and, though her progress was slow, she pushed herself more each day. She also made a concerted effort at improving her athletic skills.

If I encounter another wolf I need to have the advantage.

By the time of the winter solstice, she could run with the best of the tribe. Many in the tribe permitted her to join in the hunts, though mainly for the exercise. Only Za'Lak refused, claiming that she would bring them bad luck. He also objected to her not participating in the actual kills.

Three weeks into the new year the weather changed and snow began to fall. At first, foraging meant digging into the snow to find the remaining edible roots and tubers still in the ground. But, once the snow had begun to drift and then freeze solid, sealing off parts of the forest, change was forced onto the tribe's method of procuring adequate sustenance. While the cold allowed the meat from earlier kills to be preserved for longer, the remaining supplies were dwindling rapidly and the portions at each meal were shrinking.

By late January, with the winter showing no signs of relenting, Cassie was experiencing persistent hunger first hand, and she hated it.

I'm almost skinny, she thought, examining her arms and feeling the lack of fat around her waist. *I really am turning into Kay. I could do with her black outfit, though. These skins let too much of the cold in.*

When the snow entered its fourth week, the food situation became desperate, with occasional fights breaking out between tribe members over the enforced rationing. Za'Lak, turning even nastier than ever, suggested turning Cassie and Ka'Tor out of the tribe as, in his opinion, neither did their fair share of the tasks. He was shouted down by Em'Dor and his own daughter, El'Po. But Cassie could see that hunger was leading others to wonder if he might be right.

I really must get Ka'Tor and myself away from here at some point. But when?

It was already noon the next day when Ka'Char returned to the cave, shouting, "Tracks. Deer. Hunt now."

As had become custom he, along with most of the other men, had arisen before dawn to scout for possible prey. Hunting in pairs, they wanted to track the animals down before they had a chance to start moving on at first light.

Cassie, busy bringing scavenged wood inside the cave to dry, wanted to join them. With hunger gnawing at her stomach, the handful of fire-dried meat that had been breakfast had been far from enough.

We need to eat. If something has to die for that to happen, then it has to die.

Very few hunts had produced kills and the effect upon the tribe's health was beginning to make itself felt. El'Kek had fallen ill and despite the ministrations of her daughter, El'Po, she was wasting away. Za'Lak accused Cassie of putting a spell on her. Pe'Kat was exhibiting similar symptoms. Even much-needed warmth and a decent meal might allow them both to see the spring in.

Ka'Char's announcement had raised several of the women. Cassie saw Em'Dor, El'Ra, El'Pak and Em'Jex arm themselves with spears and knives and go to join Ka'Char. Decision made, Cassie retrieved her weapons.

"Ka'See hunt," she said to Em'Lo who was waddling around with Em'Dor's younger daughter, Oh'Sep, in her arms. Oh'Sep was partly perched upon Em'Lo's pregnant belly, which was so huge that twins were predicted. Cassie couldn't help noticing how thin Em'Lo was. If they didn't hunt down a decent meal soon, it wouldn't just be El'Kek's health that would be at risk.

"Kill many deer," Em'Lo said, resting her hand on Cassie's arm. "Make Za'Lak see you not curse us."

Cassie nodded and followed Ka'Char and the others into the forest where they met up with Ka'Char's hunting partner, Ko'Tek. In places, the tree cover had prevented the snow from accumulating but, in the more open areas, especially near the stream, the drifts had piled up, preventing easy traversal of large swathes of the woodland.

Once located, the deer tracks were already more than an hour old.

"Six," Ko'Tek said. "Two young."

The tracks headed downhill, splitting after a couple of miles. Amongst the deer tracks, Ka'Char pointed out the prints of a larger carnivore.

"Wolf," said Em'Dor, her eyes seeking Cassie's as she spoke.

Cassie shuddered but nodded, agreeing to carry on.

Ka'Char determined that the wolf had followed three adult deer in one direction. He split the party, taking Ko'Tek, Em'Jex and El'Pak with him, leaving Em'Dor, El'Ra and Cassie to the remaining adult and two juveniles.

El'Ra took the lead and, several minutes later, they entered an area where the tree cover had excluded most of the snow. Tracking became much harder.

"Here they rest," El'Ra said, examining the spoor. "This way."

Twenty minutes later Cassie grimaced as her foot snapped a twig. While her progress was almost silent, something she would have been incapable of achieving only a year ago, she was sure she would never be able to drift noiselessly through the forest as Em'Dor and El'Ra could.

It's like following ghosts.

What little sunlight managed to penetrate the canopy showed that the sun was already heading towards the horizon. Cassie's stomach protested once more.

El'Ra raised a hand and Em'Dor and Cassie halted. El'Ra's fingers pointed to a stand of denser trunks ahead of them. Without speaking she indicated for Em'Dor to move to the right of the trees and for Cassie to remain where she was. El'Ra took a path to the left and Cassie gripped a spear in her right hand, the other two in her left, ready.

She watched as Em'Dor and El'Ra encircled the target, her eyes ready for any sudden movement. El'Ra's shout startled the animals and one of the young fawns, about two-thirds the height of an adult deer, bolted from between the trunks to be met by Em'Dor's spear. The animal screeched and fell lifeless. Em'Dor, running forwards with a second spear ready, stopped to wrench the first spear from the fallen deer's body. As she did so the second fawn made an appearance, leaping to one side and escaping at speed.

One down, one escaped, Cassie thought, keeping as still as possible.

Then the adult – a female – launched itself from the hiding place, with El'Ra in pursuit. Seeing Em'Dor the doe veered in Cassie's direction. Belatedly noticing her, the animal tried to change direction. But it slipped on the icy ground, tumbling over, its feet catching in some dead brambles.

Sorry. I wish I didn't have to do this, Cassie thought springing forwards, aiming. Almost without thought, the spear was out of her fingers, flying true towards its target. She turned her eyes away, not wishing to see the results of her actions. The unearthly screech made Cassie want to gag but, with her spear embedded in its flank, the deer struggled to its feet.

Damn, it's still alive.

Cassie ran forwards, a second spear in her right hand, her knife in the other.

Shit, shit, shit. I've got to kill it. Can't let it escape. We need to eat.

But, to her relief, El'Ra had caught up with the animal and plunged her spear into its other flank. With a sigh, the deer crashed to the ground.

The meal that evening was their largest in weeks. Ka'Char and his team had also run down two of the adult deer.

"Wolf chase other off and kill it," he told them.

Another team of hunters that included Pa'Tay and Ka'Thon, had ambushed and killed a boar. Along with the deer, it was being roasted over one of the five fires lighting up the night outside the cave entrance.

Cassie delighted in sneering at Za'Lak whose hunt had produced nothing.

A few days later the temperature raised itself above zero for the first time in weeks and the thaw began. For several days the stream was a wild torrent as the melt hurtled down to seek out lower ground. But the warmth had returned too late for El'Kek. Cassie had to witness another burial in the depths of the cave.

Afterwards, Za'Lak raged for days and tried to blame Cassie for his partner's death, claiming her blue eyes had brought the snow and ice down upon them in the first place. Many defended her but even El'Po started avoiding Cassie.

Bloody primitive idiots. I wish I could time travel again and get away from here.

Morning Star

By Ka'Tor's third birthday, signs of spring were beginning to appear and the hunts were more fruitful. Even Pe'Kat, though still weak, was able to raise himself from his bed and hobble around, aided by his partner, Em'Kell.

Then, just before dawn broke one morning in mid-March, Cassie's eyes spotted a point of bright light just above the horizon.

"Venus," she muttered, a shiver running down her spine. "Shit."

"Ka'Tor," Ka'Chull announced. Standing over her, his bulk blocked the feeble glimmer of early morning spring light. He was holding a bowl.

"What?" Cassie said.

Ka'Chull placed the bowl in front of her and she could see it contained paste. "Blooding," he said, a grin plastered across his face.

Oh shit, Cassie swallowed. *It's finally going to happen. No, not if I can help it.*

"No," she shouted, pulling on her crude skirt as she got out of bed.

Having tracked Venus for over two months, seeing it rise higher each morning, she had been questioning Em'Dor and others about other tribes in the area, with a view to escaping with Ka'Tor. But, the other tribes were days away and she had no idea how to reach them.

I could probably find my way to the Valley Tribe but would they take me somewhere else? Do any of the tribes around here not do face scarring?

With no answers to her questions, she'd started to hope that Venus would start its descent and the associated danger would retreat.

Ka'Chull's presence with the bowl dashed that hope to shreds.

Ka'Tor was still in his bed, which rested next to hers in the shallow cave floor depression that Cassie used for their combined sleeping arrangements. He watched apprehensively, his eyes darting from one parent to the other.

Ka'Chull's shadow still blocked the light. "This day," he said.

"Wolf says no," she spat, putting on her necklace.

"Yes, this day. Wolf not scare me."

"Why today?" Cassie snarled, placing herself between Ka'Chull and her son, who had started to whimper. "He young. Too young."

"Is time," Ka'Chull retorted. "This day. Morning star bright. Sun rise soon."

"No," Cassie whispered. "Ka'See tribe not cut face. No cut Ka'Tor."

"This day," Ka'Chull repeated. "Not Ka'See tribe. My tribe."

Cassie shuddered, picturing the torture Zo'Mar had suffered on his blooding two years previously. The pus had oozed for days after El'Kek had lanced it but the wound had eventually healed and Zo'Mar had returned to full health. With his pain a distant memory, he even seemed proud of his scars.

But El'Kek is no longer with us and El'Po is not as experienced as her mother. If the same happened with Ka'Tor, would he even survive? No, I can't let them do this.

"No," Cassie spat. "Not today. Never."

Ka'Chull casually pushed Cassie to one side and scooped Ka'Tor from his bed. The boy screamed as he was carried off.

"Stop," Cassie screamed, running after them and pulling at Ka'Chull's arm. Turning, he swatted her across her face with his free hand. She tumbled backwards, falling hard onto her rear, her left cheek stinging. The cord of her wolf-teeth necklace snagged on something and snapped. Ka'Chull laughed as he strode out of the cave with Ka'Tor held securely under his arm.

She sprung to her feet and grabbed her obsidian blade along with a spear. Rushing out of the cave, the volume of Cassie's angry roar surprised even herself, but more than shocked all the others getting ready for the ceremony.

"Drop Ka'Tor," she shrieked, brandishing her spear at him. "No cut."

"Ka'See, no," Em'Dor implored as several others gasped. Za'Lak, arming himself with a spear, wore a smirk on his face.

Ka'Chull, his face darkening with anger, pushed Ka'Tor into the arms of his brother, Pa'Tay. Ignoring Cassie's spear, he strode towards her, his teeth bared. Many in the crowd were shouting for her to stop.

Like fuck, she thought. *I've got to disable him. I don't want to kill him, do I? Maybe I do. Bloody ignorant caveman.*

Ka'Chull tried to grab Cassie's spear but she feinted to one side and back again, attempting to stab him under his arm. He batted the point to one side but she swung it low, aiming it at his left leg. Stabbing forward, she felt it catch in the skin of his upper thigh.

With a roar, he wrenched the spear from her grip and snapped it in half over his knee. Then, as Cassie unsheathed her knife, he threw one half in her direction. She managed to deflect it, but its splintered end grazed her arm.

"You cut," she screamed, waving her knife at him, "I kill you."

He advanced, his eyes tracking the circling obsidian blade.

He's too big. How can I win against such a great ape?

Like the wolf that had attacked her, he sprung at her. But, gritting her teeth, she dropped low, rolling sideways while simultaneously thrusting the blade towards his ribcage. Ka'Chull howled as the blade sliced a shallow gouge in his side. But it failed to stop him and he twisted around in the opposite direction. Cassie tried to duck again but he smacked her around the head with one hand while snatching the knife from her grip with the other.

She rolled with the punch, using the momentum to tumble away from him. Regaining her footing, she circled around, finding herself close to Em'Jex.

"Ka'See, not do this," Em'Dor cried as she ran up to Cassie. "Is Ka'Tor blood time. Must be done. Star in morning say so."

"Fucking shut up," Cassie snarled in English.

Ka'Chull slung her knife onto the stony ground. Picking up a rock he smashed the blade to pieces and then lobbed the rock at her.

"No," Cassie cried. She grabbed the flying rock and swung it back at Ka'Chull, catching him on his arm. He roared yet again and the shouting was taken up by the rest of the tribe. Even Em'Dor was screaming at her.

Em'Jex pulled her knife from her belt but Cassie snatched it out of her hands before pushing her to one side. As others advanced upon her, she saw Za'Lak raise his spear, preparing it to launch it at her.

Oh shit, that bastard's really got it in for me this time.

She slung Em'Jex's knife at him, surprised to see it stick in his stomach. Dropping his spear, he fell to his knees to pull the knife from his belly.

"Fuck the lot of you," Cassie shouted in English, pushing past Em'Dor who sought to block her way. "I've had enough of your stupid primitive shit. I fucking hate you, Ka'Chull, you bastard and all you other morons, especially you, Za'Lak. If I can't stop you, then I'm definitely not staying around to watch you mutilate my son. I'm out of here..."

She turned her back on them and ran.

"...forever," she screamed.

Bare and Bear

Cassie ran towards the light of the rising sun. She ran amongst the tall pines whose top branches were bathed in direct sunlight hundreds of feet above her head. She ran to put as much distance between herself and the tribe, and what they were doing to her son.

She ran for miles. She ran further than she would ever have been able to before finding herself with the tribe. Despite running until her legs felt as if they would collapse beneath her, she forced herself not to stop. Even with her scarred left leg burning like fire, still she ran.

She refused to stop, even when her breath, ragged and uneven, scorched her throat. Gasping, she descended into a valley, the sound of rushing water reaching her ears. She turned in the direction the noise was loudest and, reaching the water's edge, collapsed onto her chest.

The water sped past no more than eighteen inches below her nose, hurtling over stones as it descended into a larger valley lost in the lower slopes. She plunged her hands down into the clear, icy flow and scooped several handfuls into her mouth. A similar river located in Wales came to mind.

After her thirst was slaked, she lay on her back, staring upwards through the canopy cut by the occasional beam of sunlight. She had no idea how far she had come. She might even have been lost for all she cared.

I couldn't watch it. I couldn't watch them scar him. I should have been there for him. But I couldn't remain and see them cut him, hear his screams and do nothing about it. Oh God, I hope it was over quickly.

She stood, testing her leg to make sure she hadn't caused further damage.

I'll never be like them. I don't want to be like them. Fucking primitive idiots.

Facing back the way she'd come, she muttered, "Now what?"

She listened but could detect no indication that she had been followed. The only sounds were birdsong and the rush of the stream.

I was expecting some of them to come after me. To try to take me back or kill me.

"I wouldn't have gone back. They would have had to kill me. Maybe that would have been for the best. I've lost everything and everyone – my mum, Grandad, Georgia, Ka'Tor. Even Em'Dor was screaming at me by the end. Why the fuck couldn't they see what they were doing was wrong? Morons."

With tears running down her cheeks she faced the stream. Like the one that ran past the tribe's cave, it was narrow and, even though it flowed faster, she knew it would be easy to cross. Gathering up her excuse for a skirt, she lowered her legs into the water. It was icy cold and was no more than six steps to the other side. But, halfway across, she turned upstream and walked in the water instead.

If they try to track me, this should hinder their progress.

After a couple of hundred feet, the cold began to numb her legs, so she crossed to the far side. Hauling herself out onto the bank, she refused to look back and carried on towards the sun.

Still hot from running, it didn't take long for her legs to dry. After a couple of miles, she came to another stream. It was wider and deeper, its flow far less energetic. A narrow avenue of clear sky followed its path down the mountainside as its width prevented the tree canopy from fully enclosing it.

She stripped off her skirt, bundling it up around a large stone before hurling it across the stream, the weight of the stone allowing it to reach the far bank. Then, naked, she dived in and swam to the other side.

At least being here has finally taught me how to swim properly.

She hauled herself out and sat in a patch of sunlight to dry off.

Maybe it's time to head downhill and locate another tribe. Not the Valley tribe – they are too close. They know too many of my tribe.

"No," she shouted. "They're no longer my tribe. Not after today."

Not far from the bank she found some edible mushrooms. After washing them in the stream, she ate them one by one, savouring the tang as each slid down her throat.

The sun was now a lot higher – mid-morning.

How far have I come? How many miles? Is it enough? Was it worth it?

"Oh, Ka'Tor," she sniffed. "I'm so sorry I failed you."

Before resuming her flight, Cassie looked back towards the west seeing nothing but identical vertical trunks. Towards the east, the view was different. The nearer tree trunks were a monotonous spread of vertical lines but those beyond broke that pattern. Some leaned as if they were tipping towards the lower ground. She stood and picked up her ragged skirt, decided against putting it on, and walked towards the angled trees, intrigued. While most tipped in one direction, others were still resolutely upright and a few were leaning at random angles.

What on Earth happened here?

She picked her way past increasingly damaged pines, reaching a boundary. Behind her was the still-living pine forest – before her was wreckage. Clumps of dead splintered wood, bleached white by the sun, lay between boulders that had been ripped from the torn earth. It was as if a huge bomb had exploded. To her right, the land sloped down to the tree line less than half a mile away. Piled up against them were the remains of trees that had once occupied the land in front of her.

To her left, further up the mountainside, there were no trees at all. Ahead, across the devastation, she struggled to make out where they resumed.

Stepping out from under the last of the standing trees she entered the devastated area. The eerie atmosphere that enshrouded it became more intense the further she went. The constant noise of birds and other animals under the canopy was absent. Only the light breeze induced the occasional whistle as its eddies navigated the uprooted obstacles.

Beneath her feet, the softer ground of the forest had been replaced by harder compacted earth and uprooted clusters of rocks and stones. She continued out into the desolation. Here the ground alternated between patches of shattered rock and sandy stretches. The latter were far easier to navigate and she followed the path of a wider one. Not too far away was the remains of a fallen tree that hadn't rolled downhill.

Sitting on the trunk, she tried to take in the enormity of what she could see. Despite the eeriness of her surroundings, the sun was warm on her face, shoulders, arms and legs.

I know what caused this. It can only have been one thing. Fire in the sky. This is where it hit.

The trunk upon which she sat had been stripped of its bark. In places it was blackened, charred from the fire that had resulted from the meteorite's impact.

If this had come down directly on top of the cave, it would have killed all of us.

She shut her eyes. *Maybe that would have been better. I wasn't supposed to wake up at all.*

Once again, the tears that streamed from her eyes were impossible to halt. *Oh, Grandad, Georgia. Will I ever see you again? Mum, Mummy, help me.*

She howled and punched the wood of the trunk with both fists.

What did I do to deserve this? Oh, Ka'Tor. How could they? How dare they? Why can't I escape? Why can't I time travel? Mum, Grandad.

For how long she sobbed, she wasn't sure. The sun, warming the world, rose higher as noon approached and Cassie knew the deed must have been long completed. Her son was now scarred for the rest of his life.

Tears still running down her face, she slid from the trunk and laid down upon a patch of smooth sand using her rolled-up skirt as a pillow. The warmth of the sun bathed the whole length of her body.

I can't go back. I don't want to go back. I hate them. If I can't go home then I'd rather die here. Maybe if I shut my eyes, I won't ever wake up again.

It was only when she felt something wet on her face that she realised she'd fallen asleep. Opening her eyes, she screamed seeing a dark, furry shape inches from her nose.

The bear, reacting as shocked as she was, backed off. Cassie scrambled to her feet, jumping over the tree trunk to face the animal.

It's young, she realised. *It's barely half the size of the one that bit Ko'Lak's arm off. Dangerous, though. Mustn't turn my back on it. Mustn't run. Got to make it more afraid of me.*

The bear, now about ten feet away, stared back at her, uncertain what to do. Cassie knew she had to get the upper hand. Glancing at the ground nearby, she selected several large jagged stones, placing them in a row on the trunk. The bear remained where it was, observing her. Wishing she still had her spear and knife, she gathered more stones, arranging them on the trunk alongside the others, all within easy reach.

Now would be a good time to be able to teleport again. Can I do it?

Cassie tried both teleportation and time travel – either would have done. Nothing.

I'm probably going to be killed.

The bear took a step towards her. She swallowed.

Maybe that's the best thing. If I can't get home… if I'm never going home then let's get this over and done with. Damn it. I don't want to spend the rest of my life living in caves watching morons mutilate the faces of babies.

"Come on then, bear. Make it quick," she shouted.

The bear halted and then backed off at the sound of her voice. She screamed at it and it retreated a little further.

Not enough.

She screamed once more, but the bear didn't move so she raised her arms and shook her fists at it. This time it moved back another couple of feet.

"I don't know who's more afraid, you or me," she whispered.

The bear moved again, this time coming closer.

Oh, Hell. Am I going to die out here? What if I don't get killed but just get badly injured or permanently maimed instead?

She swallowed and picked up the two largest stones, one in each hand.

Do I really want to die?

There was a rumble from the bear's throat as it approached.

Cassie raised one hand, ready to throw the stone. The bear hesitated, looking at her raised hand, and then roared.

"Fuck off," she screamed, hurling her projectile.

Much to her surprise, the stone caught the bear just above its eye and it halted. Cassie chucked the second stone, which nicked its ear as it bounced off its skull. Gathering up several more stones, she jumped on top of the trunk, screaming, hurling the stones one at a time.

The bear, seeing multiple projectiles hurtling towards it, turned and loped off down the hill towards the undamaged woods. Cassie hurled several more, which all fell far short but she continued to make noise, which kept the bear on the move.

After more than ten minutes, the animal reached the ragged tree line where it stopped and stared back at her. Raising itself onto its hind legs, it leaned on one tree that stood damaged but far from dead. Then it dropped back down onto all fours before disappearing into the forest.

No, Cassie thought, *I'm not meant to die. I have to... stay dangerous. What does that even mean?*

The Source of Nightmares

Crush and Burn

Agony pulsed through Cassie's head, neck and shoulders. Something, blood possibly, dripped from her nose, but there was nothing she could do about it. Her feet were bare, her toes dragging along the ground.

"Lemme sleep," she muttered.

Hands under her armpits denied her the sleep she craved. Instead, they dragged her closer to the flickering torchlight that illuminated the base of a towering shadow. For a second she wondered if she was inside her map again. There was something familiar about the shape of the building but the throbbing in her temple prevented coherent thought. Cassie closed her eyes hoping for a return to darkness but it failed to materialise.

"Where we goin'?" she mumbled. For an answer, hands shoved her forwards and her cheekbone hit a metal railing.

"One more," said the man on her right-hand side.

Shouting was accompanied by the clunk of a key being turned in a lock, followed by the squeak of protesting hinges.

"Back, scum," barked another voice.

Cassie opened one eye for a moment to observe a sword being rattled provocatively through the bars of a gate. The shadows on the far side backed away and Cassie was thrust inside to join them, the gate clanging shut behind.

"She's falling, catch her," came a woman's voice. She felt more hands on her. "Is that blood on her head?" the same voice added, as the hands prevented her from collapsing fully to the ground.

Why won't they let me sleep? Must sleep...

An unknown time later she regained consciousness, still propped upright. The bodies pressing on all sides left no room to fall down.

Familiarity clicked in her head but before she had a chance to figure out why, blackness overcame her yet again, and she welcomed the oblivion. But it didn't last long enough.

"Please, there's no more room," she awoke to hear a woman cry. She wasn't the only one as, all around her, men and women were shouting and crying.

Oh God, my head feels like I've been hit by a steam roller. Where am I?

The gate was unlocked once more.

"Back, or you'll feel the prick of my sword," grated a voice.

Her vision, blurred and distorted, failed to make out any detail of the surrounding crowd. The only things she could see were the flickering flames of the torches beyond the metal gate.

The crowd around her moved as one, away from the light. Caught in the human tide, the pressure of bodies intensified.

In Cassie's mind, familiarity reared up again and, this time, it became a certainty.

"No, no," she muttered. "Cow Tower. Really happening. Not a nightmare. Oh fuck, oh hell…"

She was unable to stop herself from hyperventilating, sucking more air into her lungs than her body was allowing to escape. The scream that finally erupted from her lips pierced the night and, like an infection, was taken up by many of the people trapped around her.

Got to escape. Must teleport… must… must…

But, the pounding in her head prevented compliance and the effort had the opposite effect. With her body still trapped upright, her mind escaped instead.

When she next awoke, Cassie was wedged even tighter, and barely able to breathe because of the crush. But when she did manage to gasp the shallowest of breaths, the stench of blood, piss and filth regaled her nostrils and she swallowed to prevent herself from throwing up.

She tried to move her left arm but it was pinned between two other people.

Around her, some were groaning, but most were silent. Above her head she could just make out the underside of wooden flooring, barely illuminated by the distant torches. In her time, the ground floor of the tower looked right up to the sky. In 1549, it was still an intact, working building.

The face of a woman rested on her shoulder. The woman's flesh was cold against her skin. She looked down to see the head of a young boy, his nose buried in her stomach. Her right hand, trapped between his body and hers felt the clamminess of what might have been one of his arms. If that was his arm – and she was far from certain – then he was as dead as the woman.

The ground beneath her bare feet was damp, the mud or worse clinging to her toes. Behind her left shoulder, the sound of trickling liquid was followed by a warm sensation down the back of her legs.

Oh, God. Cassie closed her eyes. *Must teleport. Must teleport. Got to get out of here. Just a few yards.*

She concentrated, gasping foul air in and out of her lungs.

It's not happening. It's got to happen. Please let it happen.

She gritted her teeth and, finally, felt the process start to kick in.

Now. Got to get away, now.

Suddenly, the air and sound changed. The press of bodies was gone but, without their support, she collapsed. Her hands, numb from being constricted in the crush, hit loose stones and a dusty track. Her remaining breath was knocked out of her and, for a moment, she felt unable to inhale. It was almost as if she had forgotten how to breathe.

Her body was racked by a bout of coughing, which forced some air back inside her. Each intake of air caused pain in her ribs but, after a few minutes, she was breathing normally once more.

She had no idea where she was. Opening her eyes she found herself under starlight.

"When is this?" she muttered, but her calendar didn't want to work. She attempted to pull herself to her feet. But her head spun causing her knees to give way and she crashed back to the ground. The urge to vomit returned and she convulsed, bringing up bile and what remained of her last meal.

Once the retching was over, she wiped her face on her sleeve and looked around. Her eyes focused on something. It took her a few seconds to recognise the shape of Cow Tower more than fifty yards away, with the glow of torchlight escaping from one side.

I made it out.

She heard footsteps getting closer.

"Help," she cried weakly as the feet stopped beside her. "Help me."

"It's her," came a voice. "He said this might happen."

"She's covered in shit," another voice said.

"Ugh, sick too. Smell it, I can. Help me pick her up."

"Urr, he'd better pay extra for this."

Hands under her shoulders hauled her to her feet. But the movement made her head spin and she passed out.

Cassie's eyes opened to see stars for a second time. She wasn't certain whether they were real or existed only inside her head. She was lying on her back surrounded by twigs and smaller tree branches. Beyond them several fires burned, their flames dancing on chalky pale rock walls further away.

Three men, whose faces wouldn't come into focus, were adding more wood to the pile upon which she lay. She concentrated on one face as, despite the blurriness of her vision, there was something familiar about his profile.

Realisation dawned. "Fulke," she gasped.

His face came closer and she managed to bring it into focus. But he wrinkled his nose and backed away.

"Witch stink," he hissed, as a smirk crossed his face. "We knew you had to be a witch. Only a witch would survive that blow to the head and escape the tower."

She tried to move but her arms, legs and body were bound to the tree trunk upon which she lay.

"Now we will see if you escape from this. The Lollards were burned here and now we will burn you, Wolf Girl. It will be a pleasure to watch a witch burn."

Lollards pit? Oh no. First the tower, now the pit. It's all coming true.

Cassie screamed, which made Fulke retreat, his face betraying his fear of her. She struggled against the bindings for a moment but stopped as Fulke ordered the men to torch the kindling that surrounded her. They touched their torches at intervals to the wood which, being dry and brittle, took the flames immediately. Cassie screamed again as the fire joined to encircle her. Though the flames were still a foot away, she could already feel the heat increasing.

Got to teleport again. Now, NOW, NOW!

She concentrated.

Damn it, my head won't stop pounding. Can't think straight.

Panicking, she struggled against the ropes with an equal lack of success.

It's not going to work. I can't stop panicking. I need to calm down. But how the fuck can I calm down when I'm about to be burned alive?

An image popped into her head. It was of Laurence waking up after having been tied up by white-haired Kay in the old Norwich library.

"You're not getting out of those ropes that easily," Kay had said.

"You think so?" he'd calmly replied.

"I know so."

"Oh, really? Watch."

And then Laurence had disappeared, leaving the ropes to fall to the floor.

Oh, he was so calm and sure of himself. I need to be like that right now. It might be my only hope.

She gritted her teeth as flames began biting at her feet and legs. Despite the growing heat, she tried to ignore them and force herself to relax.

"Ow," she shouted as pain licked at the skin of her left foot.

Got to be now or never.

She did her best to disregard the heat and the flames, and to relax into the state of mind she hoped would initiate the teleport.

Calm, calm – concentrate. Got to...aaah!

She gasped as searing pain tore up her leg.

But, it was the impetus she needed.

With a snap, she was free of the ropes. Instead of being pinned to a tree trunk at night, she dropped onto the ground outside the cottage in daylight.

"Aaah," she screamed, sitting up and clutching at the burn on her leg, flinching at the further pain touching it caused. She examined the afflicted area carefully, grimacing at the blistered skin on her ankle.

Too fucking close, she thought, as tears – a mixture of pain and relief – cascaded down her cheeks. But her relief was soon replaced by the knowledge that she had failed yet again.

"Now what the hell do I do?"

Recuperation

"I really need to sleep," Cassie told herself, but she knew she wouldn't be able to sleep with the waves of agony pulsating up her left leg. Not only that, but she knew she stunk, and it wasn't only just the smoke from the fire.

"Need to wash myself. Not in any river around here."

Back at home, she would have run the injury under a cold tap and then had a hot bath.

But home doesn't exist and this cottage doesn't have running water. No, but Wales does.

She gritted her teeth, concentrating, and the cold of the Welsh mountain atmosphere hit her.

Thank goodness it worked that time.

She lowered her foot into the icy waters of the stream and gasped as the sting of the burn was replaced by the shock of the cold. She could only take it for around ten seconds, but it was enough to take the edge off the pain. She hoped the numbing effect persisted long enough for her to sleep.

But I still stink. Oh my God, this is going to be freezing.

Stripping off her clothes, she swilled them in the water and then used her knickers like a flannel to wash the rest of her body. Then she dipped her hair in the stream and gently massaged where the club had connected with her skull. The bump was prominent with blood oozing where the skin had been broken.

Having rinsed herself down and, with teeth chattering, she wrung the clothes out, hoping that she'd removed the worst.

Seconds later she crashed back onto the bed at the cottage. Slinging the wet clothes onto the floor and, with her head still throbbing, she slid herself underneath the woollen blanket.

Before falling asleep, she consulted her calendar – Wednesday, August the twenty-eighth, it confirmed.

Oh, the day after Kett's battle. Why didn't I return to July?

When Cassie awoke, her head still hurt and her leg stung. It was pitch black and, for a moment, she panicked imagining that the blow to her head had somehow resulted in blindness. But, consulting her calendar told her it was around three in the morning of the twenty-ninth of August.

She lay there trying to get back to sleep but achieving little more than a few minutes dozing here and there. Every time she unconsciously moved her left foot, it resulted in pain lancing up her leg, fully awakening her once more.

The first light of dawn creeping into the room woke her from a shallow, restless sleep. Outside, the chorus of singing birds, more raucous than any limpid twenty-first century version, prevented any further attempts at sleep.

By the time the sun fully illuminated the room, the rising heat forced her into sitting up. She leant back on the headboard, eyes shut, unable to do much more. She was glad there wasn't a mirror – knowing she'd be horrified at what might peer back at her.

"Need to eat," she told herself as the middle of the day approached. But she had no appetite and her head was like that time she'd caught the flu. Her brain may as well have been stuffed with cotton wool, for all the constructive thoughts it was able to conjure up.

By late afternoon she was still far from being hungry, but she was desperate for a drink of water.

Haven't drunk anything for ages, she realised.

Lying on the floor was the tankard she'd brought back from the camp. Inching herself off the bed, she attempted to stand but her head swam and she had to hold onto a bedpost to prevent herself from tumbling over.

The tankard, once she'd regained enough balance to retrieve it, was dry and dusty. It took her a few moments to remember that she'd last drunk from it halfway through July, even though, to her, it had been less than two days ago.

Back to Wales again.

After dressing in her modern clothes, she sat on the floor and closed her eyes, preparing herself for the cold as she returned to the welsh mountain. This time the mountainside was merely cool and bathed in bright sunlight. She crawled to the stream, dunking the tankard in several times to quench her thirst. The water, while still cold, was far from the icy shock she'd encountered before. As she drank, she dangled her left foot in the water. It was cold enough to reduce the stinging pain but not icy enough to chill to the bone.

Returning to the cottage, she dried her leg off gently using another of the blankets from the chest.

Finally, she was beginning to develop an appetite.

Cassie checked her calendar. It was still the eighth of September – the same as it had been when she'd checked it earlier. She'd been in the cottage for ten days. The bump on her head had gone down, and the headaches and dizziness had receded, though she still had quite a bit of neck pain.

She examined her ankle and leg. The skin, while still tender in places, had mostly healed. The burn had left a ruddy splodge that curved from the front of her calf around to end just below the ankle. A few scabs still remained

"I'll be full of scars the way I'm going," she muttered, trying to force herself to sound cheerful.

It wasn't working. She knew she was procrastinating. Apart from stealing food and, occasionally, some milk from farms in the area, she had done nothing to alleviate her situation, to figure out a way to repair the damage she'd caused.

Will anything I do just make things worse? Is it worth even trying?

She sighed. She was becoming depressed and lethargic, unable to come up with any concrete solution that suggested a positive pathway through her problems.

I need advice – to speak to someone who understands all this. If only I hadn't lost the disc. The device would have known what to do, wouldn't it? But now there's no one left – the version of Robert Kett here is now the wrong one, and the domes are cutting me off from undoing what I screwed up.

Cassie could feel the emotion building up into tears.

"Damn it," she shouted. "I've cried enough – it doesn't help at all. But I just can't think of any way to undo all the shit I've caused – and I daren't do anything more in case I just make it worse."

But what could be worse than losing my friends and family? Fuck – I wish I'd never let Kett talk me into coming back here. What would he say to me if I told him that letting him win would kill my family? Maybe I should go back to 2019 and tell...

"Oh," she said. "Is that what I have to do? Would he listen? Could he somehow undo it? Will he even still be there?"

Well, if he's not there then I haven't lost anything. But if he is – and if there is a chance he has the answers, then I've got to try it. I'm doing nothing here. I'm no good to myself or Grandad.

Her mind made up, she changed back into her normal clothes.

2019, she thought, and disappeared.

Haunt Me No More

Cassie sat at the top of Kett's Hill, exhausted. This third enforced halt had prevented another impending blackout brought on by the effort of traversing so many years. She pondered what might have transpired if she had fallen unconscious whilst time travelling.

Did that knock on the head do me any permanent damage? It was never this bad before.

Here in 1846 there were few buildings to be seen. The terraced houses that would line the hill and the adjacent roads had yet to be constructed.

She checked her leg. The scabs on her ankle itched a bit and her feet were filthy. Having lost her boots after being struck on the head, she hadn't managed to locate any suitable replacements and, with no money – at least none that was legal tender until she reached at least 2018 – she couldn't buy new ones.

Maybe I'll have to steal some, she thought, which evoked a memory of her outburst to Kay. "I have NEVER stolen anything, EVER."

The sun setting in the western sky cast a ruddy glow over the hill. In this time, Kett's Heights was overgrown and wild. Below her, standing prominent across the river, was the Cow Tower. Even at this distance, it made her shiver.

Now I know why I feared that place – that and the Lollards Pit pub.

She frowned.

But how come my younger self had nightmares about it before I'd even been trapped there? Can memories travel backwards in time?

She stood up, still feeling weak but determined to reach 2019 in only one more hop.

"Here we go again," she whispered, gritting her teeth.

To her, it felt like struggling against a hurricane, but she pressed on. As she passed 1999, she moved in space towards the castle. Her head started pounding again and she had difficulty controlling both the time and direction.

Suddenly, it was 2019 and she was months past the February date she'd first departed. Not only had she overshot in time, she'd also missed the castle pathway.

Finding herself in mid-air above the castle gardens, which were located in what had once been a moat, she panicked. Even before she had fallen as much as a foot, an automatic reaction kicked in and she teleported safely to the ground.

"Damn," she gasped, collapsing onto one of the wooden seats opposite the brick-built stage of the Whiffler Theatre. "That's never happened before. Am I pushing myself too hard?"

She checked her calendar – it was a Sunday in late May at just gone six in the morning. Her unexpected appearance up in the air and subsequent auto-teleportation meant she'd materialised fully visible. She looked around, relieved that no one had been about to witness her appearance.

The day was already warm, the gardens abloom with flowers. Gazing at the array of colours put her in a better frame of mind.

Feeling her heart rate was back to something resembling normality, she stood, about to do a short hop back up to the level of the castle.

"No," she said to herself, "let's go the safe way."

She walked under the arch of the bridge which carried the castle's gateway above the gardens. Coming back out into sunlight, the heat of the path on her bare soles was slightly uncomfortable but it wasn't that which caused her to halt. Movement on the lawned area to her left caught her eye. To her amazement, a couple of wild rabbits were lazily hopping around, plucking and chewing grass. She watched them for a few moments and then ascended the steps that led up to the gateway. Several more rabbits disappeared into the undergrowth as she reached the upper pathway.

I had absolutely no idea there were rabbits living here, she thought. *I've never been up here at this time of day before.*

She turned left towards the bridge.

"Right, let's find Kett," she said, keeping to the paved part of the path that encircled the castle keep, the gravel sections being too uncomfortable. Kett had often turned up as she'd walked along the path but, after two circuits, he remained absent. She stopped where he had brushed the tangles from her hair.

"Kett," she said. "Are you here?"

There was no answer.

"Come on, show yourself. I need you."

She waited for a few minutes before starting another circuit, calling out his name every few yards.

Maybe I need to go back to before he convinced me to time travel to 1549.

Materialising on a drizzly February day her calendar said was the fourth, the drop in temperature was a shock. The pathway was cold and wet under the soles of her feet. She moved forwards a few days, then a few more – the ghost of Robert Kett was absent in all of them.

Okay, how about the exact same day I left? It was the twenty-fourth, and somewhere between nine and ten, wasn't it? I must have been talking to him for about fifteen or twenty minutes. Will my earlier self be there this time?

She moved forwards to the spot where Kett had convinced her to go back to 1549. But neither Kett nor her earlier self were present. Her only companions were birds and the noise from the occasional bus as it trundled along Castle Meadow.

"Shit," she spat once the time reached ten. "What about the future again?"

She moved forwards, keeping herself in place and only moving in time, stopping every few days when it was devoid of people to see if Kett was around. Spring was replaced by summer but Kett remained absent.

While circuiting the castle, she had received several glances at her feet. She made a point of avoiding eye contact with anyone who stared at her.

I really must get some shoes, she thought. She pulled her wallet from her jeans pocket. *At least that still remained in her possession.*

Inside it, she counted out more than eighty pounds.

It's now all the money I've got in the world. More than enough for some trainers.

Standing at the point where she'd waved to the barrow boy in 1912, she watched the traffic. Her calendar told her it was Monday the twenty-fourth of

June and the temperature was heading for the twenties. With the time just gone nine in the morning, the noise of the vehicles passing below felt like a small snippet of normality.

I need normal back in my life. But I won't achieve that until I manage to fix history. If I can...

She watched the traffic for a while longer, allowing her mind to switch off for a while, though it seemed she had no control over it.

Stop procrastinating, you idiot. Go and buy some shoes.

With the city already quite crowded, Cassie knew she wouldn't be able to teleport without anyone noticing, so she walked instead.

The Disc

Twenty minutes later found her on Gentleman's Walk wearing a new pair of trainers that had set her back thirty pounds. Passing Hay Hill she took the incline to the Forum and entered the Millennium Library. An idea had come to her while buying the shoes.

Pulling her wallet out she extracted her library card. About to book a computer, she stopped.

Oh, wait – I don't officially exist in this timeline. My card isn't going to work.

She decided not to risk even attempting to use it. Instead, she sought the history section of the physical books. Locating three dealing with the right period, she carried them to a table.

Twenty-five minutes later she had her answer as to the lack of Kett's ghost.

So much for his rebellion then, she thought.

All three books had confirmed that he had, indeed, won the battle in August 1549, holding Norwich for several more weeks. But the King had ordered Warwick, along with several other nobles, to raise a huge army to mount an even stronger counter-attack. Robert Kett, along with his brother William, had died defending the city at Saint Benedict's Gate in early October. The rebellion, whilst it had lasted a few weeks longer in this timeline than her own, had eventually been utterly crushed. Of Lord Sheffield's fate, there was no mention.

Checking other volumes revealed no changes from the history she remembered from school. While she couldn't recall exact dates for each British monarch, everything else appeared normal. The nineteenth century was dominated by Queen Victoria, and the world wars of the twentieth had progressed as before with the same outcome.

So why was my family wiped out?

Returning to the shelves, shoving each book into its designated slot, she thought, *I really must find the disc. I don't think I have any other choice.*

Exiting the library, a thought struck her and she halted outside the revolving door.

"Wait," she said aloud. "I know when it must have been taken."

"Excuse me," a man said, "but you're blocking everyone. Could you please get out the way?"

She turned to face him and, with a smile on her face, said, "Okay, if you insist."

And disappeared.

I've got to be right, Cassie thought as she hurtled back through time. *It's the only possible explanation.*

"Hell, can't this process go any quicker?"

Once more, her head began to throb intensely as the years flashed past. She was forced to slow down as a bout of dizziness hit her. Managing to cling on until it was night, she dropped back into reality, collapsing onto the ground, gasping, as soon as she materialised.

"Too quick," she whispered.

Before her rose the tower of the St Peter Mancroft church. Behind her, in darkness, were buildings demolished long before the old library had been built. A few candles could be seen flickering at the occasional window.

Her calendar dragged up the year – 1740.

Less than two hundred to go, thank goodness. I can't keep this up. At least the place is deser...

She heard a noise behind her. A rush of footsteps was accompanied by a blade held against her neck.

"Giss yer purse, girl," demanded a voice close to her ear.

"Fuck off," she screamed, elbowing the hidden assailant in the ribs, before disappearing.

Damn, that was close.

This time she moved only in space, heading out to the location of the cottage. The tangle of bushes and brambles that surrounded the ruins proved too thick for materialisation. She was shifted several yards to appear at a spot where only grass grew. A short distance away to her right a newer building showed flickering lights in two of its windows.

That's not there in 1549. Okay, slow down girl. It will still be there...

Before she resumed her backwards journey, she realised she'd forgotten the date she'd first appeared there.

I'm losing track. Think, girl, think. I went back more than a month after seeing the field of blood. It was the same date that earlier me and Kay appeared with the motorbike.

"Fifteenth of July," she said. "Wasn't it?"

After resting for several minutes she concentrated and pushed further back in time.

"I'm here," she whispered, looking up at the standing but still dilapidated cottage. Dawn was only minutes away.

She teleported up to the room, remaining invisible. The door was shut and the mattress was still rolled up on top of the larger wardrobe.

Now, I remember hiding invisible in the passageway outside after I first discovered that the disc was missing. I need to avoid that version of me. Where can I hide this time?

She squeezed herself behind the larger wardrobe, leaning on the wall. Then she slipped forwards in time until a voice saying, "Now where?" startled her back into visibility. As she materialised, a floorboard beneath her feet creaked.

"Who's there?" came a voice.

That's me – I've shot past when I first came into the room.

She didn't dare breathe.

"Damn it, now I'm spooking myself," came her voice from across the room.

Hell, I really was spooking myself, after all.

She waited until first Cassie left and then moved back ten minutes, hearing footsteps outside the door. After two more minutes, the door was shoved open.

"I don't ever fancy sleeping on that," came her voice from the opposite side of the room.

Cassie waited for her earlier self to wrench the door of the small wardrobe open. Priming herself, and listening for the clunk of the jacket and disc to hit the floor, she teleported inside the wardrobe as soon as its door was slammed shut. Stumbling in the darkness inside, she caused the whole thing to shake.

Oh shit, that was me, as well.

Trying to make no sound at all, she reached for the earlier version of the jacket she was already wearing and, with relief, her fingers enclosed the disc.

Finally, she thought.

Dangerous

Cassie teleported back two weeks and also moved several feet sideways to materialise in the room across the upper landing.

"Shit," she shouted, staring at the disc. "Why do I have to make things so difficult for myself? If I hadn't done this, my later self would have found the disc without any problem… I think."

The terms *cause and effect* and *causality* popped into her head.

"Wait, does that mean the cause happened after the effect? Am I creating yet more paradoxes? Oh hell, I have no idea what I'm doing anymore."

With the disc resting in her hand, she positioned a finger over the button.

Will it work this time? Oh, please let it work.

She shut her eyes and pushed.

The button depressed with a solid click.

"How did you do that?"

The metallic voice grating in her head caused her to jump back in surprise. Her trainers skidded on the wet leaves and she barely managed to stop herself falling over.

She gasped, seeing the device hovering in the air before her.

"Oh, thank God you're here."

"What is that you hold?"

"Huh? It's the button. The disc thing you gave me," she said.

"I gifted you no such contraption," it replied, its voice vibrating with annoyance.

"But you did. It was in my pocket after you left. No one else could have put it there."

The disc was wrenched out of her hands and floated in the air, bathed in a green glow, two inches before the device.

"Hold... scanning... decrypting..."

"What are...?"

"Be silent."

"Look, I'm sorry..."

"SILENCE!"

"Okay," she whispered. *Hell, it never acted like this before. Even when I pissed it off by forcing it to create the portals.*

The green glow shut off and the disc fell to the floor.

Cassie went to pick it up.

"Leave it. It has accomplished its purpose."

There was a flash and the disc disintegrated into dust.

"W-Why did you do that?"

"Evidence of all temporal anomalies must be erased... including your boots."

The boots that had been taken from her appeared on the floor before disintegrating just as the disc had done.

"No – they were good boots."

"They had no further purpose."

"Why?"

"Cassie Fox. You are a paradox wrapped in an enigma. You are more dangerous than even I originally suspected. And yet, you are destined to become far more dangerous."

"What do you mean?"

"You were correct. The disc with the button came from myself. But that gifting will be performed in my future."

"I don't understand."

"That much is obvious. But my future self does. And that is a paradox that I am being compelled to perpetuate. For your timeline to be restored, indeed for your whole life to exist, which is a required part of the puzzle, my future self has been forced, via the information stored in the disc, to instruct my earlier self – the me you see before you at this time – along a route that ties both of our pasts and futures together."

"What? Damn it, I don't understand. Don't you ever make any sense?"

"No, and, at this time, you do not need it to make sense."

"Why?"

"Because of what needs to come next."

"Look, I have no idea of what you're talking about. But, I think I've somehow broken time or history or something."

"Yes, you have and you, too, are broken. Damaged."

"Huh?"

"I detect recent cranial injuries. Concussion. Hold still."

Cassie was bathed in a green glow, which made her head fuzzy. Afterwards, her head no longer throbbed.

"Oh, wow. Thanks. That feels so much better. But what about my family? I went back to 2019 and I no longer exist. It's like I was never born."

"Indeed. You are, as previously stated, dangerous. A danger to this entire world."

"Really?"

"Without doubt."

"Oh. Well… can you fix it?"

"Apart from some minor shielding…"

"Shielding?"

"Yes, the disc contained details of your interference. I have therefore caused the domes you have already encountered to appear."

"Why?"

"To prevent further corruption."

"Wait, you've just created the domes that I've already encountered. And you did that after I called you back using the disc? How is that even possible?"

"Your inability to understand the intricacies of timeline manipulation precludes providing a suitably viable answer."

"Hell, more total nonsense."

"Precisely, as I have quite plainly stated, you do not have the ability to comprehend such matters."

"Okay, but what about the rest? What about my family? Can you fix that?"

"No. I have neither the authority nor the capability."

"But, but…"

"But I can call on those who can."

"Oh, thank goodness. But, um, who exactly?"

"My creators."

"What? You mean…"

"Mean what?"

"Er, aliens?"

"By your standards, correct."

"Oh, will they look like proper aliens? Not just like some actor in a rubber suit?"

"Your questions are inane. However, they will appear in a manner for which your ocular apparatus is far from capable of comprehending without suitable enhancement."

"Ocular? What? You mean invisible?"

"No."

"Oh. Well, how long before they get here?"

"While they, like myself, can transgress space-time when needed, it comes at the expense of much energy expenditure. You have yourself seen how moving even a few hundred years is exhausting. But, the traversal of a few thousand years in time is cheap compared to kiloparsecs of distance. Performing both simultaneously is prohibitive."

"More gobbledygook. Just tell me how long it will take to call them."

"If I call now, it will take them several tens of thousands of your years to respond."

"Huh?"

"Therefore I must travel that amount of time into the past and call them from back then."

The device disappeared and Cassie was left perplexed for about ten seconds.

Then the device reappeared but something else began to appear alongside it. Cassie gasped, even looking at the whatever-it-was made her eyes water, as she appeared incapable of focussing upon it. If it had a shape, then her brain refused to acknowledge it. In her head, sensations manifested, accompanied by a noise like static coursing through her brain.

Then it stopped for a second, to be replaced by a multi-tonal screech that seemed to come from both the creature and the device.

"Ah, my head. W-What the hell is that?"

The noise stopped. Cassie tried to bring the creature into focus but it was as if her senses couldn't take it all in at once. She had to turn her gaze away to stop the nausea.

"I will translate," the device said.

"You mean that was talking?"

"Correct. A verdict has been reached."

"Verdict?"

"Indeed. Your alterations to the timelines in this sector have been deemed a criminal action."

"But you were the one who showed me how to do it."

"Correct again. The influence of the one latterly named Laurence in reducing the levels of safeguards within my construction, along with your subsequent interactions, resulted in you gaining information and abilities for which your species is not suitably primed. Especially those whose DNA is weaker, such as your mother."

"Oh, Mum. But she was only trying to save me from Laurence."

"It is likely I will be analysed and used to develop stronger security protocols."

"But what about me?"

"Termination has been recommended."

"W-What do you mean? Termination?"

"That is the verdict."

"You're going to t-terminate me?"

"I repeat. That is the verdict."

"You're actually going to… to k-kill me?"

"That was the recommended solution."

Cassie's heartbeat, which was already pounding, increased even further.

"B-b-but, don't I get a say in this?"

"Do you have any words of defence?"

Before she could reply, there was a noise from the alien. The device replied in a similar fashion.

While it was going on, Cassie eyes caught a movement in the far corner of the room. For a moment, she had the sensation that three people were standing there. Then she blinked and the suspicion that they had ever existed was gone. Although she hadn't been able to see their faces, one had resembled the outline of Georgia, whilst another looked like herself. The third had been unrecognisable.

"What's it saying this time?"

"Shadows."

"What are you talking about?"

"It suspects there are shadows here. I replied that I detected no such thing."

But they were really there for a moment, Cassie thought. *Is it lying? Yes, I'm sure it is. How do I know? Just what the hell's going on?*

"Should I speak in your defence?" the device continued.

"Huh? What? Oh, yes, please. I don't want to be, er, t-terminated."

The noise went on for several seconds. Then there was silence and Cassie was aware that the creature was no longer present. She was alone with the device.

"What happened? Did it work?"

"I argued that terminating the lives of higher animals has long been considered immoral."

"Animals? Are you calling…"

"The verdict has therefore been reconsidered, as I knew it would."

"Uh, how?"

"The contents of the disc enabled a full preview of my interaction with both yourself and the creator who appeared."

"Oh. And?"

"You are still considered dangerous but my arguments were persuasive. Something I learned from both yourself and the various incarnations of your father."

Cassie sighed with relief.

"Oh, my God. Thank you, thank you. Will it put things – um, time – back as it was?"

"Indeed. It has already been done."

"My family are all back?"

"No."

"What?"

"They are not due to appear until the twentieth century. They will return then."

"Damn it," Cassie muttered. A memory of her mother saying 'You have to ask the right questions' appeared in her head. "So, why did me saving Kett and Lord Sheffield wipe out my family in the first place?"

"It didn't."

"But…"

"Apart from the lack of his ghost at the castle, his revised history had little impact upon either yourself or your family."

"Huh? So what did?"

"It was the boy you waved to in 1912. His name was, or will be, once he is born, Arthur Fox."

"Oh, my God. My great-something grandad. What happened to him?"

"Watch. I can simulate his altered timeline."

The room was replaced with a vision of Castle Meadow in 1912 as she remembered seeing it for herself. The point of view swung down to street level. It was as if Arthur Fox, gazing up to the battlements of Norwich Castle, was standing right beside her. He waved and Cassie saw herself wave back in response before disappearing. Arthur, frowning, took a step forward, unaware of the tram until it clipped him, hurling him backwards, flipping him onto and over his barrow. He crashed onto the cobbles of the road, clutching his right leg in agony as the vision faded.

"Oh no. Did he die?"

"No, although not fatally injured, his subsequent incapacitation resulted in being unable to fight in the upcoming war. Therefore, he neither met nor married Charlotte Rendell, preventing your great grandfather, Charles Fox, from being conceived."

"Oh," Cassie said, shocked that such a little thing could have had such devastating results. It made her wonder what other damage she might have caused. It was all too much. "Is that all fixed now?"

"Yes, the original timeline has been restored."

"Thank goodness," she muttered. "Can I go back home now?"

"No."

"What? But you said you got the verdict changed, didn't you?"

"Indeed. But, as previously mentioned, you are dangerous. I have been instructed to withdraw your ability to time travel. Also, I have been authorised to erase your memories and diminish your mental abilities. You will then be transferred a minimum of five thousand years into the past as well as to another part of this planet. As a simpleton, you will do no further damage. Your current personality will effectively sleep and Cassie Fox will never wake up again."

"WHAT?"

"That was the verdict."

"And you agreed to this?" she screamed.

"I will... have to comply."

Why do I feel it's lying again? Hold on, that thing it said a while ago...

"Wait. Earlier on you said something about tying our past and future together, didn't you? What future is that?"

"Because you will be projected into the past, to avoid contamination, you will be stripped of everything."

"You didn't answer my question."

"The process has started."

"No, please don't..."

But, to Cassie's horror, she found herself moving backwards through time. However, as if she had just stepped onto an express train, the centuries were hurtling past faster than the days had when she had been under her own control. And her built-in calendar had already counted the passage of far more than five thousand years. It accelerated to hit fifty thousand, and it wasn't slowing down.

"You lied," she screamed, as the number reached one hundred thousand years. She was being projected south- and eastwards away from England, across Eastern Europe to pass over the Black Sea.

Then, at around one hundred and thirty thousand years, her clothes were shredded away to nothing. As her ability to think began to do likewise, she heard the device one final time.

It said, "We will meet again. Remember, you are dangerous. You were never meant to wake up. But my future self has negated that and also instructed me to pass on one specific message to you. And that is: *Stay dangerous, Cassie Fox, stay dangerous.*"

Then, naked and with her head emptied of all coherent thought, she materialised in a pine forest. Her legs collapsed and she cried as her bare skin encountered thousands of soft pine needles that covered the forest floor.

Hauling herself to her feet, she gazed around. The exercise resulted in little reward, as she failed to make sense of not only *where* she was, she also had no idea *who* she was, either.

She knew only one thing for certain.

She was cold.

Circle Complete

Scar

With the sun past its zenith, Cassie, dressed in her skirt, the only clothing she still possessed, approached the centre of the devastation.

She stopped at the lower edge of a huge scar in the ground. Seventy to eighty feet in width, and twenty feet at its deepest, it was evident that something had come in at a low angle from west to east. But it hadn't stopped here, having churned a path that continued up the mountainside. Cassie tried to see where the scar ended but it was lost in the haze that enveloped the mountaintop.

"It could be miles away."

She tried to imagine what it would have been like to witness the meteorite landing here.

"That's odd," she said, observing how the scar travelled up the mountain. "Surely, it should have buried itself deep in the mountainside here. It's like it hit and then skimmed further up the mountain. Is that normal? Wouldn't it have just exploded instead?"

Oh, but what do I know about such things? Maybe the rock this mountain is made from was too tough for the meteorite to bury itself so it had no choice.

She ascended the mountainside walking alongside the scar. It grew narrower the further up she went and the treeline grew closer. As she walked, a sensation began gnawing at her that was both unexpected, whilst also familiar.

What is that? It's a bit like a mild version of being close to Cow Tower or Lollards Pit.

She remembered the nightmares from her childhood that had coalesced into terror after she'd gone on that ghost walk with Georgia.

"I never did find out where those..."

She stopped walking and frowned.

"Wait. I do remember. One of Fulke's men knocked me over the head. Then I was trapped in the tower. After I escaped, Fulke tried to set fire to me at the place the pub was built over."

Cassie felt dizzy and had to sit down quickly.

Oh, why is this happening now? All these memories flooding back. Didn't I go back home and seek Kett's ghost out? Yes, but he wasn't there.

"I remember now. I went back to 1549 and found the disc and pressed the button. Didn't I?"

Yes, I'm pretty sure I did. And the device turned up and then that thing... that alien or whatever it was, that I couldn't even see properly. And then...

"Damn it, I can't remember anything after that."

She stood up, frustrated, and continued to follow the scar upwards. After half an hour, the treeline to either side of the scar petered out, though this was nothing to do with the meteorite. She was entering a region too high for trees to exist. The air here was clear of the earlier haze and the view across the landscape was spectacular. She could see over the top of another peak to the west, one that wasn't high enough to attract a covering of snow and ice.

I bet the tribe's cave is down from that peak. Damn them, I didn't want to think about them ever again.

To the south were spread the mountains that she had observed almost every day since she'd arrived in this time. From the cave, only the nearest could be seen. Here, she could count twice as many snow-capped peaks, their tops still thousands of feet higher than the mountain upon which she stood. They ranged both east and west as far as Cassie could see. Those to the east were lower and free of snow. Halfway to those distant peaks, she knew the land dropped down to the plain where the Valley Tribe lived, but her current elevation hid all view of it. She suspected the sea also lay in that direction.

Despite the sun, the heat was being leached away, which made her shiver. Beside her, the scar was becoming narrower and, not far in the distance, it ended. Beyond it, the rugged mountainscape looked as it had probably done for generations.

Standing at the point where the scar ended, she gazed down at it. It was as if some giant had sliced into the rock with a massive knife.

Probably nothing left of the meteorite now, she thought.

"But there's still something that's definitely spooky. And it can't be me spooking myself this time," she muttered, remembering the room in the dilapidated cottage. "At least, I hope not... Or do I? If it's me then does it mean I figure out how to time travel again?"

She shivered once more but wasn't sure if it was the lowering temperature or the atmosphere of the place.

"It's going to get really cold once the sun sets. I'd better head downhill and get under some trees for the night. Find something to eat as well. I'd better rig up a new spear and maybe an axe if I want to eat anything other than roots and mushrooms over the next few days."

Oh hell, that means I'm going to have to kill something.

As she descended the mountain, this time coming down the opposite side of the scar, she picked up some flints, selecting them based on how easy they would be to knap into spear tips or axeheads. Once she reached the eastern tree line she carried three potential candidates. She entered the woods at a point where the meteorite scar was only about fifty yards from the treeline. As she stepped beneath the trees, she hunted for suitable straight lengths of branch to use for shafts. Given the damage, the choice was plentiful and she selected two lengths she was certain she could work with.

Further under the familiar canopy of branches, the return of the birdsong and other natural noises were comforting. Cassie encountered another small stream barely twenty yards into the forest. It was fast-flowing, icy-cold and deep in places.

I won't cross it, she thought, not wanting to be soaked just before nightfall.

Close by, she found a thicket, a small clump of trees and bushes, with a small defensible clearing within. There was just enough room to lay down. While it wouldn't keep out smaller animals such as rabbits or mice, it would be enough to make it difficult for the larger hunters to approach her without warning.

With the sun starting to descend she hunted out some edible roots and mushrooms, washing them in the stream before eating them raw. The stream also had some reed-like grasses growing on one side whose leaves were tough and fibrous. Cassie wondered if she would be able to pulp them, extract the fibres and then weave them into string.

If that works, I think I could make a fire lighter, if I can whittle some bits of wood into shape, that is.

After attempting to make the thicket more animal- and waterproof – not that she thought rain was on the way – she enclosed herself within her makeshift den and tried to find a comfortable position. But, the ground, while not completely solid, did not make a good bed.

Wish I had that backpack that converted into a cloak and a bed, she thought as darkness started to fall. But then her thoughts turned back to her son and tears flowed yet again.

I'm so sorry, Ka'Tor. I wish I could have stopped them. I wish I could have protected you. But Ka'Chull was too strong, Za'Lak wanted to spear me and all the others were against me as well.

Although she failed to get comfortable, the exhaustion from running and walking most of the day caught up with her. Before night had fallen, she had plummeted into a deep sleep.

Midnight Fire

Shouting awoke Cassie from a nightmare that had been dominated by people's skin being cut, punctured and sliced. But, these unknown characters were indifferent, happy to accept what was being done to them, while Cassie experienced all their pain for herself.

Sitting up quickly, her head brushed the branches of the surrounding bushes. Disorientated and forgetting where she was, she had trouble suppressing a squeal. It took her a few seconds to remember she was no longer in the tribe's cave.

The shouting came again. *That's definitely people – not animals. It's coming from where the meteorite landed, I think.*

Determined not to make a sound, she listened, trying to estimate how far away they were.

Hearing a voice she recognised, she gritted her teeth in anger. *That's Ja'Mutt. Bloody well leave me alone, you morons.*

But it was his call of, 'Ka'Tor, Ka'Tor,' that changed Cassie's mind about remaining hidden.

She pushed her way out of the thicket and, with her eyes trying to adjust to the darkness, she picked her way to the edge of the forest. Remaining hidden, she observed flames from three hand-held torches wavering in the distance. Another voice called.

That's Pi'Tut. Is Ka'Tor really here?

"Up mountain," came Ja'Mutt's voice again.

"Rocks move. In hole," came a girl's voice.

Em'Dor – it has to be. Why is she with them?

Cassie's emotions were ambivalent. Em'Dor had become such a close friend over the past few years. But the events of the previous twenty-four hours had severely damaged that friendship. Cassie knew she would never be able to forgive Em'Dor for her inability to see how wrong their so-called customs were.

The torches changed direction, moving up the incline.

Cassie crept out from under the canopy, stepping over several broken branches. She picked one up. It was very close to the shape of a club.

Just in case, she thought. *This could do quite a bit of damage if need be. Oh...*

She had another one of those déjà vu moments, remembering when she'd picked a log from the woodpile in Erin's garden just before she struck Jason over the head with it. *Yeah, that did some very necessary damage.*

Feeling slightly more confident now she was armed, she started to parallel the others, keeping close to the treeline, hoping they wouldn't hear her. But they were making enough noise of their own that there was little chance of that. She kept her eyes peeled for any movement just ahead of the hunting party.

Ka'Tor must be further up. Can I find him first and rescue him from them?

A sudden sparkle of light further up the incline was followed by what, to Cassie's ears, sounded like a shower of stones being thrown at the three hunters.

What on Earth was that?

There was a cry from Pi'Tut and one of the torches fell to the ground, extinguished.

"Ka'Tor, we not angry," Em'Dor shouted. "Not understand, but not angry. Spirits did it. Not you."

What are they talking about? If anyone should be angry then it's Ka'Tor and me for what they've done to him.

The two remaining torches converged on where the other one had fallen. A moment later all three were lit again and they resumed their upward motion.

Did Ka'Tor run away? How did he manage to get away from them? Has he been running all day and night? How can a three-year-old child evade such expert hunters?

Cassie, her eyes now acclimatised to the darkness, picked her way through the rocks. A thin slice of crescent moon gave enough light for her to make out the larger obstructions, though little else.

Maybe their torches will blind them to anything further away. Hopefully, they won't be able to see me at this distance.

For more than ten minutes she crept up the incline, keeping behind the level of the others to reduce the chances of them spotting her. Already the trees were thinning out on either side and she knew she would be even more exposed once she was above the tree line. Before her, the mountain appeared black while the sky was the merest shade lighter, though it sparkled with thousands of stars.

She heard stones moving some way ahead of the hunting party.

"He fall," Ja'Mutt said adding, a few seconds later, "He get up."

"He so fast," Em'Dor added.

He always was, Cassie thought. *I don't know where he got the energy from most of the time.*

"See him," Pi'Tut said. One of the torches parted from the other two as the bearer broke into a run. The other two did the same.

There's no way I can reach him first. But I've got to try. As far as I can remember there weren't too many obstacles when I came down this way earlier on.

Cassie decided to risk it, hoping she wouldn't trip over anything. Running as lightly as she could, she angled away from the last of the trees and towards the scar, aiming for where she'd heard the rocks tumbling.

That has to be him trying to escape them, she thought, spotting a movement against the just visible skyline. Increasing her speed, she crouched low as she ran, hoping not to be silhouetted against the stars. But her foot dislodged a loose stone and it tumbled, taking several others with it.

Shit. Didn't need that.

"Animal," Em'Dor shouted, waving her torch in Cassie's direction. "It hunt Ka'Tor."

They must mean me… or is there something else out here with us? Cassie slowed, glancing about herself but could detect nothing else moving. *Maybe they think I'm a bear or something. Good, if they hesitate, it might give me a chance to get to him first.*

She gripped the log, prepared to use it. Keeping her head low, she aimed in the direction she thought her son might be.

Is that him just ahead? It sounds like he's digging. Yes, that shape – it must be him.

She was about to call out his name when there was a flash and Ka'Tor was at the centre of it, his body silhouetted against a circle of intense brightness.

What the…? Cassie gasped, turning her face away. The glow was almost painful.

Down the incline, there were shouts from the others.

"No. Spirit wake," Em'Dor screamed. "Ka'Tor, spirit bad. Spirit kill Ka'Chull. No more kill, Ka'Tor."

What? Is she saying Ka'Chull is dead?

Cassie hesitated, wanting to know more.

"I hate you. You hurt me," Ka'Tor shouted. "Spirit thing hate you. Spirit not let you cut me more. Spirit friend. Spirit save Ka'Tor."

"Em'Dor, Pi'Tut, Ja'Mutt," Cassie shouted.

"Huh? Is Ka'See," Ja'Mutt shouted back. "Ka'Tor call spirit. Spirit call Ka'See."

"I here since day past," Cassie shouted back to them. "I run. Not want to see Ka'Tor cut."

"Oh, Ka'See," Em'Dor cried. She rushed up and tried to embrace her.

Cassie pushed her away. "Ka'See angry. Not want Ka'Tor cut. But you not listen to Ka'Tor mother. Thought you friend, You not friend. I run as can't stop cutting."

"You right," Em'Dor whispered. "Ka'Tor call spirit to stop cuts. Spirit come."

"Huh? What happen?"

"Ka'Chull make cut," Em'Dor said, pointing to her right cheek. "Ka'Tor scream. Ka'Chull make cut." This time she pointed to her left cheek. "Ka'Tor scream loud. Ka'Chull fall dead. Pa'Tay fall dead. El'Car fall dead. Pe'Kat fall dead. Many fall. I fall. Pi'Tut fall. Not dead but head fill with mad talk – spirit talk. Head hurts."

"Ka'Chull dead?"

"Yes."

"Why Pa'Tay? Why El'Car? Why Pe'Kat?"

"El'Car take Ka'See place," Em'Dor sobbed. "Pe'Kat, Pa'Tay hold Ka'Tor while Ka'Chull do cuts. Then all dead."

"Za'Lak?"

"Dead. Za'Lak bleed from knife you throw. Said only hurt little. But he die later."

"Oh…" Cassie couldn't help feeling guilty.

"After Ka'Chull dead, Ka'Tor run. Ka'Tor call spirit. Ka'Tor run like wolf, like deer, like bird, like wind."

"What is spirit?" Cassie whispered.

The glow surrounding her son was fading. It was no longer an intense white, but was changing hue first to yellow and then to a less blinding green.

Oh, fuck. I know that colour.

With his outline becoming clearer, she could see that he was holding something.

Cassie left Em'Dor, hurtling towards her son. "Ka'Tor, Ka'Tor, drop it. Danger."

Coming close, she could see where the incisions had been made. Halting, she saw how the blood still oozed from both wounds.

He didn't move. Facing her, his eyes locked onto her own, feeling as if they penetrated to the depths of her soul, an experience she had fought against only once previously.

She broke contact to stare at what his hands held. The black and green of its outer casing writhed: the device.

What are you doing here? she tried to say to it. There was no response. *You were the fire in the sky. Oh, of course. Now I know exactly when this is.*

She dredged up a memory of when the device had told her about its first owner after it had come to Earth. It had said, 'It was near-human. Your archaeologists refer to the species as Denisovan. Close enough to homo sapiens to allow interbreeding.' When she'd asked what year that had been, the device had responded, 'Approximately one hundred and forty thousand years ago.'

Oh my God. That means that I…

She held out a hand, "Give me, Ka'Tor. Please?"

"No," Ka'Tor snarled, snatching the device away from his mother. "Thing mine. Spirit talk to me. Not you. They cut me. Ka'See run. Ka'See not save Ka'Tor. Hurt lots. Kill them. Hate you all. Kill you all."

"Please Ka'Tor. That thing is dangerous."

He turned the device around in his hands and it opened up. Cassie's eyes clamped shut against the intensity of the light. She felt herself being enveloped and trapped within its rays as if they were solid.

"No," she tried to cry, aware that Em'Dor and the others had come closer. But the device had immobilised her.

"Go away," Ka'Tor shouted. "Thing is mine. Hate you. Not want mother. Not want father. Not want anyone. Only want spirit thing."

Unable to move, Cassie was certain she was about to be obliterated. *Is this how everything ends?*

"Go away," Ka'Tor yelled again.

Yes, I want to go away from here. I want to go home. Mum. Grandad. Please let me go home, Ka'Tor.

"Leave Ka'Tor alone. Thing is mine. MINE!"

As Em'Dor and Ja'Mutt tried to rush Ka'Tor, there was another flash followed by an abrupt sensation of disconnection. Floating in darkness Cassie thought, *Is this it? Is this what happens after death? Just an endless nothing?*

For what seemed like minutes, she floated in a kind of limbo. The impression that she had begun moving grew but, with no reference points in the darkness, she couldn't determine what sort of motion this might be. The sensation accelerated, accompanied by flickering on her visual cortex.

Am I still alive?

The flickering grew stronger.

Wait, I know what this feels like. Oh, can it really be happening?

More minutes passed before Cassie finally dared to admit to herself that she was hurtling through time.

How did that happen? Am I finally getting away? Oh please. Yes, and I'm going forwards in time – I'm sure of it.

But that wasn't all.

My calendar's back, she cried as the years fell away. She could detect that a hundred had passed, then a thousand. After a hundred thousand, Cassie found herself gaining control over the process. She could slow it down and speed it up.

Everything's coming back. I daren't stop. Got to keep going all the way home, all the way back to 2019. Oh God, I hope my family still exist. Am I really going to see my grandad again? Please… please.

As she transitioned into the final thousand years, she regained the ability to move in space. She pushed herself westwards crossing into Europe by 1290, reaching England by 1342, and then up to Norwich by 1363.

Passing 1549, she thought, *I never want to see that year again.*

Slowing as she passed 1900, she added, *No stopping in 1912, either.*

Passing the year of her birth, she positioned herself within the kitchen of the house she had shared with her mum and grandad. Tears of relief ran down her face as its décor matched her memories.

What was the date I left? Can I even remember? Ah, Erin's birthday party was on the twenty-third of February – a Saturday.

Slowing, she passed the date of the party and then it was Sunday the twenty-fourth.

I'm home, I'm actually home.

"Oh," she gasped as she materialised, seeing the shocked expression on her grandad's face. *I forgot to stay invisible.*

"Jesus Christ, Cassie, what's happened to you?" he shouted.

They both jumped at the sound of the front door slamming and the cup he had been holding dropped from his fingers, to smash on the floor.

Home

For a few moments they stared at each other.

"Grandad," she whispered. "It's really you? I'm actually home?"

"Y-Yes. But that was also you just going out," he said, a tremor in his voice. "You said something bad happened at the party last night."

Cassie found it weird hearing English outside of her own head for the first time in years, but she was just relieved that her past had been reinstated. It wasn't the only thing. All her memories, including what the device had said to her back in 1549, had returned as well.

He stared at her as she sank down onto one of the kitchen chairs.

"Cass," he whispered. "Just where on Earth have you been? And what are you... nearly... wearing?"

"Oh hell," she said, realising that all she had on was her animal skin skirt. She wrapped her arms around her chest, embarrassed about her near-nakedness for the first time in years.

"You promised," he whispered.

"I'm so sorry," she sobbed. "I really wish it had never happened."

"How long this time?"

She shook her head. "Something like four years, I think. Might have been more."

"Four years?" he gasped. "Really?"

"If I could stop it, I would. But I've just come from a hundred and forty thousand years in the past, and I'm absolutely exhausted. I know I really messed up but I don't dare try anything more."

"You might not," he said. "But what about me? What if I catch up with younger you and try to stop you?"

Cassie stared at him.

Would that even work? What will happen to this me, right here and now?

She looked down at herself, at her tanned skin, at where her muscles had replaced the fat of four years ago, at the mark on her left foot where Fulke had tried to burn her at Lollards Pit, and at the scars on her leg where the wolf's claws had raked her thigh.

If he succeeds, then this me will get wiped out of existence. All that crap I endured will be erased as if it never happened. Would that be such a bad thing? Maybe I will get the chance to live as I should have done, not as some primitive savage.

"Okay," she whispered. "Do it."

Her grandad nodded, saying, "Stay there. Don't do anything."

In the hallway, he changed from slippers to shoes, and grabbed his jacket and hat. Thirty seconds later she heard the front door open and close.

"So, what happens now?" she said to herself. "Do I wait until I just stop existing? What happens to all the stuff I interacted with in 1549? Oh, but that all got fixed, so it doesn't matter, does it? But what about back with the tribe? Well, at least I won't have to go through childbirth until I'm properly ready for it. So, Ka'Chull won't… get me into bed and Ka'Tor won't be conceived."

And then she frowned.

"Wait, if I don't give birth to Ka'Tor then he will never get the device and grow up to steal more bodies. He will never become Laurence. But if Mum never meets Laurence then I won't be born."

And didn't Mum say that Laurence was looking for close relatives? Something about DNA compatibility, wasn't it?

"Shit," she shouted, jumping from the chair. "I've got to stop him. If he talks me out of going back, then it will wipe out the whole family all over again."

She went to open the front door.

Hold on, this is 2019 – if I go outside looking like this, I'll get arrested or something.

Not knowing what to do she hesitated, her hand resting on the door handle. She heard footsteps outside and saw someone coming up the front path.

Panicking, she retreated to the kitchen. But the doorbell wasn't rung and, instead, she heard a key opening the lock.

She peered from the kitchen to see her grandad coming in. He shook his head.

"I saw you, earlier you that is, up by the shops. I called out but you ignored me and, suddenly, you were gone."

"Oh, thank goodness," Cassie said.

"What?"

"Look, I'll explain properly later but, while you were out, I realised that you stopping me would have made things worse. A lot worse."

"Really?"

"Believe me. It could have stopped all of us existing in the first place."

"You're sure?"

"Absolutely. Do you remember me telling you after all the portals stuff what the device said about where Laurence came from?"

"Oh yes, something about him being thousands of years old."

"That's right. Well, anyway, I went back to when he was born."

"Why on Earth did you want to do that for?"

"Didn't have any choice. I was sent back there."

"Who by?"

"The device."

"Oh, so that damned thing is back again, is it? And did you actually see him being born?"

Cassie paused and closed her eyes. Then she whispered, "Saw it, felt it, experienced it in its entirety."

"What do you mean?"

"Oh, Grandad," she cried, the tears bursting from her. "It's because I was his mother. I gave birth to him."

His mouth hung open, while he tried to digest the information. He didn't have much of a chance as Cassie threw her arms around his shoulders and sobbed. "Oh, my baby. I've lost my baby. I let him be cut. My baby turned into Laurence."

He led her through to the lounge and sat her down beside him on the sofa.

It took several minutes for her tears to subside. Then she said, "You know what I really, really want right now?"

He shook his head.

"A hot bath. I haven't had one in years."

"I really can't go back to school tomorrow, Grandad," Cassie sighed, trying to comb her hair in front of the hallway mirror. The smell of roast chicken drifted from the kitchen. It was nearly half-past two and she'd soaked in the bath for well over an hour before spending three hours in bed. After years of laying on animal skins and dried grass, it had been luxurious.

"Why not?" he said.

"It's been four god-damned years for me! And I look different, don't I?"

"Well, a bit thinner, maybe."

"Thinner? I had a damned baby, for goodness sake. These clothes don't fit me properly. Everything feels so wrong, especially the shoes."

"Wrong? What do you mean?"

"I got used to wearing animal skins, of being barefoot all the time," she said, trying to adjust her bra. "Even my tits are a completely different shape."

She pushed her face up close to the mirror. "My face looks a lot older. Yeah, weathered," she added, thinking of how Em'Kell had looked to her when she had first got her memories back. "Damn it – people are going to notice."

"Oh, come on, you don't look that different. I bet no one actually notices at all. Anyway, you can't drop out of school just like that."

"Why not?" she said, close to tears again. "I've almost totally forgotten what it was I was supposed to be doing there. How can I pretend that everything's normal?"

There was a noise outside the front of the house and Cassie froze, seeing a figure approaching the door through the frosted glass.

"Oh no, I can't let anyone see me like this."

The doorbell rang and Cassie recognised the fuzzy profile on the other side of the frosted glass. "Georgia," she whispered.

"Well, we can't leave her standing out there," Bill said, pushing past her to open the door.

"Hey, Cass," Georgia said. "How did it go last night with J–"

Georgia stared open-mouthed at Cassie.

Cassie looked at her grandad. "Told you," she said.

"Oh my God, what's happened to you?" Georgia said.

"Come into the lounge," Cassie said.

"You look… well, you…"

"Four years older?" Cassie said, sitting down.

"Four years? Oh no, not again. But you promised."

"Yeah, well, you can blame your nearly boyfriend for that."

"Mark?"

Cassie shook her head.

"No, not Mark, never Mark. I wouldn't imagine Mark ever… well… Let me rephrase that. How about my no-good, bastard-of-a-definitely-never-going-to-be-anything-other-than-an-ex-from-now-on boyfriend?"

"Huh? You mean… Jason?" Georgia said, looking horrified when Cassie nodded. "W-What did you mean by 'nearly boyfriend'?"

"An alternate timeline where you and Jason – a much improved version, I should add – well, you got it together. A timeline where me and Grandad don't exist and Jason's dad still does."

"What?"

"It's a long story."

"Even longer than last time?"

"Four years longer, I'd say. Oh, Grandad?"

"Yes," he said, his face appearing in the lounge doorway.

"Got enough chicken and stuff for another plateful?"

"Yes, of course," he said with a nod.

"This is going to take so long, you might have to stay for tea as well," Cassie added.

"Right, I'd better let Mum know," Georgia said, pulling out her phone.

There was a pop and another person joined them in the lounge.

"Got enough for four?" asked the newcomer.

All three of them gasped. It was another Cassie. But this one looked more like Cassie had done before she'd left for the picnic, her hair short and straight.

She grinned at them and said, "Right, this is where it *really* starts to get complicated."

Epilogue

6 December 2000

Patrick pushed open the door and caught Christopher's eye as the latter looked up from his paperwork. They both glanced up at the wall clock – it said thirteen minutes past noon.

"Late again?" Chris chuckled.

"Ten minutes-ish."

"Fifteen, more like."

"Yeah, sorry Chris," Patrick said, doing little to stifle a yawn.

"Enjoy your day off?"

"Day off? You're kidding me. It was more work than being here."

"Problems with the little 'un again, eh?"

"He's keeping us both up," Patrick sighed. "Elise reckons she didn't get any sleep last night, either. Barely got a couple of hours, myself. At least she's still got two months paid maternity left."

"Novelty's wearing off, then?"

Patrick sighed. "They don't tell you all the bad stuff, do they?"

"Nah, I remember when mine were small. No matter how much you're told or you read up, you're never prepared for the reality of it all. How old is little, er, Jacob now, anyway?"

"I keep telling you, it's Jason."

"Oh yeah, ha ha, sorry – Jason."

"Five weeks. Feels more like it's been five months."

"It will go past quick enough."

"So they say. Not sure I believe it. So, what's been happening?"

"You didn't catch the news, then?" Christopher said.

"What news?"

"He's in number seven."

"Who?"

"The guy with his head sliced off."

"What, really?"

"Yep, in broad daylight yesterday afternoon. Some mad motorcyclist with a sword. Happened right outside here on St Stephen's – in front of loads of people."

"Wow. Did they catch the guy that did it?"

"The last I heard was that he took the police on a high-speed chase down Grapes Hill and Dereham Road, and then crashed his bike in Earlham cemetery."

"So what happened to him?"

"Killed himself in the crash – what a nutter."

"We got them both here, then?"

"Nah. Just the head-sliced-off guy. No idea where the other one went. This one is bad enough – not a pretty sight – face all mashed up like something drove over it."

"Bloody hell. Number seven, you said?" Patrick said, looking at the list. There was only the date and time of arrival written in. "No name?"

"Wouldn't tell us. Actually, I don't think they know for sure. I'm calling him Horace."

"Horace?"

"Yeah, Headless Horace."

Patrick laughed, but it turned into another yawn.

Christopher continued, "I did ask the officer with the crew that brought him in if they knew his name. He said a witness had provided one and they'd found documents on the body but they didn't seem to match up properly with Mr Headless here – way too old for the identification or something. Though how they could tell from that mess, I've no idea. Anyway, not for us to worry about. The police want to take another look at him later on. You want to get him ready for that?"

Patrick snorted at the barely disguised order. For someone who worked in a mortuary, Christopher tried to avoid as much contact with dead bodies as he could. "Yeah, I suppose. Not before I get a coffee inside me, though. Didn't have time for breakfast."

"Hah, you'll get used to it in a year or twelve."

"Thanks."

"Right, I'm off for lunch. See you in an hour."

"Pick me up a sarnie, will you?" Patrick said, pulling a five-pound note out of his wallet and handing it to Christopher. "Oh, and a bar of chocolate – something to keep my eyes open."

"Ha ha. Okay, will do. Right, sweet dreams. You look like you need 'em."

"Yeah, don't I just."

Christopher donned his jacket and headed for the exit.

Patrick logged his start time details in the timekeeping book as a minute past noon – who cares, he thought, no one checks – and wandered off to make a much-needed coffee.

Once he'd returned and sunk a couple of hot mouthfuls, he felt a little more human. Sipping the rest, he flicked through the notes on the resident of morgue drawer seven. But there was little additional information, other than a sheet of paper indicating that the police were due to do a further inspection at half-two. He donned his thicker work jacket and went into the cold of the morgue to stand beside the drawer marked with a seven.

"Ok, Mr Headless Horace No-name. Let's see how pretty you are."

He slid the drawer out and, as the feet and legs came into view, Patrick could see that the corpse was still dressed in an ill-fitting suit. Presumably, these were the clothes he'd been wearing at the time of his unexpected demise. Separated from the shoulders by a gap of six inches, the head lay at an angle. Patrick inspected the cut.

"Well, that's a neat and tidy slice. Sorry, Mr H. Neat or not – there's no way that's ever going to get re-attached," he chuckled and then frowned. Christopher had stated that the face had been mangled but, while it showed a good number of contusions and lacerations, it wasn't anywhere near as bad as he'd been led to believe.

"Hmm, not that mashed up are you? But definitely a bit green around the gills," he said. The green colouring was strange – not at all the colour of gangrene.

"Weird – never seen anyone go quite that colour before, headless or otherwise," Patrick muttered, trying to find the source of the colouration. It was almost as if the head was emitting its own light. And it was just the head, for the rest of the body looked as normal as it could, considering it had been dead for the best part of a day.

Perplexed, Patrick leaned in for a closer inspection.

It was more than just his breath that got caught in his throat as the corpse's eyes opened and glared into his own.

Patrick froze – it wasn't voluntary – he was being held motionless, his eyes locked onto those below. Unable to tear his gaze away, the eyes of the corpse grew in size, the pupils expanding until they filled Patrick's entire vision. Patrick felt himself dropping, as if falling into a deep, inky-black well.

In the darkness, he heard words in his mind that did not originate from his own consciousness.

The voice said, "You will have to do for a while. You're close enough."

Patrick's own mind no longer exerted any dominance over his body. He felt as if he had been shut into a tiny cell whose walls were shrinking in about him.

Sounding like an echo in the distance, Patrick heard his own voice say, "But right now, I have a daughter to catch."

The End (for now)

Cassie will return…

Acknowledgements

I am indebted to Bob Goddard and Ross Chettleborough for reading through the manuscript, pointing out errors and inconsistencies, as well as helping to hone it into reasonable shape. I'd also like to thank Michael Heppell, 'Penfluence' (especially HJ Brown) and others from the Write That Book 2022 Masterclass who provided the impetus to keep the wheels rolling on this meandering bus – it probably wouldn't have been published in 2022 without their help and encouragement.

Notes

The primary historical references used in the writing of this novel were:

Jary, Leo R, *Kett – 1549 Rewriting the Rebellion*, Poppyland Publishing 2018.

Russell, Frederic William, *Kett's Rebellion in Norfolk*, Longman 1859 (available to read in various places and also as a download from the British Library and the *archive.org* websites).

The sources of other details were found by searching the Internet. Some of it might even have been accurate!

There is some contention around the date upon which Lord Edmund Sheffield was killed, with some stating July 19 and others a few days later (22 to 24) but the majority seem to agree that it occurred as part of the "Battle of Palace Plain", which is thought to have taken place on either July 31 or August 1. The latter date is commemorated on this wall plaque on St Martin-At-Palace Plain, which is not far from the Adam and Eve pub. So, for the purposes of this novel (and for other *obvious reasons*) I have used that August 1 date.

Also by David Viner / Viva Djinn (Horde) Publishing

Splinters

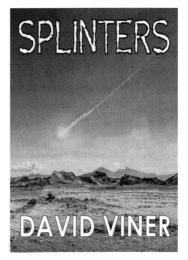

The year is 2156. The moon colonies watch in horror as an asteroid, far larger than the one that wiped out the dinosaurs, plummets towards the Earth.

The collision leaves the planet blackened and lifeless.

But is the Earth as dead as it appears?

First published 2020 – ISBN: 978-1-913873-00-4 (paperback), 978-1-913873-01-1 (ebook)

Time Portals of Norwich

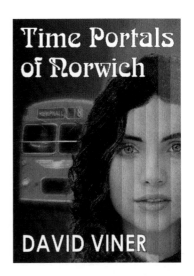

Cassie's life has never been simple. Orphaned at nine and raised by her grandfather, the past has never left her alone. By the time she is seventeen she sees ghosts, hears disembodied voices, and events from history have a habit of rising up to haunt her.

On a visit to the Castle Mall shopping centre in Norwich, the past crashes on top of her. Cassie finds herself transported back to the early 1990s in the company of a woman she's never met. And the woman not only looks familiar but claims she's encountered Cassie many times before.

First published 2020 – ISBN: 978-1-913873-02-8 (paperback), 978-1-913873-03-5 (ebook)

Time Enough for the World to End

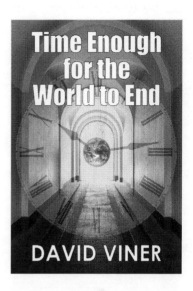

How many ways could civilisation, mankind or even the whole world come to an end?

Is time travel something that can be controlled? But what if time travel controls you?

Here are eighteen short stories from the author of Time Portals of Norwich and Splinters that seek to explore both themes, some with humour, others nightmarishly horrifying. Some even manage to combine both themes.

First published 2021 – ISBN: 978-1-913873-04-2 (paperback), 978-1-913873-05-9 (ebook)

Beyond Between

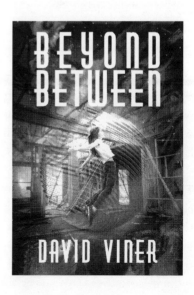

What happens when the barriers between the worlds break down? What might come through from those worlds into our own?

What could we find when we go exploring in those not-quite-familiar alternatives?

Will there come a time when, after hundreds and thousands of years, Earth will become nothing more than a forgotten memory?

First published 2022 – ISBN: 978-1-913873-08-0 (paperback), 978-1-913873-09-7 (ebook)

The Redwell Writers Anthologies Volumes 1 and 2
(in association with Timbuktu Publishing)

Published in 2017, the first Redwell Writers anthology contains, as the title suggests, an assortment of sixteen short stories from various members of the Redwell Writing group.

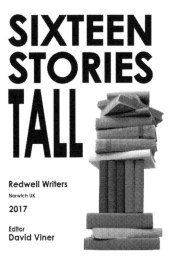

SIXTEEN STORIES TALL

Redwell Writers
Norwich UK
2017

Editor
David Viner

First published 2017 – ISBN: 978-0-956351-83-8 (paperback), 978-1-913873-91-2 (ebook)

A lover's secret. A mysterious neighbour. A woman scorned. A best friend's promise. A man on the edge of sanity. These are just a few of the tales for you to relish in this second tantalising collection of short stories and poetry from the Redwell Writers Group (Norwich).

There are nineteen well-crafted works from authors of all walks of life brought together to tease your emotions and demand your attention.

some of this is fiction

Redwell Writers
Anthology Volume Two
Edited by David Viner

First published 2020 – ISBN: 978-0-956351-86-9 (paperback), 978-1-913873-90-5 (ebook)